AUG – – 2015

Dinner
with
Buddha

Center Point
Large Print

Also by Roland Merullo and available from
Center Point Large Print:

Vatican Waltz

**This Large Print Book carries the
Seal of Approval of N.A.V.H.**

Dinner
with
Buddha

ROLAND MERULLO

CENTER POINT LARGE PRINT
THORNDIKE, MAINE

This Center Point Large Print edition
is published in the year 2015 by arrangement with
Algonquin Books of Chapel Hill,
a division of Workman Publishing.

This is a work of fiction.
While, as in all fiction, the literary perceptions and
insights are based on experience, all names, characters,
places, and incidents either are products of the author's
imagination or are used fictitiously.
The text of this Large Print edition is unabridged.
In other aspects, this book may vary
from the original edition.
Printed in the United States of America
on permanent paper.
Set in 16-point Times New Roman type.

ISBN: 978-1-62899-658-6

Library of Congress Cataloging-in-Publication Data

Merullo, Roland.
 Dinner with Buddha / Roland Merullo. — Center Point Large Print
edition.
 pages cm
 Summary: "Eight years after *Breakfast with Buddha*, skeptic Otto
Ringling and Mongolian monk Volya Rinpoche set off across America
on another unexpected road trip of discovery—from Indian reservations
and farming towns to Colorado's New Age culture and the nonspiritual
streets of Las Vegas"—Provided by publisher.
 ISBN 978-1-62899-658-6 (library binding)
 1. Buddhists—Fiction. 2. Self-actualization (Psychology)—Fiction.
 3. Large type books. I. Title.
 PS3563.E748D56 2015b
 813'.54—dc23
                                              2015015453

For Zan and Juje
stars in our sky

Though we do not wholly believe it yet,
the interior life is a real life,
and the intangible dreams of people
have a tangible effect on the world.
—James Baldwin

Dinner
with
Buddha

One

───≋───

"I had a dream last night," my sister said, and I knew, by virtue of some mysterious sibling intuition, that I was about to enter a territory of great risk.

I had just arrived from the airport in Fargo—rental car cooling in the driveway, bags not yet unpacked. Seese and I were sitting on the porch of what had once been our parents' house, a wood-frame, white-clapboard structure that overlooked two thousand acres of prime North Dakota farmland. It was nearly dusk, the high-plains August heat had eased a bit, and we were relaxing in wicker rockers on the shade of that old porch, sipping from glasses of my sister's magnificent mint lemonade, and gazing across the acreage, leased now, that still produced durum wheat with a vibrancy the gods themselves envied. We had been speaking of her daughter, my niece, a seven-year-old girl named Shelsa. According to my sister, Shelsa was a great spiritual being who'd been born in this time and place to save the world from cataclysm. Other people—sane, good, intelligent people—seemed to believe this as well. As for her uncle, yours truly, Otto Ringling of Bronxville, New York, I preferred a

11

compassionate neutrality on the subject. Shelsa was a wonder of a child, yes. Beautiful, quick-witted, graceful, often mature beyond her years, and she loved me with a pure love I clearly didn't deserve. But a great spiritual incarnation? A kind of saint? A female Dalai Lama of the American Midwest? I simply could not make myself go there.

Much as I loved her—*adored* her might be a truer word—and as much as I loved my sister and her famous guru husband, Volya Rinpoche *(RIN-po-shay)*, there were limits to my open-mindedness. When it came to my sister, especially, there were limits to the kinds of words I liked to hear, the kinds of food I would eat, the kinds of ideas I'd allow into the cluttered manger of my mind. I did not, for example, believe in one of her many specialties: past-life regression. I respected vegans and vegetarians but knew I'd never join them. Thanks to Rinpoche's kind tutelage, I had been a diligent meditator for a period of eight years, and, even with everything that had happened to me in that time, I still clung to the meditation practice as if it were a tree branch in a stormy lake and I was a novice swimmer. But in almost every other way I'd made a sharp turn away from the disciplined life. During those years there had been several emotional and psychological body blows—I'll go into detail a little later—and I'd started keeping irregular hours, gained weight, wandered off the spiritual path into an All-American backwater of TV watching and semi-indolence, a therapy of game shows, take-out meals, and bottles of red wine. It was a dark night of the soul, maybe. Or maybe just a kind of tiredness that left me living inside an old shell of decency, devoted fatherhood, and a sophisticated cynicism I associate with greater Manhattan. I wasn't sure, any longer, that there were answers to the big questions: why we suffer, why we die, why we're born in the first place. I wasn't sure there were answers, and wasn't even sure I wanted to ask the questions.

In a series of handwritten letters sent over a period of many months, my brother-in-law had assured me that my difficulties represented nothing more than one stage on a long spiritual journey. Perhaps I should have embraced that idea. The spiritual life, was, after all, his profession. But some pouty childish voice in my "thought stream," as he called it, proudly resisted. Whatever the benefits might be, I did not want, just then, to do any more interior "work." I wanted to laze in the Jacuzzi of the well-fed life. I wanted mindless, harmless distraction. I deserved, I told myself, some rest.

"It was an amazing dream, Otto," Seese was saying. "Some kind of spirit—it had no face or body but seemed to be a woman spirit—was speaking to me. She had a strong accent. Her voice was gentle and absolutely certain, quiet, like a breeze across grass, but there was nothing conceited about it. She was just absolutely sure, unbearably kind. She was speaking to me the way a loving mother would speak to her daughter."

I took a long draft of lemonade, swallowed, nodded agreeably, watched the tips of the wheat shudder in the evening breeze. "What was the woman saying?" I asked, to humor her. I knew, from my sister's tone of voice and from other conversations in our long history together, that all this was leading someplace. And I suspected it was someplace I didn't want to go. I was having a psychic moment. I was reading the aura of her words. My hopes for a restful North Dakota vacation were, something told me, about to be sent up the well-known creek.

Seese (also known as Cecelia or Celia) hesitated, made a quiet humming sound, lay her head back against the top of the chair, and smiled. "She was telling me that Shelsa was destined to meet one of the other great spirits who's on the earth at this time. She was saying—it was so convincing, brother—that Shels and this spirit were going to meet very soon. Actually, we are supposed to help them meet."

"*We* . . . meaning you and I?"

"You and Rinpoche, I'm sure—almost sure— were the people she had in mind. But the important part was that they had to meet. Very soon. The world's in crisis."

"I've noticed."

"And the two of them are supposed to help lead us out of the danger zone and into a new era."

"What does the new era look like? Did the woman say?"

"Are you making fun?"

"Not at all."

"She didn't say. But I could feel it. They'll usher in a world with less violence done to each other, and to the earth. Less divisiveness, less hatred and greed. Not paradise, exactly. Just . . . something better, kinder. Maybe some sort of new religion with one commandment: *Don't hurt other people.* I'm not sure."

I rocked back and forth, trying hard to imagine Seese's kinder universe, trying, through the curtain of my well-honed, East Coast cynicism, to picture a world without torture and war, an America that didn't have hungry children and billionaires living within a mile of each other, an international agreement to spend massive sums on medical research and education rather than on weapons systems, a planet that was nurtured rather than poisoned.

It didn't work. I watched the tips of the wheat, our own amber waves of grain, shiver and go still. It seemed to me that it was precisely the news of the world, this harsh, real world, that had chased me from New York to North Dakota for what I told myself would be a restful three-week summer vacation on the old homestead. From every direction came reports of shootings and sexual abuse, extremism, corruption, political stalemate at the expense of the poorest among us. Two Americas, as a famously disgraced presidential candidate had once said. The rich getting richer, the schools in trouble, the environment in ruins, the NSA listening in, bombs at the Boston marathon, plus radical Islamists killing people in Africa and the Middle East, in the name of their vengeful God. . . . Sadness on all fronts, it seemed.

Of course, that was and always had been part of the human condition, and I was a fool to think I could escape it, even for three weeks. If North Dakota had ever been a refuge of the quiet life, all that had gone away with the discovery of a method of squeezing oil and gas from the stone that lay beneath its surfaces. If our childhood home had ever been a paradise of small-town safety, of neighborliness and simple faith, much of that was gone now. I'd stopped for a leg-stretching stroll in Dickinson, the nearest city, and it had seemed hot and dead—bars, empty storefronts, chain restaurants peddling unhealthy food. Now, during every hour of the day and night, much of North Dakota was kept awake by enormous trucks carrying away the lifeblood of the Bakken oil fields. Tough men and hard women had

invaded the Peace Garden State. We could feel the change all around us: bright lights on the prairie at night, traffic clotting the roads, prostitution, fistfights on the street, no eggs on the grocery shelf, a stabbing in Bismarck, people locking doors that hadn't been locked in generations.

"It sounds good," I said to my sister. "A world like that."

"I can tell you don't believe in it."

"I'd like to believe in it. I really would. There's just so much evidence to the contrary."

"That's why we're here," she said. "That's why you and I met Rinpoche. That's why Shelsa was born."

I clung to a diplomatic silence. I loved my sister. I did. I loved her very much.

"This woman spirit said you needed to go into the mountains," Celia went on. "It was so clear, Otto. She said it several times. The mountains. You have to go to the mountains and find the person who's going to help Shelsa change the world."

More silence. Though I wanted to, I couldn't quite look at her. I could feel a roar—*NO!*—forming in the space between my lungs. I didn't want to go to the mountains. What did the mountains have to offer? Serpentine roads, provincial mindset, poor Internet reception, and an absence of pad Thai. I didn't want to go anywhere. I could feel her looking at me but I k

my eyes forward, fixed on our fields. At last, after considering and abandoning several harsher remarks, I said, " 'The mountains' is not exactly a precise destination. There are mountains everywhere, all over the world."

"I know," Cecelia agreed, sadly.

I waited.

She said, "I think you and Rinpoche are supposed to start with the closest ones and go from there."

"Why don't *you* and Rinpoche go? He's *your* husband. Shelsa is *your* daughter."

Now it was my sister's turn at silence. I could feel a refutation forming inside her. It would be more or less fact based, impossible to contradict. At last she said, "Maybe Shelsa and I could join you at some point, when you find the person. But you're Rinpoche's . . . *disciple*. Really, that's the only word for it. *Disciple*. You have a destiny to fulfill, something you've never really been able to accept about yourself. You're special. I'm just his wife."

As predicted.

I heard voices and lifted my eyes. On the dirt road that ran past one of our outbuildings I saw, above a line of bushes, a young face, dark hair, joyous eyes. Shelsa seemed to be riding on horseback, bouncing up and down, but all I could see were her eyes, forehead, and hair. Then the beautiful smile. Then her slim shoulders, one arm

waving. "Uncle Ott!" she was calling. "We are coming to kiss you, Uncle Ott!"

A dog barked, their beloved Jasper Junior, named after my own lost friend.

Another two seconds and it became clear that Shelsa was perched, not on the backbone of a horse, but on her father's shoulders. I heard Rinpoche's laugh, a throaty bellow. I saw his face—wide, deeply tanned, hairless—then his big shoulders and arms. He was built, this eccentric Russian monk, like a noseguard on a very good division three college football team. Five-seven or five-eight, square as a block of quarried stone, and yet somehow as limber as a ballerina. He was dressed, as always, in his traditional maroon robe with gold trim, and he was laughing and bouncing his daughter as if all the world's troubles had blown north on the evening breeze, as if fracking, civil war, arms dealers, and drug cartels could never touch people like us. He might have been forty and he might have been seventy; no one seemed to know. Rinpoche seemed not to care. But he was in tremendous condition. With Jasper prancing happily at his feet, Rinpoche jogged the last twenty yards with his daughter on his shoulders, then swung her down in a sweeping motion so she landed lightly in front of him. "Otto, my friend!" he called out happily. "My brother-and-waw! I'm good to see you!"

I set down my glass and stepped off the porch

into our yard, and the affection I received there—
Jasper's warm muzzle, Shelsa's tender hug, and
then Rinpoche's, the grasp of a grizzly—was
almost enough to alter the world for me. Almost
enough to make me believe in my sister's finer
universe and the promise of Shelsa's miraculous
future, almost enough to shake me out of the skin
I'd lived in for fifty-one years, the assumptions
about what was real and not real, about why we
had been born and what we might expect to find
here, in our cauldron of pain and trouble.

Two

While this joyous reunion was taking place, my
twenty-three-year-old daughter, Natasha, was out
running errands in Dickinson. It had been four
months since I'd seen her, and though we spoke
on the phone two or three times a week and passed
e-mails and other digital burps back and forth
through the ether on a daily basis, I missed her
terribly. My son, Anthony, was in college on the
East Coast—there already for preseason football—
and during the school year I made a point of
driving up to Maine to see him every third
weekend or so. I'd take him and a friend out to
dinner. We might attend a track meet or baseball
game. We'd joke and catch up, talk sports and

classes, and I'd give him a firm handshake and a hug, slip a twenty into his hand, and get in my car and head back to my empty life in Bronxville.

But things were different with Tasha; they had always been different. We'd always had a particularly close relationship, and from the time she was about four, I'd felt, strangely enough, that she'd arrived in my life to teach me things that no one else could teach me. Jeannie, her mother, felt the same way, and we'd had many conversations about that. I am not a humble man, but I am humble enough to recognize, in my twice-tattooed and occasionally moody eldest child, a strength and wisdom I do not possess. Two years ago, when her mother—and my beloved wife—passed away, Natasha had dealt with that blow not by overeating and watching too much TV, not by losing faith in the possibility of some Divine Explanation, but in just the opposite fashion: She left school before the start of her junior year at Brown and moved out here, to the retreat center run by Rinpoche and Celia, and devoted herself to the spiritual search. She told me she wanted to understand what had happened with her mother —why such things happened—before settling into a more traditional life—career, marriage, children. In short, while her father was floating away from the big questions, clinging to his meditation lifesaver, she was swimming a hard crawl stroke right into them.

21

A quarter hour after the hugfest, Natasha arrived in the retreat center's antique pickup, nicknamed Umâ, raising a plume of dust behind her as she came. There were more warm embraces. A few minutes of packing away groceries and making small talk, and then, while Shelsa fed the dog, and while Seese prepared some kind of tofu burgers with miso mustard on top and made a salad composed of leaves and stems no one in my circle of friends had ever heard of, never mind eaten, Tash and I went out for a stroll. We did this by instinct, without having planned it, and without discussing it. There were no meditation retreats in the month of August, no earnest strangers wandering the grounds where Seese and I had played and done chores as children and where our parents had worked and sweated, no sound of the meditation bell or Rinpoche's basso chants echoing across the wheat fields. A beautiful silence had settled over our land, a curtain of quiet broken only by the crunch of our footsteps on the gravel road and the occasional happy burst of song from a meadowlark. For a little while then it was the North Dakota of my imagination.

"Things good, Dad?" my daughter asked, in her cheerful, hopeful way. She had my mother's northern European aspect—the wide-set pale eyes, the pale freckled skin—and her own mother's mouth, a heartbreaking mouth that stretched effortlessly into the saddest of all smiles and flexed into frown when she was troubled. She was tall, slim, athletic, beautiful to my eye, capable of great things, and I worried almost constantly that she'd wither away here in this dusty outback, remain single and unhappy, sprinting down a dead-end road into middle age.

"Good," I fibbed. "Fine. And with you?"

"Nice. I have what you'd probably call 'a love interest.'"

"Wonderful! Good guy?"

"Older," she said. "Kind. Really into meditation."

What leapt to my lips was: *How much older?* But I'd learned long ago to tread lightly when it came to Natasha's love interests. I was happy she'd found someone, but she had, in this arena, a genetic similarity to her Aunt Cecelia: Both of them had loved their way through a string of unusual boyfriends—the wild, the nerdy, the addicted and arrested, handsome and not so handsome, tall, thin, stocky, short, brilliant and rather slow; men, young and not so young, who inhabited the fringes of the masculine nether-world. I'd learned to accept it and hoped now only for one outcome: that my daughter's romantic explorations would end up where my sister's had, with a good man who treated her well.

So instead of probing I said, "And how's that going? The meditation, I mean."

"Rinpoche's guiding me. He says I'm making progress but it doesn't feel like progress. It just feels like a gradual, I don't know, a gradual becoming more myself. I'm not afraid of the things I used to be afraid of."

"Such as?"

"Such as Bakken creeps coming on to me in the market. Such as going out for long walks on the farm roads at night. Such as being out on my bike in a thunderstorm."

Keep going, I thought. Soon it will be not afraid of getting into cars with strangers, not afraid of jumping out of airplanes, not afraid of working as a guard in the state prison, not afraid of. . . . I said, "As a fearful man, I have to say I'm jealous."

"Little things, Dad, but it's nice. And it's because of the meditation. Are you keeping up with your practice?"

"Sure," I said. "It's the last bastion of discipline for me. I sometimes think that, without it, I'd drown in a sea of wine and television."

"You've gotten fat."

"Thanks."

"Are you still working out?"

"Not as much."

"Are you depressed, Dad?"

"Not so much."

"What do you do all day?"

"Oh, you know. I meditate for twenty minutes or half an hour, morning and night. In the middle of the day I keep busy. A little tennis. Reading. TV. Seeing friends."

"You're depressed."

"Right."

"You should come out here and live with us. Rinpoche's an expert on depression."

"And never experienced it a day in his life, I bet."

"No, but still."

"It's good to be here, hon. Nice to see you in the flesh, to see Rinpoche and Aunt Seese and Shelsa. But after all these years of city life, being here is like downshifting from fourth to second. It's very pleasant, refreshing. But it's not the life for me, Tash. I left this life a long time ago. I can't go back."

"And Aunt Seese drives you nuts, right?"

"I love Aunt Seese. I admire her. I'm happy to see her so happy."

"But . . ."

"But she can drive me crazy, still, yes."

"Have you ever really looked into that, Dad?"

"As a matter of fact, I have. Many times."

"And?"

"I think it's because she refuses to see the world as it actually is. She believes that if she eats carefully and prays a lot and is devoted to Rinpoche and Shelsa—all good things, by the way—then she'll escape pain and death, she'll somehow come to inhabit another earth where people don't cheat and murder. We were just talking about it, as a matter of fact. She dreams of a different world, which is all fine and good, except that, as far as any rational person knows, that world doesn't exist. She's been that way since she was a girl. She hasn't changed."

"She thinks," my daughter said, in a measured, thoughtful tone that was new to her, "that if she clears her mind down to the deepest level then three things will happen: she'll never be afraid; it will be easier to love people; and it will be easier to die."

This, coming from a girl who'd recently watched her own mother die, stopped me in my tracks. Not literally—we kept walking; we were going past the solitary retreat cabins now, tidy and small, with unpainted wood siding and metal roofs. In my better days—only a few years earlier—I'd made a three-day retreat in one of them. I marked that as the end of my optimism, the high point of my spiritual attainment. Since then I'd been gliding down, slowly, almost without noticing. Down and down. My dog had died. I'd grown a belly. Even with the meditation practice, on certain days, in certain difficult hours, my mind was a circus of despair.

"You say that," I told Natasha, then I paused, "you say that in a way that's different from Aunt Seese. She sounds like she hopes it's true, you sound like you know it's true. Is that just what Rinpoche tells you, or—"

"Rinpoche is enlightened, you know that, Dad, right?"

"I believe I do, yes. I'm not sure what it means, but I believe it."

"It means that he doesn't identify with his body and his personality, his *I*. His mind has exploded out into something much bigger. In Christian terms it's like Jesus saying, 'Not I, but the Father who lives in me.'"

"I can feel something like that from him. I've always felt it. I just don't see it happening to me. Your aunt calls me his 'disciple.' I think that's absurd. I'm his brother-in-law, his friend, his admirer. Period."

"Enlightenment happens in stages, Dad. You have your ups and downs and then, if you keep trying, it comes over you when you least expect it."

"Even if you don't pursue what you call 'the spiritual life'?"

"Eventually. Sure. Just living makes it happen. The act of being alive is, in and of itself, spiritual evolution, unless a person purposely resists it. All the pain and pleasure, it's all a lesson. But a spiritual practice is like . . ." she twisted her lips to one side the way I'd seen her do five thousand times. "It's like the difference between a kid who goes to school and learns and a kid who goes to school and learns and comes home to parents who are reading to her and talking to her about the world, showing her things, teaching by their actions. Like what you and Mom did for us."

I couldn't speak.

"It's the difference between somebody who wants to be a good tennis player and goes out and plays once a week and somebody else who wants to be a good tennis player and takes lessons, practices, reads up on the sport, plays a lot."

"Maybe I'm too lazy for that, hon."

"I don't want you to be."

"Why?"

"Why didn't you want me to hang out with Judy Millen when we were little?"

"Because her parents were racist homophobes who believed God loved them and hated your mother and me because we didn't go to church on Sunday and sometimes voted for women."

"Why didn't you want me to binge drink in college and sleep with just anybody?"

"For obvious reasons, and I don't see the link between binge drinking and the spiritual life."

"If you love somebody you want what's good for them, that's the link. I don't want to see my father fat and depressed—sorry, Dad—and giving up on life. Mom wouldn't want her death to do that to you. I don't want you to grow old and die that way. I want you to really understand what a great person you are, which is something you've resisted all your life. I think there's some weird, I-can't-possibly-be-special, North Dakota fake humility there. Have you ever looked at that?"

I didn't answer. We walked along. On the heels

of her loving assault I tried to think of something funny to say, some wise remark, some deflection. Natasha had always been able to pierce that artfully constructed armor of mine, an armor that worked so well with my New York friends. At the office, at parties, meeting a neighbor at a café in town or on the front lawn during leaf-raking season, we had a repartee, my acquaintances and I, a hail-fellow-well-met bravado, in some cases a pattern of minor-league jousting. Harmless, to be sure, but an armor all the same. Here, in a few sentences, she'd pierced it again. I felt raw, unguarded, shaken up, afraid of something I couldn't name. We went along for another while and then—again, without talking about it—turned around and headed back. Only a weak yellowish light remained in the western sky, the last promise of day. Finally, when we were again within sight of the farmhouse, I said, "So tell me about this new boyfriend. Name. Age. Characteristics."

I could feel her smiling next to me. I remembered what it felt like to smile at the mention of a lover. I remembered, so well, saying the word "Jeannie" to my friends and the warm feeling it raised in me. I remembered it as if it were yesterday.

"His name is Warren," Natasha said. "And he's got some of that same North Dakota neohumility I was just talking about."

"It has a good side."

29

"Sure it does. I love you, I love him. It's just that sometimes I can clearly see those self-imposed limits and it makes me nuts. He's thirty-eight but he looks much younger. He's six-seven, 240 pounds. He played tight end at UND until he got hurt. He's a woodworker, a great one. He has a little furniture shop in Bismarck. He used to have a drug problem, long ago, after the injury, and he went to jail for a few months—just the county jail, just for shoplifting. But he's way, way past that now. He comes here on retreats three or four times a year and is a huge, huge fan of Rinpoche. He's going to be staying here to help us out while you and Rinpoche are traveling."

I thought: *Thirty-eight! Very nearly twice your age! My daughter involved with an ex-con giant with drug problems! Walking alone on the country roads! Fending off Bakken creeps! Bike riding in thunderstorms!*

I said, "How did you know we'd be traveling?"

"It was all set up," she said guilelessly. "Aunt Seese has been seeing you in dreams, on the road with Rinpoche. She's been having the dreams for months now. She planned this a long time ago, at least in a loose way. Now she's trying to set up some speaking engagements for him, too, I think, so it all works out."

"I came up here to spend time with *you,* not to travel with Rinpoche, much as I enjoy his company."

"I know, Dad. I think . . . I mean, I've heard hints and bits of conversation . . . I think there's something big, a bigger trip, coming up, maybe next year or something, and all of us are going. I'll miss you, too, more than you'd believe, but I think it's important that you go wherever it is that he's going."

"Into the mountains, apparently," I said, and I couldn't keep a droplet of sarcasm from the words.

Natasha looked up at me. She stopped, took hold of my shoulders and kissed me just to the right side of my mouth. "You lost Mom. You lost your job. Jasper. Us. You're depressed in the house. Can't you see, Dad? Everything's pointing you toward something else, a different route. You're not going to be allowed to be just one of these suburban retirees, playing tennis and taking exotic cruises. That's not going to be your fate in this life. Don't fight it. Just let Rinpoche lead you toward something bigger. Just trust him, okay?"

"Playing tennis and taking cruises doesn't sound so bad at the moment."

She smirked, smiled her sad smile. Jasper came bounding down the path.

I said, "Can't you and Warren come with us, into the mountains?"

"We need to get the place ready for the September retreatants. If you stay here for a

31

while after you get back we can spend some time together then. There are things I want to show you here."

"I grew up here, hon."

"New things. I'd like you to get to know Warren, for one. I'd like us all to go camping in the grasslands. Will you?"

I was under the spell of her warmth and love and youthful wisdom then, the very things that had been missing from my life. I was under her spell, and I understood, in some semi-conscious way, that I'd come to the retreat center to be healed again. Failure that I felt myself to be at that moment, I was at least humble enough, in the depths of my secret soul, to admit that much: I had come here to be healed. If healing meant going into the mountains with my sister's guru husband in search of a companion for his spiritually special child, then I would do it. If it meant camping in the grasslands with my daughter and her thirty-eight-year-old flame, I'd do that, too. I told myself I was finished with my regimen of coffee and pastries, gourmet pizza with french fries on the side, TV and lonely brooding. That was behind me now, merely a stage, a dark night.

"I won't even unpack my suitcases," I said. "Enlightenment in the mountains, here I come. Reserve a campsite for my return."

Natasha wrapped both arms around me and said, "That's my wondrous Dad."

Three

"You've gotten fat, Dad. Are you depressed?" are not exactly the words one hopes to hear from the daughter one hasn't seen in months. There was no meanness in them: Natasha was a young woman constitutionally incapable of meanness. But she could be blunt, a trait inherited from the maternal side. My wife's mother—in public a woman of substantial social graces—was known around the dining table to make comments such as, "If you marry him, your children will have rather large ears."

The "him" in this case was her newish boyfriend, Otto Ringling—who happened to be standing at the top of the stairs in pressed pants and his only dress shirt, heading down for his first family dinner.

I paused there, waiting, wondering how Jeannie would respond and what weight rather large ears carried (not true, in any case—they are and have always been perfectly adequate ears, neither more nor less, in no way out of the norm) in the difficult decision a woman makes about who will father her children, and I heard Jeannie say, "And rather large penises, should they be masculine." (Also, I should add here . . . well, see above regarding ears.)

Still standing at the top of the stairs, I stifled an urge to applaud.

Moms, as she was known, waxed apoplectic. "In my house we will not have that kind of talk!" (Etc. etc.) Jeannie's Uncle Gene, another summer visitor, couldn't stop laughing. And yours truly descended the stairs and inquired, "What's the joke?"

The joke, of course, is that bluntness tends to engender bluntness in some bloodlines. In Jeannie's case, and in Tasha's, thankfully, the bluntness had stayed but the nastiness had leached out.

Still, Natasha's comment rang a stinging note in my inner ear as I reluctantly made my preparations for the road. *Fat* is not a nice word. There are many good substitutes—I've used them all in reference to myself. *Big* works well. *Corpulent. Heavy. Stocky.* Even *chubby* is better than *fat.*

What made it worse in my case was that I knew the term fit, and knew precisely where the responsibility lay. The equation for weight gain is really very simple:

$$\frac{i-o}{m} = wg$$

Though, of course, the psychology is anything but. What you take in *(i)*, times what you burn off *(o)*, divided by *m,* where *m* is the mysterious workings of one's metabolism. For example, a

Polish American Bronxville friend named Francisco Wardeski could consume three slices of pecan pie at lunch twice a week and five beers at a friendly dinner party, take no more exercise than that required to walk from bedroom to BMW in the morning and back again at night, and he had the belly of a college swim captain.

My own father ate like a rhinoceros—I can still see the six-high stack of hotcakes on his breakfast plate, next to an order of toast and mayonnaise, bacon, coffee with whole milk, maybe a buttered corn muffin. But he'd spend the whole day in the barns or fields, so his large *i* was matched by a very large *o*.

My own love of food was legendary; in fact, for the twenty-eight years that I'd been an editor of food books at a prestigious New York house called Stanley and Byrnes, food had been central to my profession. During those years, thanks to my own vanity and because my wife was not attracted to corpulence, I'd made a concerted effort to get to the gym in winter, the tennis courts in summer, and to kick the soccer ball with my daughter and jog with my son at every opportunity.

Until, that is, things fell apart. Since Jeannie's diagnosis—903 days—and especially since the tripartite blow of her passing, my loss of work, and the kids' departure, my formerly respectable waist measurement had gone the way of the 2013 Dow Jones.

I had, in other words, let myself get fat.

Thinking all this, feeling a tide of shame rising like a septic overflow around my ankles, watching the purple-black cloud of depression creeping in over the horizon, I heard someone padding up the stairs and then saw Rinpoche standing in the doorway with a hand on each side of the frame. "I am wery, wery happy," he said, and you could see it was true. His eyes were lit like Fourth of July sparklers. The enormous smile caused the skin around his ears to wrinkle.

"Glad to hear it. Why?"

"Because," he said, "in this wifetime, the greatest, best fun for me is to be in the road with my brother-and-waw!"

On the road, I wanted to say, correcting. But I couldn't. Fool that I was, lonely, sentimental, wounded, fat, depressed fool, I felt a familiar spasm in the muscles of my throat. Volya Rinpoche, world-renowned spiritual master and husband of my wacky sister, actually seemed to mean it. "Rinp," I managed after a few seconds, "one question."

"Any questions, man!"

"Why is the Buddha so often shown as a fat man? We even have the term *Buddha belly* to describe the well-known spare-tire abdomen. Why is that? I mean, he was famous for eating practically nothing. What happened?"

Rinpoche peered at me as if seeking out the seed

of idiocy in the center of my brain. "Because he eat up everybody's karma all around him, man," he said. And then, after a pause that seemed atypically indecisive, he added, "Like Jeannie did."

"Jeannie was always thin. Always. Even after she had the kids, she——"

"Not talking food, Otto. Jeannie with the pain, the sickness, the dying early—she was taking other people's karma onto herself. You didn't know?"

Four

Though it is named Stark County, the territory of my youth actually has a certain complex beauty to it, in the nonwinter months, at least. The fields are sloped and slanting—western North Dakota isn't flat, not at all—and on hot summer days the fathomless sky is painted a sharp, wildflower blue and often decorated with rows of puffy cumulus —grand, purple-fringed, towering—that march eastward like the army of some resplendent king showing off on a celestial parade ground. Gravel roads run in a loose grid across land planted in durum wheat, hops, alfalfa, and sunflowers. Rolled bales of hay await collection by the roadsides, or spot the vast landscape like curlers on a head of golden hair. West-central North

Dakota is, in mid-August, a palette of gold and green below and purple, blue, and white above, though in winter it better warrants the Stark name and turns white and gray, crackles with cold, and is inhospitable to everything that breathes.

On the morning of August 16, 2013, Volya Rinpoche and I—accompanied by my sister and niece—set out across that landscape in search of God knew what. Enlightenment. Healing. The soft, bright heart of my sister's silly visions. Or possibly the spiritual being who would form the perfect other half to my remarkable niece. Rinpoche and I were headed, supposedly, to the mountains. But on that morning my state of mind was such that I didn't really care. I had planned to spend a few weeks in Dakota, taking walks with my daughter, playing hide-and-seek with my niece, enduring my sister's watercress and balsamic sandwiches on bread so fibrous it resembled some sort of by-product from the plywood factory in Williston. Now, however, my daughter had a lover and my sister had visions. I would go along, then, change my ticket, put more miles on the rental car, spend a bit of time at the farm upon my return. What else did I have on my schedule? I was a brittle, brown, November leaf scuttling across an abandoned lawn; I would go where the next breeze took me, and make the best of it.

Sometimes now I ask myself this question: If I

had known on that mid-August day where my sister's visions, where that uneasy breeze, would lead me, would I have kissed Natasha good-bye and gotten into the new Ford SUV with Rinpoche, Shelsa, and Seese? Or would I have stayed around the farm for a while, soaking in old memories and the comfort of my daughter's affection, then headed back to Bronxville and the empty house, the familiar pleasures?

I chose to repack my barely unpacked suitcase and hoist it into the back of the shiny new Ford. Hold my daughter close. Climb in behind the wheel. Toot twice at Natasha and wave. Throw up a cloud of dust and head west, toward Belfield, North Dakota, and Shelsa's favorite "eating-out breakfast place" with one last look in the mirror at the white clapboard farmhouse on its rise and my daughter there, beautiful in the prime of her young womanhood, waving, turning away.

"Where to?" I asked in a tone of what can only be described as manufactured bonhomie.

Seese was sitting in back with her daughter. Rinpoche was busy wrestling with the buckle of the seat belt, so there was a short pause before this comment came to me: "Going away now. Maybe not coming back." I looked across to see if the monk might be making one of his famous jokes, but there was no sign of humor on his face.

"You running away from my sister? I'll get out my dad's old shotgun, I'll—"

"Who's running away?" Shelsa asked from behind me.

"No one, honey," Seese said. "It's just your uncle making a bad joke. Let's play mok."

"Maybe now the change for us," Rinpoche said quietly.

"Meaning what?"

A shrug. An uncharacteristic sigh. "Celia seeing that now we go another place, all of us. She has the dreams."

"I know those dreams. Sometimes they're eerily on the money, sometimes crazy."

"Thanks, Otto!"

"It's true, Sis."

"Not about money," Rinpoche said. "We have plenty."

"It's an expression. *On the money.* Sometimes her dreams are accurate—on the money; other times they're just wrong."

"Sometimes is everybody wrong," he said, and he turned his head away from me, out the side window. "What is the word for light, the different lights, one kind to the other?"

"Spectrum?"

"Yes. I like wery much this word. On the spectrum you can see some colors wery good, yes?"

"Sure."

"And the others you don't see, yes?"

"Right. Ultraviolet, for one."

He nodded and turned his head forward again, then toward me. "Doesn't mean the colors isn't there."

"Exactly," Seese said, between the seats. "Precisely. Thank you, my love."

"You welcome."

The Trapper's Skillet restaurant occupied most of a dusty lot just off Interstate 94, on the west side of U.S. 85. Eighty-five is a 1,500-mile road with some character, and one on which I'd spent a certain amount of time as a young man, dating a woman whose parents owned a farm along it. The road runs from Saskatchewan to the Mexican border, slicing down through the Dakotas like a straight blade through dry bread. The terrain it crosses is, in fact, dry. And it does, in fact, at least in the Peace Garden State, include some land where wheat is grown. Eighty-five is one of those old American roads, like its better-known cousin Route 66—a road with the scent of stagecoach and covered wagon still lingering at either shoulder, a relic from the days before the interstates, when you still felt the soul of a place as you traveled through.

The Skillet, as they all called it, had apparently become one of Shelsa's favorite spots, a café her father liked to take her to early on Saturday mornings in order to give Seese a chance to sleep. It seemed just a bit odd to begin our trip with a

41

pit stop—we could so easily have eaten at home—but Shelsa insisted it would make her very sad if she and her mother didn't join Rinpoche and me for the first part of the journey, spend a night with us, and start with a meal at the Skillet. Her mother had relented without much fuss. The whole voyage had a weird feeling to it. No itinerary, no destination, no direction at all other than "the mountains" and a couple or three potential speaking engagements that were being set up, last-minute. There was something refreshing about the weirdness, however, at least on that first morning, at least for me. It was the kind of trip a young person might take, a trip that promised spontaneity and the risk of minor discomfort. Just the tonic for lardy middle-aged discouragement.

Because my sister is made nervous by any driver who even approaches the legal speed limit, we went along at a turtle's pace and pulled into the restaurant's Winnebago-cluttered lot as if we'd run out of gas and were rolling to a stop at the pump. One of the Winnebagos had a Smart car attached behind. A family of environmentalists, apparently. "So, Shels," I said, when we'd finally parked. "This is your favorite place, huh?"

"You will love it very much, Uncle Ott!" Her smile showed the typical second-grade gaps in her teeth. In that way, at least, she was an ordinary girl.

"What should I order? Pancakes?"

"Egg samwich," she said in her grown-up way.

We walked through the hot morning air, pulled open a door made for weightlifters, and found ourselves in a gift shop that was a menagerie of kitsch. There were posters promoting gun ownership in the strongest terms, small metal placards showing a canoe and the words, UPSHITZ CREEK. NO HOPE, NO PADDLE. There were plastic tags for every birthday and common first name. There were hunting knives, clichéd photos of running streams and mountains, wall hangings with sayings like YOUR HUSBAND CALLED AND LEFT THIS MESSAGE: BUY ANYTHING YOU WANT and I SAY DRUNK THINGS WHEN I'M STUPID.

To our right was the restaurant. It was the busboy's day off, apparently—half the tables showed crumpled napkins, plates of unfinished sausage and gravy. We found a clean one near the far window and settled in. Perusing the menu I kept hearing the word *fat* in my inner ear, and that situation wasn't improved by the arrival of a waiter with veins striping muscled forearms and the belly of a college kid, which he was not. When my turn came I ordered a bacon and egg sandwich on wheat bread.

"Cheese?" he asked.

"Sure. What kind do you have?"

"Two kinds. American and white American."

"Just plain, then, thanks."

"No cheese?"

"Not today." I patted my midsection. "Changed my mind. Diet."

The waiter sent a hard glance at me and at the berobed Rinpoche, who'd ordered oatmeal with a scoop of butter on top and forgotten to say *please.* "You run the whatever it is, the mosque or whatever. In South Heart," he said to the famous man.

"Meditation center," I corrected quickly. He didn't turn his eyes.

"You should wisit," Rinpoche told him. "Three-day retreat, no eating." He laughed.

The waiter studied him, not kindly or unkindly now, but simply as if he were a rare specimen in these parts, a migrating crane swooping in for butter and oatmeal. He squinted, started to say something else, then turned away.

When he was gone, Shelsa remembered that she'd left her stuffed mouse in the car. Topo Gigio was its name. It had been Seese's comfort object more than four decades earlier, a gift from my parents, who enjoyed the Ed Sullivan variety show and adored the little Italian mouse who spoke to Ed with a squeaky accent: "Ed-dee, kees me good nait!" I have only a faint memory of the actual show—a memory refreshed by YouTube clips I showed my children—but I remembered how attached Seese had been to the little rodent, the fits she'd throw when it went missing, the care she took with its grooming. These are the things that lodge in the mind of the older sibling.

Seese asked if I'd give Shelsa the keys so she could go out and fetch Topo. I was shocked. "You'd let her go out there alone?"

"She'll be fine."

Fine? I thought. *Fine,* as in snatched by some sex offender cruising Route 85 on the alert for solitary kids? *Don't you read the news?* I wanted to ask my sister, but, most likely, she did not. She sat looking across the table at me with an all-too-familiar, condescending smile pinching her cheeks. *She can't be hurt in the ordinary ways, don't you know that, Otto? She's protected from all that. Someday you'll understand, brother,* the smile seemed to say. *Until then, I'll humor you.*

At that moment, waiting for an already-delayed breakfast to soften my mood, there were several things I wanted to say in the direction of that smile. *I'm* the one who watched his wife die of cancer. *You're* the one who used to read palms for a living. *I* worked in Manhattan for two and a half decades, Manhattan, the epicenter of reality. And I also volunteered for eighteen of those years in one of the city's poorest neighborhoods. *You* live on a farm in North Dakota, and while it's true that the state has changed for the worse of late, you don't get out much. I raised two children, without major incident, watching them like a father grizzly when they so much as left the table for the restroom at a local café. *So please,* I was tempted to say, *spare me the superior smile.*

But Rinpoche was watching me, and I had the sense, as I often did with him, that he could read my thoughts, that he saw the run of old sibling irritation as clearly as if it were tattooed on my left cheek. It was more than not wanting to look bad in front of him, more, even, than wanting to keep Shelsa from seeing her uncle's ugly side. Rinpoche's presence was a reminder that there were different ways of doing things. One did not need to indulge one's every irritation. One could watch it rise and let it fall, without denying or embracing it, the way one did with one's thoughts in meditation. I launched a wish for peace, happiness, and sanity in my sister's direction. I said, to Shelsa, "Uncle Ott wants to see Topo, too. Let's go get him before the food comes."

Out we went past the kitsch museum to the SUV. Topo was rescued, clutched to a loving breast. As we walked back to the entrance I noticed a suntanned man in a cowboy hat staring at my dark-haired companion. Standing there idly with his lecherous eyes locked on her. I wanted to snap a picture with my phone and present it to Seese as evidence in the court of sibling disagreement. But as we passed, the man said kindly, "That's a special gal you got there." And, to Shelsa, "And that's one fine rat you're holding."

"This," she said in her adult-like tone, polite but sure, doubtless, "is a mouse!"

The man laughed in the most unlecherous of ways and apologized and I felt, as I sometimes did in those difficult days, quite small.

The egg sandwich, served on a hamburger bun, not wheat bread, was perfectly okay. The coffee, drinkable. The hash browns and biscuit were, in the great western tradition, unimaginative and filling. But I have to say that a certain sadness hung over the table, the understanding, on my part, that I'd have my sister's and Shelsa's company for only a day or two.

Rinpoche insisted on paying. As we stood at the cash register he struck up a conversation with the waiter, who'd been giving him something resembling the evil eye on every trip to the table, and who was now doing double duty as cashier.

"How could you makin' out?" asked the bald, berobed holy man, whose books were studied by seekers all over the globe, and whose presence was enough to draw the spiritual minded from every continent to the wilds of Stark County to live in a simple dormitory room, to eat my sister's cooking, and to sit and watch their thoughts for eight hours a day. How could you makin' out. It was his best imitation of a Dickinson rancher.

The man looked at him hard. "How'm I makin' out? Not bad. Thanks for the nice tip."

"You welcome, man."

"I'm just workin' here till I can get up to the Bakken."

"The oil place," Rinpoche said. "Good money, yes?"

"Bet your ass."

"Bet your ass," Rinpoche repeated. He seemed to be making a study of the local dialect, trying hard to fit in. It was odd, given the fact that he'd said, not an hour earlier, that he might be leaving.

"Three grand a week, my friend."

"What is this *grand?*"

"A thousand bucks. Three thousand bucks a week."

"But work wery dangerous."

"I can handle it. . . . How *you* makin' out?"

"Road tripped now."

"Whereabouts?"

"Big mountains, maybe."

A grunt. "What is it you all do, over at that mosque or whatever?"

"Frackin'," Rinpoche said, with an enormous smile.

"No way." The man flexed his forearms and, until my brother-in-law spoke again, appeared ready to inquire about work.

"Inside-the-person frackin'. We put on a pressure and things inside come out."

"Like what things? Which kinds of things?"

As I somehow knew he would, Rinpoche reached across the counter and, with one hand, fingers splayed, grasped the man's skull, just above the forehead. Palming a basketball.

The man frowned and leaned back, out of reach.

"Sit, sit, meditate, meditate, frackin', frackin', and all the old ways to think come out. Makes you a new man. Jesus say so."

Suspicion had now been replaced by abject confusion. The waiter looked at me, at the dark-eyed girl clutching her stuffed mouse, at the stunningly beautiful middle-aged woman in a hippie dress, then back at the monk who'd given him a big tip then fondled his head. He said, "Well, the Jesus part I could maybe relate to, but the rest of it all, you know, that's some weird shit, man."

"Best shit ever," Rinpoche said agreeably. "Bet your ass."

A woman waiting behind us in line coughed and scowled. The waiter laughed nervously, as if another part of his body might suddenly be taken hold of if he kept on with the conversation. We thanked him, wished him luck, headed for the door, and had nearly made it when a leather-clad motorcycle couple, fresh from the famous Sturgis rally, crowded through, all wind-burned cheeks and coal-black boots. Like most of the rally goers, they weren't part of some organized gang, just people who enjoyed riding in the open air. I knew this, and was all set to offer them a hearty North Dakota good morning, when the woman muttered "freak show" as we passed.

No one else in our group seemed to hear.

Five

〜

As we left the Skillet's lot and climbed the shallow rise of 85 South, fields of gold and green parted before us like the Red Sea. Eighteen-wheelers rushed past in the opposite direction, and every time she felt the car rock a bit from the air they pushed, Shelsa made a noise like "ooh!" There were lots of bikers, too, the road so straight for so long they appeared, at first, like a new species of ant out there in the shimmering distance. Once in a great while we passed a modest farmhouse, built close to the road in the days when it had been red dirt. Some of these had been abandoned, overtaken by weeds and weed trees. Windows empty of glass, roofs sagging, they put me in mind of lonely old men, all of modern life rushing past as they huddled in their broken bodies, watching, watching, awaiting extinction. With my eyes on the tar strip and my thoughts running along such happy lines, I had a desire to engage Rinpoche in conversation. The man had a way of shining lamplight into the cavern of self-pity, making me see the world's sorrows from a different angle. But he'd decided to sit in back with his daughter for this leg of the journey. They both loved an elaborate form of Himalayan tic-tac-toe that was played in three dimensions with a plastic apparatus that resembled a miniature jungle gym. *Mok*, it was called, and it was ideal for a long trip because one game, or match, could take thirty minutes or more to complete. Seese was riding shotgun, hands folded in her lap. She said, "I found an old-style hotel for tonight. Lots of character. I think you'll like it."

"Where?"

"Deadwood, South Dakota."

"I thought we were headed for the mountains."

"Eventually. But there's an easy bus back to Dickinson from Deadwood so we can spend the night with you there, then head home."

"I figured Wyoming. Montana, maybe."

"You have a touch of mockery in your voice, brother."

"Sorry." I watched the telephone poles go past, cedar crucifixes holding wires of charged atoms, voices, information, life. "I think I should be allowed one period of mockery daily, with a thirty-minute maximum, because I agreed to take the road trip to nowhere. I think it only fair that I have a mockery allowance. Or, at least, an irony allowance. One can't survive in Greater New York without it."

51

"*Mok*," Shelsa said from the back seat. It meant she'd won the first round.

I, on the other hand, had not. My sister had fallen silent and was looking straight ahead. To our left, donkey derricks pumped away like nodding cartoon animals. You couldn't travel anywhere in North Dakota now without being reminded of the liquid and vaporous treasure that lay below the surface. Lucky farmers were making millions and the nation was approaching fossil-fuel self-sufficiency.

"In Bismarck," I said, hoping to make peace, "I stopped in to see my friend Sia. You know, the guy who runs the coffee shop."

"I adore him," Seese said. "We always go there when we're in. Shelsa loves those flavored Italian sodas."

"He was telling me horror stories about the way the state has changed. He was saying that just across the street from his place the police stopped a van filled with prostitutes being sent up to the Bakken. Six women. Three from Russia and three from the Philippines."

Seese didn't reply or move her eyes from the road. For a moment I worried she didn't want me talking about such things within earshot of her daughter. But then I remembered another parental quirk of their family: They talked about every-thing—everything—in front of Shelsa. Sometimes I thought they took a good approach too far.

"Not the kind of thing that used to—"

"We're moving," my sister said.

I glanced at Rinpoche in the mirror. He was immersed in his *mok.*

"I was going to talk with you about it but I wanted you to enjoy the farm . . . in case it was your last visit."

"I'm . . . you want to close the meditation center? And go where? What about Tasha? Warren?"

"The feeling of the place has changed, Otto. We've had some . . . incidents."

I could feel a primal fatherly instinct rousing itself from sleep. "Such as?"

A pause. A glance over her shoulder at the *mok* players. So there *were* some things she didn't want Shelsa to hear.

"Natasha's safe," she said quietly. "We had a security system installed."

A security system! I suddenly wanted to turn the SUV around. My parents hadn't locked their doors, ever. It was a point of pride. When I'd first moved to New York and come back to visit, my father's opening remark was, "I hear they have deadbolts on the doors, even inside the apartment buildings—is it true?" accompanied by a knowing smirk with life-is-better-in-North-Dakota written all over it. Now, in these United States, isolated heartland farms needed security systems. Now, madmen slaughtered children in kindergarten.

Now, there were three million Americans behind bars, and our elected officials argued and pouted and stamped their feet like five-year-olds instead of governing the country. What plague had infected us while we were watching shoot-em-ups on the screen and laughing at Topo Gigio? What had happened here?

Just then I saw on a grassy knoll to our right an old-style gas stove sitting there, a forlorn monument to other times. The rusted burners, the porcelain face, the oven door ajar. My sister said, "It's not about that, really. We're perfectly safe, Otto. I just feel like our North Dakota karma is finished."

"But you've put so much time and money into the Center. What are you going to do, just abandon it?"

"Not at all. Rinpoche has three or four senior students who want to take over the day-to-day. He might still come to visit once in a while, the way he used to do with the European centers when he lived there."

"They're still in business?"

"One in Italy, one in Croatia. The Lithuania one closed because of political trouble."

"But where will you go?"

"I don't know," she said, and I had visions of them dragging Natasha to Togo or New Guinea or Tierra del Fuego. "We'll wait for a sign."

"But how do you know you're going at all?"

"I just know, that's all. It comes to me. Dreams, thoughts, signs. I know you don't believe in those things, but that's how I've always lived. Rinpoche understands it and that's all that really matters."

By this point I was squeezing the wheel, hard. "Where you lead my daughter matters. To me, anyway. I don't want to have to go to the ends of the earth to visit with her."

"I think you're coming with us, wherever we go."

"Not likely, Sis."

North of Amidon, a spot that seemed from the Rand McNally to be an actual town but that would turn out to be composed, from what I could tell, of exactly three buildings, Shelsa announced that she had to pee. How well I remembered this drill! I could hear my thirty-year-old self saying, "Tash, why didn't you use the facilities back at the restaurant ten minutes ago?" and her reply: "I didn't have to go then, *Dad.*" But Jeannie and I had never made trouble out of nothing, never indulged our exasperation when it came to tiny matters like bathroom stops or spills at dinner. Without abandoning our parental duties, we'd been the gentlest of disciplinarians and we'd raised thoughtful, caring kids. A college football player who was neither a bully nor an egotist. An Ivy League daughter who'd left school to nurse her dying mother and then to pursue goals that had nothing to do with a huge house and a Mercedes-Benz.

On certain sad days I comforted myself with the thought that I'd done that one thing right, at least, in this life. One important thing right.

Not so far past Burning Coal Vein Campground and near signs for White Butte—at 3,507 feet above sea level, the state's highest point—Shelsa made her pee plea a second time. We stopped at Amidon's sole commercial building, the White Butte Trading Company, which occupied three downstairs rooms of a tiny house. Inside, a most attractive woman about my own age sat behind a counter, minding a museum of half-old objects. Earrings and cigarette lighters, church hats and porcelain cups, campaign buttons, advertising posters, metal wall hangings that claimed IT'S HARD TO BE HUMBLE WHEN YOU'RE NORWEGIAN.

After using the bathroom, Shelsa took a sudden interest in an old loop of rosary beads. "Only five dollars, Mami. Please!" Her mommy was, as far as I knew, a practicing Buddhist. Her daddy was one of the world's foremost Buddhist masters. Plus, my sister is . . . well, *frugal* is the nice way of saying it. I expected the famous, "Not now, honey," but Seese didn't object and Rinpoche produced a five from the folds of his magical robe. "Wery, wery great meditation master," he said, indicating the small metal Jesus on his cross.

"I know," Shelsa said. "That's the Jesus." And

56

then to me, "Uncle Ott, why are the people hurting him like that?"

"Because they couldn't see who he was," I said, without thinking about it.

"They were blind?"

"Sort of."

"Why didn't the people who could see help them?"

"They were afraid," I said, and a tremor went through me then. Another of those inexplicable afflictions I was prone to in Rinpoche's company. And, now, in his daughter's.

At that moment, Rinpoche came over to us where we stood near the counter. He was wearing a white Stetson. "How did it look?" he wanted to know, beaming.

"In some very weird way it suits you," I said, because in some very weird way it did. The gold-trimmed maroon robe, the stocky body, the square, rust-brown face set on a thick neck. He looked like the cowboy from the old Camel cigarette ads, only in drag.

By the time Seese emerged from the bathroom, the second purchase had been made. She looked at her husband—who was grinning crookedly at her—and shook her head as if to say, *you're hopeless*. But, and this may seem strange, it was at that moment that I realized how deeply she loved him. The small headshake, the smile, the hint of laughter in her eyes—it reminded me so much of the way Jeannie would have reacted that I had to step outside, too quickly, and stand in the gravel drive, staring back up the road in the direction we'd come. Back in time.

Just then the phone rang in my pocket. When I heard Natasha's "Dad?" in my ear, I didn't even say hello. I said, "What's wrong?"

"Don't get worried," she said. Which is the single most worrisome thing a parent can hear.

"What happened?"

"Nothing, maybe, but it was a little strange. I forgot to buy something for supper and I was shopping in Dickinson a little while after you guys left and I was in the Kroger parking lot and this big dark blue SUV pulled up and a man got out. Very stocky. Chinese, I think. He came over to me. I was putting on my seat belt and I'd rolled down the window because it's been hot and the car had been sitting there, and, without even saying hello, he said, 'Is the Rinpoche with you?' with kind of an accent, though he pronounced Rinpoche correctly."

"Was he threatening?"

"Not really. He looked like he could have been, but he wasn't. I told him Rinpoche was away and he asked, 'Away where?' and I said on a driving trip to the mountains and he just turned and got back in his car. But when he turned away from me it looked like he had a gun in a holster inside his shirt. There were other people in his car, I think, but the windows were tinted and I couldn't see them."

"Where are you now? Where, exactly?"

"Home. At the center."

"Is Warren there?"

"Yes."

"Is the security system on?"

"We only put it on at night."

Just then my trio of fellow travelers emerged from the White Butte Trading Company. By instinct I turned and walked a few paces away. "We can be back there in a little over an hour."

"Dad! Never! I shouldn't have called you. It was just, I don't know, a little weird."

"Would you do me a favor, hon? Would you just call the state police and let them know? And go stay at Warren's for a while, or go visit Anthony at school, or go home for a week or something?"

"You're overreacting, Dad."

"Maybe not."

"It didn't have that feeling."

"You said he had a gun, Tash."

"I *think* he had a gun. Everybody has a gun here now. And if he wanted to hurt me, he could have hurt me right then."

"In the Kroger parking lot? With a hundred witnesses?"

"It was *Rinpoche* he asked about, Dad. I was just calling to ask you to tell him because he doesn't answer his phone."

I looked over and saw Rinpoche with his white Stetson on. He was sending me a big smile. I beeped the car unlocked so they wouldn't have to stand in the sun.

"Dad?"

"I'm here, hon. I'll talk to them right now. I'm worried. I'm concerned."

"I think you're flipping out a little, Dad. Rinpoche will know what to do. Enjoy the trip. Love you."

Walking back to the car I kept a grim little smile on my lips. I got in, started it up, pulled back onto the highway. It had always been Dad who would know what to do, at least in the early years. Now Dad was flipping out. Rinpoche had traded seats with Celia and kept his hat on. The Chinese, I was thinking. Murderers of a million Tibetans, torturers of monks and nuns. The people of Tiananmen Square, five hundred executions a year, supporters of the North Koreans, who kept their political prisoners in cages and worked them to death à la Hitler. The Chinese, against six-seven Warren with his pellet gun and nighttime security system and my daughter with her three-week women's self-defense course from senior year in high school. I glanced at my sister in the mirror. I looked sideways at the Lone Rinpoche. From even before Shelsa's birth they'd been telling me what a special child she was and what a special role I was supposed to play in her spiritually illustrious future. A godfather of the first order.

I'd never truly believed it. Not in my depths. And at that moment, gliding south on 85 past a billboard that advertised QUALITY SHOPPING IN FRIENDLY BOWMAN, ND, I wanted nothing so badly as I wanted my niece to be a perfectly ordinary seven-year-old, as unremarkable as the flattening dry landscape, as safe as the North Dakota of my youth, as unthreatening to the Chinese haters as a wildflower in a field. I wanted only that.

From behind me she said, "Did you give Tasha love from me, Uncle Ott?"

"How did you know it was Tasha?"

"I had a dream she was going to call."

"When? Last night? You were home with her last night."

"A daytime dream," she said happily. "In the store. When I was holding the Jesus beads."

Six

All through the barren wasteland, the moonscape, the dry nothingness that is southwestern North Dakota and northwestern South Dakota, I thought about Natasha's call. Probably she'd be fine. Most likely the guy in the Kroger parking lot was harmless, a wannabe cop, a martial arts expert looking for some spiritual counseling from the famous Volya Rinpoche. Maybe he wasn't even Chinese. Probably the visit had nothing to do with Shelsa at all. Still, the tinted windows, the gun, the fact that he'd connected her with Rinpoche. . . . I didn't like it much.

As I drove—Bowman, the state line, an eighty-mile stretch of grazing land unsuited for the growing of human food—I kept a piece of my attention on the cowboy beside me. There he sat, still, happy, unruffled, while swarms of worries, fears, regrets, and hopes buzzed my brain, hornets in a jar. He wasn't aloof, never uncaring, hardly naive; it was just that he'd somehow learned to use his mental energies in a way that was fundamentally different from the way I used mine. In the midst of a violent, speed-obsessed world, peopled with lunatics, how did one become that kind of human being? Focused, undistracted, not battered this way and that by dark wisps of paranoia?

I would have asked him that question except for the fact that he'd been answering it for eight years now, since the first hour we met. He'd sent me books—his own and others. He'd given me meditation instructions, jokingly and sometimes not so jokingly pointed out my flaws and follies, turned my attention to the heretofore ignored interior universe of my mind. The story was that

Volya Rinpoche belonged to a line of spiritual teachers—*masters* was the word some people used—men, and in his open-minded lineage, some women, reincarnated enlightened ones who volunteered to be reborn into this hothouse of pain and death for the benefit of humanity. I'd been fortunate enough to have him come into my life. . . . And what had I done with that good fortune?

What I had done, I realized, was give up. I had my reasons. You don't lose a spouse, a job, a beloved dog, have your kids leave home, and not entertain thoughts of surrender. The pain was very real. But on some buried level of my consciousness I knew that giving up solved nothing. I had been wallowing in self-pity, and self-pity always feeds its hosts a diet of sour syrup then leaves them hungry and bitter.

And yet—isn't this how the mind works?—even knowing all that, even realizing, in some abstract, intellectual way, what a stroke of good fortune it was for me to have Rinpoche in my life, even feeling the interior change he'd begun to effect in me, there was a stubborn little part that resisted, that holed up in its cold cavern, hugging itself and muttering complaints. This part of me had its own distinctive voice; I could, at moments, hear it clearly.

Rinpoche burped, smiled, gazed out at the bleak landscape, which was dry and nut-brown and spotted here and there with scrub brush and sage.

"Papi, say 'excuse me,' " came the gentle order from the back seat.

" 'Scuse me."

I wanted to tell him about the Chinese visitor, and I would, of course I would. But I didn't want to be mocked for worrying needlessly. So I worried, needlessly, that I'd be mocked.

Well beyond Big Nasty Creek, beyond Custer National Forest, and Buffalo, South Dakota, beyond Redig and Castle Rock Butte I saw a sign that read, CENTER OF THE NATION, and, without really knowing what it meant, I made a sharp right turn onto a gravel road. From my very first driving trip with Rinpoche I'd taken onto my shoulders the responsibility for educating him about America. I don't have any idea why I felt such a need. He'd never asked me to do that; Seese had never asked me. This education wasn't exactly the kind of thing a Ph.D. advisor would approve: I'd taken him to a Hershey's factory to see how the Kisses were made, to a Chicago Cubs game; I'd shown him the Coulee Dam and Yellowstone, the burnt-out iron cities of Ohio, and the elegant farms of Amish country; let him listen to talk radio for a few minutes at a time, occasionally dipped into politics and history. He seemed interested, sometimes fascinated. Maybe it was just that, since he was giving me so much in the way of spiritual teaching, I felt I owed him something in return. And America was a subject I knew. Raised on a high-plains farm, seasoned in Manhattan, denizen of the well-off suburbs, I'd seen a good part of the American spectrum, and I paid attention to the rest. I cared about my country, maybe more than I should have. I followed the news—on my computer, on TV, radio, in newspapers and magazines. When the national mood turned sharply in some new and bizarre direction, when our leaders failed us, I took it personally. I wept when the kids were killed in Connecticut; I laughed when *Saturday Night Live* mimicked Bush, Obama, or Schwarzenegger. I cringed at Katrina. Cheered for the Yanks. It would be foolish to say I was a perfect representative of an American citizen—I was a white, upper-middle-class man, educated, financially secure—but, at the same time, I took a back seat to no one in my American-ness, my pride in history's greatest experiment in democracy, my shame at its failings.

So when I saw the sign for CENTER OF THE NATION on the side of Route 85, there was no chance of *not* checking it out.

"What's here?" Seese asked from the back seat.

"Dirt," Shelsa said, and we laughed.

Down the long gravel road we went, empty grazing land right and left. Ten minutes of it and we saw the Stars and Stripes flapping on the other side of a barbed wire fence, a pile of stones there, a two-car turnout, a smaller sign. I parked and we all got out. Happy to be free, Shelsa trotted up the road in the sunlight, black hair bouncing. "I think," I said, "this must be the point that marks the geographical center of the United States if you include Hawaii and Alaska. It's too far north and west to be anything else."

We looked across the fence at the pile of rocks. You couldn't walk up to the actual Center of the Nation because, apparently, this was private property and the owners didn't want just anybody treading on a small piece of their ten-thousand-acre, next-to-useless land. After all, what if someone tripped, broke a finger, filed suit? What if, thanks to some weird clause in the law, letting a few dozen tourists a year walk to the actual spot ended up leading to the de facto loss of a few hundred square feet of property? What if, years down the road, some Hollywood type wanted to make a movie here, and would pay for the privilege, and the owners had forfeited that right?

That, too—lawsuit mania, selfishness, obsession with property—was America, though I decided not to explain it to my companion.

"This place has a very spiritual feeling," my sister said, and I agreed. Once you got off the highway you felt some kind of good spirit breathing there, in the stillness, the quiet, the space. Time seemed to shimmer rather than move. It seemed reflected in the small breeze, just a breath really, that touched the tops of the alfalfa plants. You felt presence rather than movement; you wanted to *be* more than *do*. I imagined myself making a three-day retreat in an isolated cabin here, if such a place existed.

Shelsa trotted up and leapt into my arms. I hugged her close and swung her in a circle, the smiling faces of her mother and father passing in and out of view like planets, like moons. I thought: *This is the center of your nation, of your world. Hold this moment. Appreciate this.* And I did.

We stopped for lunch at a lonely, general store/ café outpost, run by a couple who were trying to sell it. Fox News was on their TV and so everything was bad there—a dip in consumer confidence after a six-year high. The stock market going down after a long rise. The NSA listening in on phone calls. Egypt and Syria exploding. I sat with my back turned to the television and ate my turkey and onion sandwich and shared a bottle of chocolate milk with my niece. There were times of late, many times in fact, when I wanted to tune out all the news—Fox and otherwise—and focus on the little slice of life over which I had some small influence. I worried that with our demonizing, our penchant for conflict, our knee-jerk angers, we were moving too close to 1920s Germany, too many of us marching under a righteous banner, too much hatred for each other, too much divisiveness, a craziness loosed upon our world. I looked at Shelsa. I remembered what Seese had said about her. I wondered what it would take to save us.

We decided not to make an offer on the middle-of-nowhere grocery/deli. We went on through the humble city of Belle Fourche, past darkly forested hills, *mok* games in the back seat, the road winding and climbing to almost five thousand feet, a brief temptation to visit Mount Rushmore, and then, at four p.m., after a quick descent, we pulled into Deadwood.

Deadwood, South Dakota, turnaround point for my sister and Shels, is a National Historical Landmark and bills itself as an authentic Wild West town—complete with casino gambling. We found the hotel my sister had chosen—the Silverado-Franklin—without trouble. Four floors, brick front, sloping concrete patio with wood columns holding up a low roof, it looked to be something right out of gold rush days, which, in fact, it was. Teddy Roosevelt and William Taft had stayed there, then Babe Ruth, John L. Sullivan, John Wayne. In 1929 the hotel went bust, along with the rest of the country, and then, in an ironic twist (wasn't it gambling, of a sort, that had made the country go bust?), when South Dakota legalized gambling in 1989, the Silverado-Franklin was reborn.

We had barely made it through the front door—held open by a friendly doorman—when we were greeted by the clanging bells and neon of a bank of slot machines. Here was the check-in desk, and there, a few paces beyond it, a circus of noise, light, and dreams of easy money.

"Wery good place, Otto!" Rinpoche said as we stood at the desk, signing in. I felt a splash of guilt. It was one thing to show him America, something else entirely to corrupt him with its vices.

Celia was smirking, Shelsa leaning into the protection of her mother's hip. I was recalling a moment from the first road trip Rinpoche and I had made, eight years earlier, New Jersey to North Dakota. Somewhere in Minnesota, on Indian land not far from the headwaters of the Mississippi, thinking I'd show my traveling companion another intriguing facet of Americana, I'd taken him into a casino. It was a sad place, really, just sixty or so chrome-and-glass machines with a dozen old folks spinning the reels in desultory hypnosis. Rinpoche had had the bad fortune of winning on his first spin and was instantly hooked. The clank of coins in the tray, the celebratory bells and sirens—*Free money, Otto!* He kept playing, kept winning, kept ignoring my pleas to quit while he was ahead. I'd ended up having to physically remove him from the premises, and I never knew for certain if it had all been an act, or if the allure of money-for-nothing was too much even for a great spiritual master like him.

"Can we play?" he asked excitedly in the Silverado lobby.

"I tell you what. Come with me to park the car. Seese and Shels can follow the bellman up to the room and settle in, and you and I can gamble away a few bucks before dinner. Good?"

"Good, good," he said, clapping me on the back forcefully enough to make the cowboy hat tilt sideways on his head. He touched my sister's hand—so tenderly—planted the Stetson on Shelsa, and out we went to bring the SUV around back.

In the hotel lot I told him what Natasha had told me—the Chinese guy, the car, the gun.

"What means?" he asked.

"I thought *you* would tell *me.*"

"I ask what means this *tented?*"

"Tinted. Darkened. Windows made so you can't see through them."

"For why?"

"So you can't tell who's inside. It's a style favored by criminals, the ultra rich, hip-hop artists, and politicians."

"Oh," he said.

"*Oh,* is right. Somebody's looking for you."

"Lot a people looking for Rinpoche."

"Somebody with tinted windows and a gun is

looking for you. Or maybe for Shelsa. Somebody Chinese, it seems."

He turned his eyes forward, away from me, spent a moment pondering, then nodded.

I'd been worried he'd laugh at me, but now that he wasn't laughing, the worry bubble swelled in another direction. "Did you have some trouble at the Center?"

"Little bit trouble."

"What kind?"

He shrugged. "Few bad phone calls. Some people they painted words on the last retreat cabin one time."

"The one I stayed in?"

Another nod.

"What kind of words?"

"KILL THE MUSLIMS."

"Really?"

"Small people in their minds," he said. "Maybe the drug people."

Or maybe, I thought, one of the Aryan Nations nutcases who wanted to start a "community" in the town of Leith, North Dakota. I'd heard the main man interviewed on the radio. All I could remember—this was more than enough—was his comment about wanting to raise a flag with "a discreet swastika" on it. If there is a more perfect oxymoron I'd like to hear it.

Rinpoche clapped a hand down on my thigh. "Maybe," he said, "not to worry too much, okay?"

"Sure."

"Chinese, maybe a little bit trouble, but not to worry too much."

"Okay," I said, but the conversation had already watered my little seed of concern. The army of my protective instincts—paternal, fraternal, avuncular—was suddenly at attention, weapons cleaned and at the ready. I was not, as they say, a New Yorker for nothing.

We went inside, where Rinpoche had more casino misfortune. On only his third spin the bells went off—he won forty-seven dollars.

"A wise man would walk out now," I counseled from the neighboring machine.

"Win maybe one more time, okay?"

"Sure, then dinner."

But, naturally, he won once, then twice, then a third time, while my machine swallowed money with the appetite of an underfed hen. I don't believe there was any kind of spiritual magic involved. It was simply, as the expression goes, dumb luck, and I was sure that, in time, according to the unalterable calculus of gambling, the machine would turn against him. Or maybe it wouldn't. Maybe my brother-in-law was immune to the casino calculus, the way he was clearly immune to things like the common cold, anger, and America's vast array of material and physical temptations. Part of me worried, though, that gambling was the chink in his armor, the Achilles' heel, and that, if I didn't take him by the arm and drag him into sunlight again, as I'd done in western Minnesota, he'd be ruined. Another part of me wanted to see, not his ruin of course, but a stretch of bad luck. Let him be human; let him lose; let him learn his lesson and give up gambling forever.

And a third part of me wondered if this, too, was a trick, if he might be trying to impart some new pearl of wisdom as he sometimes did, without words.

Bing! Bing! Bing! Rinpoche was up sixty-four dollars, up eighty, up one hundred and twelve.

"I like this wery much!" he exclaimed loudly, raising an arm to encompass the entire casino and attracting stares from all directions. He had to be joking, feigning, teaching. Had to be. He gave me a sly look, eyes shifted right, hint of a devilish grin.

"There's some lesson here, isn't there."

"Everywhere the wessons," he said, yanking on the black ball with particular enthusiasm. He lost three spins in a row, betting the maximum, and then, *Clang! Clang! Clang!* Another sixty dollars.

"What is it? That money doesn't really matter to a spiritual man?"

"Matters, sure."

"That we're always wanting more?"

Rinpoche stopped playing suddenly, looked

73

for a few seconds at what he'd won, then gathered up his coins, and led me, like an experienced casino rat, straight to the cashier's window. He hadn't answered the question but I could see an answer forming in his eyes. "I like it so much, the gambling," he said, as we headed toward the entrance. "The feeling when you win, how you say it?"

"The thrill."

"Trill. Wery nice, this trill. Like the sex maybe a little bit. Like the happy feeling inside when you see your child smile."

"Like the first taste of a great meal," I said.

He laughed with his head thrown back and clapped me on the shoulder. "Like the candy. The ice cream, the how you say? Fadge brownie!"

"Fudge."

"Fadge."

"The sugar high."

"The nice feeling makes you want more nice!"

"Absolutely. Always."

"In your mind," he tapped his right temple, "like a bells ringing, lights. The trill. This casino just like a mind with a trill inside it. Just the same."

"It's designed that way."

"Wery smart!"

"It's actually insidious," I said. "It's all set up to make you happy for a while, then take away your money." But Rinpoche had gone to one of those places he went. He was beside me, fully present as always, but I knew him well enough by then to be able to detect a certain light in his eyes. As if in possession of some cosmic radar, he'd locked onto a pure truth and was trying to figure the right way of showing it to someone with limited vision.

"You now, I think, having to give up the sugar, the cake, the ice cream, the candy bras."

"Candy *bars*."

"Give up now, my smart friend. Three weeks, maybe four."

"Why, because I'm fat?"

"No, no!"

"Because I'm at an age when I need to start worrying about dental hygiene?"

"Because I want that you see the open space when there's no trill."

"What's in there?"

"Ha!" he said, his one-syllable laugh. "This is the big question! . . . You anytime see the wery small smile on Buddha's face?"

"Sure. Plenty of times."

He wrapped an arm around me and pulled me close against his shoulder. "That's what's in there, man!"

Seven

From that conversation we proceeded directly to dinner. I should interject here that whenever I left greater New York in those days I almost always experienced a dark and haunting trepidation, the fear of a restricted diet, the deep worry that I wouldn't be able to eat the kinds of food I was accustomed to eating. Mexican, real Italian on Arthur Avenue in the Bronx, French, Thai, dim sum on Mott Street, Japanese, Brazilian, Malaysian, Indian, and so on. Unlike several of the other married men I knew, I'd been perfectly content to make love with one woman. Beyond the occasional twinge of lust brought on by some Manhattan beauty, I felt very little urge to sleep around. Jeannie was beautiful to my eye, imaginative in conversation and in bed, and I had, with her, the kind of soul connection that no amount of passionate one-night stands could equal. I was content. I felt lucky, blessed to have her.

With food, however, it was precisely the opposite: I craved variety. Vietnamese, Burmese, Afghani, Nepali—New York offered eateries that spanned the entire global spectrum, and two or three times a week I took advantage of that. It was medicine for me. I was afraid to be without it.

By and large, to my way of thinking, the American West was a culinary desert. There were exceptions, yes, spots of color in a vast gray smock of beef and starch. But the settlers thereabouts were white people with pronounceable names, and such people—my own family among them—preferred a diet as steady and solid as their habits of work. A decent marinara was, to quote my mother, "spicy," which was a code word for *inferior.* A nice hot chana masala, say, or a good Moroccan stew—these pleasures were seen, by the longtime inhabitants of the American West, in something like the way the *Kama Sutra* would be seen by missionaries. Sinful, unpatriotic, spiritually perilous.

I confess that I've blocked out the name of the restaurant where the four of us ate dinner in Deadwood, ~~Colorado~~ *South Dakota*. There was salmon on the menu, I remember that, and flies everywhere— not uncommon in the West in summer. And I remember, too, that when I asked our waitress if it was fresh salmon or frozen she looked at me as if I were her guest at a dude ranch and I'd asked if geldings had testicles. "Hon," she said, by way of an answer, "this is South Dakota."

"The pork chop then, please."

I noticed on that first visit to our table that she was flirting with Rinpoche. "I'm a woman who likes a smooth head," was one line, and "You're

Sioux, I bet. I've always found that Sioux men fit me nicely."

Apparently, they didn't get many Rinpoches in Deadwood, and apparently she thought Seese and I were a married couple (we both wore rings; Rinpoche did not), parents of Shelsa, and Rinpoche was an honorary uncle visiting from the reservation. It's possible she'd been drinking. On subsequent trips to our table she put a hand on Rinpoche's shoulder, touched his arm. He seemed not to notice. Neither did Cecelia.

"Did you gamble?" Seese asked her husband in what sounded like a worried tone.

"With the machine," Rinpoche admitted sheepishly. He pantomimed a man pulling a slot lever and made a sad clown's face.

I expected my sister to ask if he'd won or lost, or to chastise him, but she said only, "I've been having all these dreams about casinos lately. It's so weird!"

"Dreams lead you to secrets," Shelsa chimed in, and I shall always remember her saying that and always remember that we "adulted" her, as Tasha used to say when she was a girl. Meaning, we looked at her and smiled but gave no weight at all to her words.

"Can I ask if you have any idea where Rinpoche and I are supposed to go once you and Shels head back?" I said, almost adding, *Have you had any recent visions? Dreams with maps in them?*

In my defense, I didn't speak those sentences. Also in my defense, I was hungry.

"Nebraska," Seese said, without so much as a blink.

"Into the famous Nebraskan mountains?"

Her smirk. My quick apology.

"Does he have a talk scheduled there or something?"

"We have a friend in the sandhills," she said. "A man I started a food co-op with many years ago, in Berkeley. Alton Smithson. He comes to the Center three or four times a year and does work for us instead of paying the residency fees. Alton's a computer specialist, a great one. He's become friends with Natasha, hasn't she mentioned him?"

"Not that I recall, no."

"Well, I had a dream last night that you should go see him. I sent him a note this morning. He's expecting you. It's less than a day's drive."

"In the wrong direction," I said. "You had a vision about mountains. The mountains are west of here. Nebraska's east."

"I know my geography, thank you, brother. It's just for one night."

"I think there's something you're not telling me."

Seese looked at her husband—Rinpoche was carving the last bits of the white flesh of a baked potato from its skin, with great care. Shelsa had finished her chicken fingers and was playing some kind of game with Topo Gigio, tilting his head left, then right, saying things like, "Tomorrow we ride the bus, Topo, but don't be afraid, okay? There won't be cats on the bus. I'll stay close to you. I'll protect you, okay? It's important not to be afraid. Your karma protects you, okay?"

The waitress checked in, sent a salacious smile toward the object of her affection, and, swinging her hips in an exaggerated way, disappeared again.

Rinpoche and Shelsa headed off toward the bathrooms and, when the bill arrived, my lovely sister said she wanted to pay and added—another moment I shall never forget—"Shels might be the next Dalai Lama."

I blinked once, slowly, holding my eyes closed to keep myself from reacting. I understood at that moment, in the fly-ridden restaurant in Deadwood, ~~Colorado~~ South Dakota, with part of a pork chop still uneaten on my plate, that my sister was a mad egotist. Other parents, more traditional American fathers and mothers, salved the wound of their own insecurities by making their sons out to be the next Joe DiMaggio, Michael Jordan, or Peyton Manning, their daughters the next Oprah, Beyoncé, or Maria Sharapova. Jeannie and I had run into them countless times at Natasha's soccer games and Anthony's football games. There was a particular kind of desperate urgency to the way they cheered for their kids, as if, suckled on the worship of celebrity as they themselves had been, they couldn't quite bear the thought that their Jimmy or Vanessa might turn out to be just a pretty good tight end or midfielder. My sister wasn't into sports or music; she was into spirituality. She was married to the Kobe Bryant of the spiritual world. So she'd convinced herself that, not only was her daughter spiritually gifted, the girl was special, extraordinary, the holiest of holies.

"Seese," I said, with as much restraint as I could manage, "the Dalai Lama is always a man. And, correct me if I'm wrong, but doesn't the present Dalai have to pass on before a new one is selected?"

"It could be different this time, Otto. There could be a man *and* a woman," Seese said. "They'd share the duties."

"Says who?"

"Someone in His Holiness's inner circle."

"He told you all this?"

"*Hinted.* In a talk I read about, not face-to-face. But it's a she, not a he."

"Then why don't you all just fly off to Dharamsala?"

"Because we're not sure. I said *might be.* And in any case we'd have to wait for a formal invitation."

"Why are we on this wild goose chase, then?"

"Because it came to me in a vision and because

the woman who gave that talk—a very famous Rinpoche—said they're still looking for the other person, the one who'll be Shelsa's partner."

"Do you realize how this sounds?"

"To whom?"

"To the average sane person."

"The average sane person wouldn't even believe in the way the Dalai Lama is chosen. The average sane person—as you call it—would never believe Jesus rose from the dead, or that the Buddha was enlightened, or that prayers have any effect whatsoever, or that dreams mean anything."

The waitress came back with the little leather book that held my sister's credit card. She looked at us and nodded, as if she'd stumbled upon yet another married couple in the midst of a post-prandial spat. Rinpoche and Shelsa returned just in time for the waitress to shoot him a call-me glance. I half expected to see her phone number scribbled on the receipt.

Rinpoche appeared to sense that we'd been discussing a difficult issue but he only sat there, hands folded, watching us as if he were a graduate student taking notes for a thesis on sibling conflict.

"Rinpoche," I said, perhaps too forcefully. "I'd appreciate it now if you'd tell me my sister isn't crazy. I want to hear you say those words."

My brother-in-law looked at me without expression, the muscles of his face firm and unmoving, the eyes steady, a shaft of overhead light reflecting from his bald head. He said, "I like wery much the potato here."

I wondered at that moment if both of them had been mentally crippled by their years of isolation on the farm. With its endless winters and long distances between towns, North Dakota could do that to people. A friend of my parents, one George "Buster" Fynch, was widowed in midlife, kept farming his five hundred acres alone, but then took to nudism. He could sometimes be seen on his tractor, naked as the Good Lord made him, singing church hymns and plowing circles on flat land.

I decided I'd keep an eye on Rinpoche as we traveled, see if there'd been any change, any slippage. We left our difficult conversation at the table and strolled the sidewalks of Deadwood for a little while. There was a series of interesting historical plaques—in the late 1800s the city's Jewish mayor, Sol Star, had made sure, during hard times, that no one in town went hungry; in 1876, Wild Bill Hickok had been killed while holding a great poker hand; Calamity Jane was buried next to him; the buildings of the original gold rush town had burned to ash in 1879, and had been rebuilt in brick. The place had a Disney-esque feel, families licking ice cream cones, shops selling T-shirts, couples in motorcycle leather holding hands, a yuppie in a Yale cap taking photos with his iPad while his stern-faced wife and tow-headed twins trailed along behind.

It seemed somehow fitting when, at a little shop on that main drag, a waitress with a Sanskrit OM symbol tattooed on her neck sold Shelsa a strawberry ice cream cone. In a weary travelers' silence we walked back and climbed the four flights of stairs to our Silverado-Franklin suite. We had two bedrooms with forest-green carpet, torn wallpaper, an upright piano, and a huge TV in the sitting room. A framed, yellowed newspaper clipping on one wall claimed that Jack Dempsey, the famous boxer, had once slept here. This made zero impression on Rinpoche and Seese. They did their before-bed meditation with Shelsa, and I joined them there, beside the cot on which she'd sleep. Under the good monk's guidance we all envisioned a blue lake, the surface of the water ruffled at first by a small wind, and then growing calmer and calmer until it was perfectly flat and still, like the mind in deepest meditation. "Little wind blow on across this water now," Rinpoche said quietly, resting a hand on his daughter's forehead, "and then he go still again. Flat. Blue. Sleep now, beautiful child. Sleep with wrapped around you like a blanket our love."

I peeked once. Shelsa was sitting cross-legged on the pillow, eyelids steady, face set in an expression of the most perfect peace. I closed my eyes again and instead of envisioning the lake, I thought: *What would our world be like if every child were put to sleep this way?*

The prayer completed, I hugged my niece warmly and went into the sitting room so they could have a last few minutes of family time. *The Godfather* was on the TV. Part I. I turned the volume low and watched. Luca Brasi, the vicious enforcer, was handing an envelope of money to Don Corleone and saying, "And I hope that their first child will be a masculine child."

I turned off the set and sat on the worn leather couch in a small stew of anxiety. What if Rinpoche's bloodline, with its history of purified souls, *had* produced a kind of anti-Godfather, a blessed heir, and the line of Buddhist spiritual leaders would now switch genders? Why, in the modern world, was such a thing impossible? And then, close on the heels of that idea: What if, instead of power madness and envy leading to the assassination of a mafia figure, it led to the assassination of a spiritual figure? My niece, to be exact. Wouldn't it be better for her to keep a low profile, if she turned out, as her mother claimed, to be this special spirit?

Seese emerged from the bedroom, long hair falling on her Scottish plaid sleeping shirt, which did not go at all well with her red-checked pajama pants. She closed the door quietly behind her and came and sat opposite me. "I don't like to upset you," she said.

"I'm fine."

"I could see the change in your face in the restaurant. I know what you must have been thinking about me."

I shrugged.

"Don't you see that Shels isn't an ordinary girl?"

"Sure, I see it. She predicts the future, she stands outside in the snow and warms herself up by *thinking,* for God's sake. She talks like an adult half the time. But it's a bit of a stretch to go from that to being the next Dalai Lama, don't you think?"

She slanted her eyes away and back. "In every life, brother, there comes a point where you have to make a stand inside yourself, spiritually. You have to say, I believe this and I don't believe that. I'll commit to this, I'll abandon that. It's in the Bible, the Torah, the Sutras, the Vedas, the *Tao Te Ching.* Muhammad said surrender to God is the only way to salvation. So here's your moment. You can think I'm just a flake, a nutcase, a mother who wants her child to be special to compensate for her own failings. Or you can give me enough benefit of the doubt to travel with Rinpoche for a little while and see where it leads. If I turn out to be wrong, then you can tell me I was wrong and I'll apologize for wasting your time. But you're at a spiritual crossroads. I know you're discouraged and God knows you have reason to be. But now you have a choice. You can listen to the skeptical voice and go back to New York and the life you were leading there, or you can see all the awful things that have happened to you as a preparation, a turning over of the soil so it will be ready for a new crop to be planted." She stood up, more agitated than I'd seen her in years. "I love you. I'll always love you, but I don't want to keep fighting with you. I *see* things. I *feel* things. I sense things before they happen—not always, and not perfectly. Sometimes the message gets mixed up. But this time . . . I think I have it right. I love you. Shelsa loves you. Rinpoche loves you. Good night!"

door behind her. I switched off the lamp and sat there in darkness. The shouts of drunken revelers reached the window from the street below and filtered through the glass. I tried to remember the last time Cecelia had spoken to me with that much intensity. For the most part, over the course of our adulthood she'd been background music. By her own design, I think. Always blending in, helping out, keeping the lowest of profiles, a beautiful bird in the foliage, singing quietly, urging me, cajoling me, sometimes, as in my first road trip with Rinpoche, tricking me. But on that night she'd turned into a lioness, a match for her remarkable husband.

I sat there for a long time, pondering. She was right about at least one thing: I was at a crossroads. Spiritual, psychological, emotional, midlife—whatever the term was didn't really matter. I faced a choice, I knew that, and the choice was more than whether to believe in her visions or not.

On my previous visit to the farm, in early April, Rinpoche had held up a metal spring for my inspection. We were taking a walk through the fallow fields—I remember that there were still traces of snow in the shady spots—and he must have found the spring in one of the outbuildings. He held it in such a way that the metal spiraled upward in ascending circles. "Spirchal life," he said, touching it with a finger of his free hand. He started at the bottom coil and touched each one above it in the same place. "Feels like you go in circle, yes? Like you come again back on the same place, many times. Same trouble, same thinking. But it's not true, Otto. Meditation is like a wind here in the middle pushing you up, up. You want to go up in a straight like the rocket but you really go like this, this, how you say?"

"Spring."

"Sprin'. Good. This is how you go."

I remembered that mini-lesson then, on the couch in Jack Dempsey's room in the old Silverado-Franklin, remembered it and finally understood. Time and again I'd gotten to this place with my sister, wrestling with her flakiness, her eccentric worldview, her odd ideas, trying to love and respect her in spite of them. She read palms, she dated a monk, eventually married him, she gave birth to a spiritually gifted child, she'd helped influence my daughter to forgo her last years of college for the meditative life. With each return to that point on the circle I'd had to let go of old ways of seeing her world and allow some new idea, some scruffy, unwelcome visitor to apply for citizenship in my neat neighborhood. Clearly I was being asked to do that again, on another level, after a stretch of living that had knocked most of the confidence out of me. But this time I wasn't sure I could manage it. Having a monk in the family was one thing. Spending time in meditation was easily incorporated into what I thought of as an ordinary American life. Even acknowledging the fact that Shelsa had some special abilities—really not that difficult. But believing, or even pretending to believe, that she and some yet-to-be-discovered other special soul *might* have been chosen to play some great role in the world? There was a line there. Across that line lay one of two possibilities: My sister was a true flake; or she was right.

Four floors below me banks of slot machines flashed, sang, and swallowed money. Beyond the window someone shouted in the street, five syllables of hilarity.

I sat there in the darkness for the better part of

an hour, pinched, as I had been for years, between two very different sets of assumptions about what, exactly, we were supposed to be doing here.

Eight

~~~

In the morning I awoke to the fine light of a Dakota summer day . . . and to the sight of my niece's face. Shelsa was standing next to the bed, still as the trunk of a cottonwood tree, staring down at her uncle in a kind of loving trance. Her mother was a light-skinned Caucasian, of German-Scandinavian stock, and her father's people had settled in Skovorodino in southernmost Siberia, but they'd arrived there, ten or fifteen generations earlier, from the Tibetan plateau. Rinpoche had skin the color of a ripe acorn, his genes showed more strongly in Shelsa. She had raven-black hair and brown-black eyes and a small, straight nose that bent slightly upward at the tip. She had my sister's build—on the slender side but not skinny—and Seese's long, graceful hands.

But the expression on her face at that moment—tenderness touched with wash of compassion—belonged to her alone. Natasha had twice described these bedside gazes to me, saying she'd sometimes stir in the morning and find her seven-year-old cousin there, watching over her. "The first few times it made the hair on my arms stand up, Dad. It's like she spent the night in another world and is still partly there, like she's been in a warm place and you're cold and she's trying to heat you up by looking at you. I'm used to it now, but the first few times it truly freaked me out."

"Good morning, my dear Shelsa," I said.

"Uncle Ott, your feet were going. You were running in your sleep!"

"That's how I get my exercise," I said, and she laughed so happily, so unself-consciously, that I felt a smile stretch the muscles of my neck. A smile that had not recently been seen. She hurried away to tell her mother my joke.

There was only one bathroom and her father was in the shower, so I had to wait a few minutes to use the toilet. Rinpoche was singing in a low baritone. It took me a moment to recognize the song: one verse of an Andrea Bocelli ballad that had been popular a decade before. Nice tune, but the words were lost on me.

A Russian-monk father who gambled, had ancestral roots in Tibet, and sang in Italian; a mother who had visions; a daughter with a beatific gaze: This was not an ordinary family.

After breakfast at the Howlin' Hawg Diner (committed now to a nonsugar diet, at least for a few days, I forced myself not to order a caramel roll, not to put jelly on my biscuit), Rinpoche and I accompanied Shelsa and Seese to the place where the bus to Rapid City stopped. "Why don't you travel another few days with us," I said to Seese, by way of an apology.

She reached up and kissed me on the lips. "My brother," she said, warmly.

"You could come with us, Shels."

"I miss Tasha," she said, in the grown-up voice. "And you and Papi have work you have to do. You have a job."

"You could help us, couldn't you?"

A stern shake of the head. Topo clutched tight to her chest. "Everybody has their job, Uncle Ott. I have to help Mami and Tash at the Center. I have to show Warren what to do."

I lifted her up, held her tight, then handed her across the air to her father for another bear hug. She wrapped her new rosary beads around the center of his cowboy hat and said, "So you don't forget me, Papi," as if there were one chance in twenty billion that he could. I remembered, in a college philosophy class, being introduced to the idea that it was the pleasure of sex that ensured the survival of our species. God, Nature, the Random Whirl of Molecules—our professor left the source of the design up to our individual belief systems, but made the point that the ecstasy attached to the sex drive—"more powerful than any other impulse," as she put it— was the force that kept the earth populated with human beings. Obvious enough, it seemed to me, though I have to say it wasn't something I'd thought about before I enrolled in Professor Spencer's Philosophy 102. I've pondered her words over the years and I'm sure she was right. It can't be an accident that there's so much pleasure in the act that preserves the species. Life wants to keep itself going, or the Grand Designer wants to keep it going. Either way, it works.

But on the sidewalk there in Deadwood I had the strange urge to locate Dr. Spencer, write her a postcard, and say, "The affection of small children doesn't hurt the cause, either." It's a different kind of pleasure, of course, but something turns over in the heart of an adult in the presence of a young child. No doubt it's part of the reason why, all over the world, we celebrate birth the way we do. There's magic in the child spirit. It's more than just the cute remarks and mispronunciations, more even than the completely unself-conscious embraces and abundance of innocent physical contact, the smiles, the laughs, the kisses. There is an energy there, a *pureness,* I want to say, an absolute essence that hasn't yet been messed with by the pains of grown-up life. In troubled families, in kids who've been abused, that essence is trampled on very early, but even in the healthiest families it soon fades. Doubt intervenes. Com-parison rears its ugly head. We enter a period of biological competition for a mate, a drive set so deeply in us that nothing can stop or alter it. I remembered a scrap from my Bible classes: "Unless ye become like little children. . . ." Some people I'd met— Rinpoche was at the top of this list—managed to preserve that childishness, that untrammeled self-expression, into adulthood. But most of my fellow Americans were half-crushed by the passage of time. Our spirits were dampened, twisted, mottled, trimmed. I don't mean we all turned into semi-humans, but, well, speaking for myself at least, there was some leaching out of the vibrancy, the joy, the faith in my absolute unique-ness, in my claim to part ownership of this earth.

Shelsa was such a pleasure to be around. Even forgetting the odd and special aspects—the strange morning gazes, the seeming ability to know things she had no real way of knowing, to warm or cool herself by will, the hours sitting so still in the yard that birds landed on her shoulders and joined in the contemplative fun— even forgetting all that (and it wasn't easy to forget)—she was like sunlight in every room she entered. Once or twice in any given day you'd see a spark of "normalcy" in her: She'd whine or fidget, make demands, complain. But these moments were like highlights of spice in a glass of good wine. Complexities that added to the richness. The rest of the time she was upbeat, curious, smart, warm as the summer fields. And this was especially true, for some reason, with her only uncle. She touched me whenever she could—hugs, kisses, quick back massages if my shoulders and neck were within reach. When we walked from car to restaurant or hotel, she almost always reached up and took hold of my hand, looked at me as if I were a better man than I knew myself to be, as if I actually deserved to be an uncle to such a creature, as if I carried around the reputation of a Hall of Fame father. There were times when I felt, with an eerie certainty, that I wasn't in the presence of a child at all. "Uncle Ott," she'd asked me at one of these moments, "do you think Aunt Jeannie was reincarnated yet?"

"I don't know. What do you think?"

"I think she probably was."

"Why do you think that?"

"Because Tash came out of her body. Her wound. And if a girl like Tash was borned into a wound like Aunt Jeannie's then Aunt Jeannie must be very, very special. And if Aunt Jeannie is that special then God won't let her just rest and sleep and take naps. She would come back to some other wound and pretty soon help people."

"I miss her. How could I know which wound she was born into?"

"You can't always know but maybe you'll feel it when you meet her and then you'll know. Like I knowed when I met Tash that we were friends a long time."

"When did you feel that?"

"I feeled it all the times with her. Like with you. Like with Mami and Papi. Maybe one day Aunt Jeannie will be born into Tash's wound."

"Do you feel it with Warren, too?"

"Yes."

"With the people who come to the Center to meditate?"

"No."

"With anyone else? In town?"

"Sia at the coffee shop. The woman, Marta, who is the wife with the farmer next to us."

"Special woman?"

"Yes."

These were the kinds of conversations we had. You could look at them two ways. You could suppose she was merely mimicking what she heard her mother and father say, reflecting their rather unusual (by American standards at least) worldview, repeating what she'd heard. Or, as my sister put it, you could "knock down the walls of the little room in which we've been taught to think" and imagine the world the way she and Rinpoche described it, a place of continual rebirth, of eternal connections, of spiritual evolution fueled by certain souls who kept returning and returning to aid the rest of us in our movement toward celestial ecstasy.

I was, in this one regard, bipolar. The steadiest of men in every other way, in the realm of having faith in the spiritual legitimacy of my three companions I was, in those days, a waffler, a doubter, a fair-weather fan. I confess this with no small degree of shame.

Waving good-bye to my niece through the bus window caused me an actual, physical pain. Shelsa was pressing Topo Gigio against the glass and moving him right and left, pretending to make him speak. Seese lifted a hand, blew her husband a kiss, sent me a smile and a good-luck nod. And then, in a burst of engine noise and a puff of diesel smoke, they were gone.

When they were out of sight I sent a text to my daughter, telling her what time the bus would arrive in Dickinson and asking if all was okay. She responded immediately with this message: FINE, DAD. IN LOVE. To which I responded: GLAD ON BOTH COUNTS. MISS YOU.

I found myself remembering Jeannie's mother, and thinking: *If you marry him, your children will be giants.*

Nine

South and east of Deadwood the land was dry as dust, vast rolling stretches of it, good for almost nothing but looking at. Too parched for farming. Too sparsely vegetated for successful ranching. After an hour or so of driving we saw a sign,

ENTERING OGLALA SIOUX RESERVATION, which, in a sad way, made perfect sense: Of all the corners of this earth into which they might have been herded, the Indians had been "given" this land, the worst and most useless in the continent, land that—once the bison were gone—nobody wanted. It was like taking over a family's house after the family had been living there for millennia and telling them they could camp out in one corner of the basement but you were keeping the kitchen and living room and all the upstairs, destroying the garden in the back yard from which they'd fed themselves for generations. You'd let them buy alcohol and camp in the basement, and then you'd criticize them for not being as disciplined and "productive" as you were.

Within two-tenths of a mile we passed the Prairie Wind Casino (yes, we let them have slot machines down there in our basement). If Rinpoche noticed it, he said nothing. Another few seconds and I heard him chanting, as quietly as if his daughter were asleep in back and he didn't want to wake her. It was an eerie sound, one low note held and vibrating, then held again, like a tugboat churning along the Hudson, signaling. I knew what it meant: a prayer for these people.

To either side we saw well-spaced trailers. With a few exceptions, they were rusted and broken-down, sometimes accompanied by an old car out front, sometimes with rubber tires on the roof to prevent the metal sheets from being carried away on the Dakotas' notorious winds. There were clothes drying on the lines but no people, no kids in the yards, none of the little signals of prosperity you'd see in suburbia: adults pruning trees, raking leaves, painting trim, building sheds for their lawn mowers. The structures we saw reeked of hopelessness. They were rusted, old, flimsy, sitting back from the road on their patches of useless land, in a part of the country where a winter night could reach 40 below zero, where it was regularly 110 in summer, where the nearest jobs were thirty or sixty or eighty miles away. Here and there fir trees pocked the landscape and you could see odd-shaped white sand out-croppings like miniature strip mines long since abandoned. There were two or three horses in the fields, and patches of sunflowers, and a small herd of black cattle, and then, like one last symbol standing for everything else we'd seen, a doll—naked plastic baby—sprawled on the hot tar road.

We passed two handmade signs saying WHY DIE? and THINK. And after a moment we saw another one and I realized they marked places where people had been killed in auto accidents, and they were meant to discourage drunk driving. There were other signs, handmade and stuck into the dirt—VOTE NO TO ALCOHOL! For a hundred years it had been illegal, but a news-paper headline in Deadwood had said that, just a few days earlier, the tribe had voted on whether or not to allow alcohol to be sold on the reservation. The yes votes had prevailed by a narrow margin.

Another minute and we were approaching the Oglala Ridge General Store. Rinpoche asked me to pull in to the gravel parking lot and I did so. We were the only non-native people there. The front door, open at that hour, could be locked with barred metal grates not unlike those you saw on the first floors of townhouses in parts of Manhattan and the boroughs. Inside, it was the usual array of packaged foodstuffs, the counter area presided over by an American Indian woman who reminded me of some of the African American women I'd encountered in my tutoring days. These were people who lived in the harshest of circumstances—in a sea of violence and sorrow that would have drowned lesser souls—and yet they were unfailingly upbeat, positive, fierce spirited. I'd seen it in some of the men, too, of course, and in some of the adolescents I tutored. But it took a different form in the women. It was almost as if the life force I mentioned earlier, that enormous drive to preserve and extend the species, was visible in their eyes and the muscles around the mouth, in their shoulders and hands. You could see it working its stubborn magic. There was no surrender in them, no despair. Somehow, in a swamp of desolation, they held to the long view.

The other people we encountered in and around

the store had no such energy to them. A stooped, haggard woman of thirty years came up to me and asked for "one dollar," and when I handed over a five she thanked me with a remarkable dignity. Not proud, exactly. And not fawning. Simply as if we were brother and sister, and the gift was expected but not required, and she was grateful but not diminished. I bought a bag of pistachios. In the parking lot, while I popped open a nut and waited for my companion to finish his conversation with the store owner and emerge into the light, a man approached me. He had fresh blood on his lips, as if he'd been vomiting through a ruptured esophagus, or was tubercular. He was holding out a ring of colorful, tightly woven plastic strands that he kept assuring me he'd made himself. He seemed high or drunk or alcohol-saturated or maybe just deathly ill, and he wanted twenty dollars for the rather unremarkable piece of handiwork. I gave him ten, and he accepted it with the same quiet dignity as the woman.

We drove away, east on Route 18, the interior of the car filled with a terrible silence, as if we were in the presence of some unforgiveable travesty, as if the air above the reservation were suffused with the blood of bad history, the ghosts of slaughter and teenage suicides. We passed the Felix Cohen Home for the Elderly, then a hospital that seemed defunct, then a crossroads town— Oglala—which was composed of a gas station, a market, a Pizza Hut, a Boys and Girls Club, and a string of empty storefronts. We saw a young Indian boy sitting in a forlorn posture, with his back against the market wall, holding up a packet of what appeared to be sage wrapped in newspaper. We turned left, east, out of town, then turned north toward Wounded Knee. This detour was my idea. Why I wanted to see Wounded Knee I don't know. I remembered, vaguely, that something had happened there, some type of insurrection or revolt. We drove deeper into the reservation, past miles of low, dry, empty hills, a lonely ranch house, then pulled into a rest area where there was a billboard explaining the place's history. In what would turn out to be the final battle of the Indian Wars, in late December 1890, a group of several hundred Lakota Sioux—more women and children than men—were killed by American soldiers. I stood next to Rinpoche as we read this. For a little while I believed I could feel the weight of the injustice, the actual weight of it—the stolen land, the slaughtered buffalo, the broken promises, the massacre of human beings. The people we'd seen at the general store and the broken-down houses and trailers we'd passed felt to me like repositories of history, a hundred times more powerful than a billboard with words on it. For that little while I felt sure that all the achievements of my own tribe rested on a foundation of treachery. We'd made a shimmering world—roads and hospitals, universities and libraries. Through sweat, sacrifice, and ingenuity we'd constructed a golden universe where children owned telephones, where livers, lungs, and kidneys could be harvested and replaced. But there was a lie at the heart of it—not just the stolen land and murdered squaws, but something beyond that, an ice-hearted belief in the god of competition. Our success, always, depended on someone else's failure.

The moment passed. Not far from the information board several people had set up tables under shade awnings and were selling jewelry and bundles of freshly harvested sage. I could smell it from where I stood. Rinpoche and I walked down the grassy slope to one of the tables, and the woman there—Elvis T-shirt, tattoo across the top of her chest, no upper teeth at all—showed us a display of earrings and bracelets she herself had fashioned. She spoke almost without moving her lips, saying something about the start of the school year, and clothes for her son, and there was, about her, this same . . . *dignity* is the only word I can find. Using the word *dignity* with American Indians is the same as using the word *soul* with African Americans. There's something about it that feels both accurate and not right. As far as I knew, my ancestors hadn't killed any Indians and had arrived too late to be among those who'd taken their land. None of them ever owned slaves. So it wasn't as if I harbored any personal guilt about the plight of either group. It wasn't as if I believed that every black person and every Indian was a wonderful human being. And it wasn't as if I looked upon all of them with pity. But—and here we come to one of those places in the American national conversation where we walk semantic tightropes, where we tiptoe between a stubborn heartlessness on the one side, a refusal to admit the long legacy of injustice, and a sloppy excess of compassion on the other—there *was,* in some of the people we met at Pine Ridge, a grace one does not typically encounter. There *was,* among certain inhabitants of the Bronx's poorer blocks, an obvious generosity of heart, a spiritual courage, a depth of humanity in the midst of a level of deprivation and violence that would crush most people. But saying so, perhaps especially for a person of my standing and color, was a both a 911 call to the political correctness police and an invitation to bigots. We did that now, shoved each other into this or that cage, snapped the lock, and used the label to advance our own position. One comment and into the box you went. You were conservative, liberal, racist, entitled, professional victim or heartless bigot, too cynical, too sentimental, not sophis-ticated enough. Standing there opposite the toothless woman, I felt in my own mouth the bitter taste of all this categorization. For that bit of time I set aside all that and hoped my sister's visions might be accurate, that some new world awaited us, that a different way was possible, that some brave beast—Shelsa, her mysterious and as yet undiscovered partner—was, at that very moment, slouching toward some new Bethlehem to be born.

I bought cloth bracelets for Natasha, Shelsa, Anthony, and Seese and let the woman tie one onto my own wrist, as did Rinpoche.

We walked up a hill to a cemetery and there found graves of people who'd died in the more recent uprising, a 1973 occupation of the town of Wounded Knee that began with internal Indian politics and soon grew violent. This was the Wounded Knee story I'd remembered, however vaguely. I had been in junior high, seen something on the nightly news, been struck by my parents' indifference. Trouble on the reservation; what else was new?

As we stood there a woman came uphill from a cluster of trailers below. She held out a pretty necklace and asked if I'd buy it, and I will regret for a long while not doing so. I don't know why I so quickly shook my head and said, "No, thank you." I felt I'd spent enough, God forgive me, done enough, given enough. I didn't want or need the necklace. I've never liked being approached by people who want to sell me things. May God forgive me. At least I looked into the woman's eyes and greeted her, spoke with her. We talked for a while. She said, with that same dignity, that she was hoping to move from a tepee to a house, that the nearest work was twenty miles away, the bus was expensive, other residents of the reservation charged twenty dollars for a round-trip ride. I gave her five dollars. Five dollars! She thanked me.

I turned away, then turned back and said, "What's your name?"

"Natasha," the woman answered, and I very nearly fell over backward in the dust.

I have, I should say again here, made a promise to myself to set down the events of our road trip exactly as they occurred. For spiritual posterity perhaps. Perhaps just for my own training in honesty, in not making myself out to be someone I am not. I have sworn to include the frolic and the difficulties, the fear and the laughter, even the small details that might end up having some meaning I am blind to at present. So I have to say that I drove away from Wounded Knee, out of the reservation, south toward the state line, in a cloud of shame. I didn't understand myself. Not filthy rich, I nevertheless have more money than I know what to do with. A severance package, a 401(k), my wife's inheritance, investment income, a house worth many hundreds of thousands of dollars. What was wrong with me? I should have taken out a hundred dollar bill and handed it to

Natasha, I know that. Taken her necklace and mailed it to my daughter and told her about the coincidence. But I didn't. I couldn't keep from staring through the windshield at the broken-down trailers, the NO TO ALCOHOL! and WHY DIE? signs, the bleak landscape, the hopelessness. Neither of us spoke for a long time and then Rinpoche—riding shotgun but not wearing his cowboy hat said, "Maybe now another time you come back to this place, Otto my friend. I feel like maybe you come back. Or you write something on it in a book. Rinpoche feels this."

Ten

We left reservation land and crossed the state line, passing a government-issue billboard: NEBRASKA, THE GOOD LIFE. As if the state border marked the end of the bad life.

The other part of the sign was: HOME OF ARBOR DAY. There wasn't a tree to be seen! It was four o'clock and I was hungry and a bit weary from the road, still carrying the weight of Pine Ridge's desolation and curious, too, about the man we were scheduled to visit. Seese had told me they were friends from her Berkeley days, from a period when she'd been involved with a boyfriend named Saul, who'd been hit by a drunk driver in San Francisco one evening when they were out for a walk and died in her arms. They'd worked at some kind of cooperative, a worker-owned bakery close by the university, and Alton had been employed there, as well. How he'd migrated from there to Nebraska I didn't know, and why she was sending us so far from the mountains to visit with him I didn't know either.

Beautiful as it was, northern Nebraska didn't seem particularly hospitable to anyone or anything. I'd never seen so much empty, unpeopled land in my life—and I'm a North Dakota boy. At first, there were cultivated squares on the great expanse—corn and winter wheat, I'd guess—and even one flat, neat little town, Gordon, with a grid of residential streets and enormous white grain elevators by the railroad tracks.

And then we entered the Nebraska sandhills, which, I have since discovered, is the largest area of vegetated dunes on earth, twenty thousand square miles of green rippled land that had once been sea bottom. On that day the dunes were dusted with millions of small sunflowers and endless square miles of waving grasses. I remembered my mother and father talking about the sandhills. Mom had a relative living in that part of the world and the relative had told her that, beautiful as the land might be, it was "good for nothing except looking at." Nothing edible, no saleable crop grew in that sand, and so my parents—farmers to the core—spoke of it with a kind of pity. Even the grasses, they said, were of such poor quality that you needed thirty-five acres to feed a single head of cattle. Thirty-five acres! Everyone knew that any grazing land worth its alfalfa feeds cattle on merely a three-to-one ratio. The Kinkaid Act allowed homesteaders to stake 640 acres of land, but even that hadn't been enough to make any kind of a living. Almost all the claims were soon abandoned. Eventually they were taken for free or bought up by wealthier ranchers, so now Black Angus cattle were raised on ranches that could be five, ten, or even twenty thousand acres in size.

I enjoyed driving through it, though. Empty as it was—at one point we went fifty-four miles without seeing a house, gas station, building, or human being—the landscape was a marvelous complexity of mounds and swales, and with the carpeting of flowers all around us and the sailing cumulus above, and one shallow pond where a white pelican floated like a bathroom toy, I could have gone 154 miles without seeing anyone and still been rapt.

In the last hour of daylight we pulled into the little railroad town of Mullen. There was a lone commercial street, with a handful of other paved roads leading off it, and a railroad track along which we watched a mile-long coal train rumble and squeal. I suggested we stop and ask for directions to avoid getting lost in the hinterlands on Mullen's outskirts and Rinpoche did not disagree.

"You know this guy, don't you?" I said.

"Alton."

"Right. Any idea why Seese is sending us hundreds of miles off our route to see him?"

"Do we had a route?" Rinpoche asked.

I drove slowly along the wide main street, looking for a person of whom I might inquire and thinking that if I could just settle my mind a bit more I would come to understand that everything my brother-in-law said was a lesson. Everything he said, everything he did, simply his way of being on this earth—all of it was a lesson worth more than a new summer house or a million-dollar annuity. *Do we had a route?* No, we did not have a route. Of course we didn't. But my mind, the habitual pattern of my thoughts, felt the need to rope the future into a corral. I lacked the courage to live out my life minute by minute. I needed a route, a plan, a future that was pre-dictable—or at least imaginable—and safe, even though one second's glance at my almost fifty-two-year past would prove that no such future could ever possibly exist. *Do we had a route?* It wasn't said in a critical way. He wasn't mocking or judging, only showing me, with a kind, auto-matic straightforwardness, that no, we did not have a route, not in Mullen and not in life. It came clear to me then that, looked at with my ordinary mind, the trip seemed pointless, a wild goose chase of the first order, a colossal waste of time. But one step backward into clarity and it was all clearly intentional: I was being asked to give up the crutch of having a plan. I was being offered the chance to do what I might have done in my late teens or early twenties—just go, trust the road, see what lessons it offered, take my lumps, and savor the joys. I spotted a young woman pushing a stroller in front of a place called Red's, and I stopped the car and got out, feeling as if my mind had been knocked into an open pasture. *Do we had a route?*

The young woman had the wide-set eyes and wide, pretty, pale-eyed face that seemed to me to have been handed down from the people who'd crossed these prairies on wagon trains 120 years earlier. She was somehow big-boned and slim at the same time and she had a bearing that seemed to me to speak of inexhaustible patience. Her child lay asleep in a tangle of blanket. "Hi," she said, as I approached.

"Hi. I'm looking for a friend. Alton Smithson. The only address I have for him is 'Off Route 97, Mullen.' Would you happen to know where he lives?"

"Sure. Everybody knows Alton. The computer-fixer, right?"

"I think so, yes."

Though Alton lived some fifteen miles south of town, the directions turned out to be very simple: a turn onto 97, and then one more turn a quarter hour up the road. "He's over there on the left as you crest a hill. All kinds of antennas and stuff sticking out of the roof of his barn. You'll find him."

"How old is your child?"

"Just a year. Nathaniel Andrew Ryan, Nate for short. It's nap time, as you can probably tell."

"I have a son and a daughter, both grown. Enjoy your time with him."

Her smile was a crescent of radiance, sunlight on the plains. "I will. I do. It's nice to hear somebody say that."

"It's the best work there is," I said. For some reason, there on the streets of Mullen, I'd turned into a propagandist for parenthood.

"That's so *nice,*" she said. "Everybody's always saying how hard it is. I like it, you know. That makes me feel weird with my friends."

"That's the opposite of weird."

Her smile lifted into a small laugh, a few notes of relief sprinkled across the empty sidewalk. I thanked her and turned away and heard her say, "God bless you," over my shoulder.

Darkness was falling as I turned onto 97 South, and I decided we would very much need God's blessing if I happened to miss the turn onto Alton's road. Two blocks south of town the nothingness began again, the folded hills, the dunes, the flowers. It felt like the road had been drawn through the primeval. Rinpoche and I were racing into the heretofore unimagined. Miss this turn, I thought, and you'll drive until you run out of gas. Kansas, Oklahoma, Texas, the colonial cities of central Mexico.

But the turn appeared precisely where Nate's mother had said it would be, and after a few minutes of gravel road in the fast-fading light, I saw antennas off to the left, then Alton's barn, a dirt drive, a house, the man himself standing out front in a posture of anticipation. He seemed to be leaning slightly forward.

"Alton," Rinpoche said. And then, strangely, "Do you see the ghosts around him?"

I saw no ghosts. What I saw, as we drew closer and then parked and got out, was a tall man with wheat-colored hair lifting up from a long forehead, like teased out frosting on a rectangular cupcake. He bore a slight resemblance to Lyle Lovett, the singer, but something in his manner seemed that of a beaten man, as if there were weights tied to his wrists, ankles, and neck, as if a great weariness had overtaken him at birth, a great sadness. He bowed deeply to Rinpoche, almost an exaggerated bow I want to call it, and then shook my hand without quite making eye contact.

"Anybody follow you?" was the first thing he said after the introductions.

He was looking down the road. Darkness had fallen now and a sprinkling of stars showed already above us, the advance guard of full night.

I looked back at the road, too, perplexed. "Who would have?" I asked. "Celia's home by now, or nearly so. She and Shelsa took the bus back from Deadwood."

He smirked. At last he took his eyes from the road, ran them over me, and then fixed them on Rinpoche in a way that was almost fearful. "I'm making you a real Nebraska supper," he said, and then the words rolled out of him. "Barbecued beef, beans, corn bread. It's what the pioneers ate, though they probably ate buffalo instead of beef, but the beans and everything, coffee if you want it, come in, come on in, I'll show you where you'll sleep, I have separate rooms for you, comfortable enough, I think, without being too comfortable. Come in, come in, thank you for visiting. It means a lot."

He all but snatched Rinpoche's leather-handled satchel from his hands and led us along the short dirt path to his front porch. The house was elegantly simple and marvelously built, with wide-board wood floors, exposed beams, a hallway that led past a small bath to three modest bedrooms. It was as spare and neat as our farm's meditation room, bereft of decorations or photos of loved ones. In the living room was a brick fireplace, one jade Buddha on the mantle. That was it. "I'll put the meat on now," he said, but he sounded unsure, as if he was waiting to be contradicted, waiting for Rinpoche to declare he'd become vegetarian, or that he wasn't hungry, or that the pioneer supper was a bad idea, unspiritual, a stain on our karma. It would lead Alton to a bad next life, as a cow owned by a man who beat him. He'd be slaughtered and eaten; he'd learn his lesson then.

As soon as we'd arrived, Rinpoche had taken hold of Alton with both hands and pulled him close for one of his World Wrestling Federation embraces, and Alton had reacted strangely, almost pulling away, stiff, embarrassed. At the door to the last bedroom, Rinpoche put a hand on our host's right shoulder and looked up into his eyes. "I meditate now, my good friend. You and Otto talk, cook. When the food is for eating you knock, okay?"

"Of course, of course," Alton said nervously, but he seemed affronted. Something in his face registered surprise, almost insult, even as he was nodding and saying, for the third time, "Of course, Rinpoche."

I left my bag on the bed and followed him around back. He put three thick slabs of Angus flesh on a charcoal grill and we stood next to each other in the most awkward of silences. "So," he said at last, "you're a student of Rinpoche's also."

"Student, brother-in-law, friend. He's married to my sister."

"I know. Cecelia. I was always in love with Cecelia—don't be offended—but I never had the courage to ask her out or anything. We worked side by side for two years at the bakery and I just couldn't do it. Even after Saul . . . passed, I mean, I wouldn't have asked her *before* Saul passed, obviously, but even after, long after, I couldn't even ask her to sit down with me and have a cup of tea or anything, go to a movie, you know?"

"She would have said yes, I'm sure," I said.

Alton shot me a look, wary, on edge. It was like being with an angry wolf coated in four inches of meringue. You could feel the anger there, way, way down, and on top of it a perpetual gushing apology.

"I noticed how well-made the house is. Did you build it?"

"I did," he said, brightening some. "I couldn't bear to live in regular American society anymore, just couldn't. I inherited some money. I felt bad about that. Here I was, here we were, living the free life, sharing everything, totally unmaterial, not harming the earth at all, and what happens? The bakery folds and just as it folds my old man passes—he was a big-shot lawyer in New York, working for all kinds of rotten corporations— and he leaves me a ton of money. The money was made from representing oil companies and defending Wall Street cheaters and South African gold-mining companies and stuff like that. Dirty money. But I took it anyway." He laughed in a way that made me cringe. "I am, or was, what I think of as an Abbie Hoffman type. Radical gone Wall Street."

"People change," I said. "Grow up. See the world differently."

"Right," he said. "Definitely." But his tone was the last thing from definite. "I worked for an agency in D.C. for a while just to get my head together, use my computer skills and so on. Then I decided I'd move out here and be alone and have a spiritual practice. I was writing letters to Cecelia, hoping maybe I'd get up the courage to ask her to come out here and make a life, and then she told me about Rinpoche and told me to read his first book—have you read it?—and then I found out they had the Center in North Dakota and I went up there a few times and did some work for them—"

"Did you build the retreat cabins?"

"Only one of them, the one farthest out. Somebody local built the first two."

"I made a solitary there."

It was as if I hadn't spoken. He forked the meat, turned all three steaks. "Medium rare okay?"

"Perfect."

"Do you know how Rinpoche likes it?"

"I'm sure medium rare is fine. He isn't fussy."

"Of course not." He ran his free hand over his

eyes. "So I live here on my dirty money and try to clean my mind. I'm a hypocrite."

"Lots of people inherit something from their parents. I don't think it matters all that much how your father earned it. That was what he did, not what you do."

"Maybe."

More stars had come out. A cool breeze was gliding across the sandhills. The surrounding darkness, the smell of alfalfa and cooking meat, a coyote howling in the distance—from what little human presence we could sense with our backs to the house and barn, we might have been standing there a hundred years earlier.

"Why did you ask if somebody followed us?"

"Hmph," he said. "Natasha—that's your daughter, right?"

"Yes."

"Beautiful girl. Smart, beautiful, so spiritually developed. . . . She and I talk on the phone every once in a while and she told me about the Chinese guy who was asking about Rinpoche and I've been looking into that. I have a degree in computers. I have . . . I'll show you the barn later, tomorrow, I have a kind of unpaid job doing research for various friends. As I told you, I worked for the government for a little while before I decided to come out here, in D.C., doing, you know, research. Looking into things."

"For whom?"

"Just an organization."

"The NSA?"

"Yes, if you must know."

"Really?"

"Not something I'd make up. I know some tricks and so on. I had a clearance and they're probably going to come after me one day the way they went after Snowden and Manning, but let me simply say I don't like it at all that this guy is snooping around. The man as she described him was exactly the type of person the Chinese would send out on a reconnaissance."

"Reconnaissance for what?"

A big shrug, momentary eye contact. "We don't know. Kidnapping. Assassination."

"My daughter thought I was overreacting."

"Wouldn't an overreaction be preferable to an underreaction?"

"My thoughts exactly."

"If there is one group the Chinese government is most afraid of it's the Tibetans, His Holiness in particular. If they thought they could kill him and get away with it in the court of international public opinion, he would have been dead long ago. We're not dealing with a sweet and tender group here. Rinpoche is Russian from a Tibetan lineage. His daughter is . . . well, we don't yet know exactly what she is, but it's not hard to believe they'd be interested in her whereabouts . . . and not because they want to pray at her feet."

A ball of barbed wire was forming in my belly.

"I'd like to help," Alton went on, watching me now, gauging my reaction. "I have some skills. Should I tell you more?"

"Please."

"You're aware that they have agents all over the world trying to figure out who might be the next Dalai Lama, and they'd like nothing better than to go out and kill the person. It's like, biblical, you know? It's like Herod killing all the Jewish babies. Same thing exactly.

"Now maybe the encounter in North Dakota was nothing, an innocent inquiry by an Asian man who happened to be wearing a gun and driving a car with tinted windows. A coincidence. Harmless. We shouldn't be racist about it. But it certainly begs the question: Why haven't they done anything more? On the other hand, we don't know what they've done, who they are exactly or where they are, and what, exactly, are their motivations. I told Cecelia a long time ago I could help out and do some research and figure out if anybody's looking into your computers or following you or checking you out online—"

"You can do that?"

"I can, yes. And so I was on the lookout when you drove up."

He put the meat onto a metal plate and said he was going into the kitchen to check on the beans and corn bread and would I mind knocking on

Rinpoche's door—"But quietly, okay?"—and calling him to the table.

"Right, sure. Did you find out anything? Is anyone looking into Rinpoche and Shelsa and Seese?"

"Not sure yet. Probably they're just too savvy to let me figure it out. But I will."

I went into the house and down the hall and tapped lightly on Rinpoche's door, then stepped into Alton's immaculate bathroom to wash my hands. In the mirror I saw a worried man, middle-age, medium-sized ears, hair more than touched with gray, face more than graced with wrinkles, eyes bloodshot from the road. "Who's crazy?" I asked the mirror.

No answer.

We sat on three sides of the hand-built oak table and feasted. Meat, beans, corn bread, and beer, a perfect supper. Alton had the windows open and the air that wafted in through the screens had the sweet taste of wild grass to it. From time to time we could hear moths banging against the metal threads, wild for the light.

"Rinpoche," Alton said, after we'd each complimented him three times on the food, "I've been practicing night and day."

"Good, good."

"I think I'm going to make a breakthrough soon."

"Don't think for that too much now."

"Okay, you're right. I should meditate without attachment. You're right, of course, thank you. I was hoping you could give me a new visualization, maybe tonight if you have time, or tomorrow morning, I've been getting up really early and meditating, I find that the mind is calmer then. I've really been reaching some new places."

"Good, good," Rinpoche said, but you didn't need psychic abilities to see that he was straining to sound supportive.

There was something about Alton that scared away praise the way an electrified fence scares away cattle. You could see that he wanted it, that he was hinting for it, hoping for it—asking us how the food tasted, twice, telling Rinpoche about his experiences in meditation—but at the same time when praise was offered he peered at you as if you were lying to him. He was peering at Rinpoche now, his eyes lined with anger, the anger covered over with adulation. I could feel him ticking there, inside his tanned skin and beneath the giant tuft of hair. Ticking, ticking, a bomb with a short fuse he was always trying to hide from view.

"I think you guys should pay cash on this trip," he said now, "only cash. They can trace you by the credit cards. And they can trace you by the GPS in your phone. And the car's rented, Cecelia told me, isn't it?"

I nodded, sipped my beer, watched him over

the rim of the glass. I wondered how long it had been since he'd had people in his house and enjoyed a normal conversation.

"You know they have a chip in it, then. And if the Chinese were somehow to hack into the computer of the rental agency—which one is it?"

"Dollar, I think."

"They could probably hack in if they knew which one it was and then they'd know exactly where you were at all times."

"Why would they care?" I made the mistake of asking.

"What!"

The fuse was out in plain view now, sparking.

"If they know where Rinpoche is, what difference would it make?"

"You're kidding, right?"

"Not really."

"What difference would it make! They'd figure Shelsa would eventually meet up with him!"

"Wouldn't they already know she's at the retreat center? It's no secret that Rinpoche's there. It's advertised on the website."

"Well, what if they've just now figured out she's the next one? What if they overheard a conversation or something, tapped a phone? And they've just started connecting her to him, and just decided they want to do something about it?"

It was as if we were siblings competing for a father's love. Rinpoche was eating very slowly, chewing the meat with his usual concentration, not really paying attention. But Alton appeared to crave that attention, and at my expense.

"I had the same worry for a little while," I said. "But Tasha partly talked me out of it."

"Tasha's very smart," Alton said. "She's also twenty-two."

"Twenty-three."

"Even so. It won't do to let her decide what we should be worried about."

"Probably not. I was saying I had the same—"

"The Chinese are vicious, you know. Or maybe you don't. I have files in the barn, I can show you if you'd like. First, they murdered a million Tibetans. One million! Tortured and murdered them! Now look what they're doing to the Uighurs. They'll stop at nothing."

"I was hoping Shelsa wasn't public knowledge, I guess."

"Public knowledge? It's known already in certain circles in Tibet. It was known among some of us before she was even born."

"Right."

"Not to worry," Rinpoche said. He'd put down his fork and knife. The steak—much too large a portion for him—was two-thirds uneaten. Alton looked at the plate with an expression not so very far from terror.

"Wery good food!" Rinpoche said for the fourth time.

Alton relaxed a notch. "I have dessert," he said. "Not too sweet. I allow myself a little vanilla ice cream once a week and I've saved it for you, for my guests, but I want to show you the setup in the barn first if you don't mind. Can we walk over there?"

The rest of the night went along those same lines. Alton gave us a tour of the barn with its state-of-the-art computers and scanners and shelves of files on the Chinese atrocities and electronic eavesdropping and the history of the method by which the Dalai Lama was chosen. He took photos of Rinpoche and me and insisted on making us fake IDs—he'd stay up late, he said, have them ready in the morning, make up names for us, arrange for new Social Security numbers, license numbers, everything that needed to be done. He twitched and bubbled and looked like he was plugged into a sparking electrical outlet.

Back at the house he spooned out three dishes of vanilla ice cream and asked if we wanted nuts, chocolate sauce, sprinkles, whipped cream, fresh fruit. It was an ice cream parlor of neuroses and I found myself feeling that I had to reassure him every two minutes—that I'd had plenty to eat, that it was all delicious, that I didn't need coffee, thank you, but coffee in the morning would be fine, black or just a little cream, no sugar, one cup, yes. That the IDs were a good idea. I wanted to take his blood pressure, prescribe a dose of

Diazepam, ask about his upbringing. What had caused a soul to be this tightly strung? The big-shot lawyer father? The edicts of the counter-culture, where everything from using a plastic cup to turning on a light powered by nuclear energy was an unforgiveable sin against the earth?

Rinpoche was unusually silent. His customary jolliness had been dampened to the point where I thought I saw the edge of his remarkable patience come into view once or twice, albeit briefly. He touched Alton whenever he could, resting a hand on his shoulder, patting him on the back, literally, once even tapping him in the middle of the chest in a strange gesture, wordless, that looked to be some sort of Skovorodian folk cure for the agitated soul.

Was the bed going to be okay? Alton wanted to know. Would Rinpoche need anything special for the morning meditation? The shower was strong, we were welcome to use the soap there. He had toothpaste, a fresh tube. And on and on and on, as if the poor man was being assaulted by a swarm of wasps, singing a chorus of recrimination as they stung and stung again. At one point I was going to ask if he had children, but it seemed the question—any question—might bring up the file marked FAILURE in his mind, so I held my tongue.

At last, though he appeared to have enough energy to go on worrying and talking until midnight, Alton said, "I know you get up early,

Rinpoche, so I'll let you go to bed. You, too, Otto. Or you can stay up and watch anything on the TV if you want. It's satellite, like everything else here. A hundred-twenty-eight channels. There are books. I have shelves of them. Please make yourselves at home. I'm going to wash the dishes and go work in the barn and in the morning we'll talk about the things we can do to safeguard Shelsa and the family. I can 'lighten your fingerprint,' that's the way they used to say it in Washington. You leave a fingerprint wherever you go. I can't get rid of that but I can lighten it."

"We talk about it tomorrow," Rinpoche said, putting a hand on Alton's arm. "Otto and me now, we do the dishes. You made the food. Excellent food!"

"No, I'd never let guests wash the—"

"This is your practice now," Rinpoche said, rather sternly. "You go into the barn and work, and you meditate on how much the universe love you. Go!"

Alton made a face—Rinpoche's tone of voice had bothered him—but he performed the same exaggerated bow and went off dutifully to his ID-making . . . without saying good-night to me.

I washed, Rinpoche dried, the two of us standing at the sink in a kind of mourning. We didn't speak about Alton, but something was hanging in the air between us. When the kitchen was clean we bade each other good-night and went to bed.

Eleven

Nights like the one I spent in Alton's guest bedroom with the pine-paneled walls and the massive starlit sky framed in the window—those were the kinds of hours when it would have been a great comfort to have Jeannie beside me. I slept for a while and then something—a dream, a sound—broke that sleep and I couldn't piece it together again. Lying awake there I carried on an imaginary conversation with her. *Seems crazy, doesn't it, hon? I mean, fake IDs?! This isn't our life.*

Probably, she would have said. She was a woman who drew conclusions only after a period of thought. Sensible in the extreme. Grounded. Wise. Of good judgment.

Another few seconds and I imagined her saying, *but I remember, when we were living in Chelsea and I got pregnant with Tash and we started to look at houses in the suburbs, you said almost exactly the same thing about the idea of living in Bronxville: This isn't our life. I can hear you saying it.*

I remember. It ended up suiting us to a T. . . . But there seems to me a fundamental difference between moving from Chelsea to Bronxville because we were starting a family and there were heroin addicts downstairs, and listening to a guy who used to work for the NSA and who is, right at this moment, making us fake IDs which, for all we know, might be a violation of the law and land us in Sing Sing.

Silence—real and imagined. I felt myself teetering between two worlds again. I longed for my house, my dog, my job, my routine, my wife, my kids. My identity. Otto Ringling, senior editor at Stanley and Byrnes, husband, father, upstanding citizen, homeowner, good neighbor, half-assed tennis player. What had been wrong with the plan of having that life go on for another, say, twenty years, then the move to Florida, drinks by the pool, walks on the beach, the grandchildren visiting? Jeannie and I had been putting money away so carefully for that future. Why hadn't we been left to that, the way so many people we knew were left to it?

And then there was the other side, the other voice, the other, I want to say, reality. I didn't know what Jeannie would have said about it. She'd been so warm and giving by nature, so kind to Seese in every manifestation of her weirdness, so grateful for Rinpoche's company in her dying months. He seemed, in fact, to consider her more soul mate than sister-in-law, more fellow traveler than student. "I love my sister," I said aloud, as if Jeannie were beside me. "And I've come to love Rinpoche. I'm glad he's in my life. More than glad. I'll never forget what he did for you. The kids adore him. But the heart of my worry comes from my love of Shelsa. If she is who they say she is, if she's in danger, and if I ignored that possibility because it didn't fit into my idea of what life was supposed to be, and something happened. . . . How would I face Tash and Anthony? How could I live with myself?"

Rinpoche isn't a flaky man, Jeannie said, in my mind at least. *I think you should speak frankly with him.*

"Goofy, yes. Flaky, no. Okay."

I lay there, feeling foolish, unable to sleep. You could remember a person, but you couldn't imagine her back to life. After a time I sat up, pulled on my pants, and went out into the kitchen. I didn't think Alton would mind if I helped myself to the last of the ice cream, and since I'd broken my no-sugar fast at dinner, apparently with Rinpoche's blessing, it wouldn't hurt to have a few more spoonfuls and start the fast over again next day. I dished out the sweet whiteness and sat at the table where we'd eaten dinner, but I hadn't been there three minutes when I heard the padding of feet in the hallway and saw my brother-in-law emerge from the shadows into the light.

He nodded as if he'd expected me to be there, sitting at a stranger's kitchen table, cheating on my diet at three a.m. No smile. No greeting. Just a nod of acknowledgment. Most likely he'd risen at that ungodly hour, slipped into his maroon robe, and was looking for a quiet place to do his morning meditation. Now he was going to step out onto the cold patio and sit there cross-legged on a chair cushion for three or four hours, following, in exquisitely nonjudgmental fashion, the workings of his mind, the current of his thought stream until it quieted completely, leaving him in a still pool of enlightened ecstasy. Maybe he thought I'd be joining him, the way I had, occasionally, in the old days. Not for three hours and not at three a.m., but there had been several dozen times when we'd "sat" together, side by side. My mind was the skittering right hand of a sonata, his the steady bass left, hitting a few chords, keeping the rest of the piece grounded, sane, steady.

Rinpoche paid no attention to the ice cream in my dish, though by then I'd stopped eating. He opened a cabinet and took something out. He filled the kettle at the faucet and set it on the electric stove. A cup of tea then, instead of the meditation. Or perhaps a cup of tea as prelude to the meditation. I noticed that there were two cups in front of him. He fished around in a glass jar on the counter and lifted out two teabags, set them in the cups in a way that can only be described as lovingly, found a glass jar of what appeared to be honey, and poured it liberally over the teabags. I watched him. Silence filled the kitchen. The stove light, the stark house, the silence, Rinpoche's broad back, and then the kettle's toothy whistle and the quick gurgle of water being poured. There was the clink of spoon in cup and he was sitting opposite me, two twists of vapor rising between us.

"Thank you for the tea," I said.

And he said, "Bet your ass."

I didn't have the energy just then for yet another lesson in the American vernacular, though I found myself wondering, tiredly, if one day this new affectation would get him into trouble. In a week or two weeks, up in the mountains somewhere—Wyoming, Colorado, Montana—a tough waitress would ask him if he wanted anything besides butter with his oatmeal and he'd say, "Bet your ass," and there would be a scene. Or he'd hold the hotel door for a bull rider and his girlfriend on the morning after a rodeo and the young woman would thank him, and he'd say, "Bet your ass." Or we'd be in a library in New Mexico, there to do research on American Indian artifacts, and the librarian would ask, "Can I help you?" Bet your ass you can. Or we'd be in a rest area, the kind that were peopled by lonely men in sedans, and Rinpoche would head for the edge of the trees, curious about some butter-fly or bird he'd seen there, and one of the men would say, "Want to take a walk?" And so on. There was no end to the trouble a misplaced "bet your ass" could cause a person.

This was my mind spinning. This was my mind. These riffs were what I had instead of Alton's paranoia.

Neither of us seemed to feel the urge for conversation. When the tea cooled I took a sip—some kind of mint. Rinpoche watched me, then started to do something strange with his cup. He lifted it off the placemat, but instead of bringing it to his mouth he waved it around to the side for a moment, then set it down. He turned it around so the handle was facing the opposite way. Lifted it an inch, set it down. Shifted it four inches to the right. Picked it up over his head, so that I thought he'd be burned with hot water spilling, waved it in circles, tilted it this way and that, set it down, put his index finger in. I watched him.

At last, as this circus act went on and on, I said, "Some new ritual? The anti-Zen tea ceremony, everything as complicated and unproductive as can be?"

He set the cup down, offered me one of those smiles that warmed me from the lining of my stomach to the tips of my fingernails. Pure love, it seemed to me, and I was suddenly ashamed of my sarcasm. "Almost got it," he said.

"Almost got what?"

He pointed at me. "Almost figured it out. Good, Otto. Wery good."

"Thanks. But I'm clueless. At sea. In a fog."

"This is living," he said, bringing the cup to his

mouth and taking a sip. There was an elegance to his gestures, a steadiness. One admired it the way one admired the movement of a great tennis player hitting a cross-court backhand. "And this," he began moving the cup in jerky motions again, lifting and setting it down, tilting it. He even spilled a few drops on the table, "is the worrying."

"You don't do it as well as I do," I said, and I began moving the cup sideways and tilting it, and so on.

He smiled again, not so warmly. "Good you can make the joke, my friend. But Rinpoche thinks maybe you should just drink." Another elegant sip, fluid, athletic.

"And not worry so much, right? Not have so much back and forth and up and down."

"Wery good, my friend."

"I'm a minor leaguer compared to our host," I said, and the minute I said it I realized it was a kind of gossip, my own way of competing for Rinpoche's approval. He ignored the remark and kept looking at me.

I took a sip and tried a softer version of the same approach. "A little hard not to worry when you have an expert on clandestine computer research making you a false ID and telling you how you can basically go invisible for a little while in case the Chinese are trying to kill you or someone you love."

"Bet your ass," Rinpoche said. "Wery hard."

"So how does one do it?"

He tapped the table three times with a bent index finger. "Right now," he said, "in this good minute, in this second, Chinese killing you?"

"No."

Three more taps. "In this second, they killing you?"

"No."

"You sick?"

"No. A little sniffle, nothing really. Allergies, prob—"

"They hurting Shelsa?"

"No."

"Worry is in your mind the pictures. You think you see these men but what you now in this minute see is this," he pointed to his own face. "And this," the teacup.

"All fine and good but there is such a thing as preparation. Anticipating trouble. Assessing the probabilities of the future and taking action. Alton might be overdoing it—I believe he is— but at the core—"

"Worry is worry, man. The tea not going in your mouth, see?"

"Sure. But what if we're overlooking something? What if Alton isn't completely paranoid? What if I don't like the way my photo comes out on the new ID, and what if we use the IDs and get caught and thrown in jail? I'm sorry, forgive me, but my trust in things working out for the best has been somewhat shaken of late."

"When Jeannie she was sick, you worried?"

"From the moment of the first doctor's visit. From the second she came home and said these words, 'Doctor Kahn said she wanted to run some tests.' From that sentence I started to worry."

"It help?"

"No."

"Make Jeannie better?"

I shook my head.

"But you did everything you can do, yes? Going to doctors? Medicines, yes?"

"Absolutely."

"Okay, see?" he said.

"Not really. Worrying is natural. Show me the husband who doesn't worry when his wife is diagnosed with cancer. Show me the wife. You'd have to be some kind of passive robot. Heartless or a fool, or both."

"Was Rinpoche heartless with Jeannie?"

"You were wonderful with her. You brought her more peace with your visits than anyone else."

"Rinpoche a fool? The robot?"

I shook my head.

He reached across the table and squeezed my forearm, then held his hand there. What happened then was something that had happened only once before, in the Walnut Room of the Fields Building in Chicago, midway through our first road trip together. You will have to take my word for this.

Rinpoche wavered. Oscillated. There were two seconds when the image of him wasn't. . . . What is the correct word? Solid. It wasn't solid. It could have been something in my optical nerve, a pressure caused by stress, difficult memories, the early hour, a reaction to the tea, some noxious additive in the vanilla ice cream. It could have been, but somehow I suspected it wasn't. "Now you and me meditate," he said when he'd grown solid again. He held up three fingers. "Three hour."

"I'll be exhausted in the morning. I won't be able to drive."

"Rinpoche drives."

"Worse. You'll wobble and swerve. Cross the double yellow line. We'll be stopped. The trooper will figure out the fake ID. I'll be your cellmate in the Supermax."

It was as if I hadn't spoken. "Couch now," he said, standing and gazing down at me. "We sit together. Me and you. Three hour. When the worries come, you watch them, then you let them go out your mouth open a little. You think about how much you love Seese, Shelsa, Natasha, Anthony, Jeannie. Then you rest. Then the worries come again, the pictures, the image, yes? You look on her, you say: What is happening now, this minute? Then out the open-a-little mouth she goes into the wind, and in comes the love feeling. One thousand times you do this and pretty soon the worry is like maybe the little bird, *seep seep,* in the big field. Go on, little bird. Make the little noise. Wery nice. Big wave of love come over it and she goes quiet, okay?"

"Could I try it lying down in my bed?"

"No," he said, rather roughly. He'd made his face hard, and it was a hardness that didn't admit joking of any kind. He broke eye contact and started for the living room, snapping off the stove light as he went. I want to say here, *I had no choice but to follow.* But of course I did have a choice. I could have said no, thank you, and headed back to my room and lay there beneath my quilt of worries and eventually fallen asleep.

But I went and sat on the couch.

Twelve

In one of the books Rinpoche had given me I read this statement: "Boredom is the start of the spiritual path." It made no sense to me at the time. After thinking about it for a few years, though, I've come to believe that there can be no spiritual path if there's constant movement, constant stimulation, if we don't regularly set aside a little time to contemplate the world that lies beyond the frenzy. In older times that happened automatically: Try plowing a field with oxen or taking an all-day stage ride or sawing planks out of a felled chestnut tree. There were more oppor-tunities to confront monotony, to ponder, to observe. Now every moment can be noisified—music, e-mails, video games, phone calls, Facebook, Instagram. I took Anthony to a Rangers game at the Garden and every stoppage of play was filled with loud music, cheering, announce-ments, ads. Now farmers plow in tractors with headphones on, connected to their iPod.

Meditation is the opposite of all that, a quiet space, a recess, a superb use of time. I knew that, I believed it, and yet, it was inevitably a struggle for me to stop what I was doing and sit still twice a day. Powerful anti-meditation arguments assailed me. I knew people who never meditated a day in their lives and they weren't plagued by any particular negativity. Jeannie's spiritual practice had seemed to consist of gardening, doing everything for everyone, and saying a silent prayer morning and night, and Rinpoche once referred to her as a "secret saint woman." So why did I need to sit and watch my thoughts?

The *Times* didn't have any front-page articles on meditation. Yes, I saw one brief TV report—it might have been CNN—but I didn't like to consider myself in the same sector of society as the people who'd be shown sitting on cushions or in chairs. They looked foolish there with their eyes closed and their hands folded. Un-American. Soft. Goofy. Wasting a perfectly good half hour.

Yes, Rinpoche was a wonderful man, and he meditated, but Rinpoche came from a very different culture, he'd grown up with meditation the way I'd grown up with baseball. Try getting a visiting Siberian friend interested in the Yanks-Sox playoffs.

That was the logic that took over, and a very powerful logic it was. That was my thought stream when it came to meditation.

But I'd never quite given it up and, for whatever reason, perhaps the moment of Rinpoche's apparent insolidity, perhaps simply my brother-in-law's charm, I decided to sit with him on the leather couch in Alton Smithson's house, at three-fifteen in the morning, with my new fake ID drying in the barn workshop and my daughter, sister, and niece asleep in their beds at home, with the security alarm activated and the KILL THE MUSLIMS graffiti still faintly visible on the retreat cabin. I suppose, in a certain way, I'd come to the end of logic. I suppose I felt I had little to lose. Or maybe, as Rinpoche suggested, I'd suffered enough and so I was ready for a new under-standing about what was important on this earth and what was a waste of time.

In any case, I sat there with him, a few feet of space and leather between us, closed my eyes, and listened to him give these instructions: "The worries come, you watch. When you breathe out, let them out the open mouth they go. Then in the nose come the feeling of the love for the people you love in this whirl. You breathe that out, too. Again, again, again, again. Okay, Otto?"

"Got it."

"A blessing on you, then, my friend."

A blessing on me. I needed several hundred blessings because almost as soon as I'd closed my eyes, folded my hands, and tried to meditate in earnest, it was as if an entire tribe of ancient logicians were shooting poison-tipped thought arrows at me. Plus, my left knee ached, just under the kneecap, a new ailment as of that hour. Pulsing. Not excruciating. Just bad enough to notice.

For some bizarre reason I started thinking about the leather couch on which we perched. Where had the leather come from? Was it American leather? Wasn't Alton too sensitive to his karmic future to have the skin of a slaughtered animal beneath his ass? Why did it make a squeaking noise when I shifted my weight? What was the physics of that? I missed my leather chair at home. Jeannie had given it to me as a Christmas gift because, though I'd wanted a leather sofa, she'd been against it, and we'd ended up with something too sleek and modern for my tastes. But that was the way we worked things out. We each gave a bit. She got the sofa, I got the chair. Would Natasha work it out? Warren sounded like a decent sort, and she was wonderful, of course, but from the day of her birth she'd had a side to her that was utterly uncompromising. Where would they go if the meditation center closed? California? Would they be safe there? Probably if the Chinese man had wanted to hurt her—

At that point I caught myself. I was adrift on the thought stream, gliding along, blind to the scenery. I wasn't even worrying, which was what I was supposed to be doing, just thinking, musing, wandering the cerebral caverns with a flashlight, pointing it here and there.

I liked that image. If an author had used it I would have put a check mark next to it on the page proofs. I missed work. But not that much, really. Work had had its moments, for many years, but—

Caught myself again. I needed to worry. I started to think about Alton. He didn't look like a rational man. Smart, yes, but not rational in my definition. What if he sent us all to jail?

Okay, a worry. Out the little-bit-open mouth with it. In with love. I pictured my son, imagined him fast asleep in a Maine dormitory, girlfriend by his side perhaps. A blessing for them. I wondered if they'd get married before or after Natasha and Warren, or if marriage was passé for their generation, a relic, a foolish dream—

Caught myself. I opened my eyes and saw that the digital clock on the DVD player on the other side of the room read 3:21, which meant that I'd been meditating for six minutes. Six minutes was one-thirtieth of three hours. My knee hurt. I closed my eyes. What if it was an ACL tear? Would I ever be able to play tennis again?

Boring, useless, pointless, a tiny voice said. *Sleep is what you need, not this.* Rinpoche was still as a stone. I willed myself not to look at him. I found new worries to latch on to. The knee, my daughter, my son, Shelsa.

And so on. Three hours of it. After two hours and some—I couldn't keep myself from occasionally looking at the clock, but I was determined to prove I could stick it out—I began to have moments of either peace or complete exhaustion. A small space began to appear between thoughts. I could watch the worries float away. The words and images would inevitably return but I seemed to have reached that part of the stream where the current wasn't as fast. A thought—how good would the IDs be?—and then a nice stretch of space, just presence, and then I saw another thought riding in from the left side . . . and then . . . I fell asleep. During this sleep I had a dream of being in a Greek breakfast place on Ninth Avenue, waiting for the owner to cook me an omelet with spinach and feta cheese. I was standing there holding my tray and watching the eggs sizzle on the grill. I was waiting for them to be cooked. I was about to say something to the owner. In Greek. Which, mysteriously, I could now speak.

Rinpoche woke me with a gentle shake. The clock read 6:08. The first gray light of dawn was seeping into the room. "Now take the nap, Otto, little bit," he said, kindly. "Eight o'clock maybe we eat and go, okay?"

"Fine," I said. "I must have just dozed off at the end there."

"Today when the worries come," he put his right thumb and index finger to his lips and pushed them open half an inch. "Okay?"

"Absolutely."

"Always in your life there can be worries, you see? If you have enough of the money you can worry about being sick. If you have the money and the good health you can worry about family, the politics, how you play tennis, how you gonna get old, how you gonna die, you see? Worries are like noise in the world, always there. Don't listen too much, okay? Now sleep."

I padded quietly back to my room and for two hours slept the sleep of the blessed.

Thirteen

I woke to the fragrance of bacon being fried and coffee being brewed. Really, in this life, are there two smells that bring the non-vegetarian adult American more joy? For a few minutes I lay there in the unfamiliar bed and simply allowed that sweetness to fill my mind. I was strangely at peace. I heard a cabinet door open. Another minute of peace and I saw a wave of worry rising up like a breaker off Nauset Beach. I saw that it was a reflex with me. Habitual. Almost an addiction. A default setting. My mind turned to worry in very much the way certain flowers turn toward the sun, automatically. I let my mouth fall open and exhaled slowly. I breathed in thoughts of my children, one near each side of the massive continent in the center of which their old father had spent the night. Rinpoche was right, of course: No amount of worrying about them would have any positive effect. They would breathe in and out through their own day, with its own joys and challenges. I worried about them because it made me feel guilty not to. Which must mean that worry was a completely selfish activity, a mechanism designed to salve my own sense that I wasn't doing enough, to bolster the illusion that I was in control of their destiny . . . or even my own. For a moment then, a time oasis that lasted four or five breaths, I could sense what it must feel like to be a human being who trusted completely in his fate, who let things be, who dealt with Rinpoche's famous *now,* the actual moment, and not some imaginary horror-plagued future. No wonder Rinpoche seemed so relaxed and happy, and Alton so abjectly miserable.

I showered and shaved, wandered out to the kitchen, and found Rinpoche and Alton waiting for me, cups of tea in their hands and the same dynamic between them: Alton anxious to please, Rinpoche knocked a slight bit off his center by Alton's desperate neediness.

"Pancakes be okay?" Alton asked.

"Excellent."

"Pancakes with raspberries coming up. Rinpoche says you like coffee so I made you a fresh pot. I've learned to replace that with green tea, though I have to admit it took a while."

He went to the stove, leaving in his wake the sense that tea drinkers were spiritually superior to coffee drinkers and that perhaps one day, if I spent enough time with Rinpoche and meditated with heroic discipline, I'd come around. I let it go. I had slept in his home. He was making me pancakes. There was no competition here, no need for comparison. Alton was Alton. I let it go. Rinpoche nodded at me and asked how I'd slept.

"Like a baby."

"Babies not sleep so good, Otto!" he said, and he went off on one of his drawn-out reels of laughter.

I heard the sound of pancake batter being poured into a sizzling pan. "Where do you get raspberries out here?" I said to Alton's back.

"Connections."

"Are there farmers' markets?"

"Not here. I drove to North Platte when I knew Rinpoche was coming, if you must know."

I gave up. I said I needed to step outside for a moment to get some fresh air.

"Nowhere fresher," Alton said.

On the front porch I leaned both hands on the railing and looked out across the sandhills. I'd seen a lot of the country, a bit of the world. Few places were prettier. An elegant silence—so perfect it was almost visible—had draped itself over thc hills and shallow valleys, and it seemed to echo what was inside me, quiet to quiet. A small hawk flew across the yard, miraculous.

The pancakes were outstanding, simply superb, somc kind of whole wheat flour set off nicely by the fresh raspberries. True, in place of the real Vermont maple syrup I was used to, Alton put on the table some sugar-water mix. But there was a bottle of honey there, and plenty of butter, and the coffee was strong and rich, with real cream from a Nebraska cow. Six or seven times as I ate I felt compliments rise to my lips but I held them down, nodded, hummed my praise, tried to eat the way Rinpoche was eating, slowly, one bite at a time, with full attention.

When we were finished, Alton immediately removed the dishes and put them in the sink to soak, and then came and carefully sponged off the tabletop and dried it with a red-striped dish towel. From a side table he took a manila folder.

"This you should probably look at on the road," he said. "There's a lot to digest."

"What is it?"

"A little research I worked up last night on the Chinese. I think you'll appreciate it. I was up at 6:30 while you were snoozing away. Didn't take long, an hour or so. That's my meditation time, usually, but I have nothing going on for the rest of the day so I'll sit later. The IDs are in there, too."

"Many thanks," I said. "And thanks for the hospitality. It's been nice to take a break from hotels."

"Hotels can be fine, too," he said. "All comparisons are odious."

"Cervantes, isn't that?"

He didn't seem to hear. He wanted something from Rinpoche, that was clear enough, though what exactly it was I couldn't know. We offered to wash the dishes again; he declined. I asked him if he wanted me to strip the bed; he didn't. Once he'd handed me the folder he seemed at a loss, standing there mid-kitchen like a man who had important work waiting in the barn and wanted us to leave but felt bad about saying so. "Rinpoche," he said at last, glancing at me in a way that made me want to excuse myself and give them a private moment. Some spiteful interior voice convinced me to stay put. "Can I ask you one thing before you depart?"

"Anything, man."

"Do you think I'm ready for stream entry?"

One spark of irritation flashed across Rinpoche's features. I didn't know if Alton saw it, but I saw it clearly enough. Rinpoche took hold of his chin in one hand, a gesture of thoughtfulness I'd never seen him make, and one which looked completely insincere to my eye. He held his hand there, looking up at his student as if considering the question. Alton waited for the answer, still as a cell tower but leaning slightly forward.

"I think, maybe," Rinpoche said, "could be. . . . But if you really ready, you don't know the stream is there. See? When you don't know if the stream is there, when even you don't care if it's there, then maybe you ready, okay?"

"A kind of koan," Alton said, his face lit with joy. "I'll meditate on that."

"Good, good," Rinpoche said kindly. He reached out and squeezed Alton tight against him and held him there for at least half a minute, the taller man's arms pinned and hanging straight down, his chin on the top of Rinpoche's shoulder, eyes closed.

When they separated I held out my hand and Alton shook it warmly. "I wish you well," was all I could think to say.

"You too. Practice hard and you'll see some amazing results. Rinpoche is offering you the kingdom of heaven."

I thanked him. We went out and loaded our

149

bags into the back seat. Before I could open the driver's side door Rinpoche said, "I'm drivin' now, man. You rest." And I raised no objection.

I saw Alton in the side mirror, partly obscured by a cloud of dust. He'd put his hands together and was bent over from the waist. I couldn't imagine why my sister had wanted me to meet him.

Fourteen

South from the junction of Alton's road and Nebraska 97 it was twenty-four miles to Tryon, which one might pass without believing one had seen a town. Over that stretch the landscape gradually flattened until it looked more like what I'd always thought of when I heard the beautiful Otos Indian word *nebraska.*

Rinpoche drove with both hands gripping the wheel and his eyes locked on the winding tar strip. On those rare occasions—two, to be exact— when a vehicle passed us headed north, he stiffened and made a sound like "ay." A pickup rode our bumper for a while and then, on a straight stretch, zoomed past. A young cowboy in the passenger seat rolled down the window and shouted "asshole!" as he went by.

Rinpoche waved at him. "I am doing okay?" he asked me.

"Fine. Relax a little, though."

We crawled along. There was ample time to appreciate the scenery, to replay the past hours. "A genius like Alton," I said to Rinpoche, trying hard to sound kind, "shouldn't he be living someplace where he can do more good in the world? I mean, he's raising a tiny herd of Angus cattle, living ten miles from the nearest neighbor, fooling around with inventions in his back room. He should be teaching at MIT, or running a big charity, or designing space stations or something, no?"

"No," Rinpoche said bluntly.

"Don't you feel we're all born with certain gifts and we should use them?"

"Sure."

"His gifts are going to waste then, aren't they?"

Rinpoche took his eyes from the road for one terrifying second and shot me a look. The look there was full of pity, not the first time I'd been on the receiving end of such a thing. "People," he said, returning his attention to the road and jerking once on the wheel, too hard, "they move. One place to another, they go. Sometimes one place is right for a little some while, then not so right so they move. Could be one whole life, could be one years. Sometimes you go like Jesus for a little sometime into the desert. Jesus didn't stay in the desert, he went for a little some time, then he left. Buddha his whole life moved around."

"You're speaking of yourself. You and Seese and Shelsa. You're finished with North Dakota, I can feel it. It was your time in the proverbial desert."

"Maybe," he said, and then, "Driving now, Otto."

"Okay. Sorry."

We were heading into the city of North Platte —famous for having the largest rail yard in the world, and for its citizens' hospitality to the many thousands of servicemen who'd rolled through town on their way to war in the 1940s. The city itself—we saw little of it, even at our snail's pace—offered nothing more than a pawn shop, a few old gas stations, and the typical chain restaurants. With great care, Rinpoche mounted the ramp and headed west on I-80, where the land beside the road was suddenly featureless. With the sole exception of a Ford SUV driven by a man in a maroon robe, vehicles raced along there in a rapid parade. A hundred years earlier the travelers had been on foot, and then on horseback or in a horse-drawn stage or wagon, content to make twenty hard miles in a day. These days, fifty-five-mile-an-hour speed limit signs were tacked up on the walls of secondhand shops, for sale as curiosities; Rinpoche was going forty-eight and cars were passing on both sides as if we were in reverse. "Why so angry?" he'd famously said on our first road trip. We'd been listening to talk radio then, a pastime I'd recently abandoned.

Now I expected him to ask, "Why so fast?" When cars could safely go a hundred miles an hour, when jet technology advanced to the point where we could fly to Europe in two hours, we'd accept that as natural, of course. We'd embrace it. I had a friend who designed silicon chips and when I asked him where the industry was headed he answered with two words: "More speed." The faster we went the more we could get done in a day, a week, a lifetime. We could manufacture more efficiently, send more e-mails, surf more websites, see more of the planet, renovate more rooms in bigger houses, compete with the rest of the world, which would be on the same tread-mill. All fine and good, except that the advent of the microwave oven and instant Internet searches hadn't seemed to grant us any more time whatsoever. Nor any advances in the peace of mind department.

Plugging along at monk-speed, I couldn't help but wonder if it wasn't all some kind of trick we were playing on ourselves. Maybe the more we crammed into a day the less we actually experienced. Maybe the addictive hurry was all a kind of racing away from our existential predicament, as if we could outrun old age and death, as though, if we kept busy enough, kept moving, traveled farther, checked more items off the to-do list on any given day, then, like astronauts in orbit, we'd escape the bonds of ordinary time. Or escape, at least, the manic workings of our own minds. I turned on the radio and found some golden oldies. Creedence Clearwater was asking if you'd ever seen the rain and maybe the answer was no. We never stayed still long enough.

Big trucks, speeding cars, nothing to either side of the road but empty grazing land. "Can I ask you a question?" I said.

"Any question, anytime, you can ask, Otto."

"When a rock-and-roll band has gotten famous, put out a lot of popular CDs or albums or whatever and been around a long while, sometimes right before they retire they make what people call a farewell tour. They travel around to different cities, give their final shows, say good-bye to their fans. I can't help but think you're doing something like that on this trip."

Nothing. Rinpoche breathed in and breathed out, kept his eyes forward, his lips set in a tiny smile. He blinked.

"Well?"

"Waiting for the question."

"Are you going on a good-bye tour? Is that what this is?"

"This is road trip with brother-and-waw. Talk in Colorado tomorrow."

"Good to know. Where?"

"Lead Willage."

"Okay, fine. But I feel like you're saying good-bye to America. The way you're talking, what you just said about people moving, staying in one place for a while, doing a kind of desert retreat. You and Seese really are leaving the Center, aren't you? For good."

At that moment, still two hundred miles east of Denver, we passed a giant feed lot to our right, hundreds of cows waiting in the dirt to be slaughtered and eaten. It sat just off the highway, a dozen acres of mud and white fencing. The smell of it lingered long after we'd left the corrals behind, and for a while I contemplated the whole sad chain of killing that kept us breathing in and out. It seemed peculiar to me that, almost without exception, the animals we ate were the ones that lived on grains and grasses, the gentler ones, those that didn't depend on killing another living creature for survival. Wolves, mountain lions, sharks, bears, hawks—predators weren't part of the typical American diet. We ate cows, chickens, pigs, sometimes goats or rabbits or deer, lobsters and clams and scallops. For a stretch of bland highway it seemed a metaphor: Was it always the gentlest ones, the nonkillers, who were slaughtered? Was there, as some Buddhists and Hindus believed, a hierarchy of the reincarnational life? Insect to mammal to human. And then, within the human evolution, murderer to saint? Did we evolve toward peaceableness only to be cut into chops and steaks and cooked, nailed on a cross, or assassinated by Chinese secret police? Was that the setup?

Rinpoche wrinkled his nose. "What is smells?"

"Feed lot. The cows are getting fattened up there and pretty soon they'll be sent to a place where they're killed and cut up for the market, or made into hamburger patties and so on."

He sniffed the air, twisted up his lips, moved the needle from forty-eight to forty-nine.

"You didn't answer about the good-bye tour."

"I have a practice for you," he said.

"Okay, fine, but—"

"Eating practice."

"Okay. I've been trying to lose a few pounds."

"Next time when we stop I show it."

"Okay, good, thanks. No answer on the good-bye tour question, I guess, right?"

"Answer is yes," he said, finally.

"You're closing the Center?"

"Keeping open the Center."

"But moving."

"Yes."

"With Seese and Shelsa?"

"Of course."

"Where to?"

"Finding out now, Otto."

"Waiting for a sign?"

"Celia say to go on this trip and the sign comes."

"And you believe her?"

"Always believing. Magical wife, your sister.

Wery magical. Some people don't see it. Some brothers don't."

I said, "Okay. Message received. Awaiting sign from God."

I was holding Alton's dossier on my lap, afraid, really, to open it and take a look. I took out my magical phone and dialed my sister.

"My beautiful brother" was the way she answered.

"Everybody okay?"

"Yes. And you? And my husband who didn't call last night?"

"We were out at a strip club. He had a few too many beers. He's going to call a bit later on. Once he sobers up."

"Your idea of a joke, I take it."

"A bad one. He's driving, actually, and doing a beautiful job. We left your friend Alton's house a little while back."

"Did you like him?"

"Honestly?"

"Of course, honestly. You didn't like him, right?"

"He seemed troubled. Difficult to talk to."

"His father beat him as a boy, did he tell you that?"

"No."

"Over and over and over again. He's been hospitalized, twice. Psychiatric hospitals. Not since he started meditating, but before that. I hope you were kind to him."

"I tried. He's a hard guy to be kind to. But let me ask you something, Seese: Why did you send us out there? Rinpoche just told me he has a talk in Colorado. Nebraska's the other way. What's going on?"

"You had an extra day. I wanted you to see him, that's all."

"I know that. The question is: why?"

"I wanted you to appreciate what you and Jeannie gave to the world by raising your children the way you did. I wanted you to see what gets bred in a person when there's too much trouble in the house when they're young. Sometimes I don't think you realize what you did. What you and Jeannie did. I know you think Tash and Anthony are great. I know how much you love them. But that's something different. I wanted you to take a little credit for that. Forty percent of the credit anyway."

"I'll take thirty," I said, and I heard my sister laugh. "It was a lesson, then."

"Yes, are you mad?"

For two seconds a pint-sized puff of anger blew through me, a reflex, spurt of smoke coming off my burning pride. My sister was toying with me, giving me lessons. I breathed in and out. I said, "No." And I meant it.

"Good, then. And I also thought he might benefit from seeing Rinpoche."

"I'm sure he did." I considered telling her about the dossier on the Chinese, but held back.

"Can you pass the phone to Rinpoche?"

"I'd rather not. He's driving and I don't want to distract him. I'll have him call you when we stop, okay? Or tonight?"

"Okay, tonight. Don't let him speed."

"Not to worry."

Fifteen

Northeastern Colorado was the bleakest of the bleak, the most featureless of the featureless, more arid, even, than the most arid land we'd passed through in the previous three days. There was a prison just off the highway—that seemed right. There were high-tension wires looping between massive steel towers and very occasional patches of what looked to be feed corn, growing in irrigated squares.

By the time he'd driven for a couple of hours, Rinpoche had had enough. He guided the car down an exit ramp and at the stop sign let out a long sigh. There was a roadside café just there, a mom-and-pop establishment that promised great things . . . until the food was served. How, let me ask, is it possible to mess up an English muffin with peanut butter? I don't know. It shall remain, for me, one of life's great mysteries. Maybe the coffee had been made with recycled water from the washing machine. Maybe the English muffin had been used in the seat cushions on the counter stools for a few months until the new padding arrived. Maybe the peanut butter was made with imitation peanuts and three-in-one oil. The service, sullen as a bull moose when rutting season is finished, matched the fare.

We sat at one end of the counter, a few yards clear of the only other sufferers, a mother and her two sons. The mother and her children—probably fourteen and twelve—made me look svelte and I'm not being cruel about it. I was certainly in no position to feel superior to them. It was just a sad thing to see, young boys already carrying around an extra thirty or forty pounds, an unwanted cargo that was going to hold their lives down like a barbell attached to a balloon. In school, in sports, with girls, in their own sense of themselves, there would always be this anchor. Changing the way they ate would be harder than giving up Marlboros after a two-pack-a-day decade. They sat in the ruins of the first of two cheeseburgers and big plates of fries, trading punches and quick slaps between bites, looking happy.

I think it was the way they were eating that worried me most. God knows I've had my share of cheeseburgers and fries in my life, and fed them to my children. But the boys were shoving the second cheeseburgers into their mouths like inmates of a just liberated camp where they'd

160

been starved for years. A bite went in before the previous one had been swallowed. I wonder if Rinpoche somehow arranged that—implausible as it might seem—because the lesson he gave me was the other side of that same coin. He waited until the mother and boys had paid and left, and then he ordered two glasses of chocolate milk. "For the dessert," he said. I'd never seen him drink chocolate milk. He took hold of his glass and gestured for me to do the same. "First, you look," he said. "You see what it is that soon is going in your mouth, okay? Becoming part of your body."

"Okay. Chocolate milk, it looks like."

"Not too long, but you make sure you look at the food. Few seconds, maybe. Don't make the big show. Okay? You think, where did this milk coming from? The cow. You think about the cow maybe two seconds, okay? Then the chocolate—where comes from?"

"Okay."

"Was the question. Where comes from the chocolate?"

"The cacao plant. South America probably, I'm not sure."

"Then you pick it up like this, see? He lifted the glass to his lips and took a medium-sized sip, then set it down again. Now you. Okay. You taste the milk?"

"Yes."

"Really taste it. You feel it in your mouth, then feel when you swallow."

"Okay."

"Not reading when you eat. Not looking at the phone or the computer. Eating, okay?"

"Sure."

"That's the wesson," he said. "All done. Now you lose the weight you want."

"A chocolate milk diet?"

He looked at me, unsmiling, then shook his head. "Mister joke," he said.

"Drinking chocolate milk seems a strange way to lose weight, that's all."

"Not the chocolate milk, Otto! The way! When you eat, go a little slow. Really taste. Don't put the next one in before the first one is gone. Food, drink, the same."

"Lunch will take hours."

"Maybe a little bit more time now, yes. But maybe then you eat not so much. Just try, okay?"

"Okay," I said. "I'll try it at dinner. I'll give it a shot."

"Give a shot," he said. "Good."

We sat there sipping our chocolate milk for five full minutes. If nothing else, it took away the taste of the muffin and peanut butter. Rinpoche paid. We headed out to the car, yours truly ready to get back behind the wheel. But there was a dusty and beaten-up brown sedan parked beside us. Next to the sedan stood the mother and her hefty sons, looking bereft. Another few steps and I could see that the sedan's left rear tire was flat.

"Could you help us, sir?" she asked. She was an attractive woman, not yet forty, with lively blue eyes and a wrinkle of humor in the muscles around her mouth. The boys were carbon copies, face and body both, one slightly taller. But there was something in their eyes that was missing from hers—a devilish glint, a hint of past troubles or a promise of future ones.

"Of course," I said. I hadn't changed a tire since a flat on the old Corolla we'd bought for Tasha when she went off to college. It would be, I thought, another piece of Americana for Rinpoche, part of our ongoing exchange. He'd teach me meditative eating; I'd teach him how to change a flat.

I am the son and grandson of farmers and so, while it's true that I've spent my adult life working at a desk, it's also true that I'm better than the average Otto when it comes to mechanical things. Tuning up the lawnmower, nailing neat rows of clapboards on the garage, repointing the mortar on the ancient stone wall at the front of our yard—these were the types of tasks I enjoyed on a warm Saturday morning. They formed a nice counterweight to a week of editorial meetings and the reading of galleys and submissions. I tried to pass on some of those skills to Anthony and Natasha. In doing so I usually relayed my father's advice: "The hands go slower than the brain, Otto," he'd say, whether he was showing me how to sharpen a chisel or repair a barn wall. "When you're working with your hands, methodical is what counts, okay, son? Careful is what counts, not speed."

It struck me, as I introduced myself to the woman and her children—Edie, Jesse, and Adam were their names—and set about getting ready to change her tire, that Rinpoche would have approved of my father's approach. In its own way, the farming life, the life of manual labor, has a meditative aspect to it. Slow, careful, methodical, free of a lot of extraneous thinking. At the office I could do several things at once—drink coffee, talk on the phone, check sales reports on the computer—but try doing something else when you're sharpening a chisel. It was exactly what Rinpoche had just taught me about eating.

Changing Edie's tire, however, turned out to be slightly more complicated than I expected. To begin with, there was something amiss with the lock mechanism on her trunk. The inside lever didn't pop it. She tried the key but the trunk stayed closed. I could see that she was becoming embarrassed—the old car, the flat tire, the helplessness—and I was glad when her younger son, Adam, got a running start, jumped two feet in the air, landed hard on the trunk with his ample rear end, and we heard a *click*. When he slid off, leaving a small indentation, the trunk magically opened. We laughed, Rinpoche louder than anyone.

The trunk was filled with . . . stuff. Half-empty bottles of antifreeze, old blankets, empty beer bottles, pieces of clothing, a case of soda pop, rags, two bottles of nail-polish remover, etc. I stood aside while Edie and her sons took everything out, piece by piece, and gradually got down to the place where the jack and spare tire were stored. I set one of the blankets down on the gravel lot, kneeled on it, and showed Rinpoche how the jack worked, where it fit on the underside of the car. While I did this, I could sense the three pairs of sky-blue eyes fixed on him. Edie and her sons, most likely, had never encountered a Rinpoche in the flesh. There he was, stocky, bald, not white, wearing some kind of maroon dress with gold along the edges, talking funny, laughing at things—the way a beer bottle rolled along the tar—that were decidedly unfunny to the rest of us. For a moment I wanted to explain everything to them: *This is my brother-in-law,* I wanted to say, *my sister's husband. He's a famous spiritual teacher, born in Russia, living in North Dakota, and running a place there where people come from all over the country to sit on cushions or in chairs, or alone in little cabins, and watch the wanderings of their mind. He's a Rinpoche. RIN-po-shay. It means "precious one." He's been reincarnated so many times that he has a different view of life than the rest of us do. He's not afraid of dying, doesn't care about money, often skips dinner, usually rises at three a.m. to pray for a few hours.*

But I decided to focus on the task at hand.

"Push down on this lever here," I said to my companion. "It's like the old-fashioned well behind the small barn at the farm. Push down on it and see what happens."

He shifted the folds of his robe to one side and knelt next to me, took the black metal stick in his hand, and pushed down once, violently. The car moved up half an inch.

"Not so hard," I said. "A lever. Just push down on it not so hard about ten times and watch what happens."

He did that. The car responded as I expected it would and he was amazed, stunned. "What is inside this, Otto?" he asked excitedly. "This chack?"

"Nothing's inside it. Keep going. We need to get the wheel clear of the ground before we can change it."

Everything proceeded smoothly. The car went up, Rinpoche giggled, Jesse found the lug wrench, and the first four bolts came loose without much trouble. But then, as always seems to happen, the last one wouldn't budge. I tried. The car shook. The nut refused to move. Rinpoche gave it a shot with the same result.

"You wouldn't have WD-40 or something like that, Edie, would you?"

"Nail-polish remover works."

"It does?"

A nod into the folds of her double chin. She retrieved a bottle, dabbed some on, splashed a bit of soda on top of it, I tapped the nut a few times, and voilà, the tire was free. In another two minutes the skinny temporary spare had been bolted in place, the pile of Dollar General objects thrown back into the trunk, and Edie was showering us with thank yous as if we'd waved a wand and changed the dented old Pontiac into a shimmering Mercedes. She fished around in her small cloth purse, brought forth two dollars and held them out to me. "No, never," I said. "Thank you, but no charge. When you bring it in for a tune-up I'll charge you an extra hundred to make up for it, but today's work is free, ma'am."

The boys smiled. Edie stood there confused, missing the joke entirely. For one moment I thought she would start to cry. A gust of wind blew across the barren plain, carrying a load of grit in its hot breath. Edie said, "Then I'd like you to come home with us and have pie."

"No, really. It's nothing. It took ten minutes."

"I'd really want you to."

"We just ate, really, we're fine."

"I seen what you ate. It wasn't good. I make a good pie and I, the boys and I, we'd like for you to come and have a piece, you and, I'm sorry—"

"Volya. My brother-in-law. My sister's husband."

"You ought to come," she insisted. "It's not far. We'd like you to."

The boys were nodding, watching us, arms hanging at their sides, lips pressed together, half embarrassed by their mother, it seemed to me, but also half excited at making friends with two oddballs. I was still trying to figure out the glint in their eyes. They seemed alert and fairly intelligent, but at the same time there was something else going on, a reflection of devilry, a hint of twisted smiles. I wondered if they were about to play some practical joke on us. I looked at Rinpoche, though, really, I didn't have to. I looked back at Edie and said, "Okay. We can't stay long but a piece of pie would be nice. What is it, apple?"

"Cherry," she said. "Vanilla ice cream."

Rinpoche was nodding in a slow rhythm. I said, "We'll follow you."

From the parking lot of the Worst Restaurant on Earth we turned left, crossed the Interstate, and were immediately on a gravel road running through Colorado nothingness. Less than a mile down that road we turned left again, onto a smaller road, hanging back a bit so as not to be blinded by the dust cloud thrown up by Edie's car. Another mile or so and we began to see a few homes to either side, trailer homes mostly, with the occasional one-story bungalow. There was a striking resemblance to Pine Ridge but this wasn't reservation land; the only sign we saw was for AMALGAMATED METALS TWO MILES.

Edie turned left onto a short drive and pulled up in front of a trailer home. Rusted sides, tires holding down the roof, a short clothesline to one side where men's white underpants and a colorful bra waved at us in welcome.

The wind was stronger here. When Rinpoche and I stood up out of the car we had to turn our faces away from the flying grit. "Come on in!" Edie shouted. I was trying to place her accent. Central Appalachia, I guessed. The mountains of North Carolina or West Virginia. She led the way up three metal steps, the boys standing to either side like an honor guard, and we stepped into a clean kitchen almost completely filled by a metal table and four mismatched wooden chairs. On the wall above the sink window was a hanging placard: CHRIST BLESS THIS HOME AND ALL WHO ENTER. On a small square of counter I saw the pie.

Jesse went down the hall and returned with a folding chair. His mother fussed about in the cabinets and refrigerator and in another minute Rinpoche and I had slices of pie à la mode in front of us. The boys and Edie joined us. They were going after the pie the way they'd gone after the food at TWRITW. Edie ate with a bit more delicacy, looking at us out of the tops of her eyes. The pie was excellent, in fact, and I told her that. Rinpoche made humming noises and smacked his lips, the way he did when he liked the taste of something. "Wery good pie!" he said. "Who make?"

"I did."

"Wery the best I ever had."

"You talk funny," Adam said, and his brother swung an arm into his chest and knocked him right out of his chair and onto the floor.

"Boys!"

Adam stood up, smiling, and slapped his brother on the back of the head and then there was a small pitched battle in the kitchen, how real I couldn't tell. Elbows flying, quick kicks, rabbit punches.

"Boys!"

"It's okay," I said to her. "Rinpoche here is known to wrestle with my son, who plays football. I'm used to it."

"Boys, stop!" Edie said, and they separated and tucked in their shirts, taking the occasional slap at each other. "Sit now. We have company." And, to me. "They're good boys but they can get out of hand."

"I talk wery funny," Rinpoche acknowledged agreeably. "I was born in Russia."

"Russia!" Jesse said. "Say something in Russian!"

"Say, 'The bad dad's home,'" his brother said, "Because he is."

We heard a truck door shut, footsteps on gravel,

and then the front door squeaked open again. The man who stepped into the kitchen, just as Rinpoche was saying, *atets dohma*, was as wiry as the rest of his family was plump. Short-cropped blond hair, a face at the sight of which the word *jagged* came to mind—sharp nose, sharp cheekbones, angular mouth. He was dressed from head to toe in a navy-blue work uniform of some sort, smudged here and there with silvery swipes, and he was carrying a six-pack of beer, the cans held together with white plastic rings of the sort that strangle seagulls. At his appearance a charge went through the air. The boys especially seemed to go very still. For just a moment, one couldn't imagine them wrestling. The man looked at me first, then his wife, then Rinpoche. His first words were, "What the fuck?"

Edie seemed completely unafraid of him, a reaction I did not share. "These men helped me change a flat tire or we'd still be at Bog's."

"You went to Bog's?"

"It's Adam's birthday. I took him to Bog's, yes I did. This here is Otto and this is his brother-in-law Volda."

I stood and held out my hand. I thought for a moment that Dad would spit.

"Volda's from Russia," Adam said timidly. It seemed to me he was only trying to get his father to look at him. His father gave my hand a flimsy shake, no eye contact. He was staring at his wife.

I had the urge—highly unusual for me, I would even say unique in my experience—to slap him in the face.

After two seconds he shifted his gaze—his eyes seemed weighted—to Rinpoche, who was also standing now, also holding out his hand. Dad wouldn't take it.

"Volda wrestles," Jesse said. Now he seemed to want not so much attention as to provocation.

"Cage fighter," his younger brother added.

"Boys, stop it."

"What are you?" Dad asked.

"Rinpoche."

"The fuck?"

"A monk," I said. "A holy man."

"Get out then," Dad said. "We don't need no religion bullshit in here."

"Ethan! If it wasn't for them we'd still be out at Bog's."

"Get out, queers," Dad said.

"Hey," I said. "We helped out your wife. She invited us back for a slice of pie. How about showing just the smallest bit of respect."

"How about this," Dad said, swinging the six-pack in a wild haymaker. It was my very good luck that the weight of the beer made it happen in semi–slow motion. I managed to duck enough so that only the bottom of the cans caught the top of my head, but then, before either the Bad Dad or I could do anything else, the boys were on

172

him, several hundred pounds of boys, and Dad was on his back on the floor, and they were punching, and he was swinging his arms, and Edie, who'd stood up by this point and was in the center of my view, had streams of tears going down her cheeks. "I'm sorry, I'm sorry," she kept saying. "He's been drinking, I'm so sorry, mister!"

I was down on one knee and I could already feel the blood trickling through my hair. I watched the scene a few feet in front of me as if it were a film playing on the television and I'd slept on the couch after a night of drinking and had just awakened. Arms and legs, shirts running up the boys' backs, showing their pale white skin. From what I could tell, Dad was taking somewhat of a beating, though they made a point, it seemed, of not hitting him in the face. There was a great deal of cursing, an abundance of cursing, most of it from Dad's mouth. Edie had started weeping in a pitiful way. Rinpoche had begun chanting—a prayer for peace it must have been. I'd seen it work in the past, one time, diffusing a situation that could have turned violent. But this time it didn't work, at all. The punches ceased, but there was still a violent struggle going on. I could see that Dad had Adam by his right ear, and Adam was elbowing that arm fiercely, trying to get free. He started crying now, too, and that seemed to be too much for his older brother, who punched his father in the groin. Once, hard. Dad spat out a furious four-letter howl and let go of the ear.

"I'm ashamed, ashamed!" Edie was wailing. She'd wet a washcloth in the sink and now she pressed it against my head. "Jesus, forgive him. I'm sorry!"

The main problem, at that point, was logistical: The tangle of bodies, still writhing, though Dad had almost given up, stood between me and the door. Rinpoche had stopped chanting. I got to my feet. Edie, on tiptoes now, was trying to keep the washcloth against my scalp but it slipped out of her hand and down against my ear and neck, where I caught it. I looked at Rinpoche. "Wery bad," he mouthed in my direction.

"I think," I said to Edie, in a shaky voice, "that we're going to head out now, if you don't mind. Are you safe?"

"Safe, sure," she said bitterly. "Safe as can be."

I handed her the bloody washcloth and she said, "Thank you."

By this point the boys had their father flat on his back, arms pinned to his sides. He'd stopped struggling but was grunting and gasping for breath. His eyes shifted hard and settled on me with such a fierce hatred it made me shake. Rinpoche stepped over them first but instead of heading right out the door he knelt down and put his mouth close to Dad's ear. I couldn't hear what he said. I was still a bit dazed and, at that point, just wanting to get away from there before anything worse happened, before Edie came out of the bedroom with a gun, or the boys started to pull out their father's teeth with pliers, or a vicious Rhodesian Ridgeback materialized and took a chunk out of my inner thigh. My head hurt, but the blood was no longer dripping down across my cheek. The world was not a steady place.

"Get out while you can!" Adam yelled, but the yell, the warning, sounded half-serious. His ear was bleeding. He put a hand up to it and when he saw the blood on his fingers he smiled. It was all some kind of stage play acted out in a sociopathic community theater. They must have been getting ready to audition for a new reality show. Edie plopped down in a chair and covered her face in her hands and, with that as our final image, out we went into the gritty wind. At that point a dog did materialize, but it was a scruffy black mutt, cat-sized, trotting over from the next yard and yapping at us as if we were aliens just landed.

Then the aliens were in the car, backing it into a three-point turn, throwing up a cloud of dust that drifted back in the direction of the trailer. I asked Rinpoche if he was all right.

"Wery good, man," he said, somewhat wearily.

"There's another little piece of America for you."

"Your head has the blood on."

I reached up and touched it. Tender as could be but already scabbing over. "Stitches will not

175

be required," I said, but I was a bit woozy, the pulse still pounding, the scene replaying itself over and over in my inner eye. "There's an American expression I've never liked," I said. "No good deed goes unpunished."

"What means?"

"It means you do good things for people and all you get in return is shit."

"Ah."

"I tell you that is the very last tire I ever change for anybody in my life."

I found the interstate west and took the entrance ramp, trying as hard as I could not to turn my eyes toward the Desolation Café. I was in a strange place then. There is a way in which, as realistically as it is portrayed in films and on TV, violence has a very different flavor in real life. It wasn't as if we'd been involved in a shooting or a war, but the events at Edie's were so far outside the boundaries of what I'd lived with for the past half century that my mind seemed unable to make sense of it. I was driving along I-80 like an automaton, on cruise control, steering, checking the mirrors. But three-quarters of me was running the scenes over and over again in my mind as if the cells there were trying to settle themselves back into the orbits they'd been shaken out of. I wasn't trembling, but I was unsettled at some deep level.

I could only imagine what it must be like for

the man or woman who comes home from war, having seen true violence, again and again, and then tries to re-enter the ordinary world of eating in a café or mailing something at the post office. I could only imagine. I could only imagine what would become of Jesse and Adam when they grew older and left the nest, and what would become of their mother, then, living with her gentlemanly Ethan.

Rinpoche, of course, was as calm as ever. During the whole weird two-minute scenario, at least as I reconstructed it in my mind's eye, he'd been still, watching, alert, unruffled. "You've seen things like that before?" I asked him. Just then the highway split and I nearly missed the turn toward Denver onto I-76.

"Sometimes," he said.

"In Russia?"

A nod. Casual. Unconcerned. No volatile memories playing there. "They beat us some-times. Me and my father."

"Not good."

"No."

"I thought I saw something in the eyes of those boys when we were changing the tire."

"Those boys see it many times," he said. "Worse maybe."

"Nice way to grow up."

He made a small grunt.

Reconstructing the scene yet again I remembered the last thing Rinpoche had done before we hurried out the door. "What did you say to old Dad back there? I saw you whispering in his ear. Were you suggesting some chess moves for the after-supper game? Reciting the U.S. presidents in reverse alphabetical order?"

Rinpoche either didn't hear the question and my goofiness or pretended not to hear it. It seemed to me that, in another moment, he was going to go into one of his nap-meditations, a kind of highway hypnosis with mantra.

"You told him something."

The good monk turned his head to me, then forward again. "Told him there was money under the dish. With the pie."

"Huh?"

"I put. I said, 'Look under the dish, man.' "

"You put money there? When?"

"When he say 'fuck' the first time."

"How much?"

A shrug. "Pretty much what I had."

"Everything you had? That giant bankroll?"

He scratched a thumbnail over a small ice cream stain on his robe. He said, "Looked like they could need it."

Sixteen

On the night of what I will always think of as Our Famous Visit to Edie's, I wanted predictability. So, at a rest area off I-76 I used my phone and found us a room in a chain hotel on the outskirts of Denver. En route, we shared a pizza and played some pocket billiards at a place called Cable's Pub and Grill in Fort Morgan, where the Yankees were on the big-screen TV and the waitress located a tube of antibiotic ointment in the kitchen and let me dab some on my head.

We found the hotel without any trouble, checked in without incident, took showers, turned off the lights, and lay there in our separate beds with only a little highway noise and a bit of light filtering in between the curtains, and a hardly noticeable throbbing on my scalp.

"You asleep?" I said across the room.

"Soon."

"Before you sign off can I ask you something?"

"Always, my friend."

"Do you think it really helps at all to give people like that money? I mean, setting that one family aside, you know there's a national debate going on these days about welfare and programs for poor kids and so on. One side feels compassion for them and wants the government to help. The other side says giving them money isn't compassionate at all, only keeps them poor, takes away the incentive to find work, and it isn't fair to people who don't get anything free."

"Man was working, I think, Otto."

"Right, *he* was. I'm speaking more generally. I gave a little money to the people on the reservation, but did that really help them?"

"I don't know," Rinpoche said across the dark space between us. "I don't have the big idea. In the minute when I think it's good, I give. When I think it isn't good, I don't give."

"That's not very helpful to the national conversation."

"Big question is how much you need for yourself."

"Right, I know. Maybe you judge me, us, for the big house we have, for the nice cars Jeannie and I drove, for the vacations we took with our kids, the clothes we bought them, the gadgets, the meals out. No question we didn't need all that."

He was silent. I worried he'd fallen asleep . . . or was judging me.

"You're supposed to say, 'No, I don't judge you for that, Otto. You're a good man. You worked hard. You gave a lot to charity. You were only doing what any father would do—taking care of his kids.' "

More silence. Then, "Some teachers say the

best place to go on the spiritual life is from the middle. Too much money, maybe, you don't want to think about dying, about after dying. Not enough money, all you think about is money, where I'm going to get it, how can I eat, how can my children eat. In the middle, you have enough and you can have time not to worry, to look for something else than money."

I said, "But a lot of times the way it works is you never really rest in that middle. You have a nice car, you want a nicer one. You have money, you all of a sudden need to have a boat, a summer house, a ski house. You used to like going out for a hamburger and a milk shake, but now you can have oysters and lobster and steak and fine wine. Your tastes change. You get caught up. Your friends are going on cruises down the Rhine River, you don't want to go to Cape Cod for a week anymore, and you have the cash for more exotic things, so why not?"

Nothing. I heard a child complaining to his mother in the hallway. At that hour.

"There is a story," Rinpoche said finally, "about one monk, wery famous. This monk he has a simple house, wery small, and a small garden on the land near the house where he grow his food. He have many, how you say, student."

"Disciples."

"Sure. One day he go away on a trip some-place, maybe to see another monk that is the friend. He stays three weeks maybe. When he comes back, the disciples they have maked him a new room on his house so he is more comfortable, has the space, see? What does the monk do? He gets wery, wery angry on them and breaks down the new room all apart so he just has the house the way he used to have it."

Now it was my turn to be silent. I was translating the story into modern American. I was away for three weeks. Anthony and some college friends came to Bronxville and built a beautiful one-room addition onto the back of our garage, a second-floor room, maybe, with a dormer. Pale hardwood floors, an antique desk, excellent lighting, a view out over the neighborhood. A place for Dad to write that book he'd always been meaning to write. What does Dad do? He comes home from the trip, gets out his chainsaw and sledgehammer, and cuts and smashes the new addition to splinters while his son and friends watch.

It didn't work for me.

"As lessons go," I said, "that isn't your best one."

"It's a wesson to say, 'Enough for me now. I'm okay.'"

"How do you really help, is my question? Give up a cruise and send the money to Pine Ridge?"

"Maybe. Maybe one time you take the cruise and one time no cruise."

"Hard to find the line."

"Don't worry so much, Otto. Don't think so much about. You fixed the tire for that woman, yes? You don't have to be every second fixing the tires. You make your mind calm, calm, and then you see the minute when you can do and the time when you don't."

"Got it, thanks. I just wish the world was as simple for me as it seems to be for you."

"Because everything that happens, you think on it. You judge, judge, worry, worry, the tea cup going up and down and over and there. Now, right now, what is it to do? Sleep. Tomorrow maybe in one minute you can feel to do something else, not make the cruise maybe, not eat, give maybe. Maybe one day I see you selling your house and living in a small place like the monk. Doesn't matter so much. If you are worried all times about going a little bit wrong, then always you are thinking about you, you, you. That way you don't see clear, okay? Too much *you* in the picture."

"Okay, thanks. Good sleep."

He grunted his good-night. But it wouldn't have been Rinpoche if he didn't add this last line, just to jostle me. "I like wery much that pie with the cherries," he said, sounding perfectly sincere. "I think about it now. I remember the taste. Tomorrow we get another piece more of it some-place, okay?"

Seventeen

With its large-screen television and inoffensive framed prints, its in-room coffee service and envelope for the maid's gratuity, our third-floor room in the chain hotel could have been any room on the outskirts of any city from Kuala Lumpur to Shanghai, could have belonged to any one of a dozen famous chains. But it was perfectly clean and comfortable, with two queen beds, thick walls, and a shower with adequate pressure. I awoke from my deep dream (a dream in which I was completely bald and being awarded a tennis trophy I had not won) refreshed but confused and lay there for a few minutes running the image through my mind once or twice to see if some important message would leap clear of the vague and disconnected somnambulatory feelings. I wondered why it is that dreams so often speak in symbols and signs. Why couldn't there be message boards, text on screens: YOU ARE AFRAID OF SUCH-AND-SUCH; YOUR FATHER WAS DISAPPOINTED IN YOU; YOU WISH YOU COULD PLAY THE ACCORDION.

My scalp throbbed quietly, but there was no blood on the pillowcase. Just a nick, I was fairly sure. I wondered if the universe was trying to nudge me in the direction of a late-in-life boxing career, and I reminded myself of what I'd learned in the classroom of fatherhood: There is no need to panic at the sight of red liquid; there is so much blood in us from the neck up that even small cuts to the head can bleed out of all proportion to the damage done. It seemed, in retrospect, foolish to have gone to Edie's trailer, but lots of things seem foolish in retrospect. Jeannie would have approved, I was sure. During our years together, she and I had worked hard to stay open to adventure and experience. The last thing we wanted was to become that safe, upper-middle-class couple who arranges every moment of every vacation in advance, who places security so far above everything else on the ladder of life that all the fun is taken out of it, who rushes off to the doctor at every scrape and cough. Yes, there were times, after Jeannie fell ill, when I tortured myself with the idea that we might have done things differently, might have joined the club of those who research every possible cancer-causing agent in every medical study and try desperately to keep every plastic bottle, every spore of mold, and every impure food ingredient out of the home. But even in the depth of my sorrow I knew how impossible that would be. Cancer, that merciless modern plague, waits in certain genes like an assassin in a bedroom closet; there is not one kind of knock that opens the door.

I sat up and saw that Rinpoche had positioned himself, ass on a tower of two pillows, upon his neatly made bed, and was sitting there, cross-legged, facing the curtained windows, still as a stone. For a little while I watched him, wondering what it felt like to be inside his mind. What peaceful gardens did he wander there? What did a world absent of fear, shame, worry, and doubt feel like?

"Good morning, my brother-and-waw!" he said, still without moving, without turning to look at me. "In your sleep you said, 'Pie!' like you were happy." He swiveled around to face me.

"What time did you get up?"

"Three!" he said, just like that. Not three, but three!

"And you've been down in the breakfast nook all this time, waiting for them to put out the microwavable cinnamon buns and Styrofoam plates, am I right?"

"Bet your ass, man," he said.

"There's a pool, want to take a swim before we head out?"

"Sure, man!"

"Did you bring your Speedo?"

"Celia told me to put it."

Given the inappropriately small size of Rinpoche's Speedo, and the powerful torso and legs it revealed, and given the kind of antics of which my brother-in-law was capable, I said a small prayer of thanks, as we made our way to the elevator, that, this time at least, he'd decided to wear his robe over the bathing suit. With the exception of an extremely fit German- or Dutch-speaking couple in their fifties, we had the outdoor pool area to ourselves. The air was already warm, the morning nearly cloudless. The pool water glistened in the sun, troubled by gentle wavelets, as if the couple had finished their morning laps a few minutes before we arrived.

As I knew he would, the good monk slipped out of his robe and went into his eccentric yoga routine—grunts, loud exhalations, one leg at a time held out in front of him at waist height, head rolled around and around on his linebacker's neck. And then, as I knew he would, he ignored the NO DIVING signs and lifted himself into a two-hundred-pound swan dive, arms in the crawl stroke before he hit the water, two lengths of the pool without breathing, and then the wet shimmering face breaking the surface and showing a smile like the sun, aimed in my direction. "Colorado!" he yelled out, as if the word's secondary meaning was "perfect!"

The Germans or Dutch looked up from their *Der Spiegel,* or whatever it was, raising a quartet of blond eyebrows. *Americans, such an indecorous race.*

There was nothing scornful about them, it was just that I felt fat and sloppy beside the trim man and grumpy in comparison with Rinpoche, so, after checking to be sure there was no fresh blood in my hair, I jumped in and swam and swam until the run of bad thoughts had been washed away. From that day on, I promised myself, happy dreams of pie aside, I was going back to my no-sugar, no-alcohol diet. My sister and her husband were at peace. My children weren't sick, hungry, or depressed. True, the American political scene was starting to resemble nothing so much as a circus performance in Rome's dying days, and, true, there were families like Edie's scattered all over the landscape, rural and urban, but there wasn't very much I could do about any of that, and no sense drowning myself in my own personal version of *Sturm und Drang*. I climbed out and performed a perfect cannonball into the deep end, far enough from the other guests to keep their glossy pages dry. Rinpoche copied me, making a larger splash, laughing afterward like a kid. The couple sought refuge indoors.

Cleansed and chlorinated, baptized into my new and healthier life, I eschewed the sugary, white-flour offerings of the free breakfast and jogged up three flights of stairs. I packed up my rolling suitcase, Rinpoche his worn leather satchel, and soon we were on the road again, a mile above sea level, two souls in motion. We could see the Rockies now, jagged and majestic on the western horizon, with bands of purplish clouds streaming close above their snow-dappled peaks, and then, below, a cluster of yellow-brick buildings I knew to be Boulder. Before Rinpoche told me his "speaking" was in "Lead Willage," Colorado, I assumed Boulder would be the site of it. Boulder; Sedona; Taos; Madison; Missoula; Austin; Cambridge; Berkeley, California; and Burlington, Vermont—these are the nation's meditative outposts, capitals of the alternative universe. Sensitive, somewhat hairy, riding in sandals and jeans on the tip of the country's left wing, its citizens were either a lazy, lunatic fringe or Aquarian ambassadors pointing the rest of us toward a kinder set of laws about the way life was supposed to be lived. Boulder would be the sensible place for a speaking engagement. I pictured a café with twenty-eight kinds of coffee drinks, an audience of the young and young at heart, listening with great reverence and then going home to a dose of marijuana or Vitamin-water before bed.

But of course I was wrong. By then I should have known my companion better than that, should long ago have shed my judgments and oversimplifications. The speaking, it turned out, would be in Leadville, twice as high and half as alternative; in Boulder he just wanted to say hi to a friend.

I wanted to eat. We found a place to park on Pearl Street and then, at my urging, secured a table just as a restaurant called L'Atelier was opening its doors for lunch. Boulder seemed cleaner than I'd imagined, glistening glass and stone Buddhas in its windows, a store called Bliss, perfect pavement, healthy-looking college kids with backpacks and phones. And L'Atelier fit in well. There were spotless cloth napkins twirled into swans in wine glasses. There was a collection of ceramic statuettes. There was a waiter who delighted in telling us about the many ways in which the food on the luncheon menu was grown or raised, the way the ingredients were combined. It was a culinary-school mini-seminar and by the time he finished I was impressed . . . but ravenous.

Bouillabaisse for me, vegetarian ravioli for the monk. While we waited for the wild-caught halibut to be set into the cream from grass-fed cows alongside organic onions with free-trade spices, I devoured a basket of baguette slices smeared with cold butter. Rinpoche sat opposite in the booth, watching.

"When the actual meal comes I'll eat more meditatively," I said.

He shrugged, didn't seem to care.

"What are you going to speak about tonight?"

Another shrug. "Don't know yet."

"You don't prepare? Nothing written down? No pages of one of your books marked with Post-it notes?"

"When I sit up there I take a little tea, breathe a

190

breath, two breath, look at the peoples there, then I know."

"I would have thought you'd be speaking here, in Boulder. I think the people here would be open to what you have to say."

"Already lot of teachers here," he said.

"And you seem to appeal to a different crowd . . . at least in the other events I've seen."

"Every kinds of crowd."

"Why is that? I mean, black and white and Asian and American Indian and Hispanic, old and young, alternative, as Tash would call them, and absolute middle of the road, rich and poor and middle-class, women and men and those who inhabit the territory in between. It's a little unusual, in my very limited experience of spiritual teachers, to attract such mixed audiences. Please explain, sir."

He smiled at the tone of the question, broke off a corner of baguette heel, and nibbled at it. For a moment I thought he wouldn't answer.

The bouillabaisse and ravioli were served. I went to work immediately but Rinpoche had found one of those single-serving jars of jam in the folds of his robe—God knew what else he carried around in its pockets—and was holding it now between thumb and forefinger. "I took this from a hotel one time in another speaking. They give it free."

"They do that at some of the finer establishments. You'll notice this morning that the only thing free in the hotel was a packet of instant coffee."

He ignored me, twirled the thimble of a bottle in his fingers, then held it up between us. "This paper on, what do you call it?"

"Label. Says it's raspberry and so on, what the ingredients are, the company that makes it."

"Ah. Wery nice label, yes?"

"Well made. Tasteful."

A nod, a few seconds of label gazing. "But what you eat is the inside."

"Exactly. And, as a matter of fact, if you don't mind, a little raspberry jam would go well on a buttered baguette with my fish stew. There's a little sugar in it but it's fruit sugar and fruit sugar doesn't count on my diet. May I?"

He handed me the bottle. It opened with a satisfying *pop* and I had slathered jam on my baguette and was lifting it to my lips by the time I realized he was smiling at me.

"What?"

"A wesson," he said.

"The jam?"

"You're not eating the label."

"Of course I'm not eating the label." He watched me, waited. I hurried back across the conversation.

"Black, white, American Indian, woman, man— some people think like that, like the label.

192

Maybe Rinpoche thinks, a little more, the jam is important part. So that's maybe why different labels come to the speaking."

"Lesson has registered," I said, after a moment.

"Good. Eat."

I ate. But instead of contemplating where the fish came from, the cream, the onions, the spices, and instead of really experiencing the full taste of it on my tongue as Rinpoche had recommended, I found myself wrapped in a swirl of thoughts about what my Bronxville friends would say about this wesson. It would seem simplistic to them. Don't look at people by their category—gender, race, social standing, age—but relate to them inside-to-inside, soul-to-soul, from and to that place where we're so much more alike than different. A notion like that would be fodder for mockery. My friends and I—most Americans—lived in a stew of propaganda that insisted on the categorization of humanity. We were gay or straight, we were male or female or part of each, we were conserva-tive or liberal, black or white or red or yellow or brown or mixed or Italian or Irish or Nigerian American. We wore Brooks Brothers or Izod or Polo or Levi's, we opened our mouth and said one word about abortion or taxes or God or radical Islam or military service or Bush or Obama or Fox or NPR or we said we were from Mississippi or North Dakota or the West Village or Boulder and within the time it took to say "box" we were in one. We'd somehow gotten to be straight white males or gay African American females first, and human beings second, and if you claimed the eschewment of label you'd be mocked, dismissed, labeled as a naive rube from beyond the Adirondacks.

"How much work does it take to see past the labels?" I asked him.

Another shrug. The slow chewing and swallowing of a piece of ravioli. "I think," he said, "all a time," he thumped his chest twice, "about the hearts going in people. The heart is like a, how you say it, one end of the line of the electric."

"Electricity."

"Yes. On the other end, a bigger consciousness, the true person you are. Here, all differences, but if you go to the other end, wery the same."

"I had, at certain moments, when Jeannie was dying . . . I had a sense of that. There was Jeannie, my wife, her body, her personality, and then . . . then there was something larger than that. I don't mean the promise of an afterlife necessarily. I mean, and it was rare—most of the time I was too upset or afraid—but sometimes I would have this weird feeling that she already was keeping part of herself somewhere else, and it was a somewhere, or a someone, that had always been there. Since she's been gone I haven't felt that so much but sometimes—" I put my spoon in the dish so

194

suddenly that it made a splash and a *tink*. The waiter looked over. "Huh," I said. "I just remembered a piece of the dream I had last night."

"The pie?"

"No, it was . . . I was . . . I just had . . . I was getting a tennis trophy but instead of being on the court I was in a room with no ceiling and part of me was inside the room, standing on my feet, and this other invisible part of me had been . . . the word I want to use is *vaporized* into the air above."

"Good dream, Otto."

"Right, but I don't want to end up living in that vapor. Maybe it's true, as you told me once, that *this* is actually the dream, and that other dimension is the reality, but I want to do justice to this dream, even if that's all it is. Maybe we're so insignificant that nothing really matters either way, but I still think it's important to do the dream right, to pay my bills, take care of my kids, do a little something for the world."

"Most important thing," Rinpoche agreed, and I was glad to hear it. He chewed, he swallowed, he took a sip of water. "The farmer in the next land to us, Martin."

"Rangwohl," I told him. What I didn't tell him was that my father had zero respect for the family, as farmers, as people. "Rangwohl sloppy" was his term for a job poorly done.

"Rangwohl. On his barn at the door he has the,

how you say it?" He made a fist with his left hand and a loop with thumb and second finger above but touching it.

"Padlock."

"The padlock. Being in this body, in this world, now," he brought his fingers down lightly on the solid tabletop and tapped it twice, "this is like the padlock. You live good here is like the key. The key makes the lock go. The good living makes it go open. You let go of the body. Then the door on the other world can open. The ceiling come off like your dream. You live bad and that ceiling stay on, see? The lock stay on."

"Makes sense. For a while there I was thinking it was all just meditation that mattered. That always seemed a little . . . suspect to me. There are plenty of good people who don't know meditation from—"

"Meditation is no good if you live wrong, Otto. But eat now. Now, this minute, the right thing is to eat. Enjoy the food. Pay attention on this minute, Otto. How is feeling the top on your head?"

"Good, fine. A little sore."

"Good thing you bended down, yes?"

"I would have seen my wife in the next world."

"Maybe you see her soon anyway," he said, but I was thinking about the padlock idea, and Rangwohl, and what happened to a spirit after death, and I wasn't paying enough attention.

Eighteen

Rinpoche's friend was a young man named James, who frequented a Boulder coffee shop called the Laughing Goat Coffeehouse. We went there for dessert. There was a shrine near the door, a religious statue on a chest-high miniature altar with a candle burning in front of it. The ceramic figure bore a vague resemblance to the Virgin Mary but it was clearly not intended to be exclusively Christian. And clearly it wasn't the kind of thing you saw in a Manhattan Starbucks (or any Starbucks, for that matter).

"It's there to bless the space," the barista told me as she served my latte and Rinpoche's green tea. Monica was her name, and she had a nice way about her, not at all a way that was centered in the vaporized other world. She put her hands together and made a bow to Rinpoche, but she did it with such good humor, and explained the shrine in such a happily matter-of-fact way that the most cynical of souls would also have stuffed a five-dollar-bill in the tip jar.

Most of the tables were occupied. It was the usual scene—young people peering at laptop screens, one or two with notebooks or textbooks in front of them, someone reading an actual book, friends chatting, couples sitting close and sharing a scone or a biscotti. These places are everywhere now, part of the American fabric, our version of the hookah houses of Central Asia, or the Irish pub scene, or the outdoor cafés of Old Cairo.

Rinpoche and I took a table. After a time James joined us. He told me he'd made two or three retreats with "the Rinpoche" and he talked about the Laughing Goat with so much passion that I wanted to invest. It was, he said, "a community place." There was nightly music, all welcome. There were people—he indicated a young, dark-haired man against one wall—who wrote books here. ("That guy sold his house to write the story of his guru's life.") When I remarked on the friendly barista he smiled proudly and said, "That's Monica. She's done yoga 128 days in a row."

It was all spoken the way a café patron in the City would speak of the Knicks or the Giants or the Mets or the Yanks. In Boulder, it was gurus and shrines and yoga that sewed the social quilt together, not walk-off homeruns or fourth-quarter comebacks. I felt, yet again, that I stood astraddle two very distinct worlds, one measurable, one not; one in which conflict and violence were taken for granted, and one in which a great effort— sometimes a forced and artificial effort—was made toward peace.

"The first time I set foot in Boulder," James

said, "I knew this was my place. These were my people. I grew up in a Southern Baptist family in Missouri—we get along fine now—and when I came here it was like I found my place in the world."

"And they make a great cup of coffee," I said, and he seemed truly pleased.

An hour later, driving out of Boulder toward the high peaks, past a billboard that read, MOUNTAIN AIR RANCH—NUDIST RESORT. YOU WERE BORN NAKED! and a plain, government-issue wooden sign announcing, ROCKY FLATS CLOSURE PROJECT, as if nothing of much import had ever happened there, Rinpoche broke one of his contemplative silences to tell me what a good man James was, what a diligent student.

"I know so many people like that," I said, "people who seem to have been born into a family situation that's completely at odds with their own sensibilities. I count myself among them. The way he was talking about Boulder—that's the way I felt the second I saw New York City. I could no more have settled in Dickinson and taken over the family farm than I could have come out of my mother's body speaking Swahili. Do you know what I mean?"

"Maybe."

"I'm talking about being born someplace and then, when you get to a certain age, realizing with absolute certainty that you don't belong there. You belong in a different culture entirely. I see that a lot in this country."

He pondered for a while—the GPS had us cruising a small highway between fir-covered slopes to our right, and to our left, off in the lower eastern distance, the Denver skyline—then said, "You know how on a trip we can go over one state into the other?"

"Crossing the state line. Yes."

"Is the same with these people. They have a little bit of karma left from another life. They have to live a little bit in Missouri for a while, in North Dakota. Then, finish. A new state. A new place for them, a new life. Nothing bad inside it."

"No, but there's a strain, a kind of scar or wound or something. I used to feel it all the time. I grew up in a certain way, with certain rules, clothes, sense of humor, a certain belief system, and then I found myself in one that was so different I felt cut right in half on some days, like I didn't really belong in Manhattan and didn't really belong in the Dakotas. I still feel that on occasion, only now it's one foot in what I think of as the ordinary world and one foot in your world."

"You sew up yourself," he said, in a confident way he had, as if he were reciting a rule that everyone knew, or should know. "You can talk to all peoples now, my good friend. I see you do that. James can go and talk to the Baptist mother in Missouri, can love her. And he can talk to the Buddhist girl in Boulder, love her, too. You can know how to be in New York, how to be in North Dakota. You starting to see into the jelly inside peoples now, past the label. You making good progress this time, man!"

"You, too," I said, and he laughed in an appreciative way, as if having me around was, if nothing else, good for comic relief.

Nineteen

Not far outside Boulder we merged onto the interstate and began our climb into the serious mountains, up onto the roof of the lower forty-eight. In that part of Colorado, I-70 is a winding alpine speedway crowded with tractor trailers and maniacal Coloradans in four-wheel-drive sedans and pickups, with emergency escape ramps for those truckers unlucky enough to lose their brakes, with signs for CHAIN STATIONS AHEAD and red-and-white barred gates that close the road in big snowstorms.

The scenery was nice enough—deep green mountainsides with changing views of valleys and peaks, slopes of rocky scree, and the occasional cold lake—but I couldn't appreciate it because I had to concentrate so intently on the driving, on keeping us alive and whole, on getting the Master to his talk that night. It might have been Switzerland, and not the White River National Forest—the GPS showed an altitude of 9,163, then 10,366, and the temperature dropped like a stone in a pond from near ninety down into the lower seventies by the time we made Silverthorne. On the radio we heard a story about a ballot referendum that, if passed, would result in Colorado's secession from the United States. Why? Because the massacre in the movie theater in Aurora had given rise to stricter gun laws. It seemed to me so typical of the current political climate. More careful background checks were somehow translated into: The government is coming to take away your guns. And that led to secession, or at least the hope of secession in some quarters. It was the mentality of a child. You're making me go to bed early! Next you'll be taking my stuffed animals! I'm running away!

Fine, I thought. Secede all you want. Start your own little country where everyone carries a gun. Who cares? I had no problem with guns. Hunting, shooting. Not the smallest problem. But could no distinction be made between that pleasure and the idiocy of shooting at deer with an assault rifle? Or allowing the mentally ill to fire away in a crowd? Had we grown into simpletons?

At last, tired from focusing on the drive, the radio, the nuts, I took an exit that led us past a golf course, a condominium village, a ski area, men fishing in a small lake, and onto a two-lane highway, Colorado 91. There we wound along in quieter fashion. According to the dashboard thermometer, the temperature had dropped another sixteen degrees in ten minutes. By the time we'd gone a few miles it was fifty-five; I half expected to see snowflakes. Just then we passed a series of dams and levees and Rinpoche asked if I would stop. This was another of my companion's odd fascinations. Rinpoche asserted that he was particularly knowledgeable about geology, and there were moments when I believed him. He seemed to understand—either because he'd studied it or because of some peculiar intuition—the history of the stone outcroppings we passed. On other trips, when we'd gone by a dam, he'd become as excited as a child and begged me to stop so he could get out and admire the engineering. Our visit to the Coulee Dam in east-central Washington state had been a special moment for him: Since that road trip, one summer earlier, he must have mentioned it a dozen times in my presence, cited statistics, history, praised the architects and engineers, while at the same time expressing compassion for the lives that had been ruined in the building of it.

I pulled into a viewing area and let Rinpoche walk to the edge of the drop-off and stand and stare. Now it was forty-four degrees. August 19.

A wind that would have sent the Inuit into shelter was ruffling his robe.

In case it isn't already obvious, I'm a big fan of roadside information boards. When we traveled as a family I used to drive the kids crazy by stopping at every historical landmark and reading the story of what had happened there, however inconsequential it might be. "Oh, wow, Dad," Anthony would say in his early teenage years, "there was a courthouse built here in 1798. Amazing! Man, I'm going to tell all my friends the second we get back." Jeannie would shush him, make a case to him and to Tasha about the importance of the past, cite the famous adage that those ignorant of history are condemned to repeat it. And I'd add something like, "Those who wise-mouth their father are condemned to go without lunch."

This particular turnoff had a placard with the story of two towns that no longer existed. Recen and Kokomo had been mining camps, swelling to ten thousand citizens in the late nineteenth century when the frenzy of the gold rush was at its peak. A fire destroyed Kokomo. The people rebuilt it and clung to their cold existence here, pawing at the earth in the hope of turning metal into food. It worked, too, for a while, at least for a certain lucky group. But then the veins ran dry and the treasure-seekers moved out as quickly as they'd moved in. By 1965, according to the historical board, Kokomo's nine remaining citizens voted to abandon the town, which lay buried now beneath the dammed up river on the gravel plain. I suppose it was the image of those nine souls that interested me. I would have liked to have been present at that vote, would have liked to have heard the stories, asked about their feelings as they walked away from the places they had lived. It wouldn't have been a question of selling—who would buy? Just a walking away. From a home, a place, a life. I tried to put myself in their shoes because of late the thought—only the quickest, tiniest notion—of selling the Bronxville house had been popping up in my mind like those awful Internet ads that appear when you're trying to read the news or get the weather. I pushed away the idea, but I could feel it lingering there, a sparrow chirping at the edges of my consciousness.

Rinpoche was silent for a long time, perhaps imagining those same folk. "I remember you telling me once that you see dams as a metaphor. We were driving across the Cascades, do you remember?"

"What is this madaphor?"

"It's a figure of speech. It's when you use a word to express something but it doesn't literally mean that thing. If I say, 'money worries are a weight on my back,' it doesn't mean there's a literal weight on my back. Let me think of a better example. . . . Okay, here: When Shelsa comes into a room it's like the sun coming up. Something like that. A symbol. The cross on your rosary beads has become a metaphor. People say, 'That's your cross to bear.' Your trouble to carry in life."

He pursed his lips and nodded thoughtfully, looking down across the land—all scraped and shoveled, the dirt that had been sifted for ore now thrown up into levees and the wall of a dam, with a puddle of water behind it.

"Everything is madaphor then," he said.

"Really?"

"Your body is madaphor."

"I'm not sure I explained it correctly. I—"

"Is not literal."

"It feels very literal," I said. "In fact, I don't know if it was the mussels in the bouillabaisse or the altitude, but I'm starting to feel . . . *off*. Maybe I have a flu coming on. It's very real, I can assure you."

He laughed and looked over at me—the shining face, all warmth, forgiveness, approval. "All a madaphor," he said, stern again, despite the glow.

"I don't follow."

"You know science, yes?"

"Sure. A little bit. . . . Not that much, actually."

"You know atoms?"

"I know they exist."

"Never seen them, though."

"Never."

"You trusting the science, yes?"

"Yes, I suppose. I don't think there are many people who challenge the existence of atoms these days. Global warming is highly in doubt in certain lunatic circles. Evolution can't be taught in parts of some states. But I think we all agree on atoms."

Another laugh. Not mocking. Not even critical. Simply amused at the way my mind worked. He reached down and picked up a tennis-ball-sized stone. "Solid," he said, "yes?"

"Rock solid."

"But the scientist say no. Atoms moving around inside."

"Right. I've always had trouble with that."

He put his hand on my shoulder and squeezed. "Solid, yes. This is Otto, yes?"

"Ringling," I said, "in the flesh."

"But tomorrow different cells. Scientist say so. Still Otto?"

"Same old."

"The lake," he waved his arm out toward the dam, "when it ewaporate, makes a cloud, yes? Or makes a river that goes in the ocean, yes?"

"I don't see the connection to metaphor."

"Otto, my friend," he said patiently, tossing the rock down the hill, where it bounced and rolled for hundreds of feet before coming to rest among a crowd of its cousins. "Shelsa is not the sun."

"I know that. It's an expression. A comparison."

"Worry is not a weight on your brain."

"Not literally, no. We use words approximately, to create an image, express what we can't express literally, or what we want to say more poetically: Shelsa is like sun in the room."

"Good," he said. "In the beginning was the word. What means?"

"I haven't the faintest. I'm still half-lost."

"Maybe for God, everything is making madaphor. Otto's body is a thought in God's mind, but to make the thought to be understood you have the word, you have the body, the heart, the brain. The gold in a rock is a thought in God's mind. The symbol. If you take too literal, you suffer."

"But we have to eat. In order to eat we have to work. It has to be real on some level."

"Yes, good," Rinpoche said.

I watched a gust of wind fluff and die, lifted my shoulders against the cold. "Man, you can really make me crazy sometimes."

"West America," he said, "is like Siberia. Big spaces."

"Yes."

"Mind madaphor. Let your mind go in the big spaces now."

"I'll try," I said, but the conversation was pure confusion to me, and it was one of those times when I believed that there were two possibilities: Either Rinpoche was, not a fraud, exactly, but what Anthony would have called "a spaceshot."

So far out beyond the mainstream thinking process that he lived in a world of his own, a world that was utterly impractical, that had little bearing on my own life. Either that, or his mind was, in the spiritual realm, the way Einstein's had been in the scientific. He simply saw things most of the rest of us didn't see, so we considered him, for a while at least, crazy, eccentric, impractical, an amusing entertainment or a pest, depending. Einstein envisioned black holes before they could be proven. His understanding of relativity was purely theoretical . . . until it came time to launch satellites into space, at which point it became as concrete as the stone Rinpoche had been holding.

I said, "Even if you *are* nuts, even if what you say makes no sense to me sometimes, you're still a good brother-in-law."

"Good madaphor for brother-and-waw," he said, and laughed merrily, and we left it at that and headed for Leadville.

Twenty

On the way into Leadville we passed a small collection of very modest homes—some were trailers, some not—one of which bore this welcoming sign: TRESPASSERS WILL BE SHOT. SURVIVORS WILL BE SHOT AGAIN.

We then passed a molybdenum mine that looked, with its cupola roof and windowless metal walls, like some secret government installation where captured aliens were being held and interrogated.

But I liked Leadville from the first. I liked it, in spite of the fact that either the bouillabaisse or the altitude had turned me into a nauseous, headachy, exhausted sack of miserable metaphoric cells. The highest incorporated municipality in America, at ten thousand feet, Leadville is a mix of miners and ex-miners, outdoorsy types, alternative types, employees of the pricey ski resorts an hour down the interstate, and other assorted unlabelable souls. The main street—another historical district—sports a few blocks of red brick buildings and saloons with a distinctly Old West feel. It was like Deadwood, but harder to get to, less touristy, more real.

We checked into the Delaware Hotel, yours truly feeling so sick that he swallowed his pride and allowed the young man behind the desk to carry his bag to the third-floor room. There were no elevators in the place, no room for elevators, I suppose, because the large lobby and the hall-ways of the upstairs floors were packed cheek-to-jowl with every imaginable kind of antique, all with price tags. You could have furnished two Bowdoin dormitories with the bureaus and beds, the side tables and mirrors, the elaborately carved chairs and bookshelves, chamber pots, coat racks, and spittoons. When the host showed us the room where breakfast would be served the next morning, I came upon my favorite item, a real confessional, circa 1890, that had space for the priest between a kneeling sinner to either side. An absolute treasure in polished oak. And a steal at $7,950.

I have a soft spot for creaky-floored hotels, and the Delaware certainly fit that description. Rinpoche and I were given two rooms that were linked by a bathroom so narrow you could barely sit on the toilet without pushing your knees through the plaster wall in front of you. The windows, covered with lace curtains, must have been ten feet tall. Rinpoche's side had two queen beds and a smaller sleeping couch. I had a king, and Internet access, and I sat down and wrote Natasha this e-mail:

> Hi, Hon. We're in Leadville, CO, where Rinp has a talk tonight and where your old father is suffering mightily from what he hopes is altitude sickness. I barely have the energy to go out to dinner, and that's saying something, as you know. How are you? How are Shels and Seese? Any more action with the gun-toting Chinese? Write soon. Hi to Warren.
>
> Your father who loves you.

I waited a few minutes for a response, and when none was forthcoming, told Rinpoche I had to lie down or I was going to fall down.

"Do the lying-down meditation," he suggested, and I said that I would. And, indeed, I tried to. Despite the physical malaise, or perhaps motivated by the misery of it, I lay on my back and tried to let my thoughts settle, tried to feel every one of the trillions of cells in the body I thought of as Otto Ringling, tried to send them peace, calm, relaxation, good health. It worked, more or less. I fell into a sickly sleep, at least, and when I awoke half an hour later I felt slightly less terrible and strong enough to want to venture out in search of a meal. Rinpoche was skipping dinner—not an unusual occurrence for him—and said he would like some quiet time before his "speaking." Could I come and fetch him in two hours or so?

I paced myself going down the slanted stairs and spent a few minutes wandering the lobby. Here's a partial inventory: clocks of every size and description, a giant stuffed Santa, sets of dishes with china cups, the embalmed heads of bighorn sheep, a roll-top desk, old hats, old dresses, umbrellas, jewelry of various kinds, smooth stones, figurines, cut glass, steins, vases, a pewter service, carved canes with rubber tips, cookie jars, rings, pins, knives, candelabra, teapots, and a buffalo head.

I went outside into cold—if beautifully sunlit—mountain air, where afternoon shadows stretched across the main thoroughfare and a range of massive mountains blazed pink and purple to the west. There was a clinic across the side street. I dragged myself up the steps, thinking they might offer a homeopathic remedy for suffering flatlanders, only to discover that it was a medical marijuana dispensary, not yet fully functional. On the other side of the hotel was a fossil shop, with dinosaur tracks in stone. A little farther down the block stood the Golden Burro Café, a place with Sinatra playing on the outdoor speakers and a sign in the window, COME ON IN—WHAT HAPPENS IN THE BURRO STAYS IN THE BURRO. I saw taped-up notices for psychic readings, and for a hundred-mile running race, and such was the state of my thinking that I was sorely tempted to sign up for both. Just beyond the north end of the commercial strip stood a neighborhood of Victorian houses, some of them in good repair, some not. In front of one house stood a cairn as tall as I am, with something written in white paint on every rock: DIVINE QUANTUM ENERGY. CLEAN CONSCIENCE. On a side street I passed a stretch of homes built very close together, some of them covered in decorative shingles. There were joggers and cyclers everywhere, which only made me feel more tired, hungry, and miserable. There was the

SpiritWay Reiki Wellness Center in a brick building on the corner that bore a sign saying BABY DOE TABOR LIVED HERE. I felt that I should have known who she was. There were bumper stickers—the only ones I'd seen out West—DRILL IN THE VALLEY? FRACK NO! and THIS IS OUR SACRED LAND. One that was a simple circle with Pb in the center; another reading, LEADVILLE, WE'RE HERE BECAUSE WE'RE NOT ALL THERE.

Slowly, slowly, pushing hard at the boundaries of my endurance and will, I looped back around to the main drag, past the Kum and Go variety store (where I bought a *Wall Street Journal* and where the clerk told me that the houses on the side streets had been built close together in order to "share warmth and protect each other from the wind"). I went along an old worn wooden sidewalk in front of the Silver Dollar Saloon, 1879. There were nice brick buildings, five stories, including the Tabor Opera House, which must have had some connection to Baby Doe.

How, I asked myself, could you not love Leadville?

It's entirely possible that, suffering as I was from the thin air, enduring a kind of nonalcoholic drunken exhaustion, I was not running, as we used to say, on all cylinders. I believe the physical malaise had knocked me out of the moderately sane mode in which I usually operate. I was compromised, in other words, about to exhibit poor judgment, battered by physiological forces that would have softened up the most stolid of men. In short, I am making excuses for what I did next.

There, on a side street, stood a handful of small wooden houses in a row. I saw a sign: PSYCHIC READINGS. PALM. TAROT. PAST-LIFE REGRESSIONS. CRYSTAL HEALING. Naturally enough—more excuses here—having had a beloved sister whose ramshackle New Jersey home once boasted a similar advertisement out front, I was curious. I made a small detour in order, I told myself, to examine the operation at closer range. A part of me—not the best part—wanted to see what kind of house a high-altitude past-life regressor lived in. That same part of me, crazed by weariness and tormented by wavelets of nausea, half hoped to spy a wild-haired woman sitting in a front window, to see the porch lined with voodoo dolls, its railings draped with beads, its ceiling marked with so-called sacred signs. In other words, one precinct of my brain—bitter, injured, persistent— one nasty little piece of the old me, the piece that had somehow survived years of meditation and the company of holy men, wanted some fuel for the fire of mockery.

The idea was to walk past in a nonchalant way and catch a glimpse of something or someone that would buttress my feelings of superiority to the fleecy souls that believed in things like past-life regression.

Thirteen-year-old Otto, alive and well and still trying to reduce his younger sister to some kind of flake.

Naturally then—this must be the way the universe cures us—just as I was going past, a long-haired fellow stepped out onto the porch to take in a few breaths of mountain air. He was slightly built, with dark brown hair copied from paintings of the imagined Jesus: It cascaded onto his shoulders. He was dressed in jeans, work boots, and a T-shirt, and around his neck he wore a pendant that looked, at first glance, like one of the hats worn by New York Yankees baseball players. Perhaps it was that detail that made me offer him a greeting.

"How goes it?" I said, not slowing down.

"I see the high air's got you," he replied. He had his hands on his hips, his chin was tilted up slightly, his small shoulders thrown back in a posture almost military. "You have the aura of a lowlander out of his element."

I stopped. To rest, perhaps. "I hope that's what it is. I feel like dirt."

"Not a local, I take it."

"New York."

He grasped the Yankees pendant—strange thing for a psychic to be wearing—and held it out toward me on its chain. "Not a Mets fan, I hope."

216

"Never!"

The man flashed a huge grin, a toothy, over-sized display that had enough wacko potential to start me walking again.

"Hey, come on in for a reading," he said genially. "I'll give you a quick one. Free for Yankees fans. I don't have anyone scheduled for another hour. Come on. I see something hovering around you, some grief or something. Ten minutes and I'll clear it all up for ya."

I'm the kind of man who does not like being invited into strangers' homes, even if they are friendly strangers, outgoing, and too small-built to do me any physical harm. I like boundaries, social regulations, a polite distance between bodies. Our visit with Edie and her trio of magnificent men had done nothing to change me in that respect. And yet—here I find myself out of excuses—something made me turn and walk up the path and then up the sagging wooden steps of his porch. With the distance of some months I wonder now if it might just have been that I wanted to be finished with the nasty little thirteen-year-old that still whispered to me. Finished with mockery and superiority. Finished, once and for all, with any desire to diminish my good sister (who, in any case, seemed to have given up her regressing and readings).

In my weakened state, climbing the wooden steps was the equivalent of a half marathon. If I made it, I'd be allowed to put one of those

13.1 stickers on the back of my car. Huffing and puffing, I shifted the folded newspaper to my left hand, held out my right, and said, "Otto Ringling," and I was comforted just a bit that there weren't any circus jokes, and that the man did, in fact, shake hands rather than trying for an embrace.

"Joe John Jones," he said, and I returned the favor of not commenting on the name.

Joe John ran his eyes over my face for just a moment, then pinched up the muscles to the sides of his mouth and said, "What are you, a Jeter guy? Rodriguez? Torre? Clemens?"

"Just a general fan," I said. "I grew up in North Dakota and moved to Manhattan and that was all she wrote."

He laughed and led the way inside. The house was touched with the smallest bit of mustiness, and I sensed immediately, via my own strange psychic powers, that Joe John lived alone. Just to the right of the foyer was a square room with a fold-up card table exactly in its center. On the walls hung drawings, photos, and various artifacts that seemed to include every known religious tradition from Abraham to the New Age. A framed needlepoint yin and yang symbol made a particular impression.

Joe John motioned for me to sit at the table. He sat opposite and began staring at me. I did not like this. His eyes were a peculiar cinnamon brown, as oversized as his smile had been, his face sharply boned, forehead high. Perhaps there was some

218

American Indian blood there but, whatever his ancestry, there was suddenly a bizarre intensity to him that had not been in evidence on the porch.

"I see," he said, "some large-scale pain lingering on you."

Wanting, at that point, to go along with whatever he said, offer payment, and then make a quick exit, I started to speak. Joe John held up one hand.

"No, don't say anything, please. It's too easy for the fakers to take what a client says, twist it a little, and make it seem like a true reading. Don't speak, please. And try not to react, facially. Just let me say my little piece here and I'll let you go. I see the pain, yes. Death, illness, some kind of failure or perceived failure or some kind of unworthiness that you should let go of, man. I see that you've done something big in your life, spiritually big, but you're not a churchgoer." He blinked, held his eyes closed for a moment, then opened them again and leaned one inch closer.

"Hah," he said. "I thought for a minute that it was a personal pain but now I see that it isn't. This is bigger than just you, man. This is . . ." he closed his eyes and let out a dramatic breath, "this is about something *historical*. You have a wife, or a significant other of some sort, a sister, maybe, and you and this woman are together in this life because you died together in a previous one. I'm seeing Jewish. A Jewish star. Either you have a lot of Jewish friends or you grew up in a Jewish family, or this person and you were Jewish in this past life. There was something unfinished about that death, that passing over. It was part of something larger. A war. It was part of a war. You were in a war together and you died, and then you decided to incarnate as a couple, or maybe related at least. But there's some old karma left over at the place where you died, a communal karma. That was the pain I saw. Italy, maybe, or Germany. You keep carrying it and it's going to bring some disease onto you. That's the way things work. I see a stain, a karmic smudge, on that place. You and your friend, you're supposed to do something to remove it or soften it or something." Another big breath, and then the eyes opened again and stayed on me, blinking now, not as intense. I was nodding in what I hoped was an agreeable manner. "That's all, man. That's all I'm getting today but you're . . . well, there's something cool about you, spiritually. A little more work to do but, you know, I think things are gonna be all right."

He was looking at me in a friendly way, nodding. I was glad to hear that things would be all right, but the rest of it meant nothing to me, I have to say. If my intention in coming in to Joe John's lair had been to silence the mocking voice, that hadn't been the result. He was a nice guy. There was a settled, amicable, easy way about him, I'll say that. But the message he'd given me was what a friend in Manhattan used to refer to as "consummate bullshit."

"I'm happy to pay something for it," I said. "It was interesting."

"You don't believe it for a second, do you. Was I way off, or something?"

"No, not way off. A few details were off. The general idea of it had some merit. Let me give you something for your time."

"Wouldn't hear of it, man," he said. We were walking toward the door and he clapped me on the shoulder in the friendliest of ways. It was as impossible to dislike him as it was to believe that what he'd just said had come from a genuine vision.

"It must be a tough way to make a living," I said, at the door.

He laughed in what seemed a humble way. "You'd be surprised, man. Six figures last year."

"Really?"

"I wouldn't lie. But it's not about the money for me. I live a simple life. I have all the money I need so I do a lot of freebies."

"For lowlanders walking by."

More kind laughter. "Yeah, and other people. A lot of people tell me how much I helped them. A lot."

"You're doing good in the world, then."

"Sure. And you will, also. I see it, man. I wish I could tell you something more specific, you know, but I see you clearing away some old, historical pain."

On the porch I offered, again, to pay him, simply out of politeness, but he waved the offer away and shook my hand. "Just go forward with confidence and don't worry what people think" was the last thing Joe John said to me.

"Same to you. Thanks for the reading and let's hope the Yanks can do something next year. This one's a disaster."

He laughed and said, "I see them buying talent!" The laugh dissolved into the big smile, and he stood there in the posture I'd seen earlier, filling his lungs with the thin mountain air, believing in himself and his fake magic.

I went back to the main road without looking over my shoulder at him or his sign.

I harbor the strange notion that eating cures nausea and many other nonlethal maladies and so, when, on another side street at the south end of town, I came upon a small private home that housed an authentic-looking Mexican restaurant, I did not hesitate.

By the time I sat down I had all but erased Joe John from my consciousness. I ordered. I perused the news of the day. The sopaipilla there, served without delay on a very hot plate by a kindly Mexican woman, was superb. Delicious. Just the thing for a suffering man. We made a little conversation, and when I told her I was in town accompanying Volya Rinpoche, her face blossomed into a smile. "We're so anxious to hear him!"

"Think there will be a decent crowd?"

"Are you kidding? Huge crowd. You'll see. Leadville is really a special place."

Feeling, despite the sopaipilla and the woman's friendly air, that I'd been run over by four buses, I made my way back to the Delaware, hoisted myself up the endless flights of stairs, went into the room once occupied by the notorious Doc Holliday, and somehow, through an exertion of will equal to that of the hundred-mile racers, did not permit myself to lie down on the bed. All was quiet in Rinpoche's room. My computer showed a message from Natasha:

DAD: YOU'RE NOT OLD! I HAD A DREAM LAST NIGHT THAT RINPOCHE WAS TALKING ABOUT COWS! GIVE HIM A HUG FROM ME. LOVE, TASH.

I heard a low steady sound in the other room— a sound I knew to be one of Rinpoche's chants— and I held myself back from writing a funny message to my daughter about it. *He's mooing in the next room right now! You're a psychic like your aunt!*

When I tapped on the door between our rooms and opened it, I saw that my spiritual mentor had concluded his bovine yodeling and was modeling his cowboy hat in the mirror there, rosary beads still in place. I said, "It clashes."

Rinpoche turned his eyes to me in the mirror and said, "Good town?"

"The best. Has a nice spirit. A woman I met said you'd have a big crowd."

The crowd was bigger than big. Someone had rented the main room of a downtown social club —the Fraternal Order of Retired Mining and Road Engineers or something like that. Chairs had been set up on what appeared to be a dance floor. There was a bar at one end of the room, unmanned at that hour, with bottles of whiskey filling shelves and four beer taps standing unattended like the lifted tails of very thin brass peacocks. At the other end of the room, opposite the bar, the event's organizers had set, on a slightly raised platform that looked like a stage a band would use, a comfortable chair and a table with a teacup and teapot on it. Between bar and stage stood fifteen rows of folding chairs, probably 150 in all.

I should confess here that part of me did not understand. I mean, I knew, in an abstract way, that my brother-in-law was famous. His books had been translated into sixteen languages. He was the nominal head of three meditation/retreat centers from North Dakota to the Italian Alps. There was a waiting list of people who wanted to attend his workshops on my family farm, and I'd been to several other events at which he was the featured speaker—in Youngstown, Ohio, at Notre

Dame, in a Madison, Wisconsin, yoga studio and a Spokane, Washington, storefront. And yet, there was a way in which I half expected to walk into the room and find that three bearded alternative types were the only attendees. It was a kind of conceit on my part, a kind of pride, perhaps, an unwillingness to acknowledge a successful way of life outside the free-market mainstream. If he'd been praised by the media—as an ingenious CEO, a Pulitzer–Prize winning author of literary fiction, a movie star—the overfilled room wouldn't have surprised me for one instant. But he was a spiritual man, a master, a meditation teacher, a berobed and married monk who believed in reincarnation and the ability to change one's thought stream. That was just not the kind of figure I expected our society would value.

I stood against the back wall, not far from the whiskey bottles, and ran my eyes over an eclectic assembly of Leadville citizens, aged fourteen to eighty-eight. Big-shouldered men in work shirts and jeans, young women who looked like they might be Anthony's classmates at Bowdoin, the old, the young, the fat, the thin, the ones who appeared to be in training for the hundred-mile running race and the ones who looked like they'd been smoking cigarettes and working the mines and, at fifty-five, might have, with decent medical care, another two or three years of life ahead of them. Rinpoche walked up onto the low stage without any fuss, almost as if he were alone in the room, as relaxed as if he were about to sit down to watch the first game of the American League Division Series with a beer and a plate of nachos. He arranged the robe around his backside and sat, good-postured but calm as ever, gazing around him at the expectant faces as if someone else were the star and about to perform. Another man climbed up onto the stage with him.

"Our speaker does not need any introduction," the introducer said. He was wearing sandals and white socks, had some kind of amulet around his neck and a tattoo on one muscular forearm. I pictured him practicing his golf swing at the molybdenum mine then slipping off to meditate on his lunch hour. He arranged a lavalier microphone on the lapel of Rinpoche's robe, showed him how to turn it on, and stepped away. There was polite applause. Rinpoche sipped his tea and ran his eyes over the room, then began to speak, as he often did, without preliminaries.

"I am thinking today," he said, and then he took another sip of tea before adding, "about this madaphor."

It seemed to me that the crowd stirred uneasily. I thought: *No! No, Rinpoche, bad idea! This is not a metaphor-type group. Talk about the mountains, the crisp air, the hundred-mile race, something earthy, wholesome, something having to do with the body, the environment, drug-*

enhanced cycling trophies, the fact that, all over the world, monasteries were traditionally set in places like this, beautiful, rugged, far from the maddening crowd. Metaphor is a subject for New York City or Boston, a college setting with Ph.D.s in atten-dance and a bevy of undergrads assigned to write a report. It's too intellectual, too mental.

"I am in the road trip today with my good brother-and-waw, Otto."

At this point, to my great embarrassment, he pointed to me. Half the people in the audience turned around to look. I raised one hand in a weak greeting, sinking deeper into my embarrassment as Rinpoche said, "who is going to be soon the enlightened man. I know this. Is going to help us with one wery big project not too long now."

A few people in the audience clapped and there was one faint cheer—from a person who seemed to me to have been using the bar just prior to the event. At that moment I wanted nothing more than to turn into a mosquito and fly out through a crack in a screen.

"We are in this road trip, yes? And we are today talking about this madaphor. 'What is?' I ask my smart brother-and-waw. What means this word? He explain it to me and I think now maybe I understand. Rinpoche understand it now, yes, maybe. Tell me if I know. Madaphor is when you say, like, 'When she comes into the room the sun shines.' Or maybe, 'The moon is in the sky a

227

wafer.' Or 'The wind was the whisper across the mountains.' Yes? I'm right?"

After a few seconds it became apparent that he really did want to know, and several of the less bashful members of the audience assured him that he was on the right track. On target. He'd hit the nail on the head.

Another sip of tea. The large smile. "Seem to me then that this madaphor is a small thing that means the big. Yes? She is small but the sun is big. Wafer is small but the moon is big. Whisper wery small but the wind so big." He spread his arms wide as if to encompass the wind. "Yes?"

"Yes!" someone yelled in the crowd. It was not a sedate group.

Rinpoche smiled again as if he liked the lack of sedateness.

"Why is?" A pause. No suggestions. "I don't be sure but I think maybe is because the big is too big to understand! This spirit in the girl who comes into the room, this spirit keeps a mystery in it, yes? Is something you can't maybe take and put inside one word. Same with the moon. What is this moon? What is doing up there all the time?" He giggled and moved his head backward and forward almost like a horse neighing. "The wind!" he exclaimed loudly. "What a big it is! What a mystery! 'Breath from the angels' one person say to me one time and I like that madaphor wery much!

"This conversation with my brother-and-waw, this idea on the madaphor, it makes me think about these wery big mysteries in life, makes me think how maybe every word can be madaphor. I know some languages, you see? Ortyk my first language, but I know some Russian, too, some Italian and German, maybe a little English, and a couple other ones, too. See this table? He tapped the table beside him three times. In Ortyk we say *laht*. In Russian *stoll*. In Italian *tavola*. In German *Tisch*. In English *table*. But is the same. The *thing* is the same, only the words different. Yes? The thing is a mystery and maybe too big for our minds. So we call it a *laht*, and then it's smaller. More easy for our minds. We can understand it. I can say *table* and you can say *table* and I understand you and you understand me. But I am thinking maybe there are word madaphors and thing madaphors, too. I am thinking about in the Bible they say, 'In the beginning was the Word' and 'The Word was made flesh.' A word is a thought, sometimes, yes? You close the eyes and think *table* and you have a thought about it, you see it, yes? Maybe in the beginning God have a thought, a word, and that thought is made to flesh, to a thing. So maybe what we see around us, the mountain, the tree, the person, the table, maybe all of it can be God's thoughts, the energy of God's mind, or what the Buddhists call it 'Divine Intelligence.' I think sometimes this is why we meditate, because when we meditate we can make the thoughts slow, and in between the thoughts is becomes a space, and in this space you have maybe something like the emptiness, the not-any-word. Maybe then we start, just a little bit *start,* not finish, to see the mystery without the clothes on. The naked mystery of life. We start to see the world a little bit that it is not separate one thing from the other, one person from the other, that it is maybe all the energy of the mind of the Divine Engineer, everything connected."

To this point the crowd had been silent, either rapt or confused, I couldn't tell, but at the word *engineer* there was a small burst of relieved laughter, a smattering of applause, a cheer from one rowdy corner of the room.

"When the person does something bad," Rinpoche went on, "maybe is because he and she sees the world separate. They think: This other person is different from me so I can kill this person, hurt this person, laugh on this person in a mean way. This mountain is separate from me so I can put poison in this mountain or in this river or in this dirt, yes? But if we can know that all this might be the madaphor, that if we go past all the words that make the things separate, then we can start to see the flesh, the things, all like a part of God's energy, all connected. If I look at you—he pointed to a very old woman who seemed to be teetering in her chair on the far left-hand end of the first row—and I see not *woman,* not *person,* but piece of the energy of God, the same energy that is inside me, how can I hurt you? How can I able to think bad on you? No. You see?"

The woman nodded. A murmur went through the crowd, the kind of sound one heard after the conclusion of a poem read aloud by its author at a literary gathering. Some people, at least, had understood. I was one of them, more or less. I grasped the general idea of what he was saying, but felt I'd need to sit down and ponder it for a few months in order to see things as he saw them. It was like reading a dense stanza of verse, like seeing a film with multiple layers of meaning, like looking at a painting that showed you something new with every visit to the museum.

Rinpoche sipped his tea in a satisfied way and ran his eyes over us, as if trying to see if we were with him. "Now," he said, "now with the words you can ask me question or say anything." He laughed, hard.

There was a stretch of awkward silence, more tea sipping, a cough, a scraping of chair legs, and then, at last, a hand raised from a man in one of the middle rows. "First, Rinpoche, thank you for coming to Leadville. It's a special night for us, a special thing to have you here."

"You welcome. For me special, too."

"What I don't understand, I guess, is that, if we go around seeing the world as just God's energy,

231

seeing everything as the same, or at least fundamentally connected, then why would we do
anything? You seem to be saying that we're living
in some kind of grand illusion, that words are
unnecessary or at least deceiving. But how are we
supposed to function without them? Without
making distinctions between this and that, me and
another person. This town was built, as you may
know, partly on the discovery of silver in the
stone and soil here. Silver is silver. It's not quartz.
It's not shale. There's a difference. I'm sorry, I'm
a bit confused and maybe not expressing myself
well, but do you know what I mean?"

The man sat down. Rinpoche smiled. "Wery
good question!" he said. "Buddha talked about
absolute and relative, you know that? You are now
talking relative and Rinpoche was talking
absolute. And you are wery right! If you want to
live on this plane of life you have to know the
relative, you have to know what is silver and
what is mud, you have to say, 'I am Rinpoche,'
and you are—what is your name?"

"Morris."

"And you are the Morris! Rinpoche and the
Morris not same!"

"Not even close," Morris said, and people laughed
politely.

"Mud and silver not the same, too. Wery
impossible to go to the bank with mud in your
hand and get the money for it, yes? But, inside the

mud and the silver what is there? The atoms, yes? Same in Rinpoche and Morris. Scientists know this. But Buddha know, also. Jesus know. The great teachers they all know. The silver is a madaphor. Okay, you take the silver to the bank and get money, no problem, man! But the money stand for something else, for your work maybe. Your mining or your talking or your driving in the truck. A madaphor. That work is your energy, that energy come from someplace else, from the divine mystery. Yes, sure, Morris works and gets money and takes the money and gets food and puts the food in his mouth and he lives. If you don't work or you don't have money you don't live, yes, sure. This is the relative part of life. Not bad, this part. Important, sure. But we think all the time about this part—the part you can see, you can put a word on, you can measure. We look at the other person," he gestured to the old woman again, "and we can say, with the relative part, that she is a little bit old, maybe, yes? That she is woman. That she has a skin this color, that she did this kind of work or maybe has the children, or her age has a number. All this is okay. But maybe we don't pay enough time to the absolute part, the mystery part. She is a miracle, this woman, a piece of Divine! Sometimes we close down the mind with the words.

"Listen," he said, more animated now, gaining momentum. "Last few days we drive in the places in the country where they have the cows. How you say? Ranches, yes? The ranches. We see these cows. They are in the wery big field, the big land, lot of space there, yes? And then sometimes we see, how you say it, the little cows that live in the little white boxes with one open part for a door?"

"Veal," someone in the crowd shouted. "Veal calves."

"Weal, yes. Rinpoche doesn't eat weal because these cows they stay all day in this box, never go out, yes? Makes the muscles wery soft, the meat wery, how you say. . . ."

"Tender," the same person called out.

"This is like our mind sometimes. We live in this little box. The relative world. We have all these words around us like a wall. Okay, maybe not so bad. Maybe warm in there, safe. No one hurt us, we think. But when you meditate, when you go past the words, when you see that everything in words is madaphor for something bigger, then you have the whole big space to go around. Then you can be ranching, man!"

"You can *graze*," someone in the crowd corrected him.

"Sure, but you see? You have to have the relative world to live, to work, to make the silver, to buy the food. Have to have it. But if you have only that part, then maybe your body lives, maybe you make it eighty year, ninety, one hundred year! But then what happens? So maybe, when you are here working and eating and riding the bicycle and making sex and hearing music, maybe remember some times the absolute part. Maybe think: This music or this making love with my wife, this is madaphor, stands for something big, stands for the energy in God's mind, maybe. Because when you die, if you know this other part, this absolute, this energy, then it is not so scary, dying. Maybe you understand the bigger you then, and when the little you dies it will be not so hard, okay?"

There was a longer silence. I looked around the audience and saw that some people were nodding, some had struck pensive poses, a few were shaking their heads as if they were disappointed, confused, or simply unimpressed. After a moment, one of these people—a middle-aged woman with a bun of gray-blond hair tied up at the back of her head—stood up and said, "This seems like hocus-pocus to me. Flimflam. The world, sir, is very real. There is a very real difference between good and bad, between the holy ones and the sinners. They go to very different places after their very real death. There's nothing metaphorical at all about heaven and hell."

Rinpoche looked at the woman with his eyebrows slightly raised, as if he found her remarks—or the intensity with which they were delivered—interesting, amusing, mildly surprising. When she sat down he said, "You think when the bad person dies he burns? His body burns up all the time forever."

"Absolutely!" the woman called from her seat.

Rinpoche nodded. "How old is the person's body? The same age they are when they die? Always like that?"

"It's their soul that's burning," the woman called out.

"What looks like?"

"That's one of the good Lord's mysteries. But the person feels the pain of the fire as if they have a body."

"Why they burning like that?" Rinpoche asked her.

"Because they sinned, that's why."

"What is this sin? What did they do?"

"They killed, they raped, they stole, they committed adultery, they cheated. Surely you know what sins are as well as I do."

"Maybe in my mind a little bit different," Rinpoche said. He was looking at the woman— sympathetically I would say—as if she were the only person in the room. "If you kill, you rape, you steal, you commit the other sins, I think you make the pain in the energy of this other person."

"You hurt them," the woman corrected.

"I think," Rinpoche went on, "inside the big power that God has, the power to make the moon, the wind, the breath going in and out of you, people have a small power. You can make the

236

choose to hurt the other person or not to hurt, to hurt the mountain or not, to put poison in the river or not to, yes?"

"Free will," the woman nearly shouted.

"Good! Rinpoche thinks like the same as you. When you choice to hurt a person, the animal, the river, I think afterward the energy inside your own mind is not calm then. You feel a suffering from it."

"I disagree," the woman said. "There are plenty of people who do awful things in the world who don't seem bothered by it one iota."

"Yes," Rinpoche said, "but I think, what my people believe, is that those people stay, many lifetimes, stuck in that little box like the weal. Mind is wery fast there, wery mixed up, scary, wery much words, and when those words are made flesh again—in a person, an animal, in those atoms, the person has a lot of suffering. You," he pointed at the woman, "think they are in a fire, burning. I think the fire could be the madaphor for this suffering, this box of bad thinking. We believe almost the same, you see? If you hurt a person then you will have the suffering, only you think it's the fire and I think it's maybe something else. You think it goes for all time, and I think only lots of time. After lots of time maybe one million lifetimes, this person who hurt the other people so much or hurt this world, he starts to have a little space in the suffering. In that space, maybe he see God's energy, that the Big Engineer has love there for him, too. And in that life he starts to makes a change."

"Like the Christian purgatory," someone called out.

"Could be," Rinpoche said. "We find out, yes?" and he laughed.

A young woman only a few feet in front of me stood up. Trim and calm, she looked as if she'd been doing yoga for the past 128 days. "Rinpoche," she said in a reverent tone, "on a slightly different subject, could you talk a little bit about the self-immolations in Tibet? Just this week there was a report of another young man burning himself to death. Is it right to do something like that? Even for a good cause? Isn't he taking life by taking his own life, and isn't that against the Buddha's teachings?"

"Wery sad, this," Rinpoche answered her. "Long, long time ago my people come from Tibet to Siberia, to Skovorodino. These are wery gentle people, wery kind, hurt nobody. Dalai Lama hurt nobody, yes? But now some people, in China maybe, want that there is no Dalai Lama, no Tibet. Those people they live in the relative world a hundred percentage. They don't think about living afterward. They don't have any even a little space in the thoughts. They want the walls to be solid, they never want to go outside, they think that's the safest way, to be the weal is safe! These

238

people wery, wery afraid so they want to make other people afraid, too. And the man maybe burn himself to show you can't make me afraid, to show this life is not the only one. But, I think, maybe, we can find in the future a better way to do it."

"What's going to happen when the Dalai Lama dies?" the woman asked.

"I hope, maybe, in one hundred more year he dies. But then other spirits be there, like the Dalai Lama. Somebody else coming. Maybe one person next time, maybe two. Maybe man, maybe woman, maybe the man and the woman. Maybe in Tibet, maybe in India, maybe Leadwill. We have to see."

While he was saying this I felt a sudden gust of cold wind swirling around me, brushing across the bare skin of my neck and hands. This is not a typical reaction for me, not something I'm making up or exaggerating. I felt the cold air and actually turned to see if someone had opened a window behind me. No open window. I shook my head, hard, once. I couldn't keep myself from thinking about Alton, couldn't stop my eyes from roaming the room to see if any Chinese spies had been planted there, any assassins, any gun-toting Coloradans with a fiery hatred for the ideas of the open range. At that precise moment, in the midst of my own miniature hurricane of fear, my phone, which I'd silenced but forgotten to turn off, vibrated in my pocket. I sneaked a look at it, saw my daughter's name on the caller ID, and after a moment of temptation, decided to wait and call her back when the event finished.

"In the meantime what should we do?" the woman asked.

Rinpoche pondered his answer for longer than I would have expected. I supposed then he was going to say that we should meditate, do good works, give to the poor. "The most important thing," he said, after a long moment, "is to try, in your own life, to see things—people, mountains, rivers, birds, the deers, the stars—as madaphor. Something that stand for something else, bigger. You should still work, yes. Still eat, still run the races, still pick up the dirty paper when you see it on the ground, still buy medicine for the person you know who is sick, still wash your face and brushing your teeth, but same time, try if you can to not stay in the small box of old thinking. Try to see, in any day, when you are in that box. Maybe you see your father as a bad man. Bad, bad, bad, bad. Okay. But maybe try one time to see beyond the bad, beyond the old, beyond the sick, beyond the man or the woman or the black or the white. Try. Let the words go away a little bit. Rest in the empty place a little bit if you can. See what feels like. Thank you."

There was enthusiastic applause. The introducer announced that Rinpoche would be kind enough to stay around for a while and sign books, and I slipped out into the air—very cool at that hour—and hit my speed dial.

"Dad?" Natasha said, "Everything okay? You usually answer right away when I call."

"Fine, honey. We're in Leadville. Colorado. Rinpoche's signing books. You called in the middle of his talk."

"Good one?"

"Pretty good. I think he can be a little abstract for some people. For me, at times. He was talking about metaphor tonight, about seeing everything as a symbol of something else."

"I feel that."

"You do?"

"Uh-huh. Lately, especially. It's like I'm surprised to be alive in a body or something. Like I don't take it so much for granted. All kinds of weird things have been happening lately."

"Trouble?"

I heard her delicate laugh. "My worrisome Dad," she said lovingly. I watched a drunk staggering along the sidewalk, stooped over, then lurching sideways, limbs half obeying him. "No trouble, just . . . dreams that make no sense, new things happening in meditation. Rinpoche's advice is just to ignore it all and keep going."

"Care to provide any specifics?"

Another laugh. "Well, you know when you have a déjà vu? Well, I've been having those all the time the last week or so. And I've been thinking

241

of Mom a lot. . . . All the time, a lot more even than I usually do. And Shelsa's been going into these, I guess you could call them 'trances' or 'spells.' She came into my room the other day and bowed down to the picture of you and Mom I keep on the night table. I thought it was a joke at first but it wasn't."

"Is Seese worried?"

"She was a little at first. She called Rinpoche and he explained what they are."

"Which is?"

"He called them 'rest periods.' Before she's going to do something. Do you remember you and Mom used to talk about how much I ate when I was twelve and about to sprout?"

"You ate like the front line of the New York Giants. Night after night. And then, boom, in about a month you were four inches taller."

"Like that, I guess, though she's too young to start sprouting. . . . You have a birthday coming up, Dad."

"I do."

"I always hate to be away from you on your birthday."

"I don't know where we'll be at that point. I'll call, though."

"We have an idea for a surprise gift."

"When I re-enter the Dakota territories, okay?"

"Sure, fine. Anyway, I was just checking in. Aunt Seese and Shels and Warren send their love. Anthony called and we talked for a while. He misses you but he's not much of a phone guy. He says the workouts are going okay. Take care. Love you."

"And you take care. Love to all of you. Bye."

I put the phone in my pocket and looked up at the stars blinking above the mountains. The thought that came to me, not without a trace of bitterness I must say, was this. *My daughter is not a metaphor!* I knew Rinpoche would agree. "No, no, Otto, wery real!" he'd say, or something to that effect, but I'd wonder if he truly meant it, wonder if the belief that this life was meta-phorical, symbolic, illusory, if that belief sucked away some of the intensity we feel for a loved one. In his case, it didn't seem to. With Seese, with Natasha, especially with Shelsa, even with me, it wasn't hard to feel the force of his love. And yet, somehow, that love was missing the element of worry, of fear for our safety. There was no angst in it. Which made it, I supposed, purer. And yet, I knew that, in the old days whenever I set off on a business trip, part of what made the good-bye between Jeannie and me touch me so deeply was her "Be safe, sweet one." There was a concern in it, a caring, perhaps a measure of worry. Without that, wouldn't I have felt less important to her, less beloved?

Turning and turning in the widening gyre, my thoughts could populate an empire. By then I could hear a gentle commotion at the door of the Engineers' Club, people stepping out onto the sidewalk, alone, in pairs, in small groups, and I could feel the weight of a few curious glances. I did what I could to make myself invisible. *So he gets to travel with the Rinpoche,* I imagined them thinking. *So he knows he's going to be enlightened soon. So he's going to help with some grand project.*

If you only knew, I wanted to signal back, in some kind of mental Morse code. *If only you were inside my mind and saw what goes on there!*

I waited, peered in through the door, waited a while longer, listening to scraps of conversation that ranged from "should sign up for one of his retreats" to "not crazy about this metaphor bullshit."

When Rinpoche had signed his last book, bestowed his final blessing, hugged and been hugged twenty-five times, when he'd thanked the introducer and the organizers and the people putting away the chairs, he popped out into the cool mountain night and joined me and we started back toward the hotel. Rinpoche never asked me, afterward, what I thought of his talks. He never seemed to wonder if the audience had received his wisdom wholly, partially, or not at all. Unlike the authors I'd dealt with in my editorial days, he wasn't cranked up on an egotistical high or exhausted by the need to appear kind to so many strangers. We might have just been shooting a game of pool for all the difference I noted in him.

"Tomorrow," I told him, "we're heading south. I've been doing some research. I have a treat in store for you, some real Americana."

"Good, good," he said, but he spoke in a way that seemed uncharacteristically distracted.

As we turned the corner toward the Delaware, yours truly still dragging his body along as if it were afflicted with three different strains of flu at the same time, I asked him if anything was wrong, if something at the speaking had upset him.

"One question," he said.

"Anything. Spiritual advice. Translation services. Your nearly enlightened brother-in-law stands ready to help with all kinds of answers."

Just before we crossed the threshold into the hotel lobby he stopped and faced me, put a hand on my right shoulder. Touched by the light from inside the building, the expression on his face was all puzzlement, the purest confusion. I thought he was going to break with tradition and ask me why there hadn't been more questions, or if the metaphor metaphors had made sense, but then I detected the spark of amusement there. "What," he said, "means this thing, *ocus-pocus?* I like this word wery much. What means?"

"Magic," I said. "Fakery. Trickery. And it's hocus, not ocus. Hocus-pocus."

"Ah," he said, satisfied, at peace with himself,

with others' opinions of him, at peace with this illusory, magical world. We went up to our third-floor room, the room where a notorious Wild West gunslinger had once slept. We said good-night and took turns washing in the cramped bathroom, and I lay down in the huge bed and listened to the old boards creak, Rinpoche murmuring prayers in the other room, trucks passing on the street below. I felt the texture of the sheets against my skin, the weight of the blanket, and it did all seem a kind of code, a *madaphor,* small signals standing in for something larger and more mysterious. Even in the midst of my physical malaise, I felt, as Tasha said she did, a small amount of surprise simply at the fact that I was there, alive, embodied in this world.

Twenty-one

Something—voices in the hallway, perhaps—awakened me very early the next morning. The altitude sickness was gone. I felt 51 again, not 108. I washed and dressed quietly and went down the creaking stairs and out into the mountain air. It was cool at that hour. Even in August, you could imagine the winters, with their thirty-below-zero mornings and fifty-mile-an-hour winds. You could guess what it must have been like to come to Leadville a century and a half earlier in search of a quick fortune and find yourself living in a wooden shack in January, surrounded by other fortune seekers, coffee and beans on the cookstove, a wife and kids looking at you and wondering what they were going to eat for the day's other meals and how they were going to spend the hours and why you'd dragged them to this godforsaken place. Walking an oblong route through the city's back streets, shirt buttoned on top and hands in pockets, I wondered if it was true that we were led through life by our desires. Those desires sprouted into dreams in our mind's eye—whom to marry, where to live, what to do for money—and we followed those dreams as best we could, through a kind of maze of years. Along the way we had stretches of pleasure, and hours, weeks, or years of pain; we knew the exhilaration of first love and the torment of losing friends. We went on through the maze, following some mysterious scent, and we discovered, somewhere in the middle of life, that we were in a place we never expected to be. The edges of the old dreams had gone blurry. New, smaller ones had sprouted, like branches off the main trunk. Or maybe we'd abandoned our dreams altogether and simply put one foot in front of the next, showed up for work in the morning, washed the dishes, fed the dog, settled down in front of the TV to gaze at the lives of others, imaginary and real, as we plodded along toward old age.

On one of the side streets that sloped gently down into the valley, musing, musing, glad to be alive, I passed a series of houses built so close together that, until you were straight in front of them, they seemed attached. Their sharing of the warmth and protecting each other from the wind looked to me the perfect metaphor for marriage, for family. Human life, that decades-long trip through the maze, was a difficult enterprise. Difficult, trying, sometimes terrifying. By some embedded instinct we understood that a close companion softened the terror, lightened the load, took the bite out of the coldest winds. I remembered Rinpoche telling me that he'd made two three-year retreats, mostly silent, mostly solitary, eating only enough to stay alive and spending the days in prayer, meditation, some physical work, occasionally having a bit of instruction from an older master. What interior force that must have required! What courage, to face that emptiness alone, without the ordinary sense comforts for armor, without a partner.

I missed my wife. I missed my children. I missed my old dog.

Back up on the main drag I found a coffee shop called City on a Hill—sunlit, filled with early risers, smelling of the magnificent bean—and I sat on a stool facing out the front window and indulged. A large latte, two superb buttermilk biscuits, a cup of ice water. Again, I tried to eat as Rinpoche had instructed me, without checking my phone or reading a newspaper, really tasting the coffee and biscuit on my tongue, and for a while I managed it. Pickup trucks and bicyclists passed in the street; a line formed at the ordering counter—fit, young, lively mountain types, happy in their bodies. After a time, a fellow in a gold-trimmed maroon robe walked up to the window, beamed his thousand-watt smile at me, and came inside.

"You found me," I said.

"Last night," he said, taking the stool beside me, "I see this place and I think: This is the place for Otto in the morning."

"Outstanding coffee. Breathtaking biscuits. Here, have this one."

He broke off a corner of the biscuit with thumb and forefinger and chewed thoughtfully.

"I'll get you some tea and another biscuit to share."

The young man at the cash register—another specimen who looked like he could ride his bike to Vail and run up the ski slopes then jump into a hang glider's harness and float back across the valley to his job—said, "You're with Rinpoche, aren't you?"

"Yes. This is breakfast for him. Green tea and a biscuit. Your coffee's great, by the way, nice and rich."

"No charge for this, man. It's an honor to have him in our shop."

"You sure?"

"Sure, man. I was at the talk last night. Must be nice to know where you're headed."

"We're headed south today," I said, "to a place my sister found, kind of a—" I stopped at that point, belatedly realizing that he was remarking not on the direction of our travels but on my upcoming enlightenment. How, I wondered, was a soon-to-be-enlightened, middle-aged human being supposed to act? The young man was watching me, for clues, it seemed. I was glad I hadn't ordered one of the sticky buns, or come in carrying my copy of the *Wall Street Journal*. I felt disinclined to tell him that the Rinpoche was wrong, or joking, trying to flatter or encourage me. I formed my features into an expression that suited a spiritual man.

"Cool to travel with him, I bet."

"Unimaginably cool," I said. "But, at moments, challenging."

"What good would it be if it wasn't?" he asked, and I mumbled something vaguely agreeable, upbeat, wise, slipped two dollars into the tip jar, and carried the food and drink back to my companion. A young mother with her little son in tow was just leaving his side. She appeared to have gotten an autograph.

Rinpoche accepted the tea with both hands and

took a sip. Grateful. Appreciative. Taking nothing for granted. "You meditate this morning?" he asked me.

"I mused. I went for a walk and thought about family life, loneliness, the point of things."

"A kind of meditation," he said. "Later we do the other kind, you and me."

"Three hours?"

He laughed, broke the biscuit in half, raised his eyes to mine. "You life changes now, my friend. Big."

My instinct was to make a joke, to ask him if I was going to hit the lottery, or buy a new car, if Angelina was going to leave Brad and beg me to move in with her . . . something like that. But the expression on his face stopped me. His eyes were steady, pinning me in place. Ringing in my inner ear was the remark of the man at the register, "What good would it be if it wasn't?"

"Any hints?" I managed.

"You have the birthday soon, yes?"

"Tomorrow."

"In Skovorodino we think that day wery special. The day you decided to come into this life, wery special, man! We always go to swim in the river."

"What if you were born in January?"

"Then through the ice," he said, wrapping his arms across his chest like a freezing man. "So cold! Then we do a special meditation. Then we wait for some news to come to us on that day.

Special news. A dream, maybe. A wisit from somebody. The surprise."

"In America we eat cake."

"You can have cake, too. No problem, man! Cake, candy, the swim, the big surprise!"

"I'll use today to prepare myself," I said, somewhat carelessly.

Rinpoche answered in a serious tone that absolutely unnerved me, "I help you."

Twenty-two

From a book I once edited I knew that the Arkansas River has its headwaters not far from Leadville, and from there tumbles and wanders almost fifteen hundred miles to its meeting with the Mississippi in the state of that same name. The Arkansas runs from cold to warm, fed at first by the snowmelt in the highest Coloradan peaks and spilling, eventually, after merging with its big sister, into the Gulf of Mexico just east of New Orleans. Along the way there is said to be marvelous trout fishing and excellent white-water rafting, and ongoing legal issues, too, between Kansas and Colorado about how much water can be taken from it. I knew that the river had been at the heart of the gold rush in these parts. The Arkansas's treasure was placer gold, which is gold that has broken off an exposed rock and been washed downstream (as opposed to gold that's mined in veins), and I supposed I was still under the influence of Rinpoche's Leadville talk because that seemed a clear spiritual metaphor to me. Placer gold is easy to harvest. You take a pie pan, or something called a classifier screen, and claim a spot along the bank, sifting the river bottom silt, where the gold—a particularly heavy metal— has settled. The miners who rushed into these parts upon its original discovery reaped a rich harvest at first and then found they had to do more and more work for a smaller and smaller return, a situation that caused almost all of them to leave.

Wasn't that something like my own spiritual predicament? At first, under Rinpoche's tutelage, I seemed to have made great progress in my meditations. The rush of thoughts I'd been vaguely aware of began to slow down; I encountered a type of interior calm I hadn't ever imagined. And then, after this rich first harvest, all my "abilities" seemed to go away. I blamed external circum-stances, and I think I had a right to do that. Jeannie fell ill and died, I lost my job. The meditations became noisy sit sessions from which I stood up into a confusing and dispiriting world, so much so that I gave thought to abandoning them altogether.

For some reason, though, I didn't. Now, it seemed to me, if I was going to reap any more treasure I'd have to work harder for it, burrow down through my self-pity and sadness, the emptiness of my days, and find a vein there that I could drill in darkness, steadily, sweating, grunting, eventually coming up into the light with my mother lode.

Or maybe the history of that territory offered a different lesson. Because what ultimately chased away the prospectors was the fact that, once the easy money had been made, they found themselves searching for smaller specks and flakes in the Arkansas's heavy mud. Too much work for most of them. But then it was discovered that the mud contained silver ore, not as valuable but much more abundant. At that point Leadville's real boom began, larger mining settlements sprung up, the harvesting went on, not for a few years, but for decades. So maybe the lesson for me was not to seek exotic spiritual riches and experiences but to settle for the not-so-flashy benefits of the meditative life: less worry, more peace, less about me, more about someone else.

As we headed out of Leadville I didn't ask Rinpoche about any of this. I remembered the book *Food along the Arkansas*, and the author, one Peter Ray Greer. He'd started out with brown trout and the various ways of catching and cooking it and followed the river's course, and the different cuisines he found, until he ended up at one of the South's great barbecue joints, in Arkansas Delta country. Though it had somewhat of a spiritual feel, there was nothing about meditation in the book. In fact, in the hundred or so books I'd edited or been connected to in my professional life, I couldn't remember a single mention of meditation. Not so surprising, maybe; I was, after all, an editor of food books. But many of those books touched on American culture, and our culture was, in its religious manifestations, wholly exterior, a society of vocal prayer and services, of sermons and rites, the cross, the good deed, the Book, the bar and bat mitzvah. All good, it was, in many lives, but it seemed to me on that drive that the true golden weight of the spiritual life had settled to the bottom of the American consciousness. It tumbled along there, largely undiscovered, waiting for someone with a classifier screen to come along and sift it clear.

For me, that someone had been Volya Rinpoche. I saw that now. I understood it. Was grateful for it. On that morning there seemed little chance that I'd let myself abandon the claim again.

At first, as we followed the Arkansas south, a low, fat range of puckered dry hills rose to our left, but the scenery changed by the minute. With each turn in the winding road there was something new to look at. Now the hills resembled rows of bad teeth. Now there were round humps with what looked like dry open scars cut into them, surgical cuts that would never heal. Now, sharp rock outcroppings. This was, a sign informed us, the

COLLEGIATE SCENIC BYWAY, and the peaks just to our west—some over fourteen thousand feet—were named Yale, Harvard, and Princeton, an Ivy League of metamorphic stone. Just east of the road and slightly below it the river cut and tumbled, only about thirty feet wide, its rocky banks resembling gobs of beach sand piled one on top of the other. There were kayak and rafting businesses, signs for fishing guides, a POINT OF INTEREST billboard that talked about this being a stage route, then a mail route, then a route plied by a narrow-gauge railroad. Now we were leaving the San Isabel National Forest (I didn't know we'd entered it), and approaching Chaffee City, in the shadow of 14,420-foot Mount Harvard. Wide vistas here, with rocky hills, a flat open plain for a while, and then the mountains closer in.

Yours truly was, of course, hungry. It seemed to me that the elimination of sugar from my diet was having three consequences: I was losing weight; I was tasting food more vividly; and I wanted to eat almost constantly. "Mind if we stop for a bite?" I asked my companion, worried that, as he some-times did, Rinpoche would suggest I skip a meal or two, fast, make myself more aware of the constant interior clamoring. But this time I was in luck.

"Sure, man," he said. He'd taken the rosary beads from his hat and was fingering them. "Can you show me the prayers?"

"Love to, but those are Catholic beads and I'm a Protestant boy."

"Catholic is the pope, yes?"

Rinpoche, I was quite sure, along with the other seven billion people on earth, knew the answer to that question. I nodded, glanced at him, watching for a trick.

"The Catholic wery much like the Buddhist."

"A lot of people would disagree. Catholics have commandments, Buddhists have suggestions. Catholics have sins, Buddhists have hindrances."

"Pope is just like Dalai Lama," he said, ignoring me.

"The Dalai Lama laughs more."

"Catholic has the hell, Buddhist has the hell realm. Catholic has the beads. Buddhist has the beads, too. Buddha didn't eat sometimes, Jesus sometimes, too."

"I think the Catholics have more rules," I said, trying to nudge the conversation away from not eating.

"Catholic has Mary, Buddhist has many, many Rinpoches that are women. Famous ones. Wery, wery important in my lineage."

"Catholic women can't be priests, though."

"That's gonna change," he said confidently.

"When?"

"Sometime now pretty soon."

I pondered that. Catholics had a new pope, Francis by name, who was in the news every week that summer, hinting at changes in the Church, talking about the poor. Though it might seem an improper comparison, I wondered if he was a Gorbachevian figure—someone who'd risen up through an old and calcified system, then reached the top and turned the whole thing upside down. He seemed a decent, kind man. I wished him well.

We rolled into Buena Vista, a pleasant town, geared toward fishing and rafting, it seemed, judging by the types of stores and signs we saw. We stopped at a place called Punky's, unimposing enough, with framed photos of high school athletes on the walls. At Punky's the food was served on paper plates, something I've never liked, but the barbecued brisket there had to rate among the very best I've ever eaten. Rinpoche sipped from a cup of water and watched me slice and chew. Two local policemen came and sat in the booth behind ours and Rinpoche took the opportunity to turn around and ask if either of them understood "the Catholic prayers on the beads and how to do it."

The female officer did know. Rinpoche got up and stood beside her and she went through the beads with him. "These are for Hail Mary's," I heard her say. "These ones here are for contemplation of the sacred mysteries."

The officers wolfed their pulled pork and went out to their cruiser. Rinpoche returned to the table absolutely aglow. "The sacred mysteries!" he exclaimed. Two elderly men at a table on the other side of the room looked over at him and frowned. Another weirdo tourist in BV. Then, more quietly, Rinpoche said, "The sacred mysteries, Otto! All these things that happen, nobody understands!"

"And many don't believe."

He was nodding as if I hadn't spoken. I could see the material forming for a new talk. I savored the brisket, a forkful of beans, some coleslaw. This was the way to eat. I offered it to Rinpoche, but he shook his head.

"The sacred mysteries," he said again, under his breath this time.

I finished my meal, looked at him. "Why do they make you so happy?"

"Because one day I want that there's no more fights about religion."

"A tall order."

"Buddha, Jesus, Muhammad, Moses, Mary— all sacred mysteries, man! All picccs of God. If they were here all now together they wouldn't fight. I want that people see it."

Good luck with that one, pal, I thought. I let Rinpoche have his dreams and I cleared the table and we went out into the sun.

South of Buena Vista the road was, depending on your definition, bereft of sacred mysteries; it was all gas stations, pawnshops, storage units, places to fish. We saw an old man with a beard and a backpack hitching in the other direction.

We watched heavy purple clouds roll in over Poncha Springs, and then we were climbing through stands of what appeared to be white birch or aspen. Up and up we went, over a pass. Suddenly the blue mountains were all to the east of us, with a flat sunlit plain ahead, and a smattering of rain on the windshield. We passed a sign for a town named Bonanza and then, sooner than I'd expected, one for the Joyful Journey Hot Springs Spa—the place my sister had suggested we stay if we found ourselves in southern Colorado.

Joyful Journey. The name seemed to fit Seese's kindly worldview perfectly. And, at first, I worried that the place itself would better fit her notion of comfort than my own. It was set well back from the road, at the edge of a dusty plain with the Sangre de Cristo Mountains running north to south about ten miles in the eastern distance. At first glance there appeared to be a couple of teepees and yurts set off to one side. There was a blue strip of a building with rooms that opened onto a small lawn, a green oasis amid the dust. In one of the smaller buildings we were greeted by an attractive young woman, a few years older than my Natasha, who seemed to me—I was reading auras now—to be in the midst of overcoming some great difficulty in her life. There were all kinds of essences and beads for sale in the office, wholesome snack foods, and as I was writing down the license plate and handing over my credit card, and so on, the young woman filled us in on the healing pools, three of them, ranging in temperature from 98 to 110 degrees. Rinpoche and I walked over to our lodging, the air filled with the scent of lavender. From the outside it resembled a motel. There were thick pine posts holding up a metal roof, but inside an unexpectedly nice room, huge beds with big headboards made of pine logs and saplings. Tile floor. Even—the essence of thoughtfulness—a small black towel in the bathroom with a sign saying it should be used to remove makeup.

Rinpoche and I wasted no time changing into our suits and strolling back over to the healing pools. They were small, surrounded by fencing, and covered by fiberglass roofs, but, one after the next, they did seem to have some healing powers. Relaxing powers, at least. In the hottest of the three I told Rinpoche that I'd done a little research on the area. "Those are the Sangre de Cristo Mountains, 'Blood of Christ' it means in Spanish. An hour or so south of here there's supposed to be one of the most amazing of the American National Parks. That's my surprise for you."

"What is?"

"The Great Sand Dunes National Park. Enormous dunes—piles of sand—and nothing else, miles of them. Tonight's the full moon. I thought we could drive down there and hike up the dunes and wait for the moon to rise over the Sangre de Cristos. What do you say?"

"Show me America, man!" he said, so loudly that a woman in the next pool over, enjoying a contemplative moment, shot us a nasty look.

I'm showing him America, I wanted to tell her. You and I are used to it. We take it for granted. The millions of square miles of some of the most fertile farmland on earth, the spectacular coastlines with their golden beaches, the mountain ranges—newer and sharper out west and older and rounder in the east; the parched desert of places like this, the rainforest outside Seattle. The rivers, the bays, the islands and harbors, the great cities—I want to show him all of it. I want to see it through his eyes. I want to scrape the jadedness from my soul and experience it the way Walt Whitman seemed to, as if seeing it all for the first time.

Instead, I waved to her in a gesture of apology and told Rinpoche we needed to leave the spa now, so we could make it to the dunes in time.

"Five more minutes, man," he said. "You go take the shower. Rinpoche likes this hot water wery much. Makes my face push out the sweat. Take the shower cold, cold afterward."

"People will think we're Finnish," I said, and he gave me a puzzled look, and said, "Not yet," and I headed back to the room to get ready.

Twenty-three

The road south from Joyful Journey was a two-lane tar strip lacking either shoulders or a breakdown lane. One second of inattention and you'd find yourself either crashing head-on into a tractor trailer heading north, or plunging over a six-foot levee into the high desert. The sun was setting, the sky turning various shades of pastel pink, orange, and blue, and Rinpoche was asleep. He did that sometimes, drifted off in improbable moments. No doubt the extra few minutes in the hottest of the pools had sapped him of his legendary energy, but I knew it would return. A brief nap like this and he'd be sprinting up the dunes with the zest of a teenager.

He slept solidly as we made a ninety-degree left at a place called Mosca then raced along another two-lane road, this one, if such a thing can be possible, even straighter than the road south from Joyful Journey. No one seemed to live on this land. Once you turned off the main highway, you covered a landscape of empty grazing fields, dusty stretches spotted here and there with small cactus and tumbleweed. We were losing light fast, and I worried we'd arrive too late for the moonrise. Would there be police on a road like this? Would it be possible to push the SUV up past seventy and not get stopped? That question was answered immediately by a pickup passing me as if Rinpoche and I were in a train traveling the other way.

Another ninety-degree left, a less-straight road, an empty booth at the entrance to the Great Sand Dunes National Park and Preserve, and then, in darkness, the parking lot. Rinpoche awoke. "Let's hustle," I said, "we want to get up onto the dunes before the moon comes up."

"When she coming?"

"Soon. Let's go."

There was a stretch of flattish land between the parking lot and the actual dunes. Fifteen minutes of fast hiking before we started to climb. There before us, stretching thousands of feet into the purple sky and for what seemed miles to either side, was an agglomeration of sand the Sahara might have envied, hips and breasts and buttocks of sand, as if we were walking among a tangle of giants, all sleeping in the nude.

"This place!" Rinpoche exclaimed.

"Unbelievable, isn't it?"

We climbed the rounded spine of one dune then transferred to another, higher one, and kept going. Behind us I could sense the light subtly changing and I was surprised that no one besides a loud group of young people, far, far above, had thought to do this. By the first stage of the climb I was struggling, not quite gasping but struggling. I could feel a familiar burning heaviness in my thighs. Rinpoche, of course, was all but skipping along. Our feet sank in a couple of inches with each step, which made things harder. But it was a deliciously and—from what I'd later hear—atypically cool night. There was very little wind. We slogged and slogged, and finally, when I decided we'd gone high enough and that it wouldn't be wise to push myself deeper into the breathless zone, we stopped, turned, and sat.

The group far above us erupted in wolf howls—they could already see the moon from their perch. The sky over the jagged Sangre de Cristos moved from dark purple to charcoal gray and then we spotted the rounded tip of it, the year's largest full moon. A bit more. A little more. At last it cleared the peaks completely and sailed free there like some resplendent god-face. Rinpoche was quietly praying. I took out my phone, careful to keep the sand away from it, and dialed my daughter.

"Interrupting anything?" I asked.

"Nada, Dad. What's up?"

"The moon. Can you see it?"

"Wait a sec. Let me go outside. Warren's here. He says hi."

"Hi back."

There was the sound of footsteps, a familiar creak of a familiar door, and then, "Holy shit!"

"Something, isn't it? Rinp and I are sitting a few

hundred feet up on a dune in the Great Sand Dunes National Park. Almost completely silent here except for a few college kids yelling farther up the hill. The dunes are half in shadow, very sensuous. You'd love it."

"You should write, Dad."

"Yes, my memoirs. North Dakota kid goes east, makes his fortune in publishing, sires two saints, retires young and travels. It would sell hundreds."

"I like being called a saint," she said. "That's a first. . . . Speaking of saints, I'm saying a prayer for Mom right now, Dad. I can feel her presence."

"Still having the weird things going on? Not the Chinese visitor, I mean the other weird things, the déjà vus and so on."

"More than ever. I wish Rinpoche were here to counsel me because I feel like something gigantic is about to happen, but I can say that only to you and Warren. It's a little scary."

"Gigantic how?"

"Interior gigantic."

"Here's the interior master, then. I'm handing him the phone."

Rinpoche looked rather absurd with a phone to his ear. There was something in the way he held it, thumb on the bottom, middle finger on top, that made it seem he was measuring the side of his head for a sideburn implant. I watched him in the moonlight. He was listening, nodding, nodding, making a small humming sound. I could barely make out bits of Natasha's voice at the other end of the satellite beam. At last he said, "Okay. Have courage now like your father, okay?"

He sent me a quick look, of concern I thought.

"Make sense. We see you. No, nothing will . . . yes, okay. See you."

He closed the connection before I had a chance to say good-bye and handed the phone back without looking at me.

"Something's wrong," I said. "She's in danger. I can feel it."

He shook his head as if it were suddenly heavy. "No danger now," he said, as if implying there had been danger, or would be in a short while.

"What, then? Why is the courage needed if there's no danger? And what's this about 'courage like your father'? Does she have some other father I don't know about?"

The look Rinpoche gave me had a trace of pity in it. He did that sometimes when I joked because he knew the kind of mindset from which the humor had sprouted. "Rinpoche needs now to think on it before I tell you, okay, but no danger. Not that kind of courage, okay, Otto?"

"Okay. What kind then?"

"Other kind. Something maybe not what I thought happening, not what Celia thought."

"Happening to Tasha?"

"To us," he said. "Maybe. Not a bad happening."

"All right, but if it is a bad happening, you'd tell me, right?"

More nodding. He patted the sand beside him. "Sit now with Rinpoche. Listen me now. Watch the moon and remember what I said the other night. The madaphor. Make your mind quiet now, like the air. Take the one breath now, pretty big, slow, okay?"

"I'm with you, brother."

"Now, listen me. Make the every cell in your body go quiet, all relax. Think about Tasha and Anthony and Jeannie for a little second then let the thought go up in the air away. Now. Feel the big world around you. World is turning just the right way, yes? Air is just the right way for us to live, yes? Moon is there. Inside all this you can now feel something else, some God word, some spirit that knows. You feel it now. Feel this world with no worry in it, okay? Things going like they supposed to go, the moon, Tasha, you. Now go quiet, quiet inside, no thoughts now. Okay. Stay here and you and me we meditate now, little while."

We did that. From time to time the silence was disturbed by a muted shout from far above. Other than that, there was only a great interior peace, really like nothing I'd ever known. From time to time a little wave of thought moved across that dark inner water but it had no magnetism for me, did not carry me off. I could sense Rinpoche beside me. I believed I could feel the light of the moon on my face but I kept my eyes closed. Silence. Stillness. And then, as he had described it, I sensed something within that stillness, an essence of something, a pulse perhaps, or, better, a tone of energy. There was such a joy to the interior quietness, such a great vast pleasure. I wanted to remain there forever, truly. A blip of thought, then the beautiful energetic stillness that words could never capture. I could feel my heart beat and there was something un-taken-for-granted in that sacred mystery. Quiet, quiet joy, and then I heard Rinpoche move, and I opened my eyes, and he said, "Now we pray, Otto," in a voice barely above a whisper.

"Great Spirit," he said, "who turn this world, let Natasha's mind open out into you. Guide her now in the travel she takes. Watch her father and her cousin and her aunt and especially her great mother spirit now. Soak the love on us in this world spinning and let us go the road we supposed to go."

I was quiet and attentive during this short prayer, still wrapped in the fine tendrils of my meditative peace. But then, at the mention of my beloved late wife, something changed. The peacefulness faded into wisps of memory and I had the powerful sense that there were, before me, pieces of a puzzle I was supposed to put together. Rinpoche's tone was subtly different.

For once, he didn't seem to *know;* a troubled air surrounded him, as if he were wrestling with a complex spiritual algorithm, or assessing a chessboard on which the game could turn, quickly, either in his favor or against him.

"Something's going on," I said.

He turned and looked at me and in the moonlight I believed I could see the confusion on his face. No, *confusion* is the wrong word. What I believed I could see was more like the dawn of some new understanding. It made me think, strangely, of a child on Christmas Day, hoping against hope that he was just about to be given the gift he'd asked for, but still not sure enough to celebrate.

"Maybe," he said, looking hard at me.

A breath of wind sent a few sand grains onto the lap of his robe. He looked down at them, then back into my eyes. "When Jeannie die," he said, and then he hesitated—again, so unlike him— "who she talk to, last thing?"

"Me."

"What she say?"

"She said, 'Bye,' like that, very calmly, almost as if she were just leaving to go to lunch in town. Why do you ask?"

"What she say to Tasha?"

"I don't know. Tasha was asleep when she died. I went upstairs and woke her and she came down and hugged her mother for a long time and wept."

A somber nod.

"It would be nice now if you told me why you were asking these questions. It has to do with something Tasha just told you, doesn't it."

"Now," he said, and there was another pregnant hesitation. "Now, Otto, you have to wait, okay? You have to wait, my friend. If I tell you something now maybe isn't right, but when I know the thing sure I'll tell you. Please."

Rinpoche had said many things to me in the years of our association, but never had I heard him say the word *please*. I looked into his face. I said, "Fine," but it didn't feel fine, not at all.

If the college kids hadn't come tripping and sliding down the dunes just then I'm not sure what I would have done, but here they were, laughing and talking. One of them was carrying what looked like a miniature surfboard, or sled, or a skateboard without wheels. They skidded to a halt near us, two young men and a young woman. "Amazing, wasn't it?"

"Spectacular," I said. "Were you . . . is that some kind of board for skiing or something?"

"We rented it," the girl said. For some reason she held it out, not toward me, but toward Rinpoche, as if she intuited which of us would want to use it. "Try it, go ahead."

The chances of Rinpoche saying no to this did not exist. Under the young trio's brief tutelage he sat on the board and pushed himself over the rounded edge of the dune. One more second and he was out of sight and we could hear him, "Ah-ha-yah! Oh-oh-oh!" and another two seconds and he came back into sight, a dark lump there flying down the slope. Fifty feet from the bottom of the valley that separated our dune from its neighbor, he lost his grip. The board went right, Rinpoche left. He rolled and tumbled in a moonlit mass of ankles and robe. One sandal—I hoped it was a sandal—went flying off and Rinpoche tumbled, grunting, until he came to a stop. Taking the hill on foot, at an angle, like a beginning skier, I hustled down after him, worried he was hurt. I heard what I thought, at first, might be a whimper, then it grew louder. Three more sandy steps and I heard the sound swell into his astounding laugh, a thunder roll of laughter, "Aha, aho, aho, aho!" And when I finally reached his side the sight of him made me think of a red-robed Gulliver, tied down there, being tickled by a million invisible Lilliputians.

Twenty-four

Every race, every tribe, every nation, every people from antiquity to the silicon age has chosen certain days to be more special than others. Whether it's Easter, Yom Kippur, Buddha's birthday, or the Fourth of July, we seem to have some innate sense of the importance of cele-brating anniversaries. I think it keeps us from getting lost in a run of days that speed by, faster and faster, as the years move beneath us. Maybe we understand instinctively that we should stop and party every once in a while—dance, eat without restraint, have a parade, blow out candles on a cake, shoot off fireworks, give presents. When Jeannie was alive I always tried to take a vacation day on her birthday—and on mine. Like Rinpoche's people, we believed it was important to mark the day we'd come into this life. The celebrant would have a special homemade breakfast (corned beef hash and home fries for me, eggs Benedict for her), then we'd play a game of tennis together, or go for a long walk in the Bronxville Reservation, or we'd drive up the Hudson and have lunch at a bistro we loved, a little place called Gian's in a stone house not far from the river. In the evening there would be another special meal, and then presents and cake. We made the same effort for the kids, of course, even more so: bowling parties, sleepovers, trips to the City to see a show or a sporting event. The one birthday I'd had since Jeannie's passing had been bittersweet. Tash and Anthony made a fuss, took me out for an expensive dinner, showered me with gifts I didn't need, told me how much they loved me, what a great father I was, and so on. But naturally it wasn't even close to the same.

On that August morning—maybe it had something to do with the meditation, the mystery, and the hilarity on the sand dunes the night before—I awoke early and felt that I wanted to mark the day in something like the way Jeannie and I used to mark it. The clock read 6:48, and I saw that Rinpoche was already up and gone. I sat in a chair, facing out the window as he'd recommended, and started my day with a deep and quiet meditation. A settling of the monkey mind, a first-class peace. I always ended these sessions with a prayer for my late wife and children, for Seese and Rinp and Shelsa, and I did that again, feeling lucky to have or to have had such people in my life. Next I walked across the small distance between the motel and the main building and soaked for ten minutes in each of the healing pools. The morning was perfectly still, already warm, the mountain air bursting with light. The other inhabitants of the Joyful Journey were still asleep, busy in the breakfast room, or off somewhere saying their morning prayers or taking their morning exercise. Back in the room I took a freezing shower, standing there for as long as I could, breath coming in gasps. A contemplative shave. Shorts, a jersey, running shoes with no socks—my usual summer uniform. It seemed to me that my ample belly had shrunk another inch, and in the breakfast room I noticed that I was losing my taste for the sweet stuff. The muffins didn't tempt me. I had bagel with butter, coffee with Coffee-mate, and I enjoyed the paintings on the wall—by one Rita Berault—of Mary and the baby Jesus.

I was sitting at an outdoor table, admiring the distant mountains, and keeping my phone in view in case one of the kids called, when Rinpoche came striding along the path, beaming. "Happy birthday, man!" he said, squeezing me almost to death in his powerful arms. "How you makin' out?"

"Making out fine," I said, and I gave him the rundown on the morning's activities.

"Rinpoche's present for you is one massage," he said, and when he saw the look on my face he laughed and added, "from the woman here. Anna. Not me, man! She's the best!"

Which turned out to be true. The massage room was just off the main building, ten or twelve feet square, and the therapist, Anna by name, was hardworking, skilled, attentive. Toe to scalp she worked me over, telling me about a healing business she and her boyfriend, Walt, had started, a combination of massage therapy, counseling, and what sounded like positive thinking.

"You should open franchises all over America," I told her. "The country needs a little healing."

"A lot," she said.

She punished the tight muscles of my upper back. "I've read every single one of Rinpoche's books, you know. Walt and I nearly fainted when we saw him here yesterday. We didn't want to bother him so we didn't go up to him or anything, but, man, he has a presence, doesn't he?"

"Absolutely."

"He thinks the world of you, you know. Told me it's your birthday. Said he wanted a special treatment for his good friend and brother-in-law. He seems to really be set on the idea of your visiting Crestone, though I'm not sure how much you'll like it there. You seem like a pretty straight arrow."

"Very straight arrow," I said. "Too straight of an arrow, probably. What's Crestone? Sounds like Muzak that gets played while you're brushing your teeth or something."

"Ha," she said. "Funny. I'm surprised you never heard of it. It's a town that's set back a ways off 17, just south of here. In against the mountains. The story is that years ago some politician diverted a lot of water away from Colorado, and so, to try to stay in office, he had his wife give away all these plots of land they owned, near what is now Crestone. And the people that settled there, well . . . I really don't want to say anything else about it. It's special, I'll say that. Different. Colorado's a funny state. We have our Crestones and our Boulders and then we have these other types who think global warming and evolution are conspiracies intended to take away their livelihood. I'm Colorado born and raised and I tell you it's freakin' bipolar here. Even the landscape, in case you haven't noticed. The biggest mountains, and then the freakin' flattest stretches you'll ever want to see. Half the people claim Spanish blood, in these parts, anyway. Half of them are white ranchers. And the other two halves are Indians and people like me and Walt, old hippies, alternative types."

She told me to turn over and then said, "That's four halves, I just realized, but you know what I mean."

"I do."

"You're a city guy."

"New York now. Born and raised in North Dakota."

"Hah. Let's talk bipolar, shall we? There was another piece in the paper today about organized crime moving into the oil fields. For years and years it was the only place you could probably go in the whole freakin' country and not worry about being mugged. Now, in certain parts, it's some kind of weird hell. The Wild freakin' West all over again, except worse. It's all greed. Rinpoche paid for you by the way," she said, finishing with a gentle massage of the scalp. "So you're all set. Don't tip me, either. You don't know what a blessing it is to even ever *see* a guy like that in the flesh, never mind talk to him for five minutes. At the end, he took hold of both my hands and looked into my eyes and gave me a blessing and, I tell you, I felt like I was gonna get pregnant or something just from that."

"Name the baby Volya," I said, "if it's a boy."

"Hah. We don't want Walt to get the wrong idea. It wasn't sexual, but man what a charge!"

"Great massage, really. I've had a bunch of them and that was first rate."

"Thanks. Peaceful year to you."

When I was dressed and on my feet again I found Rinpoche waiting for me in the courtyard, still beaming. "Good, man?"

"Excellent, thank you. That's the perfect gift. It's been the perfect day so far."

"Let me show a place," he said, and he led me along a narrow footpath that ran between the office and the yurts. We walked out into the desert flora: rabbit brush, sage, prickly pear cactus. A few hundred yards and we came to a kind of shrine, four small stone benches set in a square with the remains of a campfire in the middle and miniature cairns all around. "We sit a few minutes now. Special place."

It was, too. We faced out across the long, slanted plain—the very definition of high desert—to the Sangre de Cristos. It was a painting in earth tones and blues, the air so still and quiet it absorbed even the engine noises from the big rigs on 17.

For some reason, sitting there, I had the clear sense that my life had grown too complicated. There was another twinge of thought about selling the Bronxville house, maybe selling the car, living in a totally different way. A twinge, I say.

"Now, listen me," Rinpoche said, as he'd done the night before. "Now in this meditation—not too long!—you touch the place you come from, okay? That place, the you-spirit was there before you born, Otto, still there now, waiting there after you die, okay? Now you learn to touch that place, and when the time comes you die, you remember that place, and dying not so hard for you, okay? This is your true self you going to touch now."

"Okay, ready."

"I'm saying some things and then nothing and in the nothing you touch your true big self, okay?"

"Got it."

"Listen me. Close the eyes. Far up is your father spirit and mother spirit, like another pieces of you. You send up a prayer to them now, and they send back the blessing, like a, like the satellite for the phones, okay? You feel them there now. Tasha and Anthony are not with you now, yes, but in another way always with you, see? Their big self and Otto's big self. Wery close. Now you feel that and you rest in your mind for a little while with Rinpoche."

He fell silent. I noticed he hadn't mentioned Jeannie and I wondered if the great secret was that he somehow knew she'd left me now, left all of us, moved on to some other dimension we wouldn't touch again for a millennium, if ever.

I turned away from the sadness of that. I worked with the satellite image for a few minutes then let it go. Too technical for me, too modern. There were no such things as spiritual satellites. But there was for me, intermittently at least, exactly what Rinpoche had promised: the sense that I did have an eternal self, that a piece of my consciousness resided elsewhere, outside the grasp of time. For those minutes, my body, my personality, my cares here, felt so purely temporary. Real, yes. A piece of my essence, of course. But I actually *knew* in those moments that a piece of me was still and always there, and whatever happened here, important as it might be, all passed.

That, I have to say, is an absolutely terrible description of the feeling I had during that meditation. Awful, really. But the best I can seem to do. Maybe I should just say this: It was comforting. It seemed real. For a while it left me unworried and unafraid.

When we were done, when, by the rustle of Rinpoche's robe and a certain kind of exhalation of breath, I knew we'd come to the end of the session, I opened my eyes on that marvelous vista and saw him peering at me, examining me with the gaze of a concerned doctor. I heard him say, "good," as if I'd passed a rigorous physical.

"Thanks."

"You welcome. Now Crestone."

Twenty-five

I was in what I thought of as a "birthday mood," meaning the day had a shine to it, a kind light. I was fifty-two and that seemed, for a while at least, as we packed up and left the room at Joyful Journey, like the prime of life.

We went south toward Mosca, along the same narrow, shoulderless road we'd traveled twice the night before, but the turnoff for Crestone was only about a third of the way to the turnoff for the Great Sand Dunes. Just there, just opposite the ninety-degree left, stood a building that had caught my eye on the earlier drives. COFFEE AND ART, the sign advertised, but the name of the operation was Mirage Trading Company. My kind of place. Before we even went through the front door we could smell the roasting beans.

The art was good, but it was the coffee that drew me, coffee prepared by a man who cared about his coffee. John was a transplanted Long Islander with striking blue eyes and a lingering trace of that wonderful accent. He'd settled out here, he said, "because of a girl." He talked to us about the land, about the friction between farmers who grew grain for the big beer companies and used a lot of water doing so, and ranchers, who wanted the water for other purposes. The ice cubes in his iced coffee were frozen cubes of coffee, a nice touch, I thought, and one that suggested I might bring up the subject of food. I almost said, *Today's my birthday and I was hoping for something special for lunch,* but I thought it might make me sound as picky about food as I actually am, so I went the diplomatic route: "You know, the meat around here is really good, but I have to say the food options we've encountered have been a little . . . limited. We're heading over to Crestone. Can you recommend a place there?"

"Crestone's something else," he said, and there was a touch of the same tone Anna had used, a hint of some Crestonic mystery. "Try the Bliss Café. That's your best bet."

We turned left off the main drag and drove a road not dissimilar to the one that had led to the Dunes. It was parallel, in fact, if a bit shorter and much more crooked, and it wound this way and that between scraggly rangeland before making one last turn into the 1960s. Everything was different in Crestone. To begin with, there were trees.

The town itself was a ragged grid of streets,

with small wooden houses and a handful of modest shops on one commercial corner. We drove right past the Bliss Café without seeing it, and it was only with the help of three young men in dreadlocks that we eventually retraced our route and found our lunch spot.

"Looks like a house," Rinpoche said, and it did indeed. Up a set of stairs we marched, past a boy, probably ten, who might have been the lost brother of the kids in the trailer in northwest Colorado except that he was punching people on his phone's video game rather than in person, and the people weren't his father. I said hello; he ignored me. Inside was a room with five tables and a small L-shaped bar. The door to the kitchen had a heart cut out of it. At all but one of the tables lounged people, ranging from young to very young, who seemed to be auditioning for a play set in Berkeley, summer of '68. They slumped about in postures that combined attitudes of laziness and resistance, as if the world surrounding them was all wrong, offensive, corrupt, ruinous, and they were wearily toting the truth through it, day after day. A mother sat with two children, one in a kind of sack at her breast, the other leaning against her and picking his nose. She was involved in an earnest conversation with a young couple, both in dirty clothes and backpacks.

Perhaps I'm being harsh. No doubt I am.

Growing up when I did, and where I did, in 1970s North Dakota, graduating as I did from UND in 1983, I was one-half of one generation too late for all the marijuana and easy sex (though I have to say neither was totally absent from my college experience), a bit too late for SDS marches and walkouts, too late to have friends who went to die in the jungles, too late for the summer of assassinations and the era of presidents resigning in disgrace. No, ours were the Ronald Reagan years when very, very few people protested against, say, the invasion of Grenada, or went there to die.

Still, in part because my sister had managed, even in the eighties, to live the sixties lifestyle, I felt a familiarity with that decade. In fact, she'd never stopped living it—the long dresses, the dietary fads, the insistence on building a life in opposition to the mainstream. Stepping into Bliss, I felt all over again how strange it was that, given her alternative leanings, Cecelia should have ended up with Volya Rinpoche. For all his quirks and eccentricity, he was really the last thing from that kind of alternative.

All this in mind, my birthday glimmer fading by the second, Rinpoche and I occupied the empty table and were soon handed menus by a thoroughly tattooed young woman with an efficient air. I suspected she owned the place. I began to hope that she was someone with radical sympathies who nevertheless recognized the value of making a good living. May God forgive me.

I studied the menu. Vegetarian pizza. Pasta with pesto. Spinach salad. And then something called Frank's Mom's Pasta, which looked like it might have potential. The danger in ordering pasta in a place inhabited by few or no actual Italian Americans is that one runs the risk of receiving cooked-to-death penne in a Campbell's tomato soup sauce. I'd seen it happen. Once or twice on business trips, before I learned my lesson, I'd ordered pasta in such places, ended up taking a bite or two, then left the rest of the dish uneaten, filling my belly with bread, butter, and beer. So it was a risk to go with pasta in Crestone, but it occurred to me that maybe Crestone was actually an Italian name—like Capone or Calzone—and the "Frank's Mom" part of the dish gave me added hope. So it was Frank's Mom's Pasta for me and the spinach salad for my companion. We waited. I worked to get over my distaste for the whole atmosphere but at least I understood now what had been in the voices of Anna and John, and I suspected that Crestone had been Cecelia's idea, not Rinpoche's. Probably she had friends here from the old days. These friends were growing a little weed out back, counting the hours until it could be legally sold. They didn't watch sports on TV, probably didn't own TVs. They brought their children up to wear long dresses or tattered pants, sandals, headbands. They eschewed shaving, men and women both, as well as makeup, cologne, and the two major parties. They drove cars that ran on used vegetable oil and smelled like it, too.

I had a whole riff going. It was only the meditative path that saved me from a steep descent into hardcore nastiness. I realized what I was doing, saw the run of thoughts, the dirty little stream of sardonic comparison, saw how I was just trying to put myself above the Crestonians in order to validate my own way of being.

"You know," I said to Rinpoche, very quietly, "these are true hippies. This is what the sixties looked like in this country, in certain places, in most colleges."

"Like Cecelia," he said, which more or less took the air out of my balloon.

"I think she's a little more . . . mainstream now."

He was looking at me.

"I'll be honest, Rinpoche, I feel like they live *in opposition* to something rather than with any ideas of their own. Again, not my sister. But it's like the people here are saying everything's wrong in the world that surrounds them. Cars that run on gas, wrong. People who eat steak, wrong. Women who shave their armpits and legs, wrong. I'm wrong to think this, I know, but—"

"You know these people?"

286

"No, of course not. I just get a feeling from them. Even their posture speaks volumes."

He saw right through me, of course. He kept his eyes on me, kindly enough, for a few seconds, and then from the magical robe he produced a pencil. "You have paper?"

I found a credit card receipt in my wallet and handed it over. I watched him draw a circle on the blank back side, watched the circle become a clock face, numbers, no hands. In the center he made a smaller circle, the size of a shirt button. "Look now," he said, in the tone of voice he used when giving one of his "wessons." It's not easy to describe that tone because it was a mix of absolute certainty on the one hand and a species of gentleness on the other. It put me in mind of our mathematics teacher, senior year of high school, a mustachioed World War II veteran named John Speinecke. Mr. Speinecke was a math genius and he passed on the various strategies for solving problems with a certainty that made it all seem so straightforward and irrefutable. But at the same time he taught us as if he understood the torment math could bring to certain minds. Compassionate confidence is the way I thought of it, and there was, in Rinpoche, that same blend. "Look now, Otto." He placed the tip of the pencil on the central circle. "Maybe this is the enlighten-ment, okay?" He moved the pencil tip up to the number twelve. "Maybe this is monk, see?" He drew a line from twelve back to the center, where he made the v point of a small arrow. "Monk goes to enlightenment this way, from this, how you say, angel, yes?"

"Angle."

"Maybe best angel, maybe not, but this is the monk's way to go."

Next he put the pencil tip onto the number one. "Maybe the good father or mother go to enlightenment from this way." He drew another line into the center.

Then from number two, "Maybe good sports player come this way."

From number three, "Maybe president or queen this way."

From number four, "Maybe wery poor or wery sick person this way."

From number five, "Maybe the hippie this way, see?"

"Yes."

"Anybody have the chance, Otto. Maybe some ways are easier for some people but maybe some hippies go to enlightenment and some monks not, okay? Maybe some fathers go and some fathers don't go. Maybe some sports people, how you say it, too much of themselves."

"Too full of themselves."

"Like that. And other sports people okay, wery good concentration, wery much can go past the pain, see? If you hurt people, if you make what the Christians say is 'sin,' then wery, wery hard to go to here, to this place, because," he scratched up the white space between the number 6 and the central circle, making curlicues, turning the pencil sideways, shading in the white, "because now you have the mess inside your mind, your soul, see?"

"Yes."

"Okay then. So maybe you are number one, the good father in this life. Not so smart if you worry about number five or number three, okay? Just do the best number one job you can do, best father, best brother-and-waw, best uncle, best man now fifty-two years, okay?"

"Message received. Lesson humbly learned. Thank you."

"Welcome."

At that moment the pasta and salad were served and I began, from the first bite, to give thanks to Frank's mother, who had clearly gone to enlightenment from the standpoint of a great cook, which was number ten or eleven on the clockface, and had clearly passed on her talents to her son. Olive oil, garlic, and spices—small and perfectly balanced miracles in and of themselves, but the remarkable thing was that the pasta was properly cooked. (Al dente, as the Italians say, which means "to the tooth." "Way too crunchy" would have been my mother's translation. Unlike my companion, who claimed to speak eleven languages, some more fluently than others, I wasn't much of a linguist. However, over the course of my editing career, I'd learned a few dozen foreign phrases, all having to do with food. Au jus, au poivre, al dente, coq au vin, puttanesca.) I wondered if the chef had made a mistake, been in a rush, taken the penne out of the pot three minutes earlier than he or she usually did, or if the owners of Bliss Café—Frank, perhaps—actually understood al dente, and had instructed his employees to err on the crunchy side. God knew. In any case, it was an excellent birthday surprise. Rinpoche enjoyed his spinach salad with cranberries and walnuts and gave me a taste. "Wine you want?" he asked. "Little beer?"

"Tonight maybe. We still have some driving to do. I had the thought, after our Sand Dunes adventure, that you might like to see some other national parks. There are some great ones not too far from here."

"Once the Great Canyon I saw."

"Grand, not great. When?"

He waved his fork. "Had a speakings in New Arizona. Last year."

"You drove?"

"Celia was driving. Rinpoche doesn't like the flying."

"I remember. All those times you came out to see Jeannie you drove."

"Or the train."

"I miss her on this day. She always made it special, as I did for her on her birthday. I miss the kids, Seese, Shelsa. Don't you?"

A strange twist of smile played for a moment on his features. Who could read that amazing face? Square, brown-eyed, a rather large nose and ears, but it was the musculature that gave it character: His cheeks, forehead, eye sockets, chin, and jaw were composed of what seemed a hundred sinews that could assume a thousand shapes. The smile might have been one of sadness or mischief, or the Buddha's tight grin of pure understanding. With Rinpoche, who could ever know?

"Dessert?"

"Later, maybe, we should probably get on the road."

He was shaking his head.

"What? I like Crestone well enough. I've come to accept it as the six on the clock face, but I'm ready to move, show you some of the country, check out a national park or two. I was thinking Grand Canyon but you've seen that, so we could head to Utah and . . . don't you have a talk there?"

A nod, another quick grin.

"What?"

"Not finish with this place," he said. "Big stupa here to great, great Rinpoche. Important for you now to do the meditation in that place. Maybe big surprise there for you, who knows?"

"Okay. It's close?"

"Wery close, I think. Woman, she tells us now." He nodded in the direction of the owner/waitress, who was en route to collect our plates and to present us with a perfectly reasonable bill. I complimented her on the pasta; Rinpoche asked about the stupa; and on the blank bottom half of the receipt she drew us a map. The directions were all dirt roads, easily missed turns, landmarks that consisted of bits of shrubbery and certain kinds of trees, a house with solar panels, another house with two horses in the yard. It sounded sketchy to me, as if we might end up driving into the Sangre de Cristos and spending my birthday night in the cold there, sleeping in a car with a flat tire, holding phones with no service. I asked, half-jokingly, if we should take water and supplies.

She answered with a straight face, "No, it's not that far, really. You can't miss it."

We became lost immediately. I must have turned left instead of right in front of Bliss, or she must have thought we'd parked facing the opposite direction (which would have made sense if we hadn't missed Bliss in the first place), but we became momentarily lost and wandered back through the town, where I saw a grown woman pushing a stroller that had a doll in it. She appeared to be talking to the doll. She reached down and adjusted the blanket that covered it. For one second then, an instant, a flash, I thought I saw my wife—not with this woman, but behind her, in the window of a store that sold patchouli brownies or something. I didn't see a face, but something in the swing of long brown hair, something in the hips beneath a blue dress. . . . Maybe the waitress had slipped some LSD into Frank's Mom's Pasta and I'd been hallucinating about the al dente, and was seeing things now.

We returned to the front of the restaurant, rechecked the map, set off in the other direction, a right turn, then a left onto a dirt road. We bumped along this road, the mountains close behind us, and in front of us a long, slanting, dry plain lying in sunlight. More turns. The house with solar panels, but no house with horses. We were briefly on Ashram Street—not joking—and then in a kind of suburban wilderness where the homes, well spaced, were of a design that might be called American Funky. Some of them resembled the Alamo, others looked as though they'd been built one room at a time, with any available materials, by different carpenters or stonemasons, in different moods; still others appeared to have been the work of skilled architects, with second-floor patios, sunrooms, elegant porches.

At last, when the homes had fallen behind us

and we were, after fifteen minutes of searching, still stupaless, I stopped in the middle of the gravel road and said, "We're lost."

"Could be."

"We'll retrace our steps and figure it out. There has to be a stupa here someplace. There has to be someone we can ask."

Rinpoche pointed through the windshield. "A person."

It wasn't a person, but it was a black Volvo station wagon a few hundred yards in the distance. From my vantage point, the car looked to have been pulled off the road, and I wondered, as we drove toward it, if we were about to interrupt a young hippie couple engaged in the act that sometimes results, after a period of months, in the birth of a human being. But no, thankfully, though the car was parked in a turn-out, there was only a single woman outside it. She was fully clothed. When we drew closer and stopped I saw that she was standing beside a small pool in a stream that ran beneath the road. She seemed completely unafraid of two men, one in a robe, one not, approaching her in the neowilderness of Crestone's sandy outskirts. "Hi," she said, as if we had come in peace. Her hair was wet.

"Hi, sorry to bother you. We're looking for a stupa that's supposed to be near here. It's a Tibetan structure, sort of looks like a—"

"I know!" she said happily. "Just go back a

mile or so and take the right turn there. You can't miss it!"

Believe me, we can, I wanted to say. Rinpoche had walked a few steps to one side and was examining the pool. "You could swim here?" he asked.

"I just did. It's not deep but it's clean. I'm just leaving, so you guys go right ahead. Nobody will come down this road at this time of day, I'm pretty sure."

We thanked her. She got into her Volvo and drove off. By then, Rinpoche was already lifting the robe off over his head. "Birthday swim, man!"

I wasn't quite as sure as the young woman that no one else would wander down the road. People would see the two of us naked and assume we were lovers. I had a whole busy line of worry going—they'd think we were gay, or nudists, or gay nudists, or old hippies flaunting the county's strict anti-exhibitionism laws. We'd be cited, arrested, fined, thrown in jail. And then—thank you again, meditation—I was able to let it go. Rinpoche was already immersed, splashing happily and looking up at the mountains. I joined him there. The water was cool but not icy, perfectly clean, the bottom sandy, a few tiny minnows darting this way and that. I ducked under, floated there, lounged, drifted. A baptism, it was. Fifty-two and I felt cleansed and alive, eternity stretching out in front of me, a big, true Self holding me in an invisible embrace.

Twenty-six

From that baptism we retraced our route, found
the missed turn, and finally came upon the stupa.
It was an impressive structure, probably fifty feet
high, with a white square base and a tapering,
pyramidal, gold-leafed tower, all set in a cleared
area and looking down across the valley. I knew
from Rinpoche's books that stupas were origi-
nally designed as repositories of the ashes of great
Buddhist teachers but now primarily held a
variety of religious relics. There were eight
different kinds, each representing some important
stage in Buddha's life, and it was thought that
seeing a stupa, or merely being touched by the
breezes that blew around it, was enough to bring
the seeker closer to enlightenment. Building a
stupa was an act that created excellent karma, led
to a rebirth in a kind, loving family, or as a
beautiful creature who gave joy to others simply
by his or her presence. I got out of the SUV and
approached the structure with all this in mind,
with a certain amount of reverence but also traces
of skepticism. I hadn't exactly been raised in a
stupa culture. I hadn't exactly embraced the life
of a true seeker. I felt, in a word, half-worthy of
any blessings the structure might bestow.

But something strange and wonderful happened to me there, something I will remember all my days. I'm sure Rinpoche knew it would happen. We spent a minute walking around the stupa, admiring it and the view it looked out on, and then the Master suggested we sit and meditate together, as we'd done on the Great Sand Dunes and at Joyful Journey. It seemed to be happening more and more now, meditation filling spaces in the day that would previously have been filled by other things: eating, worrying, getting lost. I didn't mind.

There were terraced stone walls in front of the stupa, on the valley side. I followed Rinpoche's lead and sat on the highest of these, my back to the stupa, my legs hanging over the wall in a more-or-less comfortable fashion. As he'd done on the dunes, Rinpoche began to give instructions. "Listen now, Otto my friend," he said, "in the order for you to go the next level now you have to believe it is right for you to go there. If you think, 'I am failure,' 'I am no good,' 'I am not this, not that, too much this, too much that,' no good for you, okay? You have the same blessing inside you the Buddha had inside him. You were always the good father. This is your main work on this life, okay? You did this work with a wery special woman. So now, in this meditation, you think of that goodness inside you, of the goodness you and Jeannie passed on to Tasha and Anthony, and all the goodness they are now passing on in this world, okay? You start now with that. Eyes closed. Mind wery calm. All relaxed in every part of the body. You see the goodness in you. You see that you are father and mother to yourself for all time, you are the child here that is loved the way you love your childs, yes? Rest inside that love now, man, and we be quiet."

It took a minute or two, but I could feel what I can only describe as a deep satisfaction enveloping me. *Satisfaction* is not quite the word, however. This was a state of being that I hadn't ever known, not in my best days as a father or husband or anything else, not in my quietest meditations. This was an absolute forgiveness for all that I was not, for all that I had not done right in this lifetime. A slate wiped clean. Not by some wishful thinking but in a way that felt like a physical fact as true as the sun's warmth on the back of my shoulders. I took in a long, slow breath and it was akin to breathing in golden vapor, not merely acceptance but a fundamental belonging, as if I held title to the very earth, as if my name were written on a document stating that fact, as if there was no possibility of my being denied my share of ownership. I'd heard someone say once that, when he first heard the term *self-loathing,* the Dalai Lama had been shocked. How, he wondered, could a person hate herself or himself? But it was almost a default setting in our society, where we were constantly being compared with some impossible ideal—judged worthy or not according to how we looked, what we owned, how much we had in our retirement account, and on and on. It fueled the beautiful, rich life we had . . . and, at the same time, encouraged us to feel perpetually insufficient.

At the stupa, I felt, for once, perfect in my imperfection.

I rested there in that velvety warmth for what must have been half an hour or more. Little wisps of thought floated across the interior screen, as insignificant and untroubling as the quick beating of a gnat's wings. I felt a kind of existential praise, simply for being. I felt that I might be destined, not for greatness in the usual sense, but that I had a limitless capacity for generosity, for good deeds, for aiding others.

I heard Rinpoche stir and stand, but for another little while I sat there, believing that when I opened my eyes and stood it would be into a totally different world. It was sweet to breathe. I wanted to hold onto the feeling and, of course, that was what eventually chased it off. I blinked, looked up. Rinpoche was staring at me intently. "When I come for you on the last day of the alone retreat your face look almost like this."

I nodded. "Feels different, though."

"Don't pay too much attention now, Otto. Don't describe. You can't hold on of it."

"Why not?"

"Because the part that wants to hold on is the part you letted go to have this feeling."

I turned and looked at the stupa, which somehow made sense to me now, whereas before the meditation it had been an interesting structure, finely made, well cared for, but not particularly inspiring. Now, it seemed to me, it had been designed to represent the experience I'd just had, or something that was its cousin. I kept looking at it. Everything else was slightly different, too, the fold of the mountains in the clear desert air, the feel of my body. It required a supreme effort of will not to talk about all this with Rinpoche, not to ask him to explain. Clearly he knew where I'd gone. Clearly he'd led me there.

"Now we can go," he said. "Natural parks! Rinpoche has to see America!"

Why would you bother, I wanted to ask. If you can travel to a world like the one I just stepped out of, what on earth would make you want to go anywhere. "One question," I said.

He held up one thick finger. "One. Then no more. Ask."

"Has Natasha . . . has she had meditations like that?"

"Yes," he said, and he gave me a fierce look that was a kind of warning: *No more now, man!*

Twenty-seven

We headed south again, through the small city of Alamosa (in winter, the Long Island coffeemaker had told us, Alamosa was often the coldest spot in the lower forty-eight), and stopped at a place called Smoothy's for an outstanding cantaloupe-watermelon juice. After that refreshing snack we headed farther south, crossing greener land and wandering through a little Mexican-looking town called Antonito (where the instructions on the gas pumps were only in Spanish). Then began the spectacular climb through the Rio Grande National Forest toward a ten-thousand-foot pass. To either side lay splendid green pastures that reminded me so much of the high fields of Yellowstone that I half expected bison to come wandering out of the trees. Deer grazed near stands of Ponderosa Pine. Far below in the valley ran the winding Conejos River.

It was several hours of curving climbs and fast descents, tough driving, but there was something so *clean* about this land, so untrammeled, so unconnected to the rest of the West, that it seemed to fit in perfectly with my hour at the stupa. Here, too, was something I'd never encountered, something not quite of this world. Rinpoche stared out the window and said nothing. I had a strong urge to pull over and spend the night in the pine needles, wrapped in a blanket—and that, I can assure you, is not a thought that commonly crosses my mind.

Eventually it came to an end; we couldn't live there, just as one couldn't stay in the meditation; we had to let that beauty go. We crossed into New Mexico and glided down into a rough little town called Chama, a railroad town, it seemed, with a few poor shops, small knots of tough-faced young men who glared at the car from beneath lowered eyebrows. It was the dinner hour, already. Frank's Mom's Pasta had long since left my stomach, and because I didn't see any eating place that looked tempting, I stopped in an old-style convenience store to inquire. A Mexican American woman sat there in the semi-darkness, perched behind a counter piled high with every kind of snack—candy bars, beef jerky, nuts, chips. Behind the piles were signs for ice cream cones. Tiny and at peace, the woman was a figurine from a temple of another era, an Incan goddess granting an audience, perhaps Seese's mysterious female dream spirit leading us into the mountains. "People like the High Country for dinner," she said, in thick, beautifully accented English.

We followed her directions and found the High Country, waited there for a table to open up, were served some very good chips and salsa and then a decent posole. Here, again, let me add a droplet of knowledge from my days as a food editor. Posole was no ordinary stew. Made of maize, meat, hominy, and chili peppers, it was served, in pre-Columbian times, only on special occasions. Feast days. Ex-editors' birthdays, things like that. Some anthropologists believe that, in those days, the meat used in posole was human.

The meat, in this case, was pork. I was there and not there. The quality of the food—good without being great—mattered and didn't matter. The fact that it was my birthday was pleasant enough, but the usual birthday shine had given way to something else, something Rinpoche said I shouldn't talk about, shouldn't even be thinking about. Which was impossible. He was sitting across from me, his rosary-adorned cowboy hat set beside him on the table, and he was munching on a corn chip as if it were the last such thing ever to be created in this land. "Sometimes Cecelia she makes the bread," he said.

"I know. I've had her bread. It's like eating compressed sawdust."

He laughed merrily and didn't disagree. "I watch how she makes, you know. First she puts in the dust."

"Flour."

"White. Then other things, the water, the salt. With her hands she mixes. I like watching."

"If you put a lot of butter on it's not that bad.

Honey or molasses or something. Needs moisture. Fiber is all well and good, but we aren't horses, we have to—"

He ignored my little riff. "Then you have to knee it."

"*Knead,* not *knee.* It's a funny word. K-n-e-a-d."

"She knees it. Hard. Like punching. In the summer it makes the sweat on her face. She makes sure everything mixed up good, yes? Then in the stove she puts and watches for it to get big."

"I'm with you. Jeannie would make bread from time to time. There's something wonderful about it. Primal. It's like watching a mason build a—"

"Wery exciting to see it go big, yes?"

"All of a sudden I'm feeling a lesson here."

"Wery exciting, Otto. But you can't eat it yet, see?"

"I see. I think if you'd used another bread maker, a different end product, the lesson would have hit me harder, but I get the message. The bread of my meditative life has risen, maybe, and that part was exciting, but I shouldn't think about eating it quite yet."

My spiritual guide reached across the table and squeezed me hard on the upper arm. "Wery good, my friend."

"Still, it's a nice feeling."

"Nice, nice, sure. Wery nice. But important to

remember one thing when you eat it: The bread gives you strength not for you, but so you can make a help for somebody else. See?"

"I believe I do, yes. One shouldn't wallow in the pleasure of it."

"Yes. At the minute you die you say: Let me to help people in the next life. Okay?"

"Got it."

"Good. Now we talk about something else, my friend."

"Well, how about this for a something else: I realized today that I'm getting used to not having my job. I do miss the routine of it—I think that routine kept me sane in a certain way, especially through Jeannie's illness—and I miss the people I worked with, and the paycheck, and the excuse to be in Manhattan most days. But I'm getting accustomed to it. One thing I liked was learning so much from the authors I worked with, not just about food but about the world. Most of the books we published incorporated some aspect of culture or history, because food is always connected to those things. That's what a lot of people don't realize, I think, and it was kind of a crusade of mine, making that connection between what people eat, how and when they eat, and all the other parts of life that go with the place they inhabit—history, climate, culture; even the religion sometimes plays a role in what people eat."

"Lot of times," Rinpoche said, but I wondered if I might be rambling again, or if he was actually interested.

"You know a lot about geology," I went on, "which is one of the reasons I want to show you some of the parks while we're out West. And I know a little bit about the history of places. Take New Mexico, for instance. There were native peoples living here thousands of years ago and they had a well-developed civilization with a mix of agriculture and hunting. They had living spaces that were underground, or mostly underground, because the climate here can be so hot in summer and so cold in winter. They had what were essentially apartment complexes. And then the Spanish came, and this one guy called Oñate, especially, was determined to convert the natives to Catholicism and make them subjects of the Spanish king. The stuff that was done to them in the name of God! Unbelievable! Cutting off the left foot of every man over twenty-five, for one example. There were these people called the *Hee car ee ya*. J-i-c-a-r-i-l-l-a is how you spell it. The Spanish did a number on them. Then, later, the U.S. government did another number on them, moved them onto one chunk of land, then they took that land away and moved them someplace else, then they moved them back again. One broken promise after the next."

"A sin," Rinpoche said.

"The very definition. We're going right through their land later on today."

"Should stay there then, Otto," Rinpoche said. "Spend some money."

"We'll see what the options are. But, here's where I'm going with all this: The life to which you've been introducing me all these years, whatever we call it—the meditative life, the interior life, the contemplative life—it seems to be something that stands at the center of your culture. I mean, you and your father were famous in Skovorodino the way movie stars, athletes, and musicians are famous in America now, right?"

A nod. His full attention.

"I'm thinking something like that was important in the American Indian cultures. The medicine men, the shamans, and so on. They'd be the ones getting forty million a year in this society. I know just a little about them, but I think they had spiritual traditions that weren't so different from what you have. They weren't as focused on material goods or competition. They had fasting, prayer, something closely akin to meditation. They also had human sacrifice, which I'm pretty sure your people did not. . . . And then the Spanish came, and their religion was more external. They wanted to, needed to, *convert* people, even if it meant using violence. And yet, at the same time, they were so much more . . . *advanced* probably isn't the correct word, but they knew how to do all these things the native people didn't know how to do—from making rifles to riding horses to drawing maps of the world to not eating human flesh to doing surgery to writing books." I stopped and looked at him.

"What is question?" he said.

"I don't know, exactly, but it seems to me there *is* a question. Our people, my people, are excellent at using the world, maybe better than any other group that's ever existed. Digging out ore to make silver objects, sending up spaceships, you name it. But there's something we're missing, isn't there? We're missing it and we don't even know it's there. I wouldn't have known if I hadn't met you. Maybe that's the source of all our addiction and violence and mental illness."

"What is question, Otto?"

"I'm not sure. It's just that, traveling this land, where you can still feel the Indian presence, which you can't feel where I live, not at all, maybe it's just the right thing for me and you right now. For me, anyway. Maybe what we're supposed to do on this land—I'm talking in the very long run here—maybe our only hope is to blend those two ways of being. Maybe we can have all this scientific and practical knowledge— vaccines, medicines, space stations, computers, great roads—and maybe we could also have the other side of the coin, the contemplative, meditative, the interior aspect of living. I was thinking about this on the drive we just took, and after the . . . the thing I'm not supposed to talk about. It all fits somehow, in my mind at least. Did you and Seese arrange this on purpose?"

The question had finally materialized out of my rambling. He ignored it. "Like what the Chinese do in Tibet," he said.

After a second I understood. "Yes. Similar genocide. Similar clash of a more 'advanced' society, militarily at least, technologically, and a more contemplative one. You're right. I hadn't thought of that."

"Long, long times ago in the mountains there, in Tibet, there was somebody who, how you say, predicts this. Like the acorn, you know the acorn? Unless she breaks open, the acorn can't make a tree. The acorn of Buddhism, the meditation ideas, the inside life, this will be broken open, he said. The Chinese broken that open. Otherwise the Dalai Lama still there in Lhasa. Rinpoche still in Russia. Then the Chinese come, the Russians come, smash us open so we go to the other parts of the world, the West parts, and teach. See?"

"I do see. It's almost as if there's some grand plan."

"Maybe." He wiped his mouth with his napkin and bowed his head toward the empty plate the way I'd seen him do a hundred times, giving thanks for the meal. There was no big show about it, no loud prayers or gestures, just this quick nod of gratitude. "Maybe," he said, "you don't listen enough on your sister."

"I'm sure I don't."

"She been telling you the same thing you just said to me, many times she telling you."

"You mean, why Shelsa has been born and that sort of thing."

"Shelsa, Cecelia, me, you, Natasha, Jeannie. Lot of people in this big plan, not just our family. *Lot* of people, man! Many years it takes but now is one time."

"Why?"

"Just is."

"What's going to happen?"

A big shrug. "Little bit, how you say, change."

"Good change?"

He lifted his hands, palms facing inward, fingers spread, then brought the fingers together and squeezed. "Maybe West and East like this. Maybe Shelsa and somebody else do this now. Maybe this new pope, he's helping. Not sure yet."

"I think that's the first time I've ever heard you say you're not sure."

"Things have to happen. Nobody sees these things all the way. Celia doesn't, Rinpoche doesn't. Nobody. Maybe nothing change. Maybe bad guys win, nobody knows."

"Chinese bad guys?"

"Lot of bad guys now, Otto. Same as always."

On that note, with the familiar shiver running along the outside of my arms, with Rinpoche looking as calm as I was worried, with me glancing around the High Country for Chinese operatives, Somalian terrorists, and crazed militiamen from the Bakken field, we paid for our chips and posole and went out into the New Mexico evening. I found myself, at that moment, giving silent thanks for having been born. I thanked my mother for enduring labor and my father for his work, and I thanked, too, the mysterious *something* that stood beyond them, beyond the realm of image and thought.

Twenty-eight

If you are a road trip person like I am, a map person, a person who loves to be behind the wheel, especially in new territory, then there will be interesting drives and fascinating drives and certain drives that stand above all adjectives and that will remain imprinted on your mind for as long as you have one. Route 18 in eastern Washington state is like that for me. Parts of Route 100 in central Vermont. An unnumbered byway through Alabama farmland near the city of Eutaw.

The road Rinpoche and I took as we headed west from Chama will now be added to that list.

I'm tempted to suggest that the intensity and clarity with which it has engraved itself on my memory had something to do with what happened to me during the stupa meditation, that the beauty of the drive was just another aspect of seeing the world as if it had been washed, as if the disguise had been yanked away. But I think I would have remembered this particular drive even with the most cluttered mind in all of America.

We were headed for the city of Dulce (which means "sweet" in Spanish, and was meant as a pairing with Amargo, which means "bitter," and which lies some forty miles down the road). Shortly after leaving Chama we entered a deserted paradise of thousand-foot buttes standing at various distances from the rolling grazing land near the road. Rinpoche began to tell me how the buttes had been formed, how millions of years of erosion had weathered away the softer rock surrounding them, leaving these royal structures standing their ground, as it were, looking like red-faced kings and queens, or great Indian chiefs, staring out over their dry plains.

Route 64 ran like a snake among these magnificent plateaus, offering different angles on their majesty, the flat tops, the eroded faces, the scree in slanted piles at their feet. It was the highway from heaven. In the midst of it we crossed the Continental Divide, which I explained to Rinpoche, and which he insisted on calling the

"Continental Decide." He went off on a riff of his own then, rather unlike him, musing on the big "Decide" we all had to make, whether to pursue distraction and superficiality or dig deeper into the mysterious interior world. "Once the water go this way and not the other way it keep going that way, yes? Same with practice. Once you go to a level, once you touch that place, you always keep going now. You can't go back."

There were ELK CROSSING signs in abundance and high fences beside the road to keep the elk from playing in traffic.

I told Rinpoche about reports, over a series of years, of dozens of UFO sightings right in this area, and rumors of an underground base, operated by the U.S. government, where captured aliens were interrogated and studied. I harbor a secret affection for these kinds of crazy notions, but Rinpoche seemed unmoved, unimpressed, bereft of UFO curiosity.

For miles and miles we barely saw another vehicle, and then, as quickly as it had turned marvelous, the roadside landscape went flat and poor, not featureless exactly, but plain, dry, uninspiring. It didn't surprise me to see a sign telling us we were entering the Jicarilla Apache Reservation, because everywhere we went it seemed the Indians had been given the least fertile, least remarkable land. Maybe they disagreed, these Apaches. Maybe they found this land spiritually essential, holy, fine. I hoped so.

But soon we came upon the same array of poor trailers we'd seen at Pine Ridge, not quite as old, the scenes not quite as desolate. Another few miles and we saw a sign for a hotel/casino, Indian run: THE WILD HORSE. The idea of stopping at another casino didn't appeal to me. But it was getting late, the hotel looked new, and I thought, as did Rinpoche, that it would be only right to spend a little money in that local economy, to begin to compensate, in the smallest of ways, for all the lies, deceit, and slaughter.

"Tell me something," I asked him as we pulled into the parking lot. "If we stay here can you control yourself, gambling-wise?"

He laughed.

Twenty-nine

First impressions can deceive, of course, but it seemed to me that the American Indians we saw on the Jicarilla reservation were happier than those at Pine Ridge. They were tiny people, dark-skinned, dark-haired, nothing at all like the TV cliché of the Apache warrior. In fact, if they had, at one time, been warriors, most of the people we saw in the Wild Horse were too old for that now. Elderly men and women perched, bird-like, in the lobby chairs. When I peeked into the casino I saw more of them sitting in a similar posture on stools in front of the machines, a contented quietness surrounding them as they played the penny slots.

Rinpoche and I checked into a clean, comfortable, standard-issue second-floor room with very weak Wi-Fi. There was an hour or so of daylight still available to us. I suggested a walk but he said no, thank you, Otto, he was going to "stick here a little" as he put it. A wisp of bad feeling trailed me as I went out the door. It seemed natural enough for him to want some alone time, to meditate or just sit quietly without having another person around; time to call his wife and daughter and have some privacy in speaking with them. But for whatever reason I had the sense he was going to gamble and didn't want me to know about it. Old worries awoke, like ravenous wolves, stretched, yawned, swung their heads this way and that, surveying the territory. I told myself he was a competent adult. He had money. He spent hours each day in meditation and had endured the difficulties of my company for nearly a week. Surely he had the right to gamble if he wanted to. Surely I could count on him not to lose the farm, as the expression goes. Still, the wolves trotted after me as I walked.

On the opposite side of the street spread a small, treeless neighborhood, trailers and a few exceedingly modest homes. I decided to take my walk there. Most of the houses had tiny yards in front of them, most of the yards were surrounded by chain-link fences, and most of them were guarded by a dog or two of various sizes and breeds. Some of these looked fierce, some not, but I felt no threat as I walked along—dogs have always loved me and I have always loved dogs. I'd gone less than a mile when this mutual attraction manifested itself yet again: A pooch started following me. He was a scruffy, cream-colored mixed breed with curly hair and a confident, officious manner, as if he might be the neighborhood census officer come to see if I was only passing through or applying for residence. When I crouched down and made ticking noises with my tongue, he hesitated only a second then hustled over, stubby tail flipping this way and that, and accepted some ear scratching. No nametag, not even a collar. I decided, for whatever reason, to call him Mister Big, a name of which he seemed to approve.

Mister Big and I went along the gravel road in tandem. He sniffed. I looked. The larger local dogs stirred, watched him; one or two let out listless barks, as if to say hello to an old friend, or as if to acknowledge, for the sake of any undocumented schnauzers or Dalmatians who might be living nearby, that Mister Big was in the neighborhood, accompanied by a two-legged foreigner who looked like he might be the type to give painful vaccinations. The fences seemed secure enough, but at one point Mister Big spotted a hole beneath one of them, and, for reasons known only to him, clawed his way into the yard, which turned out to be the province of a German Shepherd with his own small house. The shepherd stuck his face out into the air, laid eyes on Mister Big, paused one second, and came charging out across the dust. "Mister Big! Mister Big!" I yelled, idiot that I am. "Come here! Hustle!" Mister Big did not need my prompting. Realizing his mistake, he made a U-turn and sprinted back toward the hole beneath the fence. However, getting out proved more difficult than getting in. I ran over and pulled him out by the shoulders and he came within a portion of a second of losing the rest of his tail. The shepherd, having been roused from a pleasant sleep by the white intruders, leapt up against the fence again and again, barking furiously. A tiny Apache woman appeared at the door, observing the show. I sent her the most innocent wave imaginable. She watched, expressionless. Her dog snapped and growled and slammed itself against the chain-link until he reached the corner. There, he put his forepaws back on the dirt and showed his teeth. "What's the lesson here, Mister Big?" I asked my companion when we'd put a safe distance between us and the German fellow. "The lesson here is that not every place on earth is hospitable to the well meaning, the kind, the unaggressive."

I gave him another minute of ear scratching and then he trotted off along a road that led over a dry, defoliated hillside, into the sunset. As I waited to cross the two-lane highway back in the direction of the hotel parking lot, those words rang in my inner ear. I was thinking of Natasha, of Seese and Shelsa, of the inaccurate mosque references, of the anti-Muslim rants on talk radio, of the phrase "Bakken creeps." I took out my phone and tried to call my daughter but the service there was spotty and the call did not go through.

As I had feared, Rinpoche wasn't in the room. I decided I wouldn't worry about his gambling problem, but, still full from my oversized helping of posole, I washed and lay in bed worrying. Since the stupa meditation, I felt, more than I'd ever felt, that I was allowing him to lead me someplace. It was an interior place, surely enough, but I had an intuition that it would lead to exterior places, too. Natasha had mentioned some big trip, some grand plan. Rinpoche had hinted about leaving and had been saying for years that I was about to enter a period of great change. So, I didn't want him to have a gambling problem. I wanted him to be the man he seemed to be—secure, beyond doubt, a confident guide to a dimension of life that transcended things like addiction, worry, fear of death, and so on.

For some reason then, maybe because it had been an almost perfect birthday and some twisted part of me wanted to spoil it, I fished around in my computer bag and pulled out Alton's folder. Inside were seven or eight pages, printouts from websites, mostly, that detailed what the Chinese had done to the Tibetans. Mass arrests, torture, forced sterilization and abortion, the slaughter of close to one million people, many of them monks and nuns. Possession of the Dalai Lama's photograph was punishable by a prison term. And on and on. I closed the folder and decided to take one last look at my computer mail program. There was a message from Cecelia and when I opened it I saw that it was a photograph of her and Shelsa, their faces pushed close together, a single candle burning in front of them. Each of them was holding up a piece of cardboard, but they'd gotten it a bit mixed up: BIRTHDAY HAPPY it read from left to right. I tapped out a note of greeting, gazed at the photograph for a few extra seconds, sent up another word of thanks for my life, then fell into such a deep sleep that I didn't even hear my traveling companion when he finally returned.

Thirty

I awoke just after seven the next morning and saw that Rinpoche was sound asleep in the other bed. This was unusual, unprecedented in fact. I took a shower, had a short meditation, and found an e-mail on my machine from Anthony, apologizing for missing the big day and promising to make it up to me with tickets to a Yankees playoff game that October. "We can hope, right, Dad?" Rinpoche slept on, snoring peacefully. I left him a note saying I'd be downstairs having breakfast and I closed the door quietly behind me.

A series of large-format photographs adorned the walls of the hotel dining room: remarkable images of American Indian men on horseback and of American Indian women on their knees, grinding what looked like corn kernels into flour. It was a glimpse into another universe, one that bore next to no resemblance to either the casino hotel or the neighborhood through which I'd walked with Mister Big. Somehow, strolling around the perimeter of the room, studying those photos as I waited for my huevos rancheros to be served, I had the visceral sense of what had been lost in our 150-year accumulation of creature comforts. I wondered how one went about finding it again.

Just as the food was served, my brother-in-law came striding into the dining room, fresh from a shower. He sat down across from me in the booth and offered one of his massive smiles. "How could you makin' out?"

"Fine. You? Order something. The huevos are perfect."

He gave the waitress a similarly enormous smile, clasped her right hand in both of his, and ordered the usual: a pot of green tea and oatmeal with butter on top. She looked at me as if to say, *Is he serious?* I indicated that he was and she left us in peace.

"I think this is the first time in any of our trips that I woke up before you did."

The waitress brought his tea. Rinpoche sipped. Nodded vigorously, happily.

"Were you in the casino?"

"Sure," he said. "Nice machines. I sat a long time next to the Apache man and his wife. Long time. Many things they told me about this place."

A woman about my own age shuffled past and took a seat at the next table. She had an oxygen tube attached to the bottom of her nostrils and was accompanied by a very young boy and girl, her grandchildren I supposed. The girl reached up and slid a lock of hair off her grandmother's forehead. The boy put her water glass where she could more easily reach it. She was smiling, touching their arms, speaking to them in another language. The phrase that came to mind was: the gift of grandchildren.

"How'd you do?"

"Big money," Rinpoche said.

"Won big money or lost big money?"

"Won. Wery big. The bells, the lights. The man come over and take me to get the money. Papers I had to sign."

"How big are we talking?"

Rinpoche fluffed a hand beneath his robe and brought out a thick wad of cash. I spotted a hundred-dollar bill on top.

"You'll bankrupt the tribe," I said. "How much is that?"

"Wery much. I give a lot to my friends. The rest I will give now to the, how you say, people they clean the room. Little surprise."

And that's what he did. I finished my excellent rancheros, Rinpoche went contemplatively through the oatmeal, recounting the stories of the elderly Apache couple, whose forebears, it turned out, had suffered grievously at the hands of the Spanish. And then, as we were back in the room packing away toothbrushes and taking a last turn in the bathroom, he brought the roll out of his robe pocket and set it on the writing desk, using a coffee mug for a paperweight. Even flattened, the bills stood an inch high. In the man of opinions, judgments, and worry, this one act spawned another flood of thoughts of which he is not particularly proud: Would the cleaning person manage it well? Keep it all? Share it? Shouldn't Rinpoche have saved some for himself? Wouldn't the money have been better used if he'd given it to the tribal clinic or school? Wouldn't it be more satisfying to hand it to her in person and watch her reaction? But for Rinpoche, as had been the case in Edie's kitchen, it was as simple and natural as the act of piling our used towels in one corner of the bathroom so they'd be easier to collect. There was no fuss, no show. No big deal, man! When I asked him again, he told me he'd won seven thousand dollars the night before and given "maybe about half" to the couple at the next machine. The rest was on the writing desk.

I closed the door behind us and nodded to the woman with her cart of cleansers and sheets. She was about to walk in on probably three months' pay. For her and for Ethan the Bad Dad, Rinpoche was Robin Hood, which made me, I suppose, a smaller-sized Little John. Once, I wanted to tell him, was enough. But just as I was about to open my mouth I realized it was another lesson. All my adult life I'd orbited around a money sun. Earning it, spending it, investing it, watching over it, parceling it out to children and charities with a guarded generosity, but always, always, thinking about it. With two acts of crazy giving, Rinpoche had shown me a different star.

Thirty-one

The ride from Lumberton south and west across the parched top of New Mexico had little to recommend it and would have been almost forgettable to me if, near Gobernador, Rinpoche hadn't seen a simple sign, MONASTERY, and told me to take a left. The turn brought us down a mile-long dirt road that ended in what looked very much like a motel, without the signs and without the numbers on its doors. For a few seconds I thought it might be the New Mexico State Tourism Office's idea of a cute attraction. The Monastery Motel, a place to spend the night in prayer. It would be the polar opposite of most motels, where praying was the last thing that went on.

But from the dusty parking lot we saw a woman in a nun's habit. She was standing on a stepladder, washing windows. "Why are we here?" I asked my companion.

"To pray."

"You know these people?"

A shake of the head. He was already getting out of the car.

"It's a nunnery, Rinp. We could be disturbing them. Men might not even be allowed."

But he was crossing the lot by then and so, naturally, I followed. The nun came down from the ladder and greeted him. As I approached I could hear him asking if there was a place we could use "to say the small prayers."

The nun seemed strangely unsurprised. She smiled at me, shyly, without fuss, and led us to a door. She opened the door on a plain chapel, probably fifteen feet by thirty, with a crucifix on the front wall, a pulpit, and four rows of folding chairs, three per row. "Please," she said, and she left us.

"Why?" I whispered to Rinpoche.

"Has a nice feeling."

"It's Catholic."

"Yes, wery nice."

We each took a chair in the front row, an empty one between us. "Say the Catholic prayers now," he said to me, with that glint in his eyes that sometimes appeared when he was playing a trick.

"I don't know any."

" 'Hail Mary filled of grace,' " he said in a stage whisper. " 'God goes with you.' Say it like that to yourself, quiet, bunch of times, okay?"

"Sure, fine."

I folded my hands and closed my eyes and repeated those words to myself, just by rote at first, just so as not to make trouble, to indulge my friend and his bizarre notions. At one point I glanced over and saw him with his head bowed, mouthing his Skovorodian Hail Mary. At another point I found myself musing on the idea that the Catholic Church, notorious, at least in my circles, for its outdated attitudes toward women, had always kept a revered female figure at its center. She was a figure the Protestants basically ignored, and yet Protestant women in most denominations could serve as priests, were not obliged to forgo birth control, and were left to their own conscience when faced with the possibility of an abortion.

I said the words quietly to myself, over and over again, mantra style. After a while, the repetition did bring about a nice mental quiet, cousin to what I'd felt in my Buddhist-style meditations. After another little while the quiet was so refined and pleasurable that I didn't want it to end. We must have sat there for an hour. If the nuns wondered about us they didn't show it, didn't interrupt, didn't worry that we were two traveling marauders bent on rape and robbery.

At last, after our long mantra session, our mini-rosary in what still felt very much like a motel, Rinpoche stirred and exhaled once, so I could hear him. He sat there another minute, then stood and bowed with great reverence in the direction of the crucifix. I was, at this point, confused. When we stepped outside we were introduced to the Mother Superior, a woman of perhaps forty-five years, with a pleasant face and a manner so calm I felt like I was running at 350 RPMs and she was at 35. Since Rinpoche didn't volunteer to do so, I introduced us.

"It's very nice of you to stop in," was all she said.

To fill an awkward moment, to quell my very odd desire to ask her for the rest of the words to the prayer, and infected, perhaps, by Rinpoche's generosity, I asked if she had any kind of gift shop where we might purchase something, or make a donation. She led us to another motel-like building sitting perpendicular to the first and showed us a small selection of icons and crucifixes. Rinpoche pulled more money out of his robe, pointed to a painting of Mary and Jesus and gave the good nun twice what she asked for it, which was next to nothing. I bought a set of beads, thinking—I don't know what I was thinking—that I might make a gift of them to Shelsa or Natasha. We stood there for a little bit, making small talk. The mother superior told us there were nine sisters in residence, that they had another monastery somewhere in rural Massachusetts, and that they didn't like to leave the doors open too long because of the snakes. "Sister Edwina takes care of them for us," she said. "Bull snakes, mainly, but the occasional rattler. She grew up on a ranch and used to just reach down and pick up the bull snakes with her hands and bring them outside again, but she's eighty now, it's hard for her to stoop, so she has a tool that she hooks them with."

"Do you stay out here . . . *forever?*" I couldn't keep myself from asking.

She laughed and put a hand gently on my arm. "Are you Catholic?"

I shook my head. "Raised Lutheran. My friend here, my brother-in-law, actually, is a famous Buddhist teacher."

"And what made you stop in?" she asked Rinpoche kindly.

"I think the Catholics wery important in this world now," he said. "One billion maybe, I think."

"Yes, a bit more than that. And we have a new pope about whom we're very excited."

"I have a dream about him last night," Rinpoche told her. "I have a dream that he's wearing a robe like this one." He pinched the material of his robe, held it out in her direction, and laughed.

"Well, it's very stylish. And we think he's going to do great things for the Church."

"I say a prayer for that," Rinpoche said.

"That's kind of you."

"The Hail of Mary."

"Hail Mary, yes, an important prayer for us. We all say it hundreds of times a day."

"Good, good," he said. "Now I start saying, too."

I expected the nun to make some religiousy joke about converting him, but she just looked at him steadily, kindly, eyes not flickering, as if she had nothing better in the world to do than to listen to these strange visitors tell her about the Hail Mary.

For another thirty seconds or so we stood there in a little pool of awkwardness. Rinpoche was looking around the room, its bare walls adorned with a single wooden crucifix, shelves of icons, small plastic boxes of rosary beads. The nun watched him lovingly, patiently, in no rush at all.

"We should go," I said finally. "Thank you for letting us pray. I hope we didn't disturb you."

"Not at all. We don't get many visitors."

I couldn't help myself, couldn't catch the words before they slipped off the edge of my tongue, "What made you do this? I mean, I'm sorry, I don't mean to be rude, but what made you choose this life, way out here?"

Again, I expected her to say, *I wanted to devote my life to Christ,* or something of that sort, the kind of syrupy platitude I would have dismissed out of hand. But she only raised her eyebrows and said, "My mother died when I was fifteen. It made the world stop making sense for me. I thought I'd come to a place like this and be quiet and wait until it made sense."

"Has it?"

"No."

"Why do you stay then? Forgive me, I—"

"It's fine. It's a good question. I ask it to myself every few weeks, in fact. I think the answer is that from time to time I have inklings. I have a sense of something beyond the rationale of this world, a peek into another room is the way I think of it. That keeps me going. I think the other sisters would say the very same thing. The longer I stay here the more glimpses I get."

"Do you—I'm sorry, my wife died not long ago, and my daughter did something fairly similar to what you're doing; she went to live in a meditation center, run by Rinpoche here—do you feel you have some communication with your mother?"

"Very much so, yes. Not any kind of regular conversation, but a sense of her presence, a powerful sense of it. It heals a very deep wound in me. I feel it most often when I'm saying the Hail Mary, in fact. I think I'm in touch with some wonderful feminine spirit of which my mother is a part. And I'm sorry to hear about your wife; that must have been hard for you."

"Very."

"I'll keep her in my prayers. What was her name?"

"Jeannie," I said, nearly choking on the syllables.

We bade good-bye to the friendly nun and took the dirt road back to the highway, and then the highway west in the direction of the city of Bloomfield. Just as we left—you can believe this or not—I looked up and saw a cross in the sky, two strips of white cloud forming the great Christian symbol. They didn't look like contrails;

there were no other clouds anywhere to be seen. They formed a huge, slightly lopsided crucifix in the sky. That is the truth.

"Nice woman," I said to Rinpoche.

"Yes, yes, wery nice. Catholic."

"Right. What's with all the Catholic stuff lately? The rosary beads, the Hail Marys and sacred mysteries, this place? What's going on?"

"I'm having the feelings," he said.

"You going to convert?"

"I don't understand these feelings. Maybe little bit later on I understand. Now I just feel."

"What do they feel like?"

He paused a moment, looked away. "Feel like maybe a big woman spirit bringing someone into this world now, again. Special someone. I think she carry change into this world."

Even with the cross floating in the sky above us, perhaps especially with the cross floating in the sky, this was not a conversation I chose to pursue.

Thirty-two

There are things you can deny, and things you can't. Even on this lost-in-space bluish melon of whirling atomic particles, even on this relative plane, even in an existence where undependability rules, there are certain feelings and states of mind that must be acknowledged as fact. It was a fact, for instance, that my wife no longer inhabited the body I had so loved. It was a fact that Rinpoche and I were driving through northern New Mexico in a blue Ford SUV that had been rented at the Fargo airport and that now, according to a dashboard warning light, was due for an oil change. It was a fact that I couldn't see my children, couldn't touch them, couldn't speak to them face to face on that day, and that their absence caused a small web of sadness to hang around a part of every hour. On the other hand, the idea that some sacred feminine spirit was giving birth on this planet, that the odd crucifix cloud above the Gobernador Monastery was anything but a momentary fluke of meteorology, that Rinpoche and I were supposed to make some grand discovery on this trip, a discovery that would go some ways toward causing the world to be a more loving and peaceful place—these things were, of course, debatable. Unfacts. Perhaps nothing more than figments of the imaginations of people—my sister, Rinpoche—who didn't play by the rules of our scientific-minded society. Wishful thinking, some would call it. Flakiness. Wisps of idea from a dream world that ignored the all-too-factual hardship and suffering of what most of the rest of us considered real.

Scientists use the term *uncertainty principle* to

denote the relationship between perception and actuality, the idea being that what the scientific observer sees in, say, the inner workings of a cell, is not pure objective reality but reality influenced by his or her observation. It raises some large questions. If two people view human life very differently, for example, what is the actual truth of the situation? If I think life is a bowl of cherries, and you think it's a cauldron of pain, which is it? This goes beyond a mere difference of opinion, it seems to me, and beyond individual circum-stances. What I'm getting at is this: The mind is the perceiving instrument when it comes to defining reality. If the functioning of one's mind changes, then one's assumptions about life change. After the war, the combat veteran's world-view could very well be altered, but has the world altered? Isn't the spiritual search, at its essence, a movement toward objectivity? Toward seeing our predicament clearly, as it actually is, without being influenced by reflexive patterns of thought, and without being seen in the refracted light—rose-colored, tragic, or otherwise—of our life experiences? Isn't true scientific study the same thing?

I pondered these questions as we drove through the parched New Mexican landscape, along a road leading us to the city of Farmington. It seemed to me that, beginning with the meditation at the stupa in Crestone, my own perceiving instrument had changed in some fundamental way, and I was trying to describe that change to myself, to make sense of it, to find concrete markers that would enable me to speak about it in terms that weren't too vague and general.

One thing I noticed was that I'd started to care less about the label and to look deeper into people. The friendly nun, for example. I'd been able to see beyond her habit.

Another was that I seemed to have developed a different relationship to nature. I'd always loved to see new landscapes and had, since my earliest days doing chores on the family farm, been attentive to the flora and fauna of my surroundings. (I had loved, for instance, the call of the sharp-tailed grouse, the sight of the prairie rose; I had thrilled at the rare visit of a whooping crane flapping over the box elders in our yard, and even at the sight of a porcupine waddling through, quills up, hips swinging.) But now I felt what can only be called a *kinship* with the earth. The dry brown hills we were driving through—hardly beautiful—seemed to me to be breathing, pulsing, throbbing in the subtlest of ways, as if the energy field of my own body extended itself out into the sage plants and dry stream beds, the red rocks, the cirrus clouds. I wanted to ask Rinpoche about it but decided to wait. "Don't get stuck on the experiences," he'd said. "Don't pay too much attention to you, you, you." So I drove, wondered about the Mary spirit, missed my children, and worried, just a bit, about finding my way north and west to Moab, the site of Rinpoche's last scheduled talk.

Farmington, a few miles down the road, was a strange apparition. There must have been a dozen pawn shops, a couple of "Asian Massage" establishments, an adult bookstore with a billboard right next to it that showed a familiar, bearded face and the words JESUS IS WATCHING YOU. We strolled back and forth along the flat main street, perusing the merchandise in a secondhand store with friendly clerks and an absolutely incredible selection of objects from another era. Straight razors, a real barber's chair, pearl earrings, wall hangings, porcelain plates, paintings of Elvis—it was a step back into another America and I enjoyed explaining it to my companion. While telling Rinpoche what a transistor radio was used for, I had a memory of watching one of the Harry Potter movies with my kids and hearing Ron's father say, "Harry, tell me, what, exactly, is the function of a rubber duck?"

"This used to be a big oil and gas town," the woman at the desk told us, "but the oil and gas kind of disappeared and things got tough for a while. It's coming back a bit now," she said.

I hoped so. I always hoped for places to come back. I hoped, in fact, that they would never have left in the first place. I remembered driving through Youngstown, Ohio, with Rinpoche on our first road trip—he'd had an event there—and witnessing the devastation left behind after the iron and steel jobs disappeared. Walking back to our car along the hot, deserted main street of Farmington, I couldn't help but wonder what North Dakota would be like when the oil and gas ran out, when and if it was proven that fracking caused earthquakes or the spoilage of groundwater. All those people would have moved in, new houses would have been built. Would the oil workers make a smooth transition back to wheat farming and the simpler life, or would we be stuck with abandoned storefronts and Asian massage parlors, hundreds unemployed, an economy built on pawn shops, adult bookstores, a casino or two? Small cities full of friendly citizens like those in Farmington, Bloomfield, and Dickinson seemed to me a kind of smiling, generous flotsam and jetsam being lifted and dropped on great economic tides over which they had no control.

Beyond Farmington we sliced through the Navajo Nation. In the distance we could see the monolith referred to as Shiprock, an old protrusion that could, I suppose, in the eyes of a drunken cowboy or mad conquistador, seem to resemble the prow of a ship, standing 1,500 feet above the high desert floor. "Used to be underground," Rinpoche told me. "Wery hard rock it's made from. Now all the soft rock washed away, little after little, and this stays."

"Sacred to the Navajo, I've heard."

"Wery sacred."

"The stupa was a sacred place."

He looked over at me, not fooled, not taking the bait. "For Rinpoche, every place sacred, every person, every food, every cloud, every mouse and snake and deer. Sacred."

"Right, but even for you some places seem more holy than others."

"Different energy," he said.

"Some people are more fun to be around, less threatening, calmer."

"Sure."

"But sacred all the same."

"Absolute and relative, Otto."

"Right. I'm working on it. I feel a little more absolute lately, like I moved over a few inches into the absolute light and out of the relative light."

No response. Bait not taken.

In Shiprock, feeling sleepy and realizing how far we still had to travel, I looked around for a coffee shop and, finding none, reluctantly pulled into a McDonald's. Rumor had it that, since switching over to Newman's Own, they'd improved their coffee offerings, but, chain-averse as I was, I hadn't experimented. The servers were all Navajo. I asked for an iced coffee, on the dark side, and was served one as light as an eggshell in color and sweetened with about four sugars. I asked for something darker, no sugar, and, with some regret, watched the woman pour out the contents of my cup and make me another one, exactly the same. In her worldview, from her vantage point in the spectrum of life, coffee was supposed to look and taste like this. I thanked her, took it into the car with me, and didn't drink any. We stopped at a roadside flea market and bought something called kneel-down bread, which turned out to be made of cornmeal and wrapped in a charred corn husk. The name derived, the seller told us, from the days when Navajo women ground the corn-meal by hand, kneeling down to do so. I found it not to my liking, but Rinpoche nibbled away contentedly and took two sips of my coffee.

We drove then, through a wonderland of light-brown buttes and mesas, dry, flat-topped hills placed in such a way—looking at each other across the highway—that they seemed about to speak. Sacred land, without question. At one point we pulled into a rest area littered with whiskey bottles and we simply breathed in the mag-nificence of that scenery, a magnificence that no amount of roadside litter, no amount of poverty, no sweet milky iced coffee could spoil.

"If your ego is wery, wery small," Rinpoche said, almost as if speaking to himself, "then the world is wery big, wery beautiful."

"I wonder if pain is smaller then, if fear is smaller."

"Yes," he said, as if nothing could be more obvious. "The ego is like the big animal that breathes all the air in the room. The small ego leaves air for other people, other animals. Then the earth can breathe, see?" He squeezed the back of my neck like a basketball coach squeezing the neck of a guard who'd just missed a key three-pointer but might still help the team win one day.

"What would you say," I asked him, "if you had to pick one sign by which the ego could be recognized, what would that be? Just to be on the lookout for something, you know?"

He looked at me, the coach seeing now that his player had understood, that there might be hope for him after all. He turned his eyes to the flat-faced buttes for so long I thought he might not even answer. "The one thing?"

"Yes. I'm sure there are many. But give me one."

"The ego takes. The attention, the money, the things, the time, all the space in a room. Okay? But when you thinking, *I'm not taking up space, I'm giving*—little bit of ego there, too, Otto."

"It's impossible then, this enlightenment thing. It's like trying not to be."

He smiled. He said, "Bet your ass, man," and we headed west in a pleasant silence, past the tourist attraction of Four Corners, and the Ute Mountain Indian Reservation, through Cortez, Colorado, and Monticello, Utah, and then north, in darkness, along a snaking two-lane road, to Moab.

Thirty-three
〜

The organizers of the Conference on Psychology and Spirituality in the Western World had arranged for us to stay in Moab's Red Cliffs Lodge, in a completely comfortable two-bedroom cabin that backed onto the Colorado River. Rinpoche and I arrived very late, bade each other good-night, and, in my case at least, fell into a dreamless sleep.

I began the next day with a meditation, a quiet, unspectacular hour sitting out on the cabin's secluded back porch and listening to the river run. When I opened my eyes I saw a large raft drifting past—like one pleasant thought—filled with life-jacketed tourists, and then, across the way, two children and a father fishing from the bank. The kids' apparent pleasure, the dry, hot morning, the river muttering over rocks, the afterglow of the quiet hour—it was a good way to begin a morning.

We'd brought food for breakfast—yogurt, fruit, bread—and I brewed myself a cup of tea to go with it and tried to eat with as much focus as I could, paying attention to the textures and tastes, taking my time. Conscious without being self-conscious, aware without making a fuss of my awareness. Judging from the somewhat less urgent press of my body against my belt, I'd shed another pound or two on my low-sugar, high-focus, slow-eating diet, and after e-mailing back and forth with my daughter for a while ("Dad, I had a dream last night that you sold our house! It should have been sad but it wasn't!") and my son ("Man, they're working us this year, Dad. I get home from practice and shower and eat and all I want to do is hit the sack.") I went out and swam a dozen laps in the resort's outdoor pool. I half expected to see Rinpoche come striding up in his Speedo, but he was AWOL that morning, off for a walk preparing his speech, I supposed, or floating downriver after an incautious dip, drifting between the rocks, approaching a set of rapids, looking up at the sky and laughing away the last few seconds of this incarnation. He'd told me once that he existed in a near-continuous state of the meditative mind and for a little while then, while I was breathing hard at the edge of the pool, looking up into the pale blue, that actually seemed a statement that could be taken literally.

At quarter to noon I wandered over to the conference room. I mingled, more or less, with a bunch of talkative psychologists, sipping coffee and spearing at pineapple chunks with a red plastic toothpick. They were an eclectic tribe, ranging from men in expensive-looking suits to men in sandals and dreadlocks, women in short skirts and lots of makeup to women who bought their clothing where my sister bought hers, in Crestone, perhaps, or out of a Nature-Hemp catalog. I could smile at my own judgments and labels, at least; that was a start. I refilled my coffee, sat in the back row, and waited.

11:55.

Noon.

12:05.

12:15.

No Rinpoche.

Upon arrival we'd been given a list of the day's presenters and panels and I knew the schedule was tight. Volya Rinpoche was listed as speaking from noon to one, and then there was lunch from one to two and then several panel discussions (Reconciling Western Materialism and Traditional Christianity; Work and the Human Brain; The Sex-Money Link; The Eye of the Beholder; The Influence of Weather on Mood). My understanding was that Rinpoche had been paid handsomely for this talk, and I could sense, both in the restlessness of the hundred or so attendees and the facial expressions of the organizers, that his tardiness was not much appreciated.

It was unlike him, too. In all the years of our

acquaintance I'd known him to be late only a handful of times, by only a minute or two, and I'd never known him to miss an appointment.

One of the conference organizers—a tall, gaunt man with a silvery goatee—looked over in my direction and raised his hands, palms up. I shrugged. He was walking toward me and I was wondering what kind of explanation I might offer when we heard footfalls on the gravel outside. The door opened, Rinpoche strode in. He was wearing his robe, his cowboy-hat-and-rosary headgear, and an absolutely unapologetic look on his face. The introduction was shortened and, in its brevity and tone, clearly reflected the gaunt man's disapproval. I suppose he had every reason to be bothered, but at the same time there was something of the stern father in his voice and manner, a bit too strong of a rebuke to his speaker, almost the sense that he was encouraging his audience to start the Q and A with complaint.

Unbothered, unperturbed, unapologetic, Rinpoche took his place at the front of the room, in the center of a long, unoccupied table, set his hat gently to his right side, adjusted the rosary beads with some reverence, and then, smiling broadly, swung his head from side to side, taking in the gaggle of shrinks.

"I am late, yes," he said pleasantly.

Nods all around. One emphatic, "You sure are!"

His smile shrank half an inch. "I am walking,"

343

he said, swinging his arm in a circle, "all around this beautiful place. I am thinking: Where anger come from in this whirl? What you say?"

"From others being inconsiderate." It was the same voice. Far-right section of the audience. A man's voice, but I couldn't see the source.

"*You* are angry now," Rinpoche said, pointing at him.

"You bet I am. We're on a tight schedule here, and you breeze in twenty minutes late without explanation or apology. If I did that to a client, she'd get a refund, and deservedly so."

"I give you refund," Rinpoche said.

"That won't be necessary. An explanation would be nice, however."

Rinpoche nodded as if one might be forthcoming, but it wasn't. "Why other people here not as angry as you?"

"I have no idea. I'm not concerned with others' emotions. Perhaps they're just as angry and simply unwilling to say so. Punctuality is valued in our culture, sir. The society runs well because of it. And now we have, what, only thirty minutes or so before lunch!"

"I will keep you late," Rinpoche said. "Maybe no lunch for you today." He laughed. No one joined him.

"Please let's end this," the man went on. "Please just speak and allow us to leave if we do want to enjoy our midday meal."

Rinpoche held his gaze on the man for a long moment and then closed his eyes and sat there quietly, in what I thought of as a posture of meditation. There wasn't any particular posture involved. He didn't cross his legs or sit up straighter, though he did clasp his hands calmly in front of him on the table. A minute went by, two minutes, four minutes. Someone—not the man who'd been so upset—got up and left. We heard the door close hard, then the angry crunch of footsteps on the gravel outside. I sat there, watching him. Six minutes. Seven minutes. There was less than half an hour left in the session and all around the room I could hear muttering and the scraping of chair legs. A susurrus of exasperation.

At last Rinpoche let out a long breath. He opened his eyes, ran them over the room. "Now inside you," he said, "I want that you feel this anger." He took and released another breath. "Maybe good reason for this, but now I don't want that you think about the reason. I want that you feel the anger in you, that you see him there, inside. What he feels like, this anger?"

"A hot sphere," a woman said from the row in front of me. "A prickly ball, hot, thorns on it. It's moving restlessly."

"An electric line between my ears," another woman said.

"A voice babbling very quickly, snapping out words."

345

"Fear," a man sitting just in front of me called out.

"Afraid for what?" Rinpoche asked him.

The man leaned his head down a bit and I had the sense he'd closed his eyes and was trying hard to look into the anger inside him. After a short pause he said, "Of my own powerlessness. Of my having so little control over the world. . . . Possibly . . . of my own death."

"Ah," Rinpoche said, but it was a noncommittal "ah," neither approving nor disapproving, curious perhaps, interested, turning the idea over in his mind as if to examine it for truth or falsehood.

My own situation was complicated. Over the course of our married life, Jeannie had kept me waiting on at least five hundred occasions. Even in our dating days she'd done it, and there had been times when I'd been furious, and times when I'd been bothered, and other times when I was able, for one reason or another, to let it go. So I was sitting there in my customary spot at the back of the room, stewing in a pot of small confusions, a mix of my love for her, the pain of her absence, the remnants and memories of my irritation and her lack of consideration. In my own life, work and personal, I was extraordinarily punctual, early more often than not. If I happened to be on the road and a bit late for anything as simple as a date for coffee with an old friend, I'd be overcome with a restless nervousness, an anxiety out of all proportion to the situation. I'd been known to risk a speeding ticket or run along a city sidewalk just in order to be there at 10:30 as I'd promised, rather than 10:32. I was so proud of my punctuality. It made me good, better, utterly considerate. It was one of the pillars of my self-esteem.

"Sometimes maybe," Rinpoche said, touching his hat with two fingers and turning it a quarter inch, "you have the clients—clients, yes?" He looked over the rows of heads at me. I nodded. "Clients that feel for you the anger. Why is? Maybe not getting what for they paid you. Or maybe they want to talk and you say time to stop. Or maybe you tell them something they can't like. About themself. About life. You can see the angry in them, yes? You can feel. Or maybe with the children this happen. Or with the wife, or the husband, or the sister or brother or the friend, yes? Or the person you don't know. Maybe the person who drives bad in front of you, yes? Sometimes when you are the angry person you think: Good now that I'm angry so I can teach this other person not to be wrong. Teach my children not to run around. Push on the, how you say," he pressed the heel of his hand forward and someone in the audience figured it out and said, "the horn!" "Horns, yes! You push the horns to teach this other person about driving bad. Wery good! But why sometimes you are angry when the person drive bad, when the boy or girl act bad, and sometimes not so angry? Why is?"

"Depends on your mood," someone called out.

Rinpoche nodded at her. "So you can control, little bit, yes?" He went into a riff of high chuckling, solitary mirth. "So you are angry because the whirl is not controlled by you, and then you don't control what part you can control—you—and so the anger comes out even more big. Funny, yes?"

Not many in the audience seemed to think so.

"Maybe questions now."

Immediately a man on the right side of the audience snapped to his feet and when he spoke I recognized his voice from the earlier comments. "I'm not angry now," he said, "I'm quite furious and I plan to lodge a complaint. First, you keep us waiting for twenty minutes, and then you feed us this pablum. We're an intelligent group, Rinpoche. Educated. Well experienced. Sophisticated in the psychological sense. We came, many of us, hundreds or even thousands of miles, and we spent a good sum of money and took time away from our professions and families because we hoped to learn something from these panel discussions. I, for one, feel like you're mocking us, mocking this whole conference, making light of it. And I am not pleased."

Rinpoche listened attentively, unruffled. "What is this 'making light'?" he asked. "How can you make it?"

"Making fun of something," I called out from the back of the room. "Not taking it seriously."

"Ah." He looked down at his hands and then up at the angry man. "When you help people, when you are with the clients, they pay you to talk, yes?"

"To talk and to listen, yes."

"Helps them, this talking?"

"Of course it helps them! You have a hundred or so people in this room who get paid, some of us very well, for helping people."

"Good," Rinpoche said. "But maybe some people you don't help?"

"Obviously, sir. There are always going to be some for whom the therapy isn't successful. For a wide variety of reasons."

"Maybe for some people, there is another way to help instead of talking. Another therapy. Maybe works better for some people."

"Maybe so, but that isn't the point."

"Maybe it's exactly the point," a woman called over to him from the left side.

"I'm speaking to the speaker, thank you."

"But maybe you're wrong, and, excuse me, but I have as much right to speak my mind as you do. You're monopolizing here. Yes, he kept us waiting. I'm not especially pleased about that. But maybe he's trying to show us something in ourselves that's valuable, and he thought this was the best way."

"So now you're going to start arriving late for your sessions?"

"Not at all. But maybe I'll understand a client's anger in a different way."

"I can easily see how your clients would be angry at you."

"And at you," she said. "You're a boor!"

"Stop making excuses for his inconsiderate behavior."

"God!"

Rinpoche rapped his knuckles on the table like a judge with a gavel. He was smiling again but it was a rueful smile this time, lined with sadness. "Everybody angry now. Now we sit for the last ten minutes and you go to lunch five minutes late. Sit quiet. We look on the angry in ourselves. We see maybe that it comes part from us and part from the other person. We can say words. We can say, 'You were late, no good!' Okay. Maybe next day the person on times. But now we look on the part in us that we have control, okay? Ten minutes. Then big lunch!"

The audience sat in something like silence for five or six minutes. There was some coughing and shifting about, and for a little while I was distracted by it. I was thinking that, given another few exchanges, the therapists might have come to blows, the room taking sides on the question of Rinpoche's lack of professionalism. There would be shouted accusations, harsh words, perhaps even fisticuffs. A few of the attendees might get hurt. The *Moab Times-Independent* would run a headline: CONFERENCE ON SPIRITUALITY ENDS IN HAND-TO-HAND COMBAT. SHRINKS DUKE IT OUT AT RED CLIFFS.

But then I did what Rinpoche had asked me to do. I looked into my part of the anger, not Jeannie's part. She had been late, yes. Inconsiderate, yes again. It had been right for me to speak to her about it, rather than stifling it and cooking in an oily resentment for all of our married life. But had it been right to be *so* angry? Was it to be excused with the classic, "Well, I'm human"? Or "She deserved it"? Or "Maybe next time it will make her think twice about being late"? I looked deeper. I seemed then to be able to set the question in the midst of the quiet room of . . . my *stupa mind* was the way I thought of it. There it sat, the thorny ball of my old anger, still twitching, long after the object of it had left this world. Just looking at it that way made me feel a certain power. I had set aside the question of whether or not it was justified. I was observing it. I was wishing I could have observed it then, in those moments, and felt this power, instead of the semi-frantic powerlessness I'd actually felt. I wondered if it might have made a difference, if Jeannie would somehow have *heard* me when I spoke from that quiet place, instead of in anger. I wondered if it would have upset the kids less. I breathed in and it was clear to me that it was next to impossible to pray while being angry. I breathed out. I felt stronger. I felt an urge to drive through Midtown Manhattan in Friday rush hour and test that new strength and patience. I smiled at that thought, at the image of myself driving Seventh Avenue at five p.m. as a spiritual test, the calm cabbie as bodhisattva, and I heard the great master say, "Eat now, my friends. Sorry to making you late." And just about half the room erupted in applause.

Thirty-four

After lunch I suggested to my brother-in-law that we drive over to Arches National Park, said to be a place of some of the most stupendous rock formations on the planet. Rinpoche agreed enthusiastically. We packed up bottles of water and small bags of peanuts and dates and set off.

It was thirteen miles from Red Cliffs back into Moab, an extremely serpentine thirteen miles, on Utah Route 128, a heavenly road, certainly one of the great drives one can take in this land of great drives. That road carries you through a million-year-old museum, really, because over millions of years, with enormous patience, the mighty Colorado has cut its snaking path through the sandstone. On turn after turn we were presented with thousand-foot-high, burgundy-colored out-croppings—rounded, massive, proud, so sensuous that you wanted to get out of the car and rub your hands over them. Along that road the river was a hundred to two hundred feet wide, sluicing past dusty, rocky banks, cutting down and down but at the pace of a thousandth of an inch a year. One of these massifs was so huge, so dignified, so impressive, that an odd label for it came into my mind: Headquarters of the Bank of the Underworld.

"Time," was the only comment Rinpoche made, but it was the perfect comment. This red stillness beneath a bright, still sky was nothing less than a monument to time, its great, mysterious passage. It was a feeling you couldn't get in the East, where the landscape is mostly tree covered, the trees shedding leaves after a six-month lifespan, the trunks standing for fifty or sixty or a hundred years. Yes, the hills were older there—the Appalachians far older than the Rockies, in fact —but you couldn't *feel* the passage of time the way you could feel it on this stretch. You couldn't place your small moment on that giant continuum, or understand yourself to be tiny amid the grandeur.

When 128 met up with 191 the show ended. We cut briefly across a corner of Moab, headed north, and found the entrance to Arches National Park there on the right-hand side. A diorama at the welcome center let us know that the only dangerous species of snake in the park was the miniature faded rattlesnake, and it added the comforting information that "Most visitors who are bitten are trying to catch the snake." I laughed at that at first—trying to catch a rattlesnake!—then the thought came to me that it was exactly the kind of thing Rinpoche might try. Anthony had told me that when he and Rinp had played golf in Medora, North Dakota, in a river bottom hospitable to rattlers and water moccasins, Rinpoche had gone into the rough after an errant shot and ignored my son's warnings. "Nakes like Rinpoche!" he'd said, or something to that effect. "Nakes love me!"

I made sure to show him the diorama and exact a promise that he wouldn't try any snake catching on this particular hike.

We drove a ways up into the dry hills, the road turning and climbing, surreal felt-hat-gray formations appearing now and again to either side. There were arches, yes, and odd rock towers, too. But the landscape was dotted with every imaginable stony shape. We decided to stop and hike through a section called Garden of Eden, which was the home of a dozen crooked pillars. These were citizens of some other world, standing there unsmiling, chins raised, proud as the proudest chieftains. Glorious. Beyond them stretched long views under a heavy sky, the landscape pocked with other proud stone creatures standing singly

354

and in groups. Rinpoche and I hiked for half an hour along dry paths and ended up eventually at a particularly striking sandstone arch that offered a view back toward Moab. There, a group of people, an extended family it seemed, was having a conversation in another language. Rinpoche greeted them in that tongue—Italian, it would turn out to be—and you could read the surprise on their faces. Here they were, six thousand miles from home, in a section of the United States not exactly known for diversity, and who should walk up and greet them in their own language but a bald-headed *signore* in a maroon robe!

I wandered around on my own, marveling at the sights, drinking them in like a thirsty man. "There is nothing like this anywhere else on earth," I said aloud to myself at one point. "I wish you could see this," I said to Jeannie. "I wish we'd taken the kids here and seen this together."

When I returned to the big arch, Rinpoche appeared to be holding court. The Italian family— a woman about my own age, three thirtyish couples, two small kids—had gathered around him, engaged in a lively back-and-forth. Rinpoche introduced me, and the talk turned to English. Some of them were more proficient than others, but they were all so pleased to be in conversation with us, so warm, so enthusiastic, so remarkably open and friendly. *Are all Italians like this?* I found myself wondering, and I cast my mind back to the one trip Jeannie and I had taken there, to Venice on our twentieth anniversary. My parents had come east to mind the kids—who were near the end of high school by then and needed almost no minding—and Jeannie and I had set off on the one vacation we'd ever taken without them. Venice was, well, Venice. I remembered the food, the feeling of being alone with her after all those years of crowded family life, the feeling of missing our children, our regret at not bringing them, our joy in each other. The churches—in one of which Jeannie sat for a long time in prayer—the canals, the elegant old apartment houses, the food, the food, the food, the prices! Our interactions with the Italians had been limited to brief exchanges in the hotel and in restaurants. We hadn't really gotten a feel for the country and its people, nothing like what I sensed in that circle of happy souls with the shadows lengthening around us and the arches and pillars offering themselves for our entertainment.

Rinpoche was telling them about his meditation center there. Near Torino, he said, one of four he supervised on three continents. "You should come there to see me, to meditate," he said. They smiled, indulging him. I couldn't imagine them sitting still and quiet.

"What do you think of American food?" I asked, because, though I'd been to Italy only on that brief visit, I'd edited half a dozen books on the cuisine, often finding myself drooling over the galley pages.

There was a diplomatic pause. "Meat, meat, meat," the woman said, at last.

"Yes, especially in this part of the country."

"But the meat is *buonissimo*," one of the younger men added diplomatically. "Perfect meat you have. Perfect."

"Thank you."

"We have an inn near Bologna," they said, "not so far away. You and your brother-in-law should come there. You have children?"

I held up two fingers.

"A wife?"

"She died two years ago."

There was a general expression of sympathy. Even the boy and girl, who were all of five and seven, made sad faces.

"Come with the children then. Your brother-in-law speaks the perfect Italian. Come see us! We'll make good care with you, you'll see!"

It was impossible not to be infected by their warmth, by the sense that I'd known them for decades.

"I think maybe we come," Rinpoche said. "I have the feeling we are coming."

A storm was brewing in the valley. One of the children let out an exclamation and pointed and we all turned to see flashes of lightning there among eggplant-purple clouds, folded and roiling and sliding east. The older woman dug a business card out of her purse, scrawled a telephone number on it, and handed it to Rinpoche, insisting, so sincerely, that he call and come visit, that he bring his brother-in-law and nephews and nieces and wife and little girl. He had to come see them. He must!

"Nice, nice people," Rinpoche said, as we made the walk back to the SUV. "Lot of people there like that. Friends, you make, wery quick there. Wery good friends."

"Why haven't you gone back all these years?"

"Too much the flying."

"You can take a boat. That's how you came, isn't it? Before you met Seese?"

"Boat, yes," he said, wrapping an arm around my shoulders and holding me that way as we walked. "We going, I think, Otto. Soon. I have the feeling we are going."

"Count me in."

"What means?"

"Count me in? It means, 'include me.' Yes, I'll go. With bells on."

"What means with these bells?"

"That I'd be happy to go."

"You have to," he said. "No choice about."

A small remark, but it was spoken in a particularly strange tone, not light, not mildly encouraging, but as if I actually, in fact, and very definitely had no choice in the matter.

We headed down past the entrance and off into the wilds of Utah.

Thirty-five

As we drove north on Utah 191 and then turned onto I-70 West, all color leached out of the land, leaving only a palette of dry grays, a stony scene that went on for miles and miles. It was a moonscape, lifeless and somehow unkind, and the unkindness was matched by a radio program on which the host ranted coldheartedly about Muslims and lazy illegals. They seemed, in his mind, conjoined.

"What do you know about Islam?" I asked my companion.

"I like wery much that they say the prayer five times a day."

"Yes."

"Keeps you not to forget. And I like very much the Sufi. This is a part of Islam, mystical part. I like them *wery* much!"

"I remember you had a Sufi book in the retreat cabin."

"What I like, Otto, is these Sufi people they think you should be human. The full human. Not interested in special things, in big gods coming down, in special meditations, like that. They want that if you married, you are the good husband or the wife. If you work, you do the work the right way, not the wrong way. If you sick, you say, 'I am sick. This is part of my job now.' "

"They're into the nitty-gritty," I said.

"What means?"

"The everyday. The ordinary."

"Yes! Just do the best nitty-gritty and you okay, man!"

"But they're mystics. By definition, mystics are at least partly into another realm, another world. It comes from *mystery*. We have an image of mystics as being off in a cloud someplace."

"Is bad, this image. They maybe in the meditation have special feelings, sure, wery special. But what is the point in it?"

"Of it."

"The point in it, in the special meditations, is then when you come back to be the husband you wash the dishes maybe, you make your wife feel good in herself, you be kind. You love. This is the point. My father used to tell me that he walked around giving. Every time. He give to my mother, to me, to his friends, to his, how you say—"

"Disciples, maybe."

"Maybe, yes. The young people who come to hear him and learn. Give, give. But not with the big show, Otto. Just like the well. The well gives you water and gives and gives, but no show about, you see?"

"I do."

"The earth gives."

360

"Some places more than others."

"Sure. But you have the breath now. You have the muscles to move this car, you have the brain to think, you have all the food. Something gives that to you, all the time. You want to try to be like that something."

"*God* some people call that."

"Call what you want to call. Something gave you. You give back."

"And sitting around the house in Bronxville watching the Yanks and drinking Pinot Noir with my gourmet popcorn is not exactly a posture of giving, am I right?"

"You were resting," he said.

"I was?"

An emphatic nod. "God, maybe, doesn't need to rest, but the Sufi say be human, not God. Human sometimes needs a break, man. After hard work, after raising up the kids, after heavy things happening on you. Little break you took. Now you go back to work."

"Editing, you mean?"

His laugh was almost scornful, a first in my experience of Rinpoche. He said, after a moment, "Sometime, you know, I think sometime maybe you try to say wrong things on purpose."

"Why would I do that?"

"Pull over now, on the side."

"Kind of a bad spot. This is an interstate."

"Pull now. One minute."

I pulled over to the far edge of the paved shoulder. Tractor trailers roared past, too close for comfort.

"Stand out with me."

We got out and walked around to the safer side of the vehicle. The sun was hot without being merciless; the air stirred for three seconds and went still. The ground beneath our feet was gray sand, dust, useless. Rinpoche bent down and lifted up two cupped handfuls of it. "See," he said, a bit more gently now, but still with a hint of impatience in his voice. "Million years ago maybe this dirt was good to grow the food. Maybe plants here, and the big animals ate from the plants. It made use."

"It was useful."

"Million years maybe. Twenty million. Hundred million. Then, finish. Now what you grow in this?"

"Nothing."

"Good. You had the big house, yes, the good wife. In that house, with that wife, you grow the beautiful children, yes?"

"Exceptionally beautiful."

"Good. Wery good. Put your hands out like me."

I held out my hands, together, palms up. "Listen me now, my good friend." He poured the stone dust into my palms. "Maybe make you sad, but listen. The big house now like this. The editing job, like this dirt, see? Nothing grows for you

362

there. Finish, that life. Now you rested, now you give a different way, understand?"

I nodded, but without a great deal of enthusiasm. This wasn't the model, this constant giving into one's sunlit years. The model was to raise your children, to drive them everywhere they needed to be driven, to counsel them, support them financially, to see to their teeth and health, to speak with their teachers, to clothe them, comfort them, advise them, attend their dance recitals and athletic contests, rush them to the emergency room when necessary, make them costumes for Halloween, shower them with gifts at Christmas or Hanukkah, accept the warm fire of their love, see them off on their own adult adventures and then . . . spend the winter months in Florida or Aruba, take a train through Europe with your wife. Read the *Times* and have dinner with friends; drive up to see the kids, the grandkids, and stay at a nice bed and breakfast so as not to inconvenience them; gather the whole clan on the Cape for someone's birthday. The idea was to relax, to rest, to do a bit of volunteer work, maybe, but basically to suck at the pleasure faucet for your last ten or twenty decent years and then to pass on as peacefully as modern medicine would allow. It was supposed to be like that, I wanted to tell him, because the idea of it being like that had been engraved into the stone at the base of my thought stream. I'd seen dozens of older friends do it. Even my parents and Jeannie's mom had enjoyed their own versions of a stretch of years like that. It was the natural pattern . . . at least for the educated American upper middle. Before I could explain all this to Rinpoche, however, before I could make my small protest, he said, "The editing now, the house," and pulled my hands apart so that the pile of stony powder fell onto the toes of my running shoes. He looked hard into my eyes and said, "Finish."

Thirty-six

We had lunch in the town of Green River, which billed itself as "Utah's Desert Treasure" and was, in fact, located in a kind of oasis. The oasis had seen better days. Along the main drag stretched a row of small stands selling melons, but many of the stores and eating places were closed up and exhibited a forlorn look. One of the only surviving establishments, a place called Ray's Tavern, resembled a biker bar from the outside but wore a sign saying THE PLACE FOR EVERYONE, so Rinpoche and I went in. At Ray's we enjoyed a fine lunch of slightly overcooked pork chops, thick as the phone book, coleslaw, fries, and a decent draft beer shared between us by the ratio of 11 to 1. There was a glassed-in collection of

T-shirts on the wall, as exotic as those from Ivy League rowing teams and as mundane as one from a local construction company; behind the bar a man stood over a grill, flipping burgers that bore no resemblance whatsoever to the thin strips of so-called meat in the fast-food chains. As we ate, a gaggle of bikers did, in fact, come through the door, but they wore jackets saying COMBAT VETERANS AGAINST CHILD ABUSE and had gray beards and gray ponytails and were the last thing from threatening. I asked the waiter, as diplomatically as I could, what had happened to Green River, why the closed-up shops, the quiet streets?

"Used to be a missile range here," he said. "That's closed now, but what really hurt us was when the highway got built." He waved an arm to the south. "People used to drive through town and stop to eat or get gas. Now they just go right on by."

It seemed so sad. Here was a place with character, with homemade coleslaw and a welcoming air, and it had been cast aside in favor of highway rest stops with paper-thin hamburgers, chemical additives, interior design that was as bland, upbeat, plastic, and inoffensive as some consultant in Chicago could make it. For a little while it seemed to me that all the blood and zest were being siphoned out of the American landscape in the name of convenience and low prices. We eviscerated whole towns, fed our kids with less care than we fed our cattle, put people in uniforms and set them to work for eight bucks an hour. And we called that progress.

Maybe I simply didn't want any kind of high-speed modernity just then, on the heels of our conversation by the side of I-70. Maybe I was seeing America through the lens of my own drama: I didn't want the house in Bronxville and my life there to be "finish." A fine film of nostalgia had wrapped itself around me. Against all hope and reason, I still wanted to be husband and father, the guy kicking the soccer ball in the back yard and washing the dishes after dinner. Even as I saw, so clearly, that Rinpoche was right, a part of me still wanted him to be wrong.

We finished our food and hit the road again.

Just past Green River was a sign: NEXT SERVICES ON I-70 106 MILES. It was that kind of place, empty land, eyed lustfully by the makers of missile bases and the dumpers of nuclear waste. Soon we turned off the highway and headed southwest through another wonderland of rock formations. In Goblin Valley State Park the stone hills, layered in horizontal grays and reds, looked like big slabs of steak stacked on their sides. The plains were dotted with tufted grasses, sagebrush perhaps, burnt sienna in color with hints of pale gray-green. One half expected to see saguaro cactus against the crumbling hillsides. We passed a place called Temple

Mountain, which looked like nothing so much as a dry castle rising from the desert floor. Off to the south we saw the bottoms of clouds being tugged toward the earth in bands of gray vapor, and my phone started giving off an alarm that severe weather was close. Rain. Flash floods. Caution was urged. As if fleeing just as Noah was finishing the ark, pickups raced past in the opposite direction, many of them towing speedboats. Lake Powell lay to the south of us. It was Saturday. Vacation was over and people were heading home.

The windshield had ceased to be an insect burial mound. Nothing lived here.

For a hundred more miles we went along like this, the landscape watered very lightly by the edges of the storm, small towns like Hanksville and Caineville, with trailers, horses in pens, junked pickups in fields. Out Rinpoche's window now was a vista of bluish mountains behind gray stone fortresses that had never been occupied. It was a world made by the children of some sand-castle-champion god.

Now it changed again—a green field, sudden, packed with Angus cattle. Then dusty gray slopes, veined with rain runoff, looking like manmade piles of slag, and then stone that appeared to be bleeding from maroon veins. A sign on an abandoned cement mixer read, UTAH VOTE NOT FOR HILLARY, as if, summer of 2013, she'd already declared her candidacy, the primaries were in full swing, and there was one chance in a billion that Utah might *not* vote NOT for Hillary. The rocks had turned pink again now, closer to what we'd seen in Moab. In Capitol Reef National Park there were Swiss cheese holes in the cliff sides, and pellets—armchair sized—of dark pebbles strewn on top of the sandstone, like crumb-cake crust.

I was hungry.

Soon, we were ascending into the clouds, literally, the scenic overlooks on State Route 12 of little use because of a dense fog, though we stopped long enough at one of them to read a placard saying that this was the last part of America to be mapped.

Of all the places on this vast section of the continent, we were standing in what was arguably the last American place left alone, in the shadows, in mystery, undeveloped, unused. Free.

The idea of that seemed strange and wonderful to me. I felt then that I had entered unmapped territory myself, though it was interior territory. This new place in me was unspectacular, not suitable for any particular designation, nowhere that would attract hordes of tourists, and yet, in its mystery and anonymity it felt like a door to some secret room. It was as if I'd parked the car and walked off into the wilderness, but there were no dangers, no rattlers or wolves, just peaceful Alpine fields where one might walk or camp anywhere one wanted.

A strange side effect of all this was that I didn't want to look at Rinpoche. I don't know exactly why. We were descending now, coming down out of the clouds beneath an unsettled sky that showed flashes of blue. Three deer stood nonchalantly beside the road. Then sunlight streamed through, lighting up a carpet of yellow wildflowers as if setting them ablaze. I knew that my wise companion had led me to this interior place, through years of small nudges and larger shoves, books, comments, meditation tips, and, mainly, by his example. But now that I'd arrived in this happy unmapped territory, I didn't want to look at him. I was worried he might tell me, *No good, Otto. Do not stay in this place.* And I wanted to stay there.

We left Dixie National Forest, passed Anasazi Indian Village State Park, saw llamas in a field to our right, and palomino ponies grazing there. It was late afternoon, the temperature back up in the low seventies, and we were curling along a canyon bottom now, looking up at rocks that reminded me of light-tan cake batter poured into a pan and not yet touched with a spoon. There were dead trees here—the arthritic hands of tortured souls—and then we found our resting place, the Slot Canyons Inn, and were still for a while.

Thirty-seven

At the Slot Canyons Inn our host went by the unusual name of Joette Marie. She showed Rinpoche and me to a two-bedroom suite just off the wraparound porch. Jacuzzi tub. Fireplace. King bed for me with a large-screen TV, and a separate room for Rinpoche behind the curtain. On our various road trips together, we'd developed a routine: Upon checking in to a new place we left each other alone for half an hour or so, settled in, read, meditated, sent e-mails or texts. It was our way of giving each other a respite from our constant, if good, company.

I flicked on the TV for a few minutes, just long enough to hear more about the Syrian government's chemical attack on its own people, then opened my computer and read through a few new e-mails. There were notes from Anthony and Tash. And, from my wonderful sister, the following:

> **Dear Brother, We've all been tracing your route on the map on the kitchen wall and wish we could be with you. We are well. No need to worry. I have a favor to ask you. I'd like you to take my beloved husband to Las Vegas. Though**

I don't think Rinpoche will like it much, I think it's important for him to see that part of America. Would you do that?

My response:

Dear Seese, I'm glad you are all okay. I miss all of you very much. But I have to tell you I think the Vegas idea is the worst one you've come up with in a long time. And that's saying something. You know how much I love and admire your husband—more each time I take a trip with him—but I have to tell you that it seems to me he might have a little gambling addiction thing going on. I haven't confronted him about it but it worries me. Taking him to Vegas would be like taking a reformed alcoholic to a bar. I was thinking more along the lines of Taos or Sedona.

Her reply:

Otto: I had a vision, a very, very strong vision, that you should go to Las Vegas.

I held myself back from writing this: *You had a very strong vision that we should go into the mountains, too. We did. And absolutely nothing came of it.* And out of a calmer, kinder place, wrote:

How about Salt Lake City as a compromise?

Neither my sister nor I are the compromising type:

Brother, really. This isn't the kind of vision to ignore. I'm not worried about the gambling.
I'll make a deal with you: If you go to Vegas I'll pay for Natasha to fly down there as a birthday present. It's supposed to be more family oriented than it used to be. You can see a show, swim in the hotel pool. Natasha is dying to spend time with you. Please!!!!????

I reclined on the king bed with my head propped on the pillows and the computer on my lap and felt an old big wave of aggravation rising up over me. *Story of my life* was the phrase that came to mind. Or *our* lives, at least. For as long as I could remember, my sister had been shunted this way and that across the continent by various visions, ideas, boyfriends, jobs, notions, gurus, offers, enthusiasms, and wacky plans. One time she settled in northern California, in the college town of Chico, simply because she'd pulled off the road to get gas there and a man selling flowers from a roadside stand had smiled at her! She was a gorgeous woman. At the time she'd been in her mid-twenties. Men smiling at her was not a rare occurrence, but she took that particular smile as a sign, and she rented an apartment, and found a job, and stayed almost a year.

Out of this vapor of lunatic notions she would periodically contact Jeannie and me and ask us to do this or that. It was never about money—Seese had always paid her own way—but these requests usually involved some minor inconvenience. She wanted me to send her a particular photo of us when we were kids; she wondered if Jeannie could possibly make a batch of cookies and deliver it to her spiritual friend in Queens; was there any chance we could house-sit two of her cats for a year while she sailed to Jamaica with her new boyfriend; could we please help her find a good lawyer for Jake, who'd been wrongly accused of selling speed. Etc., etc., etc.

Since she'd married Rinpoche these requests had all but disappeared, but now here was another one. Las Vegas of all places. I'd been there twice for book conferences and once as a college student on a crazy road trip and I had never quite managed to see the appeal of the place. People I knew went to Vegas on their honeymoons, or saved up all year for a week of slots, shows, and buffets, or chose it as a place for a family reunion. I associated it with noise and alcohol, with mindless distraction and moneymadness; in short, the polar opposite of the types of things I considered spiritual.

So, naturally, after pondering for a while, I wrote back and said:

> Okay, sure. Two nights maximum on the condition I am able to spend time with my daughter. . . . But you owe me.

> Dear Brother! The best brother of all time! No wonder Rinpoche says so many good things about your spirit-heart!!!!

Spirit-heart, I thought. That was perfectly Cecelia. I signed off with love, as always, but at that point it wasn't my spirit-heart I was concerned about; it was my spirit-stomach.

Thirty-eight

This may sound immodest, but I consider myself a pizza aficionado. As is the case with all my other culinary tastes, I'm not particularly interested in gourmet, just good. I don't care if the maker of the pizza uses artisanal cheese or a whole-grain crust or adds some unexpected topping like butternut squash or andouille sausage; what I care about is that the pizza is made with care and suits my taste. When we used to go to Cape Cod we'd often find these "pseudo pizzas" as I called them—much to the amusement of my children, who ate them with delight and considered me a snob—often made, it seemed, by Greeks (I adore Greek food, and I admire the Greeks' passion for cooking, but I think they should stick to stuffed grape leaves and moussaka and gyro and baklava and leave the pizzas to their fellow Mediterraneans). These pseudo pizzas had thick, doughy crusts and too much cheese. But even the Italians don't always get it right. In Venice on our one visit we found the pizzas to be fairly good but the crust to resemble matzo (again, I love Jewish cuisine, am particularly fond of a good knish, but it wasn't the Italians who fled across the desert and needed unleavened bread). This, in Italy, was a particular disappointment, but it turns out there are, when it comes to food, at least two Italys, and my taste in pizza runs more to the Neapolitan.

The problem with pizza is the problem with driving: Almost anybody can do it, but not so many people can do it well. Lovemaking, the same. Any two people can jump into a bed. Anyone can throw some cheese and tomato sauce on a circular piece of dough and slide it into an oven. But to make the perfect crust (thin, but not too thin, bubbles at the edge, but not too big bubbles), to use real mozzarella so that strings stretch from mouth to table, to get the tomato-to-cheese ratio just right (roughly 3.4 to 2), and most important, to create a pie that is oily without being greasy . . . this is an art form. Whole books have been written on the subject of making the perfect pizza. I know: I edited two of them.

At seven-thirty p.m., after our solitary hour was finished, Rinpoche and I wandered through the main part of the house and out onto the Slot Canyons Inn's back patio, which was pressed up tight against a natural wall of brown stone and covered with a canvas roof held up by poles. There, a young mother named Mandy served us an excellent spinach-artichoke dip accompanied by a just-baked baguette and then a good, perhaps very good but not quite excellent, oven-fired pizza with onions on top. Rinpoche, who had a particular fancy for onions, ate one slice of the pie, and I ate the rest, contemplatively. I badly wanted a beer but I held back, ate slowly, and enjoyed the sight of Roscoe, the inn's Catahoula, who wandered from table to table, begging with great dignity. I slipped him some food, of course. Among my other weaknesses: I am constitutionally incapable of refusing a begging dog.

This particular Catahoula—a breed famous for its ability to hunt wild boar and other mammals and to herd cows—looked like an overgrown beagle, with the same floppy ears and sorrowful eyes. To me, all dogs are irresistible, but Roscoe was particularly so. As soon as we checked in he'd come and sat on the porch outside our door, waiting patiently for a bit of affection. I gave him that, in spades, and gave him bites of the baguette and then a mouthful or two of the pizza.

We also enjoyed a conversation with Mandy. A single mother of two kids, she worked full-time at the electric company and several nights a week at the inn. On that night, her fourteen-year-old son was with her parents, bow-hunting deer and elk. Her six-year-old daughter liked to sleep outdoors under the stars and pestered to be taught to shoot a gun with the same passion that my Natasha had pestered to be taught to drive a car when she was about to turn sixteen. "I love hunting, too," Mandy told us. "I can't wait to get back out there."

"This is not New York," I told Rinpoche when Mandy had left us to our meal. "In New York we tend to look down on people who hunt. It's a savage activity, barbaric . . . and we say this as we're ordering our pasta with venison sausage at some upscale bistro in the West Village."

He nodded with his mouth full, let out a small grunt.

"We'd no more sleep out under the stars, with all that darkness and all those snakes, than we'd root for a Boston sports team, and yet we think nothing of crossing a Manhattan street while the DO NOT WALK sign is on, or going up to the eightieth floor of a building in a metal box."

More nodding, a swallow, a sip of water.

"Until recently I would have said that the great thing about America, the great and unique thing, is

377

that we're really a dozen countries all sewn together by a fluke of history, and yet we seem to get along well and feel a certain sense of patriotic unity. Lately, though, I'm not so sure. Somehow this awful political divide has formed, a Grand Canyon separating the two Americas. We used to be able to talk across that divide. Then for a while we used to be able to shout across it. Now we're so far apart we just stand on one bank or the other and yell insults up into the air. It worries me, I have to say."

More nodding. Rinpoche said, "I like wery much what you tell me these things about America, my friend. I like to understand this country."

"I love the place," I said. "But I have to say lately I wonder if we might be just another of history's great empires on the downward slope."

"I don't understand this."

"All the great empires in history—the Incas, the Aztecs, Persia, Greece, Rome, Portugal, Spain, Britain, the Soviet Union—had their moment in history where they were powerful and thriving, and then something happened and they went into a slide and either were conquered and overrun or just slowly lost their zip, their edge. Slowly declined and ended up either out of business altogether or as just another country."

"All comes from the mind," Rinpoche said.

"I suppose."

"There is the individual karma and the, how you say, collection?"

"Collective."

"Collective karma. Sometimes, in the collective karma, the thinking makes a change. Seems wery small. Just thoughts in a mind. Just things people say. But with a millions of people this makes in the history a big change."

"And what can you do about it? I'm not going to run for the senate, not going to start a talk-radio show. If I write a book—which I've been thinking about doing lately, for some reason—it's not going to be a book that changes the collective karma."

"Everybody has a thing they supposed to do in this life."

"I feel like I've done it. My thing was to raise good children and I've done that. Since they've gone out of the house I feel empty. Without purpose."

"Maybe some new purpose coming."

"Maybe."

"What book you wanna write?"

"I don't know. About food, probably. That's my area of expertise, more or less. The problem is, after all these years of editing food books I'd have trouble coming up with a new idea. So many areas have been so thoroughly covered. Any suggestions?"

"Write the book about America!"

"Big subject."

"Sure. But maybe the book to change the American karma. More focus on the world inside."

"The thought stream."

"Sure."

"All books do that, to some degree, don't you think? Maybe that's the whole purpose of the book, moving a tiny rivulet of the communal thought stream a little this way or that way. Every movie. Every song. Every radio and TV show. Maybe every word and every action of every citizen moves it a little this way or that."

"Big responsibility, being a person."

"Can make you nuts if you think about it."

"Sure. Just do the laughing meditation little bit every day."

We fell silent for a bit, Rinpoche sitting with his arms crossed over his big chest, and yours truly churning through the last two slices of pizza. Just to the left of my left foot Roscoe assumed a new pose—balancing on his spine, belly up, forepaws bent at the wrist, head turned slightly toward me, and eyes wide and pleading. It seemed to me a version of the laughing meditation. "You," I told him, "have a great future in film."

"I miss my dog," I said to Rinpoche. "There's no love like the love a dog gives you."

"You give food, you touch, you make him not too cold and not too hot and everything okay."

"And here we are, the master species, wanting ninety-seven million different things to be just a certain way. More oil on the pizza, a green car instead of a black one, a new face, another trip, a granite countertop. Always more money, no matter how much we have."

Rinpoche flexed his lips but made no other sign.

The words "more money" caused me to think of gambling and to recall, with some pain, the recent e-mail exchange with my sister. The memory of it was something like a bureau-sized alien spacecraft coming in for a landing just on the far side of Roscoe's belly. It sat there, looking completely out of place on the inn's peaceful patio, in the windless desert night, amid talk of deer hunting, communal karma, and the Great American Book. It was impossible to ignore. I hoped Rinpoche would say something to move the conversation in a new direction, away from the alien craft, but he was silent. I fussed with the last crumbs of pizza crust, asked Mandy for a water refill, sneaked glances at a young couple having what appeared to be a contentious discussion on the other side of the patio. At last, I cleared my throat and said, "Um," and then, two seconds later, "I just had an e-mail exchange with your wonderful wife."

"Wery wonderful," he said. "You and me, wonderful wifes we got."

"You miss her."

"Big," he said, spreading his arms wide as if he needed, at that moment, some body-to-body affection. He reached down for Roscoe and lifted the Catahoula onto his lap. Roscoe didn't resist.

"Yes, very good woman . . . except that she wants me to take you to Las Vegas."

"What is this, Lost Wegas?"

"Las Vegas. It's a city. In Nevada. Maybe, I don't know, five or six hours' drive from here. The problem is, if I had to pick one American city that seems unspiritual, Las Vegas would be at the top of the list. Nothing else even close. Lot of prostitution, drugs, gambling."

"The machines?"

"It's pretty much where the gambling machines were invented. There are machines in the gas stations, in the convenience stores, in the airport. There are dozens of hotels with casinos in them, huge casinos."

"I think," he said carefully, thoughtfully, stroking Roscoe's head, "that Lost Wegas is important for me to know about America."

"There's no place like it, really."

"Tomorrow we go then."

"Okay. Fine. Seese will be happy."

"The machines," he said, with a particular glint in his eye. "The other ones, too, we can try. Cards. Like that."

"Cards, dice, sports betting, whatever you want. I'm not going to worry about it anymore.

But, if you lose too much money, please just stop, okay?"

"I win," he said.

"Yes, so far. But that doesn't always last."

Rinpoche nodded without much conviction. I was tired of fighting and tried to tell myself that, unless he had massive sums in the bank, or a huge limit on his credit cards, there was only so much money Rinpoche could lose in a day or two.

Still, when we paid and thanked Mandy and complimented the two young men working the pizza ovens and went back to our suite, I sat outside on the deck for a while and looked at the stars and pondered. It seemed to me that I'd become rather passive since Jeannie died. Seese wanted me to go into the mountains with her husband, so I went. She wanted me to go to Las Vegas, so I went. What would be next? Skydiving? Moving to Thailand? Opening a frozen yogurt shop in Dickinson? At that point—it must have been the Froyo idea—the power went out and the inn's lights died. Through the open window I could hear Rinpoche snoring lightly in his sleep and I looked up into the sky and saw more stars than I saw in a year in Bronxville. A nice new peacefulness settled over me. In the midst of that peace I understood that I was a drifting man. It wasn't so unpleasant to drift. I had enough money; I'd never want for food. Yes, I was lonely, but Jeannie had told me she wanted me to date other women after she was gone, and though I'd resisted the idea for two years now, it was starting to seem like something I might try. I wouldn't tell Natasha and Anthony at first, wouldn't get involved in anything too serious. But I'd have some company at least. I could take in a show, a symphony, go out to dinner again without feeling like the Solitary Man every moment of my life. Sex didn't matter as much to me as it once had. And probably it wouldn't be a sexual relationship in any case, not for a while. What I wanted was the company of a woman.

But how else to fill the time? Dating was all well and good, but one didn't date from breakfast until bedtime. Where was my purpose in life now? What was I supposed to do, beyond the meditation practice and keeping the house more or less in order? I'd mentioned the idea of writing a book but, really, that was pure fantasy. There were plenty of books in the world already—food books and otherwise. And probably I didn't have the self-discipline. And, even if I did, it was such solitary work, exactly what I didn't need.

I looked up into the blackness, dusted with stars, and I said, "Honey, if you can hear me, send me a little advice now. I'm fifty-two. I could live to be eighty or ninety and what am I going to do with myself for all those decades? No one wants to hire a fifty-two-year-old ex-editor, and I'm not sure I want to go back to working full-time in any case. I'd give anything to be able to sit down with a glass of wine and talk this over with you. I'm adrift. Help me out if you can."

The stars glistened and shifted. Roscoe came by to say good-night. I scratched his ears for a while then went in and lay on my bed in the unelectrified blackness and soon fell asleep.

Thirty-nine

In the morning Rinpoche was not to be found so I enjoyed a serving of Joette's delicious sausage-and-egg concoction with my coffee and talked with her for a while about Mormonism. At its essence it seemed to me not so very different from the other associations human beings had put together in order to face the baffling predicament in which we found ourselves. There was a central figure/holy man—Joseph Smith, in this case. There was a story, embellished, perhaps, of illumination and struggle. There were rules set in place to provide some guidance, to suggest limits on the massive array of choices we all faced. There were even, Joette told me, culinary suggestions: that Mormons should eat lots of fruits and vegetables and only a little meat. She was a kind and friendly woman, and, just as I finished breakfast, she handed me a *Book of Mormon* as a gift.

Since Rinpoche was still AWOL, and since we had an hour before checkout, I sat in a straight-backed chair in our room and had myself a long meditation. Perhaps the only way I can describe the strange pleasure of that hour, the joy of the settled mind, is to contrast it with its opposite. We've all had times—often in the middle of a sleepless night—when the mind races and races, thoughts coming in a waterfall of words and images, a billion droplets of worry, fear, frustration, or desire. My meditation that day was the polar opposite of all that, a stretch of interior openness and ease. When I heard the scrape of Rinpoche's sandals on the porch and opened my eyes, I was shocked to see that an hour had passed; it seemed like minutes; or, truer still, it seemed as if time had loosened its grip on my life entirely. Yes, it churned steadily on. And yes, it wrought the unpleasant changes I could already see and feel in my body: hair growing where I didn't want it and not growing where I wanted it; aches; stiffness; the graying, the wrinkling, the once fine set of teeth turning not so fine. But, for a little while at least, those seemed merely like chapters in a book with no end, an interesting book, intriguing even, with painful passages and funny passages, always moving, yes, true, but not toward anything that stood still forever and ever. During that hour and the hours immediately following, death seemed like nothing more than a dip in a cold ocean. One resurfaced after the shock of it. One kept going, on and on, in a different form, no doubt, but the form didn't matter to me then.

In that state of mind I felt reconnected to my wife.

At nine a.m. the great spiritual master and I loaded up the SUV and set out across the dry and rocky surfaces of Joseph Smith's state. According to the temperature gauge it was 65 degrees. In Tropic, Utah, we stopped for coffee at the Bryce Canyon Inn, a little oasis of sophisticated bean brewing set amid orange-hued hills. We cut across one edge of Bryce Canyon itself, where the stones were the color of salmon flesh, and as we left Route 12 for 895, with the sky brightening a bit, we passed a sign contending that Orderville, Utah, was THE HOME OF THE HO-MADE PIES (a choice slice of Americana I did not even attempt to explain to my traveling companion).

At the entrance to Zion National Park, beneath a suddenly darkening sky, we were informed by a ranger named Lance Cleaver, who bore an eerie resemblance to the Red Sox–turned–Yankee outfielder Johnny Damon, that the twenty-five-dollar entrance fee was waived because that day was the ninety-seventh anniversary of the founding of the national parks.

Zion greeted us with a mile-long tunnel, then a

switchback road that led in downward curlicues into a cliff-ringed valley so grand, so king-sized, so surreal, that it was all I could do, on the hairpin turns, to keep my eyes on the rear end of the Winnebago in front of us. Rinpoche was literally oohing and aahing. Zion had been drawn on the scale of the giants, all greens and grays, massive. We pulled into the visitor center and hiked up the Watchman Trail in a light rain, Rinpoche holding an umbrella and yours truly wearing a water-proof jacket. It was like hiking through an anteroom to ordinary life, an enclave, a private, U-shaped, mountain-fringed wonderland. We went along a not very steep, slick, rocky path with the faces of cliffs rising to our immediate left and a hilly pastureland to our right leading to the base of another cliff. We saw a bighorn sheep picking its way through the rocky slopes there, and by the time we'd circled back to the car my boots were caked with red mud and Rinpoche was holding his sandals in one hand, the umbrella in the other, and carrying clods of earth on the bare soles of his feet. He laughed about this, of course, and I laughed with him. The rain was falling harder. We were doing the laughing meditation, washing feet and boots in a parking lot puddle, chortling like boys in some baptismal ceremony for the free-minded and slightly loony.

The whole day to that point had been suffused with the fragrance of a strange other life, so it seemed only fitting that, in rain that was now a true deluge, we discovered a Thai restaurant just beyond Zion's gates. On the wall hung a photograph of a decidedly androgynous Buddha, sitting in meditation and looking fierce, confident, all powerful, one who'd loosed the chains of suffering and death. Nearby stood a small altar on which the owners had placed offerings of fruit and candles. This, at the gates to an American National Park, really and truly. Pad Thai in rural Utah, honestly. Oh blessed day.

Soon, drying out slowly, we were in Virgin, Utah, where there was Virgin Books, Virgin Goods, Virgin Cactus Jelly, and so on. The rain eased there, just as we reached the town of Hurricane (I could not possibly make this up). There was a handmade sign for RON PAUL REVOLUTION and then a stretch of reddish stones topped with smaller black stones, like pepper grains on loaves of bread.

"You had, this morning, the special meditation," Rinpoche said, without turning to look at me.

"How did you know?"

"Your face."

"The world seems a bit different to me today, a bit surreal."

"Like the dream, yes?"

"Something like that."

"Feels like if you die it doesn't so much matter anymore, yes."

"Yes. . . . Though I'd be sad not to see my kids get a bit farther into adulthood before I go."

"You will see many things before you go, my friend, before you move across from this world. I see this. My good wife see it."

"Some of the things she sees don't exactly work out the way she sees them, though, if you don't mind me saying so."

"You be surprised."

I left it there. On that day I was open to all mysteries, to an encyclopedia of unlikely outcomes. Having found good pad Thai in Utah, I supposed that all surprises were on the table. All my sister's wacky visions might turn out to be true. Ron Paul might be elected president and there might actually be some doubt, three years down the road, as to whether Utah would vote for or against Hillary Clinton.

In the city of St. George, there were McMansions on the buttes and a strip of the kinds of things we hadn't seen in a while—fast-food eating places, palm trees, landscaped developments surrounded by stucco walls, traffic. According to the news, 85 percent of Americans were against involvement in the Syrian civil war; we were approaching the fiftieth anniversary of Martin Luther King's March on Washington; a group of people who called themselves "Sovereign Citizens" were putting false liens on judges, marshals, and sheriffs to ruin their credit ratings; and a five-year-old girl with cystic fibrosis, whose parents had had to fight a legal battle to get her a lung transplant, was going home from the hospital, not quite ready to cross into that next world. It was, in other words, the human circus, amusing or tragic, depending on your viewpoint and your place in the karmic parade.

We were gliding down out of the mountains now, with the Virgin River winding in and out of view and the faces of gray cliffs in shadow and sunlight. The descent went on and on, great dry swoops out of the high country, and then, at last, it ceased, and we were running across flat desert. The second we crossed the Nevada border we found ourselves in a different circus tent. The Eureka Casino. The Oasis Resort. And then, PRISON AREA. HITCHHIKING PROHIBITED. Las Vegas's tall, steely hotels lay visible in the western distance, covered by what seemed to be a fog of sin. There was the Love Store, open twenty-four hours. There was a billboard advertising THUNDER DOWN UNDER, some kind of Australian men strippers show. A billboard advising, ARRESTED? LAWYER UP. Another for THE CHEETAH TOPLESS CLUB. The next for ULTIMATE FIGHTING, and then, of course, one that read, BE NOT DECEIVED—GOD IS NOT TO BE MOCKED.

I asked Rinpoche if he could sense the

difference between the state we'd just entered and the one we'd just left.

"Sure," he said. "One lets you play the machines, and one maybe not."

Forty

Strangely, however, when we'd located the Vegas strip and then the Monte Carlo hotel and carried our bags up to the twentieth floor (we'd requested two rooms and been given a suite for Rinpoche, a two-bed double for me), Rinpoche expressed exactly zero interest in visiting the casino. He wanted to swim, he said.

It was late afternoon, mid-eighties, a cool day for Vegas in August. Still, the extensive swimming complex was crowded, all the chaises occupied or reserved, couples drinking from thirty-ounce margaritas, a few kids watched over by lifeguards who might have worked as fashion models in their off hours.

The Monte Carlo swimming complex offered something called a "lazy river," a form of entertainment unknown to me prior to that afternoon. Encased in cement, this chlorinated stream, six feet wide, four deep, carried its revelers in a large, irregular circle. Rinpoche and I rented inner tubes and waded in. The problem, it turned out, was how to mount the inner tube. After watching others for a moment, Rinpoche thought he had it figured out. He set the inner tube on the surface of the water, held it in place with one hand, and then leapt up and sideways, aiming, ass first, for the tube's center hole. He missed. Or partly missed. His weight landed on the inflated rubber ring in such a way that it ricocheted up and away from him, landing in the laps of two men and a woman who were sitting on the tiled edge enjoying what appeared to be their fourth or fifth margarita. They were not pleased. "Sorry, sorry," Rinpoche told them once he'd surfaced again. "Wery sorry." One of the men shoved the tire back at him; none of them spoke.

Rinpoche tried again. I observed, ready to intervene in case the inebriated trio completely lost patience with him. This time he managed to get into the center of the tube, but there was another problem: As he floated away I saw that one leg was stuck down in the donut hole, and the other hooked over the top. Off he went, one leg up, one down, making, in his pink Speedo, a magnificent fashion statement.

We spent half an hour like that, floating in circles past bikini-clad, huge-breasted women who might or might not have worked for the escort service we'd seen advertised on passing pickups; past drunken thirty-year-olds in small gangs; past fathers and mothers herding their children along. I was the oldest person there, and, except for the kids and Rinpoche, undoubtedly the most sober. The smell of chlorine, the squeak of rubber, the enormous drinks, the casinos lurking on the other side of swinging glass doors—what on earth were we doing here? Considering this question, I began to suspect some kind of trick. Seese and Rinpoche had cooked up another "wesson" for me, and just when things in the interior world seemed to have taken such a kindly turn. That was the deal, then: The motto of the spiritual life was No Rest.

I'd stay alert, I told myself. One step ahead of them. In this world of Thunder Down Under and Girls Who Will Come to Your Room in Twenty Minutes and topless clubs and bottomless buffets and twenty-four-hour hundred-dollar blackjack, I'd keep my sanity, hold tight to my new peace of mind, resist judgment and distraction.

Rinpoche paddled up close and grabbed onto my right big toe. "Later we play the machines," he said.

And I said, "Sure. This is Vegas, after all. What would be the point of going to Vegas and not playing the machines?"

Something was afoot.

Forty-one

But, of course, you can't be ready for the things life throws at you. Not really. Not entirely. Being ready in that way would be like trying to cling to a particular state of the meditative experience, or like trying to stay young all your life. It would mean stopping the roulette wheel of time on your number and having the dealer pay and pay and pay without ceasing while the sirens sounded and lights flashed. It would be the extinction of surprise, which would mean the absence of learning. The world is not made that way.

Rinpoche and I went upstairs, showered off the chlorine, and changed into our walking-around outfits. His robe and sandals, my shorts, jersey, and tennis shoes. Outdoors again, in a lazy river of tourists, we made a promenade along the strip, where red-faced men and women sat on the pedestrian overpasses with signs like this: WHY LIE? I WANT MONEY FOR BEER. YOU PAY, I'LL DRINK. and RAIN WASHED OUT MY CAMPING SPOT. ANYTHING HELPS.

Very small Mexican men and women stood mid-sidewalk, flapping strip-club cards in just the way they did in Midtown Manhattan. We passed a young guy wearing a T-shirt that read: COVER

ME IN CHOCOLATE AND THROW ME TO THE LESBIANS. Loud music blared from speakers in front of souvenir shops. Hawkers sold tickets to country-music shows and excursions to the Hoover Dam. There were women in tiny skirts and tall heels. A fake Statue of Liberty. A fake Arc de Triomphe. Beside me I could feel Rinpoche taking it all in, making mental notes, maybe, for a future "speaking." It was a museum of appetites, a promise of FUN, whether your idea of fun was the roller coaster roaring on its tracks near the Monte Carlo, the exotic dancing clubs on the edge of town, the escorts, the clubs, the chain restaurants, the jewelry shops, or even the glass-walled chapel, where a couple exchanged vows while a small crowd gathered on the sidewalk to watch. That, in particular, seemed so tawdry and sad to me. Were they actors, being paid to pretend to swear fidelity? Were they drunk? Were they really making a mockery of marriage that way?

We took a break from it all for a superb Indian meal in a second-floor restaurant set back from the revelry behind a courtyard with booths selling belts and hats. We walked some more, strolled through the Venetian with its fake canals, three-year-old frescoes, and phony gondoliers; we stood for a while in front of the fountain display near the Bellagio.

And then Rinpoche said he was ready for the machines.

Up the entrance ramp we went, past the illuminated hundred-foot-high fountains, past the stretch limos and glamorous women, past the midwestern families of four and the T-shirted couples, and into the Bellagio's lobby. There were tiled walls, vases of exotic flowers posed on marble tables, chandeliers, leather sofas and chairs in a comfortable arrangement . . . and a few steps to our right, thc casino. Rinpoche moved toward it like a conquering emperor and we wandered for a while, savoring the atmosphere—the lights, the bells, the neon, the somber men at blackjack, and the lively scene at craps. And then, as if drawn and held there by an evil magnetism, he hovered near something called the Big Six, a roulette-like wheel with plastic-encased one-, five-, ten-, and twenty-dollar bills instead of numbers. After a moment, he took a seat on a high stool and I joined him, watching, ready for a lesson, telling myself not to worry. He purchased one hundred dollars' worth of ten-dollar chips and fielded the most curious of glances from the Thai woman behind the felt. It seemed to me that she'd given him the Evil Eye. On the first spin he lost twenty dollars. On the second spin he lost twenty more. On the third spin, enthusiasm untempered, he lost twenty again. More than half his cash gone in the space of two minutes. I was secretly glad, I admit it. He then placed three chips on the joker, at forty-to-one, and the wheel spun and spun, flashing, flashing, promising great things. Gradually, inexorably, the forces of friction took over and the wheel slowed, clicked, the rubber tongue bending one last time over one last pin and coming to rest . . . on a two-dollar bill one notch beyond the joker.

Unperturbed, Rinpoche fondled the last two chips, made them into a short stack, and set the stack on the five-dollar spot. The dealer yanked on the wheel, the bills blended into a glassy blur. A man pushed in too close on my right. I suspected a pickpocket and reached for my wallet and at that moment saw that he was Asian, built like a wine barrel, with hair cut in a low bristle a quarter inch above his scalp. He was dressed in a dark sport coat and dark shirt and he was looking at me with the blank expression of a killer. The wheel slowed, I could hear it, but I was no longer looking at it. I was looking over the man's shoulder at his twin, or something like his twin, who was standing on the far side of Rinpoche. I saw that he'd put one hand under the back of Rinpoche's arm. "Now you come with us," I thought I heard him say. The wheel clicked in a dying rhythm. I heard the dealer announce, "Ten." There was a hand on *my* arm now. I stood and tried to shake it free but the man did not let go. A thick neck. Steady black eyes. He seemed amused. "Come with us now."

"I will like hell come with you!" I said, perhaps

too loudly. The dealer looked up, ready to summon security. The other gamblers stared. Rinpoche had turned around on his stool and was standing now, too. "No," I half shouted. "We're not going."

"Come now," Rinpoche's man said, rather gently, I thought, but, at the same time, in a tone that offered very little chance for disagreement. This was it, then. These were Natasha's parking-lot Chinese goons. We were about to be thrown into the back of the tinted-window SUV and driven into the Nevada desert. We'd be interrogated there, tortured, left to the vultures. The Chinese assassins would then find their way to our loved ones. A hundred scenes from various violent films showed in my brain.

Rinpoche was his usual calm self. The four of us shifted position so that we were a few steps away from the stools at the Big Six and I said, in a quavering voice, "Whatever you want to ask us you can ask right here."

The man holding my arm gave me a small smile. His friend said to Rinpoche, "Ila Rinpoche is upstairs. She would like to speak with you."

"Rinpoche, it's a trick."

"No, no, fine," he told me. "No problem. We go, Otto. I know about this person. Don't worry."

My Asian friend released my arm and put a hand on my back, guiding me in the direction of the elevators. I calmed down by about 3 percent. The elevator arrived. We stepped in. I found it somewhat reassuring that the men were no longer gripping our arms and that several other people —three drunken guys with RONALDINHO T-shirts—had squeezed in with us. They exited at the nineteenth floor. We went all the way to the top. If the assassins took us out onto the roof. . . .

But the two men led us to a door marked PRESIDENTIAL SUITE, and infected perhaps by Rinpoche's confident posture and by the odd gentleness of the two legbreakers, I'd gone from red alert to orange. One of the men knocked. The door opened. We stepped into yet another bizarre Las Vegas tableau, a luxurious living room that had been turned into some kind of temple. There were bright crimson, blue, and gold sheets of cloth hanging from the walls, statuettes of the Buddha on side tables. Until I saw those brass Buddhas, and perhaps even for a second after seeing them, I worried that the forces of evil had brought us there for a mass murder. The spiritual lineage to which my brother-in-law belonged would be extinguished now, in Las Vegas of all places, the final insult.

All this happened—as things do in these cases— in a minuscule portion of a second. I had time only to feel a last cold wash of fear and then, as if it were background music in a film, I heard a voice speaking words that sounded like this: *Ys din diim patdr*? and then I heard a one-word response—*haie*, in a voice I knew. I turned toward the far end of the long room in time to see Shelsa practically sprinting across the carpet. She leapt into her father's arms and for just a moment Rinpoche's impregnable fortress of calm cracked open. There was a glint of moisture in his eyes, a glistening lens of the tenderest love. He held his daughter against him, twirled her in a circle, all the while making a sound like, "Haaaaaah!"

My turn next. The glorious embrace. The "I missed you so much, Uncle Ott!" And then Shelsa had her feet on the ground again—she seemed to have grown a few inches in our brief absence—and was taking my hand and turning me toward a middle-aged woman sitting near the windows. This woman, wearing a gold-trimmed robe not unlike Rinpoche's, sat on a meditation cushion that had been placed on a platform raised a foot above the carpet.

Rinpoche bowed to her, so I did the same. I suddenly felt grossly underdressed. The body-guards had stayed near the door. Rinpoche and I were motioned onto cushions. I would have felt more at ease by then except for the fact that the woman four feet in front of me bore a frightening, a terrible, a spectacularly eerie resemblance to the framed Buddha on the wall of the Thai restaurant at the entrance to Zion. She rested her eyes on my eyes—not even glancing at my shorts and running shoes—then on Rinpoche, and while she was assessing us, or greeting us, or blessing us in this fashion, Shelsa sat down beside her, on a second cushion. This seemed strange to me, that she should sit with a stranger instead of with her father. It was almost as if she'd found her place in the world, as if every dust mote in the room was now offering formal recognition that she was, in fact, something more than a cute and loving little girl.

When the woman spoke it was in English and in a voice as quiet as summer wind on a field of grass. There was an accent, unlike Rinpoche's, and I will not try to replicate it here except in her first sentence, which was: "Iss goud goud dhat you kaim."

I could not seem to squeeze out a syllable.

"Do you know who I am?" she asked, speaking into my silence. She was looking at me with a peculiar warm intensity.

I shook my head, no. I was sitting cross-legged, not in the full lotus position, of course. The outsides of my knees were already beginning to hurt but I barely paid attention to that because the woman was mesmeric. Calm to the thirtieth power. The air close to her face was vibrating, I'm sure of that. I could not stop looking.

"I am Ila Rinpoche."

"I'm Otto," I managed. "Ringling. Volya Rinpoche here is married to my sister," I gestured to my right like a fool.

She smiled beatifically. "I know."

I kept watching her.

She said, "I work with His Holiness. The men you met are my bodyguards."

"Oh." I looked at Rinpoche, who had turned toward me, eyebrows raised, amused. I felt, for some reason, very young.

"We have been trying to find you for one week now. You move around very much!"

"Road trip," I said, stupidly. I could feel my heart slamming about in my chest and throat. I shot another sideways glance at Rinpoche, who had turned his face forward. In profile he looked the way he always looked, patient, at peace, pleased, mildly curious, unsurprised. I thought I saw him wink at Shelsa. I wanted Ila Rinpoche to stop staring at me, and at last she shifted her eyes to Rinpoche, and I saw something there that was—well, *love* is the word that comes to mind, though at the same time I was almost certain they'd never met. To say she saw him as an equal doesn't quite do it justice. She seemed to see him as herself. Shelsa reached out and put a hand on Ila Rinpoche's knee and there was so much pure affection there that I wondered—this is the slithering energy I carried into that room—if my sister would feel jealous.

"I wanted to find you and tell you in person," Ila said.

Rinpoche nodded. Confident. Unsurprised.

Tell you what? I thought, but I was biting down hard on my tongue.

"The child has been born," she then said, shifting her eyes to me and holding them there.

I heard Rinpoche say, "Wery good," in a pleased tone.

The woman turned back to me. Her eyes were black and bottomless. Kind, but, it seemed to me, capable of severity. In service of the truth, perhaps, but severity nonetheless. "Do you understand?"

"Not really. No. I don't understand any of this, actually. None of it. My sister—"

"A great teacher has been reincarnated. We knew this would happen, and when it would happen, but it has taken some time for us to find exactly where. Now we have done that. This spirit and Shelsa should meet now. You are to help them manage this."

"Me?" I said. "Where? I mean, the reincarnated. . . . I mean, where is this person?"

"In Italy," Ila Rinpoche said, "in a secret place." And then she added these famous, unsettling, and unforgettable words: "In the mountains." She paused without moving her eyes from me. I kept looking into those eyes, which seemed to open onto worlds as vast as the Nebraska sandhills, as stunning and massive as Zion, as soulful, deep, and full of old suffering as the Pine Ridge plains. An absolute peace came over me, and stayed with me—one second, two, three—until I heard her speak again, at which point a tickle of sour memory, of doubt, broke it apart. "This," Ila Rinpoche said, "is the work now for Shelsa and for you and for her parents. To go there, to clean the pain from that place. The pain of war and history."

I tore my eyes away from her and glanced again at Rinpoche, who offered only the raised eyebrows, the tiny smile. My mind went scurrying back across a series of comments and encounters—Seese's casino dreams, Jeannie so atypically at prayer in the church in Italy, the chance meeting with the Italian family at Arches, the absurd predictions of Joe John Jones. I would, no doubt, have felt that I'd descended, at last, into the epicenter of my sister's illogical world, except for the fact that the woman sitting a few feet in front of me had a presence like no other human being I had ever encountered. If Rinpoche was a thousand-watt bulb, she was the sun. *Radiance* is the word. An absolute stillness at the heart of every word and movement, and, at the same time, a vibrating radiance. In the face of that, though I tried hard to resist, my doubts, my old assumptions, my entire former life, was a shallow puddle, evaporating by the second.

"I can see that you are surprised. I thought you would have been prepared for this."

"I. . . . Not one bit."

I expected her to ask me if I believed what she was saying, but she didn't do that. She kept looking at me with this severe, loving gaze. She watched me, assessing. As a boy, on those few occasions when the cold services of my parents' Lutheran church had actually made an impression on me, I'd imagined what it would feel like to meet God after the moment of death. You would be seen, judged, loved. Something would be expected of you, an impossible blend of reverence and fearlessness. That is precisely what it was like in the Vegas hotel room.

At last, Ila Rinpoche said, "Your daughter is here."

What came out of my mouth then were these words: "I love her." And then, "Here where? In Las Vegas?"

A stretching of the lips. "We have spoken earlier. What a fine soul."

"Thank you. Can I see her?"

"Take Otto to his daughter now." Ila Rinpoche nodded toward the people behind me, speaking to them in a tone of absolute, quiet authority. "Shelsa and her father and I will speak."

She bowed to me. I was shaking. I tried my best to bow back. I shifted my eyes to my niece and offered her a shaky smile. I looked at Rinpoche, who was beaming. I stood up, shaking, on creaky, aching knees and took a few steps backward into the care of the bodyguards. Sinner that I must be, I have to admit here that the second I was released from Ila Rinpoche's gaze the doubts came flooding back, the snake slithered. A voice from my old life, with all its rules, assumptions, and intelligent certainties, began to chatter. The craziness of it all, the weirdness.

In a kind of post-anesthesia daze I let myself be given over to the company of one of the bodyguards. He led me out of the room and a short distance along the hallway to a door, where he gestured for me to knock. I did so. My daughter opened it, wrapped me in a magnificient hug, and said, "Dad! Isn't it great!"

Forty-two

By now I hope I've made it clear that I'm a rational man, a more or less middle-of-the-road American who, while acquiring a Buddhist brother-in-law and developing an interest in meditation, has nevertheless retained a certain basic normalcy, a sane ordinariness. I am not, in other words, my sister. I am not a flake. I consider myself open-minded about many things, but I am rational in the extreme, a friend of science and logic. And so, being told, by a woman in a maroon robe, a woman with a remarkable presence, that some twin soul spirit to my beloved niece had reincarnated as a child in the Italian mountains, a child with some special mission, a mission that

I was somehow going to help facilitate . . . well, I perhaps don't need to say that a resistance rose up in me. As much as I doted on Shelsa, and as much as I loved Celia, Natasha, and Rinpoche, I didn't envision myself leaving everything behind to follow some child around the Apennines in an attempt to wash the historical pain from the soil of Italian hill towns.

"Give me a few minutes before we talk about it," I told Tasha when I'd released her from our strong embrace. "Let's go out. Let's go out into the real world and take a walk and get an ice cream or something and then discuss it, okay?"

"Sure, Dad. It's a shock, isn't it."

"Shock isn't the word. Please, let's take a walk. Let me have a minute to think."

We went down in the elevator and out onto the street. I needed, then, to see the fake Statue of Liberty. It was somehow reassuring. I needed to see the strolling partiers from Missouri and Louisiana and Minnesota and Vienna and London and Ouagadougou, the ads for alcohol, even the shops selling thongs with WHAT HAPPENS IN VEGAS, STAYS IN VEGAS printed on them in silvery script.

Natasha hooked her arm inside mine. I tried, and failed, to calm my mind. It was as if, in Rinpoche's company, in Ila's, my doubts had settled quietly into an underground tunnel. Now, walking the Vegas strip with Natasha, I felt as if

I'd tripped over a hornets' nest and they'd all come out and were intent on stinging me. I had a strange urge to flee. *It's real then,* a squeaky interior voice kept saying. *Celia was right. It's real. Shelsa has a mission. You're supposed to help. It's real.* And then came something saner, something more *adult* is the way I thought of it. *If you buy into this one, Otto, my man, then surely all hope is lost. . . .*

Natasha and I walked along the sidewalk without speaking, crossed the strip, and stopped to buy a couple of ice cream cones. We walked another little ways and sat on a bench with the whole American circus passing in front of us, and she said, "*This* is what you call reality, Dad?"

"I'm sorry. I can't . . . I just can't . . . there's only so far I can stretch my acceptance. I feel like I've reached my limit. Really, honestly, it calls everything into question."

"Everything? The kinds of experiences you've been having in meditation?"

"How do you know about that?"

"You're a stream entrant now, Dad. Rinpoche told Aunt Seese on the phone. Ila Rinpoche confirmed it. Do you know what that is?"

"No, and I suspect I don't want to."

Her marvelous tinkling laughter floated in the air above our heads. "It means you're on, like, a conveyor belt. Another few lifetimes at most and you'll be enlightened and you won't have to live on this plane of suffering ever again if you don't want to. It's a kind of guarantee. You really can't screw it up at this point. Do you have any idea how wonderful that is?"

"It's absurd, is what it is."

"Nice, Dad."

"I love you, I'm sorry, but right now the only stream I feel qualified to enter is the jet stream. I should fly home. I've . . . it's gone too far, hon."

"Is it the idea of reincarnation or just that Shelsa really is someone special?"

I looked at her. "Tasha, I've just been told that I'm supposed to go and help out some little baby in the Italian mountains and believe that baby is the reincarnated spirit of some great teacher who is going to save the earth from cataclysm!"

"It's only weird by our standards, Dad."

"Our standards are the only standards I know. I'm American, Christian by birth and upbringing, a rational man."

"The Christians believed in reincarnation for five hundred years after Christ, Dad. They changed it at some meeting, that's all. Now it's one of the main things that divide East and West, spiritually, can't you see?"

"Reincarnation, sure, maybe. It's a nice theory and it makes a lot of sense—why should we have only one shot at living? And why should some people have such an enjoyable time of it and others endure a kind of hell? But if it is, in fact, true, then I want to find out after I die, not now. How am I supposed to believe that . . . a reincarnated holy teacher, I mean, baby, child . . . who'll work with Shelsa to unite East and West, spiritually! Tasha, please. It's . . . beyond absurd."

"The entire Buddhist world worships Ila Rinpoche."

"I can understand why. But that's not the point here."

"You don't see that Shelsa is special . . . in that way?"

"I suppose I do. Yes. She's a marvelous girl, but—"

"But she could never be *that* marvelous, right, Dad?"

"What is she, what are they supposed to do? Walk from Venice to Rome with their Chinese bodyguards?"

"Taiwanese, Dad."

"Become the next twin Dalai Lamas? It's nuts. My sister has brainwashed all of us. And why didn't she come with you, anyway?"

"Why?" Tasha tossed her paper napkin in a trash barrel to her right and hesitated in a way I recognized. "Because she didn't want you to be embarrassed. Because she predicted it just this way and you . . . doubted her."

I stared out at the street.

"We don't know exactly what Shelsa's supposed to do," Tasha went on, "but it's good, it's special, and it's supposed to begin over there in the mountains—just as Aunt Seese predicted."

"Don't rub it in."

"Maybe they'll write or teach or something, give talks, start a new religion that combines Christianity and Buddhism. We can't know yet."

"Tash. They are seven and a newborn."

"The Dalai Lama was four when they found him. Don't you believe he's special?"

"Of course I do." I went silent. I felt, for lack of a better word, grumpy.

"So what is it then, Dad? That something like this could never happen to you because you're not special enough? Mom wasn't? Anthony isn't? I'm not? That it's okay for Rinpoche to be a holy teacher, respected all over the world, but the people who revere him are a little messed up, or that it was some kind of accident that he married your weird sister? A fluke? Can't you just accept what it is you're being asked to do?"

"No. I'm too modest for that. Too humble. I'm ordinary, Tasha. I think I was, am, a good father. I was a decent husband. But I'm not special."

"That's a kind of conceit."

"It's the opposite of conceit."

"No, it really isn't, if you think about it. There are teachers who say that one of the main obstacles, spiritual obstacles, for westerners is a sense of unworthiness, a self-limiting sense of what's possible for them in a human life. You personify that, Dad. At least at the moment, and you're not humble enough to let your logical Western mind take a backseat for a while. A lot of these people," she waved an arm at the passersby, "are just hoping for a little pleasure in their lives. Some sex, some food, some drink, a little partying, a new boat or a house or a nice kitchen. They kind of go along, working at some job maybe they don't love, grabbing these little pleasures, and there's this, like, whole enormous golden life inside them that they've never been allowed to imagine. They're miracles, all of them, but everything tells them they're not special, not worthy of anything more. They hope to hang on until they die and then maybe be let into heaven."

I sat there, held in a silent, grumpy stubbornness.

"The thing about Aunt Seese, Dad, is that she understands what I just said. She sees beyond the little pleasures. She sees that there's another dimension to life and that every one of us has been put here to pursue that dimension. Why do you think Rinpoche married her?"

"Because she's nice looking and because she owned part of a farm."

"You don't really think that, Dad. You can't."

"Sorry, you're right. I don't. I used to, at first. I worried she'd be taken advantage of, but I don't really think that way now."

"Let me tell you, Dad, from working at the

Center there's one thing I'm sure of . . . there are a *lot* of very rich, very nice-looking women who'd marry him in a nanosecond."

"And he chose my sister."

"That's right. *Your* sister. A flaky North Dakota girl. And he chose to be *your* friend and teacher, to take trips with *you.* And the weird thing is, you think that's just an accident. That's a kind of pride in your own thoughts and a self-hatred mixed together, isn't it, Dad?"

"I've let him guide me, Tash. You have no idea what I thought of meditation and those things—guys wearing red robes—before I got to know Rinpoche. At least give me credit for that: I've changed a lot because of him. Abandoned friend-ships, changed my diet, sat in meditation all these years—"

"Okay, but the one thing you've never really changed is how you think of yourself. He's been trying to get you to do that. What would happen if you at least went and met this child? Aunt Seese and Rinp are going, you can bet on that."

"Bad choice of words."

"And you know Shels will be absolutely devastated if you don't go. I'm going. If I get there and it feels too weird, if this kid seems like just another ordinary kid, if I get some sense that there's a mistake, or somebody's trying to put one over on us, then I'll admit that and come home and probably go back to school or something. But nothing, nothing I've seen or heard or experienced at the farm makes me think that will happen. I'm not flaky, Dad, and not stupid. Are you afraid?"

"Probably."

"Well, is that a good reason for not going?"

"No, it isn't. If they just hadn't brought the war and Europe into it, history, the karmic stain. . . ."

I stopped myself there, unable to tell my daughter about Joe John Jones, the Leadville psychic. But the guy was haunting me. The Jesus hair, the embroidered yin and yang, the stuff about dying in a war and a karmic stain and Italy and having Jewish friends . . . as if there were a soul in New York who *didn't* have Jewish friends! The idea that Joe John had seen or predicted even *one tiny piece* of my actual past or future was more than I could bear at that moment.

I couldn't look at my daughter, but I did have the presence of mind to reach out and take hold of her hand and rest it on the bench between us. "I feel like," I said, and then I had to wait for a noisy bus to pass in front of us. "I feel like it was one thing to believe in this stuff, abstractly, but that if I let myself act on it, leave everything, follow Shelsa to Europe, then it will be like I'm dropping my whole life off the Verrazano Bridge. I'm standing at the rail, a thousand cars going by behind me, the skyline I love there in the distance, and I'm holding a huge bag that contains every-thing I think of as 'my life.' You and Anthony are in there, memories of Mom, Jasper, friends and relatives, our house, my job, all the hours and years we spent together living according to a certain set of assumptions. Everything I believe to be true about life. I say yes to this and it's like letting all that go, letting the bag drop, watching it sail down and down and splash into the water and then gradually sink. There's no getting it to come up again. It would be like dying." I turned to look at her. "That's what it feels like for me."

She looked back. My mother's eyes, gray-green, widely spaced, wet but unwavering. She said, "Exactly, Dad. Exactly like dying. . . . That's the whole point," and she started to cry.

I remembered then, strangely perhaps, something Jeannie had said to me in the latter stages of her illness. "This wasn't the way I imagined for myself, Otto. When it happened, when we got the diagnosis, I kept saying to myself, 'No, no, this isn't right. This isn't going to be my path. I have a different life, a different death planned out for myself.' I kept saying no, no, no, and then last night, for some reason, I said 'Yes, okay.' I don't like it, but last night it came to seem right for me. Unavoidable. Intended. Do you understand?"

I sat there with one arm around Natasha, the girl who'd lost her mother, then turned her back on an Ivy League education in order to find, for herself, the meaning of life and death, a truer purpose to our being here, something beyond food, sex, pain, and fear. I held her until the tears subsided and then, for no good reason I could think of, just to have something to say, just to put some sound in the air between us, I said, "What language were Ila and Shelsa speaking when I walked in? I'd never heard it. It's not Italian. What was it, Tibetan? Greek?"

Tasha shook her head and a tear went sliding over one cheekbone. She squeezed my hand, once, and said, "Yiddish, Ila told me it was. They talk to each other in Yiddish, Dad! And Shelsa mostly understands. How weird is that!"

Forty-three

Yiddish.

Tash told me she'd agreed to meet Rinpoche and Shelsa for an hour of meditation and she asked if I wanted to join them and I said what I needed just then was some thinking time, not some nonthinking time, and she said she was glad I hadn't lost my sense of humor, and I said that would be the last thing to go, and I hugged her warmly and watched her walk off along the Vegas strip. I watched her, in fact, until she'd crossed the busy road and disappeared into a building on the other side, and then I headed off in the opposite direction and wandered aimlessly. Away from the main drag the city had a somewhat—and I emphasize this *somewhat*—more normal feel to it. There were shops selling things and offering services that ordinary people actually needed. There were ordinary-looking places to eat. One occasionally saw a small child.

After a while, walking and walking without any destination in mind, with the harsh afternoon light beginning to fade toward evening, I found myself tracing back over the route of my life. The North Dakota childhood with its wealth of open spaces and dearth of familial warmth; the sometimes confused, often happy liberation of college life; and then Jeannie: the first passion, our years of young love and semi-poverty in New York City, the start of real careers, her pregnancy, the risky decision to buy a house we couldn't afford and become suburbanites; the tremendous joy and amazing exertion of having young children. Then some financial security, travel, teenagers, meals, arguments, celebrations, a settled and marvelously satisfying family life with good kids, a good marriage, good health, good work. And then her illness and death and the general unraveling. I went over it and over it again, searching for some clue that would make any kind of lasting sense, some identifiable pattern that could guide me out of the strange realm into which I seemed to have stumbled. What, exactly, was the point of it all?

I thought about how much my life had changed

since Rinpoche appeared in it. The things I did now that I never would have done before meeting him. The very different angle from which I looked at the world. The kinds of thoughts I held on to and the kinds of thoughts I dismissed. It seemed clear to me that, from almost the first week of our acquaintance, I'd let him have more influence over me and my family than any other single person or event in my fifty-two years. The fact was that I'd either been saved or brainwashed by a bald man in a gold-trimmed robe. My sister, my daughter, my son, and my precious niece—we'd either been saved or brainwashed.

But which was it? And how could a child understand a language she'd never heard and warm her body, outdoors, in a North Dakota winter, by meditating? And how could Seese and people like Joe John see the future and past—however imperfectly? And what caused the weird radiance around Ila Rinpoche? And was I a stream entrant or a man on the verge of insanity?

I walked and walked, back on the strip now, where the neon had not yet quite taken over from ordinary daylight. The gambling, the music, the shows, the food, the fun! Another kind of brain-washing, maybe, or maybe the real purpose of being alive: Enjoy what you could, while you could in the midst of this kettle of boiling pain. Don't be afraid of pleasure. Seize the day!

I was passing by the Venetian again and so,

thinking of Jeannie and our Venice trip, I walked in and went along beneath a fake sky, past the fake canal with its pretend gondoliers. In a food court I decided, after a moment's indecision and with a twinge of guilt, to order a cappuccino and a chocolate-covered brownie, paying something like twelve dollars for the privilege. I carried my illicit little feast over to a plastic table and sat there alone. Took a sip. Had a bite, chewed, swallowed. The sugar left a sourish film on my tongue. I took another bite to get rid of it. Same result. In a posture of defeat I leaned against the back of the chair and looked around me at the glittering surfaces, the shine and polish, the crowds of tourists wandering, wandering, buying, looking, searching, it seemed to me, for some elusive lasting joy, the fulfillment of the promise this rich, rich nation had made to them. I sent Anthony a text: "How was practice today? What's the story with the Yanks this year?" I waited for several minutes. No answer. I looked down at the remains of the brownie, then abandoned it there, and went out into the last of the light and headed back along a side street I'd strolled an hour earlier. The old-fashioned, vintage, real American barber shop was still open, if barely, one of two barbers finishing up with the day's final customer, his colleague washing combs and razors and lining up bottles of cologne. "Am I too late?" I asked, and the second barber, African

American, about my age and height, blessed with a gracious manner, simply gestured toward the empty chair then snapped open a clean sheet and swung it around under my chin with a practiced ease.

"What can we do for you tonight, my friend?" he asked, and it was like a song, his voice. He seemed gracious, generous, delighted to be alive. In his eyes I thought I saw something of what I'd seen in Ila Rinpoche's eyes, an odd mix of full attention and complete detachment, as if he were a great actor playing a beloved role. A barber in this life, king in another, female Rinpoche in a third. "What's your pleasure?" he asked.

I looked at myself in the mirror for a five count and said, "A shave, please." And then, after one last moment of hesitation, "Not my face . . . my head."

"That's the new look nowadays," the man said delightedly, reaching for the electric clippers. "Lots of guys going for that look. Down to the skin, yes?"

"Exactly. Can you do that?"

"Not a problem," he said. "Not a problem at all, my friend."

And I watched him in the mirror as he set to work.

Acknowledgments

First thanks, as always, to my wife, Amanda, for her patience, advice, and support, and for loving the road as much as I do. Thanks to our wonderful daughters, who have made our three adventures with Otto and Rinpoche so much fun, and who've contributed valuable suggestions to the stories. My thanks to everyone at Algonquin Books for their efforts on my behalf. Though I've never meant these novels as manuals on Buddhism, and though I've taken some liberties with the tenets of that faith, I do try to keep Rinpoche somewhere in the general territory of Buddhist thought, and my friend the Zen monk Allyn Field has been helpful in that regard. Peter Sarno, who publishes my monthly newsletter and a number of my other books, has been a loyal friend and a continual inspiration. I'd also like to express my gratitude to people who help in less specific ways, simply by virtue of their ongoing friendship and encourage-ment. In no particular order: Craig Nova, Tim Murphy, Jessica Lipnack, Peter Howe, Bob Baker, Suzanne Strempek Shea, Tommy Shea, Frank Ward, Vivian Leskes, Arlo Kahn, Matthew Quick, Bill McGee, Neal Smith, Rob Phipps, Lianne Moccia, Peggy Moss, John Beebe, Cynthia Goodyear, Joe and Susan Merullo,

Peter Grudin, Dana Wilson, David Weber, Bob Braile, Bob and Martha Patrick, Sarah Stearns, Tom Mottur and Jen Stearns, Anne and Gary Pardun, Joel Thomas-Adams, Jessica Patrick, Chiemi Karasawa, Ed Shanahan, Cecilia Galante, Davis Bates, Sally Mixsell, Tony Pelusi, Wick Sloane, Randy DeTrinis, Jan Hryniewicz, Renee Gold, Art and Pat Spencer, Steve and Theresa Merullo, Ken Merullo, Eileen Merullo, Gene and Terri Aucella, Joanie Pratt, Derek Campbell, Deborah Schifter, Dan Davies, Dean Crawford, John and Maria Recco, Mike Murphy, Rich and Sue Clarendon, Charlie Johnson, Bill Fields, Lee Hope Betcher, Meg Montagnino Jarrett, John DiNatale, Alex Gonzalez-Mir, Sterling Watson, Mary Remmel Wohlleb, Marty Wohl, Steve Weiner, Ed Desrochers, the late John Aucella, the late Peter Greer, the late Joe McGinniss, and the late Robert Stone. All of them offered a good word or more at various times in the writing of this book, and I remain grateful for that community of good will.

Center Point Large Print
600 Brooks Road / PO Box 1
Thorndike, ME 04986-0001 USA

(207) 568-3717

US & Canada:
1 800 929-9108
www.centerpointlargeprint.com